Published by Accent Press Ltd 2017
Octavo House
West Bute Street
Cardiff
CF10 5LJ

Copyright © Kate Field 2017

ISBN 9781786152381
eISBN 9781786152374

To Molly

With hope that one day you will love books as much as I do.

CHAPTER 1

It couldn't be him – could it? Helen stopped dead and scanned the crowded pavement. Her head and her heart battled over what they wanted the answer to be. Her head won. Instinctively tightening her grip on Megan's hand, she pushed open the nearest door with her bottom and backed inside, out of sight. She peered through the grimy glass window, anxiety thudding through her chest.

'What are we doing, Mummy? Are we hiding?'

'Yes.' Helen's attention was still outside. 'Isn't it fun?'

'Is it the Gruffalo, Mummy? Are we hiding from the Gruffalo?'

'Hmm, that's right.'

'Can you see him?'

She couldn't: the phantom figure had vanished. She looked up and down the street, and saw nothing but ordinary families going about their shopping. Nothing to be alarmed about. Nothing to make her lungs freeze. She risked a tentative breath.

Helen felt a little hand squeeze hers. She turned away from the door and looked down. Megan was gazing at her, bright blue eyes – so like his that she couldn't have forgotten him, even if she'd tried – screwed up worriedly.

'Is he there? Outside?'

'Is who there, sweetheart?'

'The Gruffalo.'

Helen hauled her attention back to reality and bent down to kiss the top of Megan's head. The familiar scent of strawberry shampoo wrapped round her like a comfort blanket. 'Don't worry, I was only playing hide and seek. I thought I saw someone I knew.'

But how could she have done? Rational thought trickled back into her brain. It was impossible that it had been Daniel. He was thousands of miles away. There was no need to panic, unsettled by the tilt of a man's head and the roll of hips that had looked so desperately familiar. She should have moved on from these false sightings years ago. And that treacherous flicker of hope, defying all logic, that he might have come back for her... She wished she knew how to move on from that.

Helen reached for the door handle but a manicured hand blocked her way.

'Is it a family holiday you're looking for? We have some fabulous offers on Disneyland Paris at the moment. Free child places!'

Helen stared down at the brochure that had been thrust into her hand, silently cursing her bottom for steering her into the travel agents. Megan's eyes widened at the images of Mickey Mouse dancing in front of her. Helen's eyes were trapped by the happy family pictured on the front cover: mother, father, children. The contrast with her own life almost robbed her of breath again. She stuffed the brochure in her bag, and dragged Megan out of the shop as fast as they had come in. She steered a determined path through the shuffle of Saturday shoppers clogging the centre of town and up the hill past the shopping arcade, not slowing until the doors of St Andrew's sealed shut behind her.

This was Helen's sanctuary. A red brick church dominating the skyline on the northern edge of this faded Lancashire mill town, St Andrew's had long since been deconsecrated and for the last fifteen years had been run as a craft centre. Eight retail units were tucked along the sides of what had once been the centre aisle, underneath the first-floor balcony, and the third along on the left, sandwiched between designer jewellery and handmade stationery, belonged to Helen. Crazy Little Things sold everything a needlework enthusiast could want, from tapestry threads and cross-stitch kits to dressmaking patterns and buttons.

Helen's real passion was crazy patchwork. Irregular pieces of fabric, in any colour or texture, could be joined together and decorated with embroidered motifs, intricate seams and embellishments, to create a stunning piece of art – the more sumptuous the better. Some of her simpler work was on display at St Andrew's: cushions, a woollen scarf, trinket boxes and hanging hearts. There wasn't a huge return on these from the hours of love she put in to creating them, but they were priceless advertising for larger commissions, and had led to this afternoon's appointment with a couple who wanted an embroidered family portrait. It was hard to survive a lifetime of being treated as decorative but useless

3

without believing it; but against everyone's expectations she was beginning to make a success of the business. She was earning enough to support herself and Megan. It was all she wanted. Almost all.

Helen hurried over to Crazy Little Things.

'They haven't arrived yet, have they?' she asked Kirsty, her friend who ran the shop on Saturdays.

'No, but they're not due for another twenty minutes, are they?' said Kirsty, glancing at her watch. 'What's the matter? You look like you've sprinted all the way here.'

'We've been playing hide and seek,' Megan piped up helpfully. 'Mummy saw someone she knew.'

'Did she?' Kirsty looked at Helen with a question that Helen chose not to answer. Perhaps their pace up the hill had been a little brisk. Megan was looking quite pink.

'I'm thirsty,' Megan said, in a plaintive tone perfectly calculated to capitalise on Helen's guilt. 'And hungry.' She took a few hopeful steps in the direction of the coffee shop that had been created in the chancel at the head of the church. Helen laughed and caught her up.

'Okay, let's go and see what Joan can find for you.'

Joan was more than happy to hand the coffee shop over to the charge of her Saturday girls and help Megan with her colouring. Leaving Megan settled with a glass of milk and a slice of chocolate cake, Helen returned to her shop.

'How's business been this morning?' she asked

4

Kirsty. There wasn't a single customer in St Andrew's, which was worrying on a Saturday afternoon.

'Not bad, actually. The usual bits and pieces, and I sold a couple of those Kaffe Fassett tapestry kits. But wait until you hear the best bit. A lady came in to look at your work after seeing your advert in the magazine.'

'Already? It only came out this week.' Now that Megan was past the age of needing constant attention, Helen had taken her first tentative steps to promote her crazy patchwork, rather than relying on interest drummed up by the shop. She had placed a quarter-page advert in a free local magazine: £30 she could scarcely afford, but perhaps it was about to pay off. 'Did she like it?'

'Loved it. She's coming back on Tuesday lunchtime to discuss some ideas.' Kirsty grinned. 'You can celebrate tonight. How did you get on this morning? Are you all ready?'

'Not quite. I still need to finish the hem on my dress, and then it will probably take a few hours to plaster on the make-up so I look halfway presentable. I may be going to a fortieth birthday party, but I don't want to look like *I'm* anywhere near there yet...'

Helen's voice trailed off. The doors of St Andrew's had swung open and let in two women, one in her early sixties, one mid-twenties.

'What a charming little place. Who would have thought it could exist in this town?'

Helen could never have mistaken that voice, even

5

if she hadn't recognised the older woman's face.

'I'm not here,' she gasped, and dived behind the curtain that marked the private section at the back of the shop. Her heart racing faster than was good for it, she lurked behind the thick velvet, her eye pressed to the gap as the new arrivals advanced along the aisle.

As Helen was wondering whether to try a silent prayer for them to leave, the women's attention was caught by the fabulous displays of jewellery next door. From her hiding place, Helen only dared risk the occasional peep, and she saw that the younger woman – a tall blonde she didn't recognise – was poring over the glass cabinets until the impatient fidgeting of her companion hurried her on.

Helen retreated behind the curtain again. Surely they must be leaving now? Then she heard a voice, scarily close outside.

'Look at this evening bag, Val. Isn't it amazing?'

Helen pushed herself even further back. They must be looking at her crazy patchwork, but the compliment hardly even registered. Val? Since when had anyone dared abbreviate Valerie Blake?

'And these cushions would look beautiful in your house, Val.'

'Yes, I suppose they are quite attractive.' Helen flinched at the memories stirred up by the tone of faint surprise. That tone had been directed at her frequently in the past, as if Valerie had found it astonishing when Helen had said something intelligent or done something useful. 'But I expect it's all done by machine.'

6

That slur was almost enough to drag Helen from her hiding place. She heard Kirsty launch her defence.

'Actually, all the decorative detail on these pieces is done by hand,' Kirsty said, adopting a much politer tone than Helen could have mustered. But then Kirsty didn't know who she was talking to. 'It's beautiful, isn't it? It's a technique called crazy patchwork. All these items were designed and created by Helen, who owns this shop. She has a diploma from the Royal School of Needlework. She undertakes commissions, so do take a card.'

Helen stiffened. Under any other circumstances, this sales pitch would have been perfect, but was it too much to hope that Valerie Blake could see her name and not recognise it? Clearly it was. Helen heard a slight choking noise, and then Valerie's voice again.

'Helen Walters? Helen Walters did these?' There was that note of surprise again, now veering on disbelief. There was an undercurrent, too, of something that in anyone else Helen would have described as panic. But Valerie Blake didn't do panic.

'And is she – Helen – here today?'

'No, she's not.'

Valerie's relief was almost tangible.

'Are you okay, Val?' The younger woman had an accent that Helen couldn't quite place – Australian? New Zealand? 'Shall we have a drink? There's a café over there.'

There was no time to think. They mustn't go to the coffee shop. Megan was there. If Valerie saw

7

Megan… Helen simply couldn't allow it to happen. In desperation, she knocked a box of scissors to the floor, flinching as the sound crashed and echoed round the church. A second later Kirsty's head appeared between the curtains.

'Don't let them go to Joan's,' Helen hissed at her. 'Tell them I'm about to arrive. Do whatever it takes.'

Kirsty nodded, a good-enough friend to overlook that Helen had gone mad. Helen heard her call out.

'Excuse me? If you're staying for coffee, you'll be able to meet Helen. She's coming in this afternoon to see a client. I'm expecting her any minute now.'

Holding her breath so tightly it felt like her navel was glued against her spine, Helen listened as the footsteps stopped.

'I think we'll have to forego that pleasure this afternoon.' Valerie's voice rang out, more confident now. 'We're in quite a hurry. Perhaps another time.'

Not if Helen had any say in the matter. The footsteps started again, and she tried desperately to work out which way they were going, braced to jump out if the café was the target. At last she heard the front doors bang shut, and instantly the curtains in front of her were whipped aside.

'What the hell's going on?' Kirsty demanded. 'Who was that? And why are you acting insanely and destroying your stock?'

'That,' replied Helen, collapsing onto a chair to relieve her wobbling legs, 'was Valerie Blake.'

'And she is…?'

'Daniel Blake's mother.'

8

'And he is…?'

Helen hesitated. Could she say it?

'Megan's father,' she whispered.

'What?'

'Don't look so surprised.' Helen managed a smile as Kirsty's mouth dropped open. 'You've heard enough stories about the life I used to lead in London to be sure that it wasn't another virgin birth.'

Kirsty pulled up a stool.

'You told me about the amazing parties and premières and all that sort of thing, but you've never mentioned him. I've never even heard his name. I assumed…' She stopped, and grinned.

'That I didn't know it?' Kirsty nodded, without a shred of embarrassment. Helen laughed. 'I was never *that* bad.'

'So what was it? Come on, I've been dying to know for the last four years, but you've been like a clam on the subject. Was it a one-night stand?'

'No, we were together for over two years. Happy years.' It was an inadequate way to describe what they had shared. Sometimes only silence was big enough to say what words could never explain.

'Two years? And you've told me nothing about him?' Kirsty's eyes narrowed. 'He abandoned you when he found you were pregnant, didn't he? What a bastard.'

'It wasn't quite like that,' Helen said. Quite the opposite, in fact. She sighed, as a familiar swell of longing spread through her. She really didn't want to be thinking about him. It had taken years to climb to

9

the level of fragile resignation she was at now. She couldn't let one encounter with Valerie Blake bring her crashing back down.

'So where is he?' Kirsty wasn't going to let this drop, full of the moral indignation of a happily married mother of two. 'Why has he never visited Megan?'

Helen looked across at Kirsty – her best friend – the only real friend she had. They had shared everything over the last four years, every physical and emotional detail, except this one thing: the truth about Helen, the truth that no one else knew. Would Kirsty condemn her for what she had done? How could she not, when Helen condemned herself every day?

But it didn't matter. The near miss with Valerie had made her reckless. She needed to confess.

'Helen?' Kirsty's gentle nudge made up Helen's mind.

'He's never visited because I didn't tell him I was pregnant.' Helen saw confusion cloud Kirsty's face and pushed on quickly, before she lost her nerve. 'He doesn't know that Megan even exists. And as far as I'm concerned, he's never going to find out.'

But as Helen fell silent, waiting for Kirsty to react, she was attacked by the thought that had been buzzing round her head, desperate to see the light since the first glimpse of Valerie. The initial shock of adrenalin faded, and the enormity of the coincidence sank in. Valerie Blake had appeared, minutes after Helen had thought she'd seen *him*. It could still be

10

coincidence, of course it could. But what if it wasn't? What if Daniel Blake wasn't thousands of miles away after all?

CHAPTER 2

Craig's fortieth birthday party was already in full swing when Helen arrived at the small country-house hotel in Cheshire hired exclusively for the event. She had never left Megan overnight before, and though she trusted Kirsty and her husband Ben implicitly, she'd still lingered too long over saying goodbye. The unexpected sighting of Valerie Blake had unsettled her, making her more reluctant to leave Megan than she had been before, especially for a night out where reminders of Daniel were sure to assault her at every turn.

She hesitated outside the door leading through to the bar, arrested by the laughter and chatter leaking from the room and the memories the sounds evoked. This had once been her natural habitat: one, maybe two parties each night, always at the centre of the pack and never doubting that was where she belonged. Now unfamiliar nerves flickered in her stomach, and when a guest held the door open, indicating for her to go in first, she stole through, avoiding the attention she would once have expected and even courted. She ordered a sparkling mineral water while she scoured the crowd, trying to spot a friendly face, and could hardly disguise her relief when she saw Sally, Craig's wife, threading through the guests towards her, right hand vigorously waving.

'Helen, where have you been? I've been looking for you for ages.' Sally kissed Helen's cheek, then frowned at the drink in her hand. 'What's that?' She took a sniff. 'Water? You're not having that. White wine, please,' she called to the barman.

'I'm pacing myself,' Helen explained as Sally steered her away, a large glass of wine now replacing the water in her hand. 'It's one of the joys of being a single mother. I can't get drunk. What if there's an emergency with Megan?'

'You call a taxi. How is Megan?'

'Very excited to be having her first sleepover. I phoned Kirsty earlier and she'd gone off to sleep okay, so...'

'I don't mean about that... Oh for God's sake,' Sally said. 'Uncle Stan has had too much already and is trying to start a conga. I'd better stop him. Hang on here a minute, there's something I need to tell you.'

Sally dashed off, and Helen waited obediently, sipping at her wine. But when Uncle Stan proved harder to settle than expected, Sally made apologetic gestures at her across the room, and Helen wandered off. She lost sight of anyone she knew until Craig grabbed her as she was sneaking past the disco.

'Hello!' Craig shouted, still at disco volume. 'It's my birthday!'

'I know!' Helen laughed. 'Are you having a good one? This is quite some party.'

'Isn't it? Sally has excelled herself. Are you on your own?' He looked behind her, as if there might have been someone lurking there. 'Not making the most of your night off with a hot young stud?'

'Damn, they must have run out of them by the time I reached the buffet. Just my luck!'

Craig laughed, and put his arm round her waist. 'Have a hot old one instead. Come and dance. Don't shake your head. When else can I get my hands on so many gorgeous women without Sally complaining?'

He winked, and Helen let herself be dragged to the dance floor. The DJ was playing classics from the last forty years, and Craig danced with abandon, flinging out his limbs exuberantly and keeping up a largely incoherent conversation. But then, for a heart-stopping moment, she thought she heard the word 'Daniel'. She lost her rhythm for a second, but Craig was still dancing and smiling as if nothing untoward had happened. She was imagining it, she told herself firmly, and vowed to stick to water for the rest of the night.

'Come on Eileen' brought a surge for the dance floor and Helen escaped. The party was spread through the downstairs of the hotel, and she'd hardly seen any of it yet. She headed down a corridor until she found herself in a quiet sitting room, where some of the older guests were having tea or a nap. The end wall was covered in a montage of A3 and A4 photographs of Craig on various birthdays, from chubby baby to sullen teenager. Helen pored over the photos as they became progressively more recent, until her gaze was snagged by the picture of Craig's thirty-fifth birthday party.

Helen remembered the night well. Sally and Craig were part of the crowd that Daniel had introduced her to when they had moved from London to Lancashire about a year into their relationship: hard-working, respectable people – quite a different crowd from the one that Helen had left behind. The party had been tame by her London standards, but for the first time she hadn't felt such an outsider in the group. Sally had organised a barbecue, and they had stayed outside eating and drinking by candlelight long after the feeble autumn sun had faded. It had been almost morning before she'd rolled into bed with Daniel, and even then, they hadn't slept for hours. It was one of the memories that had both tortured and comforted her when Daniel had left a few months later.

She stared at the Helen in the photograph. Her arms were wrapped around Daniel, her head resting on his chest, her expression adoring. It was a long time since she'd seen herself looking like that. The long blonde hair had gone, cut back to an easier shoulder length in its natural shade of brown. Since Megan's birth, skirts had covered her knees and not just her knickers. But there was something more than physical that marked the difference between the Helen she had been, and who she was now. The photograph had been taken a lifestyle ago.

'Hey Danny, come and take a look over here, isn't this you?'

The voice startled Helen. Lost in the picture of her former self, she hadn't noticed that other people had wandered over to look at the photos. Heavy footsteps thudded across the room and the movement created a draught that made her shiver.

'Where?'

One word. Such a simple word, too, nothing significant about it – or not to anyone but Helen. Because it was Daniel's voice that had spoken it. He was in the room, somewhere behind her – perhaps within touching distance – and she closed her eyes briefly and took a deep breath, as if to inhale his presence.

'Here.' A long finger and slim arm reached past Helen and pointed towards the very photograph she was still staring at. She edged cautiously to one side, trying not to draw any attention to herself, though she was aching to turn round. 'It is you; I'd know that gorgeous smile anywhere. But who is that you're with?'

'Craig and Sally.' There was a slight hesitation. Helen stopped shuffling, and held her breath. 'And Helen.'

'Helen?' The unknown woman laughed. 'You've never mentioned her.'

The stem of Helen's glass almost snapped under her fingers. Never mentioned her? That couldn't be right. He wouldn't airbrush her from his past like that. But she would never previously have believed that he could stand so close to her and not instantly know her, however much she had changed.

16

'Nothing to tell. It was a long time ago.' Daniel's tone buried the subject. 'Come on, let's go to the bar. I need a drink.'

Footsteps faded behind her. Helen couldn't help herself. She glanced over her shoulder. It was him, it really was him, her Daniel – though plainly not her Daniel anymore. She could never not know him: the shape of his head, the broad set of his shoulders, that firm bottom... She had to turn away, to stop her eyes devouring him until he was out of sight. She wasn't prepared for this. Why had no one told her he would be here?

Avoiding the bar, Helen prowled round the hotel until she found Sally, and dragged her away from her friends.

'Daniel's here,' Helen said, stopping in a quiet corner where they wouldn't be overheard.

'Yes. I hope it's not too awkward. Of course it had to be plus one, so we couldn't object to Tasha.'

'Tasha? Who's Tasha?'

'Daniel's girlfriend.' Sally frowned. 'God, I'll kill Craig, birthday or not. He didn't tell you, did he? He promised he'd spoken to you and you were fine about it.'

'But what's he doing here? In England?'

'Who, Daniel?' Sally asked. 'He's come back. Surely you knew?'

'No, how could I? We've not been in touch since he took the job in Hong Kong.' And then it all began to fall into place, why Sally had been so keen to speak to her earlier on. She had been trying to warn

Helen about Tasha, in case she didn't know that Daniel had a new girlfriend. It had been kindly meant, she supposed. But what if Sally and the others had been doing the same with him? What if they had warned him about Megan?

Helen gripped Sally's hand. 'Please don't let anyone mention Megan to Daniel. This is really important. Will you make sure everyone knows?'

'We've never talked about you to him. You asked us not to.' Sally extracted her hand from Helen's. 'So he still doesn't know that you have Megan?'

'Why should he? Megan has nothing to do with him.'

The lie had never felt so heavy on her tongue. Sally looked at Helen sharply, with the accumulated suspicion of many years rampant in every feature. And who could blame her? It was amazing that Helen had got away with her secret for so long. Logically she should never have become involved with their mutual friends again; but she had never been logical where Daniel was concerned. She had run into Anita, another of the gang, when Megan was a few months old – when the absence of sleep, of money and of Daniel were overwhelming her – and the appeal of maintaining a link with him, with their past, had been impossible to resist. It had always been a risk, continuing the acquaintance: the ultimate game of Russian roulette, gambling with exposure not death; and perhaps, deep down, she had hoped she might lose, and that it might bring him back. But now she was confronted with six foot

18

of solid reality, she knew better. She mustn't lose. Because what would happen if he found out the truth? What if he tried to take Megan from her? *He couldn't find out.*

Helen fled to the ladies, and sank onto a closed seat, her head heavy in her hands. What the hell was she supposed to do? Her first instinct was to rush home, grab Megan and – what? Run? Hide?

Her second thought was a better one. She would have to face Daniel at some point; now would be as good a time as any. She had the advantage over him: she had gone past the first shock. There were plenty of people about to make a scene unlikely. She had had enough to drink to give her the courage to do it. And – though she wished it wasn't a consideration – she looked her best. She would be in control of this first meeting; and perhaps by forcing it now, it would lessen the risk that he might ask about her and hear of Megan. It had to be now.

Acting before she had time to reflect, she refreshed her make-up, combed her hair, and went to the bar. She ordered a large vodka and tonic and turned to survey the room. There he was, by the window, brushing arms with the tall blonde whom Helen had seen with Valerie Blake earlier. Tasha, Sally had called her, whatever sort of name that was. But it wasn't the name that made Helen stare at her – it was the way she looked. It was as if the old Helen had stepped out of the photograph and taken her rightful place at Daniel's side. And seeing them together, Helen realised that she had deluded herself all these years. She would never be resigned to this. It would take more than the passage of time to make her feelings for Daniel any less than they had ever been.

Helen transferred her gaze to Daniel, and allowed herself a few moments to absorb those familiar features again. Then she took a generous swig of vodka and nudged her way through the crowded room to the window.

'Hello Daniel.'

He broke off from what he was saying, and looked at her for the first time in over four years. Initially his face was blank, polite; then he bent forward a little, and studied her. His eyes travelled slowly up and down. She waited, gazing steadily back, amazed by her own stillness.

'Helen?' It was barely more than a whisper, and caused a tremor in her out of all proportion and expectation. But the sight of Tasha flashing gleaming white teeth, and rubbing her hand up and down his back, was the slap she needed to recover control.

'Danny? You look like you've seen a ghost.'

Ignoring Tasha, he stared at Helen.

'You look... different,' he managed at last. Then he actually shook himself, and straightened up. 'This is Tasha. Tasha, this is Helen... Is it still Walters?'

The chip of ice in his voice took Helen by surprise. Goosebumps crept up her arms.

'Yes, of course it is.'

'You haven't married since we last met?'

'No. Have you?'

20

'No. A bad experience put me off commitment.'

There was nothing in his eyes but anger. He couldn't be faking this. He really did seem to hate her. They stared at each other, his eyes hostile, hers confused, then Tasha laughed and linked her arm in his.

'But I'm trying to put you back on to commitment, aren't I?'

'If you can't, no one can.' Daniel turned his head and kissed Tasha hard on the lips. Helen felt it like a punch. But what had she expected, really? That he would see her again and take her into his arms, the last four years forgotten? She gulped her vodka, knowing that part of her had hoped for exactly that, and had done since the day she had let him go.

Tasha was either oblivious to the tension, or tactful enough to change the subject. Helen didn't feel inclined to give her the benefit of the doubt.

'That's a fantastic bag,' Tasha said, stretching out and fingering Helen's crazy patchwork bag, which was dangling from her wrist. Instinctively Helen moved her hand away. 'I saw some just like it earlier today. Do you know all those fancy stitches are done by hand?'

'I do. And those hands happen to be mine.'

'Wow! I thought your name sounded familiar.' Helen couldn't help a flash of satisfaction at Tasha's evident admiration. 'Hey Danny, you didn't tell me you had such clever friends.'

'I was only doing it as a hobby before,' Helen replied. 'What do you do?'

Small talk with Daniel's girlfriend! She had never imagined that it would be like this if they met again – and in over four years apart, she'd had plenty of time to role-play every possible scenario in her head. But it had honestly never occurred to her that he would simply stand by and shoot her with looks of animosity. And this was before he found out that he had so much more reason to dislike her than he knew.

'I'm a personal fitness trainer,' Tasha said, running her fingers through her long blonde hair, and tying it up loosely in a scrunchy that had been decorating her wrist. Helen used to do that with her hair. 'People hire me for one-on-one exercise sessions. It's a dream job. Getting paid to keep fit!'

Helen nodded, though she had always been too lazy to keep fit, and living with Daniel had provided her with as much exercise as she could need. No wonder she'd grown almost two dress sizes since he left. And look what had happened to him: he'd found a new Helen, several years younger than the last one, blonder, with white teeth, and not an ounce of flab on her. Was he even conscious of the similarity? Had he picked Tasha because of the resemblance to the Helen he had known, or did he merely have a preference for tall, slim blondes? Helen tucked her hair behind her ear, for the first time regretting what she had done to it.

'Well,' she said, turning to Daniel with what she hoped would pass for a natural smile. 'It was good to catch up with you again. I'm glad you're doing so

22

well.' Though he hadn't actually told her anything. The fact that he'd bagged himself a personal fitness trainer was the only achievement she had found out. But she'd had quite enough now. The first meeting was over, and she had survived. Time to quit while she was ahead.

By midnight, Helen was worn out by the effort of avoiding Daniel, and headed upstairs to her bedroom. She was fumbling with her key, blinking away tears of exhaustion – or so she told herself – when she heard steps behind her. Glancing round she saw Daniel. She could tell at once that he was drunk. He used to be able to hold his alcohol well, but his eyes were unnaturally wide and bright, and there was a slight stagger in his walk. He had always been a funny drunk, but there was nothing funny about him now.

Helen tried to force her key in the lock, but she wasn't fast enough.

'Why did you do it, Helen?'

'Do what?' The words jerked out as a reflex response, but as she turned and saw his face, his anguished expression told her that it was too late to prevaricate. He must have found out about Megan, and her heart reared in apprehension about what might follow. But before she could speak, he carried on.

'Why did you stay here? Why didn't you join me in Hong Kong? We had it all planned – the new job, the new life out there together – all the arrangements were made. It was what we wanted. You were looking forward to it. Why didn't you come?'

Helen's relief was so overwhelming, she almost missed his next question.

'Was there someone else?'

'No. There was no one else.' She fiddled with the key in her hand, unable to meet his gaze.

'Don't lie. You were always a rotten liar. Who was he?'

'No one. I didn't stay because of another man.' She could look at him now she was telling the truth, although only half of it.

'Then why?'

She smiled. Now that the moment had come, it was easier than she had expected, but then this was a scene she had rehearsed well over the years, as she had imagined what might happen if they ever met again. She knew exactly what she had to say, what smokescreens she had to create to protect her secret until he was safely out of the country again. Because she had to protect it: seeing him here in front of her, still in every way the man she loved, convinced her that there was no alternative. She couldn't bear him to find out what she had done to him and couldn't bear to consider the consequences if he did.

'I realised it was too big a step. I couldn't follow you there. It was too much commitment.'

If anything, his eyes grew wider.

'And it wasn't a commitment when you moved from London with me? You didn't hesitate then.'

'Hong Kong hardly compares with Lancashire. From here I could be back in my old life in a couple of hours if I changed my mind.'

'So it was never serious?' He took a half step back, and leant against the wall. 'Is that why you weren't concerned about having a six-month visa? Was it only ever a temporary thing until you decided to go back?'

His voice sounded strained. She was clearly a better liar than he gave her credit for. He wasn't really believing this, was he? Could he have forgotten what they had together?

'You shouldn't have expected anything else.' Helen ploughed on, determined to finish, however much it pained her. If she destroyed herself, he would surely never make any effort to contact her in future. 'You knew what I was like. I skimmed from one relationship to another before you. I'm not cut out to make an effort or do long haul, in anything. You should have listened to your mother. Didn't she warn you against the blonde tart?'

He didn't deny it. He couldn't. Helen had overheard Valerie say it. She could see from his face how he was thinking, how he was reassessing all their time together in this new – false – light. It felt like she'd taken a cheesegrater to her heart.

'And what about Alex?' he threw at her at last. 'Did you have to dump her too? Was it really necessary to hurt her as well?'

Helen flinched. He had deviated from the script here. Of course she had never wanted to hurt his sister. Alex had been one of her closest friends, as good as a sister to her too. But what choice had she had? Alex could never have kept Megan a secret from Daniel.

'I wish we could have stayed friends,' Helen said. 'But it was impossible.'

'Nothing is impossible. You couldn't be bothered, could you?' The weariness with which he said this, as if he expected no better from her, hurt Helen more than any words would have done. 'Typical selfish Helen, not stopping to think of anyone else's feelings. Aren't you even going to ask how she is?'

'I don't need to. Sally mentioned she's engaged. I'm happy for her.'

'Even though you don't believe in commitment?'

Helen let this pass. There was only so far she could go in defending a lie, and she was already close to the border. She turned her back on him, and put the key in the lock. She had to get away. She had wanted him to think she was shallow and frivolous, so that he wouldn't look further into why she hadn't gone with him to Hong Kong. Her job was done. Nothing good could come from prolonging this conversation.

'I came back for you, you know.'

She stopped.

'What?'

'I flew back. After you emailed to say you weren't coming. You didn't reply to my messages and your phone number wasn't recognised. I couldn't get away for the first six weeks, then I pleaded a family crisis, took a week off, and came home.'

Helen turned back to him.

'And what happened?' Though it was silly to ask – of course she knew he hadn't found her. But what if he had seen her, bump starting to show?

'I couldn't find you. The house was sold, and neither the new owners, nor the estate agents, nor our solicitors, had a forwarding address. I tried Adam, but he pretty much refused to speak to me, as if I were the guilty party.'

Helen said nothing. By that stage she must have told her brother she was pregnant, and failed to disabuse his assumption that Daniel had rejected her because of it.

'I even went to the police, but they weren't interested. As far as I could tell, you had vanished into thin air.'

Exactly what Helen had done, at the time, while she tried to get her head round her new future, and grieve for a relationship she had murdered.

Someone walked down the corridor between them. It gave Helen a moment for reflection, but not long enough to prevent the question hovering on her lips from tumbling out.

'What would you have done if you'd found me?'

Instantly she regretted her weakness, as his alcohol-glazed blue eyes regarded her without a trace of emotion.

'By the sounds of it, from what you've said tonight, I'd have made an even bigger fool of myself. But at the time, I would have said or done anything to persuade you to come with me.'

'It would have made no difference,' she said

27

quickly, desperately. 'I could never have gone to Hong Kong.'

'Then I would have come back. Hong Kong was never that important.'

It was the last thing Helen wanted to hear. She didn't believe him – she couldn't allow herself to believe him, or what had been the point of the previous four years? The job in Hong Kong had meant everything to him, the culmination of years of ambition and hard work: she had been convinced of it, or she would never have made the decision she had. He had spent several weeks there on his own, while she stayed behind to arrange the sale of the house, and he had loved it. She still had emails he had sent her, raving about the place, and what an amazing life the two of them would have there. But by the time she was due to fly out, it hadn't been the two of them any more. The new life he craved was no longer possible – or not if she joined him. She had let the flight go without her.

'You're kidding yourself,' she said, her voice sounding harsher than she intended. 'From the moment you were offered that job, there was never any question of you turning it down. Oh, you went through the motions, consulting me, listening to your family, taking me to see what it was like. But you were always going to go, whatever I did. It *was* that important.' He opened his mouth, but she hurried on. 'You would never have been happy if you had stayed here. I couldn't have let you do it.'

'Come off it, Nell,' Daniel said, shaking his head

28

dismissively. She shivered at the name only he had ever called her. 'Don't try to pass off what you did as some sort of grand sacrifice for my sake. I may have loved you, but I was never blind to what you are. You always put yourself first. You didn't come to Hong Kong because you didn't want to. Don't make out there was any other reason.'

The key bit into Helen's hand as she clenched her fingers together, and clamped down her teeth to stop herself spitting out the truth. Then he made a small shrug, a gesture so like Megan she almost gasped.

'As it happens, it turns out you were right.' His gaze was steady, despite the alcohol. 'I was probably happier there than I've ever been. And as I had no ties, I could suit myself. I could work whatever hours I needed to, travel wherever I wanted, stay out all night with whoever I chose. From Hong Kong I moved on to Tokyo, and then Australia, where of course I met Tasha. So really you did me a favour. I was soon glad you weren't tagging along.'

He meant to hurt her, that was clear. But he didn't realise that the darts he flung so savagely grew wings and landed softly on their target. Every word watered down the guilt she had carried round with her for so long. The night had turned out badly, but she felt an unexpected release in her chest.

'I'm happy it worked out for you,' she said at last. She turned away and opened the door. 'Good night.'

She'd taken two steps into the room when she heard movement behind her and he grabbed her arm. He was a surprisingly nimble drunk.

29

'Helen.' Something about his voice made her face him again. 'Was it ever real? Those months in London, at least? Did you ever love me?'

It took an immense effort to stand still, not to reach out for him and put her hand on his, not to smooth out his frown with her fingers as she had done so often in the past. The truth was gagging in her throat. But she had left it far, far too late to alter her course now.

'It was fun. More fun than I'd had with anyone else.' He dropped her arm, his face sagging. 'Goodbye, Daniel.'

CHAPTER 3

Helen checked out early the next morning, abandoning the chance of a lie-in and skipping breakfast. The sight of Daniel and Tasha sharing a postcoital glow would have ruined her appetite. No doubt Tasha had already enjoyed her own very special full English.

Megan was blatantly disappointed to see Helen return so soon, and wriggled out from her hug.

'She's had a great time,' Kirsty said. 'What about you? I can't tell whether you look like you've had an amazing night or an awful one. You could carry coal in those bags under your eyes.'

'I didn't get much sleep.'

'That sounds interesting.' Kirsty closed the door as the children ran out. 'Tell me everything. Did you not sleep with anyone in particular?'

Helen laughed.

'If only it had been that exciting...'

'Wasn't it?' Kirsty looked disappointed. 'Your first night of freedom and you didn't make the most of it? Did no one catch your eye? What did you pull that face for? There was someone, wasn't there?'

'No.' Kirsty opened her mouth, ready to continue her interrogation, and Helen caved in. '*He* was there.'

'He... oh! You mean Megan's...' Helen nodded. 'Does he live round here? How have you managed to

31

avoid him with Megan?'

'He's been working in the Far East until now.'

'Really? So how long is it since you've seen him?'

'Four years.' And six months, two days. If she'd been counting.

'So how was it when you saw him again last night? Had he changed much?'

'He was older.'

'Gone to seed? Big belly? Lost his hair?'

Helen laughed.

'That sounds more like me! Time has definitely been kinder to him. Salt-and-pepper hair, maybe, but he's the sort of man who can carry it off.'

'Right. So you still think he's gorgeous?'

'He's still got it. But he's also now got an equally gorgeous girlfriend, a blonde Australian fitness trainer.'

'Ah. So no happy reunion then?'

'That was never going to happen.' Only in her head. It had happened a hundred times there. But so, as the years wore on, had the unhappy-ever-after, where he had returned and punished her by taking Megan away. 'It was hard to ignore how much he hates me.'

'He didn't take the news about Megan well?'

Helen took a sip of coffee and moved her head slightly in what could have been interpreted as a shake. Kirsty wasn't fooled.

'You didn't tell him, did you?'

'No,' Helen admitted. 'It wasn't the time or the place.'

'But you do plan to?'

'No. This is probably just a flying visit for Craig's party. He'll be gone again soon. He doesn't need to know. We're fine as we are.'

'But he deserves to know! And what about Megan, don't you think she might be interested in having a dad?'

There was no answer to that, or not one that Helen wanted to give.

'You've never said Megan was missing anything before.'

'Because I thought you didn't know who her dad was. I didn't realise there was a perfectly decent man out there who was losing out on knowing her.' Kirsty squeezed Helen's arm. 'You know I'm not judging you. But if he's back for a while, amongst all your friends who know about Megan, it's only a matter of time before he finds out, isn't it? You can't go on hiding this. You have to tell him. You have to do it for Megan.'

Helen flopped down onto the sofa. Kirsty had hit upon the only argument that could make Helen pause and reconsider what she was doing. She had spent four years striving to do what was best for Megan. How could she stop now? Of course it had occurred to her before, to wonder if Megan would be happier with a father. But she had become adept at burying those wonderings, because they challenged the decision she had made. Was she still being the typical selfish Helen that Daniel remembered? For Megan's sake, did she have to tell him, while he was here?

Helen closed her eyes, and stroked the chenille nap of the sofa, taking comfort from the familiar feel of fabric. She couldn't bury the truth any more. She knew she had to do it, and face whatever consequences followed. She just wasn't ready yet. She couldn't imagine ever being ready.

'So he hates you before he even knows about Megan?' Kirsty asked, when Helen stayed silent. 'After so long apart? And though he has the hot new girlfriend?' Helen nodded. 'He must have loved you an awful lot.'

'Yes, he did. But don't go dreaming of happy-ever-afters,' she warned, seeing Kirsty's eyes begin to sparkle. 'I can't compete with Miss Australia.'

'But you have a huge advantage that she doesn't have.'

'If you say age or experience I'll throw the rest of this coffee over your lovely cream sofa.'

'You wouldn't dare. And that's not what I meant. You have Megan on your side. Miss Australia isn't the mother of his child, is she?'

'Thanks for that glowing review of all my desirable assets.'

'Hello, this sounds interesting.' Kirsty's husband, Ben, came in, a crying toddler in his arms. 'Sorry to interrupt, but Tommy isn't happy about the amount of attention I'm paying to the vegetables. Can I leave him with you?'

'I'll take him.' Helen stood up and prised Tommy away from his father. 'Shall I take him out in the

34

pram? He might be glad of a nap before lunch.'

'But it looks like it's going to rain,' Kirsty protested.

'I don't mind.' Helen was already pulling on her coat. 'Some fresh air would probably do me good.'

'I thought you were looking ropey,' Ben said, with more honesty than tact. 'What did you get up to last night? Or is it not suitable for a man's ears?'

'It would be suitable for the Pope's ears. I had an early night.'

'Is that what you call it now?' Ben laughed. 'I believe you. I hope you weren't worrying about Megan. She had a great time, and we loved having her. She played quite happily with Jenny this morning, and we had the best lie-in we've had for ages...' He winked at Kirsty, whose dirty chuckle left no doubt over what he meant. 'In fact, if you want to leave her here every weekend, I won't object...'

'Now I definitely need some fresh air to blow that image from my head.' Helen laughed, and fastened Tommy into his pushchair. 'Back in an hour or so, okay?'

She pushed Tommy out of the house, and walked towards the park, where she wandered round idly, wishing the blustery wind could blow the relics of last night right out of her head. When Tommy fell asleep at last, she headed back to Kirsty's, taking a quicker route along the main road, but as the rain started in earnest she had to stop to fasten on the raincover over the pram. It wasn't easy: the wind took hold of the plastic and blew it around on one side as she attempted to tie down the other, and the rain running down her face made it difficult to see anything.

'Hey! It's Helen, isn't it?'

Helen looked up, pushing rain-soaked hair from her face, and saw that a new BMW had pulled up at the kerb beside her. The front passenger window was wound down, and a smiling Tasha was leaning over from the driver's seat – across a most definitely not smiling Daniel. He was pale, unshaven, and clearly suffering from a horrendous hangover. Helen's heart lurched. She knew exactly what he needed to make him feel better. She wondered whether Tasha did, and whether she'd already administered his medicine that morning.

'Hello,' Helen replied, gaze firmly fixed on Tasha. There was no hint of a hangover there: she looked as blonde and perky as she had last night. Helen felt more conscious than ever of how frightful she must look herself, the weather having put the finishing touches on the devastation resulting from a sleepless night. 'I didn't expect to see you up and about so early.' Or anywhere near here, she could have added. She'd assumed they were staying with Valerie in Cheshire.

'Blame this darling man for that,' Tasha replied, flashing a bright smile at Helen, and ruffling Daniel's hair. Helen imagined the coarse texture of that hair under her own fingers. 'He drank far too much at the party, and kept me awake all night – and I don't mean in a fun way!' She laughed. 'We were up early

36

and he wanted to go home, so here we are.'

Tommy suddenly let out a scream, which was uncanny, because it was exactly the sound Helen was making in her head. Tasha looked like that after a sleepless night? And what was that about going home? Surely they weren't staying round here, where she might run into them at any time, with Megan?

'I didn't know you had a baby,' Tasha said, appearing to notice the pram for the first time. 'Is it a little boy?'

'Yes.' Helen could see out of the side of her eye that Daniel was staring at her. 'He's not mine, though. I'm taking him for a walk while my friend makes lunch. The weather wasn't quite as bad when I set off.'

A sudden gust of wind blew the raincover off again, and Tommy let out another scream as he was attacked by a face full of rain. Helen turned back to him, and struggled once more to pin down one side while the other flapped. The next thing she knew, Daniel was out of the car, and within moments he had Tommy securely encased beneath the cover.

'Thanks,' Helen said. She was going to leave it at that, but she couldn't stand his silent scrutiny. 'I would have managed it myself.'

'The poor child might have caught pneumonia by then.' He stared at her, rain streaking down his face, but he made no move to get back in the car. 'Who on earth would trust you with their baby? You used to be barely capable of looking after a cat.'

'I've changed,' she said, biting her lip to hide her

37

reaction to his words. He had thrown so many darts last night, but this one hit the bullseye.

His eyes flicked over her.

'So I can see,' he said. His expression left no doubt that he didn't mean it as a compliment. Personal insults now! After all they'd been to each other, how had they come to this? She felt another stab of pain, and to prevent him seeing it, she went on the attack.

'I don't need you to tell me how crap I look. You're not looking so hot yourself.'

'So not everything has changed. Still just as quick to fly off the handle, aren't you?'

'Only with you. It seems your ability to wind me up is as strong as ever.'

She saw, then, the memories flash across his face. Their relationship had been a passionate one in every way, and she knew he was thinking not only of how they had wound each other up, but of how they had wound down afterwards.

'Are you getting back in, Danny?' Tasha's voice floated over them, bringing them back to the present. 'You're drenched, and I expect Helen needs to get on.'

'Yes, I'd better return Tommy to his parents before they panic.'

Tasha laughed as Daniel climbed into the car.

'That's exactly the sort of child I like best. One that can be handed back!' The passenger window rose, then stopped and lowered again. 'Hey, will you be at the christening next weekend?'

'What christening?' Helen knew it was a stupid question as soon as the words left her mouth. How could she not have seen this coming?

'Is it Anita's baby? I lost track of all the names last night. I can't even remember what it is. I know it made a lot of noise... I'd have had to switch that monitor off!' Tasha laughed. 'Will we see you there?'

'Yes, I'll be there.' Helen had no choice: she was Sophie's godmother. She'd been thrilled when Anita had asked; now she wished she was an ordinary guest, and could feign a sudden illness to avoid the event. Thank God Tasha had mentioned it, so she could at least stop Megan going.

Tasha waved goodbye, and raised the window again. Daniel looked fixedly ahead while they drove away. Helen walked back to Kirsty's house, hardly registering the rain now that a bigger cloud hovered over her head. She'd had a lucky escape with the christening, but it had confirmed what Kirsty had said earlier. Daniel was going to find out, whether she was ready for it or not. And though a cowardly part of her thought how much easier it would be if he heard it from someone else, she still cared for him too much to allow that to happen. He deserved better.

'I thought you'd have been back ages ago,' Kirsty said, opening the door as Helen pushed the pram up the path. She looked at Helen's face, and frowned. 'What's the matter? Did Tommy not sleep?'

'Yes, he's fine. We were delayed by an encounter with Miss Australia.'

39

'Really?' Kirsty scooped Tommy out of the pram and stared at Helen. 'What was she doing round here? Was she on her own?'

'Daniel was there. I think they must be staying nearby.'

'And was the second meeting any easier than the first?'

'No. Worse, if that's possible.'

'Did you tell him?'

'No, it was hardly the time... standing out in the rain... and with Miss Australia there...'

'You're going to run out of excuses eventually.'

Not if she tried hard enough. She was known for her creativity, wasn't she?

'Talking of Megan,' Helen said, ignoring Kirsty's last sentence, 'is there any chance you could look after her next Sunday? Sorry to ask again so soon. I'll swap you for two evening babysits whenever you want.'

'Aren't you at the christening next Sunday? I thought you were taking Megan.'

'I was, but now I think she might be bored, and it will be difficult to look after her if I'm busy doing godmotherly things.'

Kirsty saw straight through this.

'He's going to be there, isn't he?'

Helen nodded. 'But that's not the reason...'

'Of course it's not.' Kirsty oozed scepticism. 'Okay, I'll look after Megan, on the condition that you use the opportunity to tell him about her. Agreed?'

'I'll try,' Helen said. It was the best she could do. Because she had no idea how she was ever going to make a confession of this magnitude; or how she would deal with the fall out when she blew her world apart again.

CHAPTER 4

As soon as Helen walked into St Andrew's on Tuesday morning, she could tell that something was wrong. The other shop owners were gathered at the base of the pulpit, which was where they normally caught up on each other's news after being closed for two days. It wasn't normal to see the miserable expressions they were all wearing today.

'This isn't the happy smiling face we want to show to our public,' Helen chided them, as she joined the group. Not that any members of the public were there. Tuesday was always a quiet day. As was Wednesday. And Thursday. St Andrew's was on the wrong side of town to benefit from the visitors to the popular market on the days it was open. 'Come on, you can't all have had such a bad weekend!'

'We've all had letters,' Malcolm said gloomily. A local artist in his late fifties, Malcolm had been selling his work at St Andrew's since it opened as a craft centre. Although, as he was often heard to point out, recently it had felt more like exhibiting his work than selling it.

'What sort of letters? Clearly not love letters judging by your faces. Not poison pen, are they? Are they constructed from cut-out newspaper headlines?'

No one returned Helen's smile.

'There's one for you.' Fiona, the creator of fantastic handmade stationery, held out an official-looking brown envelope. Helen took it.

'It's from the council,' Saskia interrupted before Helen had even managed to tear the first corner. Saskia was Helen's neighbour on the other side from Fiona, and sold the jewellery that Tasha had pored over on her visit to St Andrew's. 'They're kicking us out.'

'What?' Helen yanked open the envelope, pulled out the letter, and read it through. As she did, she could feel the same expression of blank misery settling over her own features. It was true. The council had leased St Andrew's from the local diocese, but the lease was about to expire, and they had chosen not to renew it. All the owners of the shops were given three months' notice of the closure. 'They can't do this, can they?'

'I'm afraid they can.' Ron, the oldest trader at St Andrew's at almost seventy, waved a folded paper at Helen. 'I've dug out my contract. The council only needs to give three months' notice. It's here in black and white, and I expect we all agreed the same terms. By Christmas, these doors will be closed for good. At least we might catch a bit of the Christmas trade before they do.'

The others nodded in resignation.

'Surely we're going to fight this, aren't we?' Helen demanded, looking round the group. 'We can't let this happen. There's nowhere else like this in town. The council should be keen to promote independent shops. I know we've been quiet recently...' This caused some raised eyebrows: for quiet she could as

43

easily have said dead. 'But it's always been a struggle through the school holidays, and things usually pick up from autumn through to Christmas. We could start a campaign, do more advertising, hold some events... They haven't given us a chance.'

'They won't,' Malcolm replied. 'We're snookered. Three of the shops have stood empty since the wood turner left last year. No one wants to take on these units, not with the economy the way it is. Keeping the place open probably costs more than they get back from us.'

His Eeyore-like gloom was infecting everyone. Heavy sighs echoed around the church. Helen couldn't let this happen. St Andrew's was more than a shopping destination: it was a community. She knew she wasn't the only one who had found solace here. Fiona had opened her shop in her mid-forties, when she had finally found the courage to leave her bullying husband. Saskia had turned her hobby into a career when she'd been made redundant. For Malcolm, St Andrew's had been a place to grieve when his disabled son had died. Ron's story was unclear, but there was no doubt that something drew him here, past the age when he would normally have retired. Surely there was something that could be done?

'I'm going to ring the council,' Helen said, looking at the letter again. 'Let's see what this Miriam Priestley has to say for herself.' And she strode off, her mobile phone already pressed to her ear.

Ten minutes later, she rejoined the others, who

44

hadn't moved from the foot of the pulpit.

'We're too late,' she said, screwing up the letter and throwing it to the floor. Fiona quickly bent to pick it up, hating any assault on paper, however plain. 'Even if the council could be persuaded to change its mind – which I doubt, if Miriam Priestley is typical of the lack of imagination there – it would do no good. The diocese has already agreed to sell the building to an evangelical church movement. The deal is done, and the paperwork all signed. They want to hold their Christmas service here, then they plan to strip out all unwelcome signs of commerce – that means us – and move in permanently by February. St Andrew's is going to be restored as a church.'

'I suppose it is what it was built for,' Fiona said.

Of course she was right, and as Helen gazed round at the vaulted roof, the ornate woodwork, and the original stained-glass windows, remnants of her Catholic upbringing kicked in and whispered to her that it was fitting that such a beautiful place should be given back its heart and purpose. But then her eyes fell on Crazy Little Things, and those whispers were quashed. She had put her whole heart into that shop, and the business had given her a purpose she had desperately needed in the post-Daniel days. What would she be without it? Where would she go?

'It's like bloody redundancy all over again,' Saskia grumbled, her otherwise attractive face marred by a familiar scowl. 'Except this time there isn't any payment to sweeten the pill. What are we meant to do now? Did the council give us any thought at all?'

'Apparently there are lots of available shop units in prime locations in the town centre if we're interested,' Helen replied, pulling a face as she quoted Miriam Priestley. 'By which I assume that she means the derelict buildings between the pound shops and the takeaways. The rent is probably twice as high as here.'

'It's all right for you,' Saskia said to Helen, with ill-concealed bitterness. She had a chip on her shoulder large enough to feed a whole school of hungry children. 'You'll be okay if you set up somewhere else. You have a following. We all know that eighty percent of the people who come in here are visiting your shop. Our business hangs on your coat tails, or on a few curious visitors that come in to browse. Even Joan's cakes are more popular than my jewellery. I could never justify my own independent shop. I'm finished.'

As Helen glanced round, she saw that everyone else was nodding in agreement, even Joan, who had been listening silently to what the others had to say. They had all given up. There would be no battle to save St Andrew's unless she undertook it herself. Her first instinctive thought was that she couldn't do it: it was too much on her own; and she had no idea where to start. But as she felt the despair of the others seeping under her skin, she gazed over at Crazy Little Things again. She wasn't useless. She had created that business, and had invested huge amounts of time and energy to keep it alive. She was not going to give it up now.

'Perhaps we can find a similar set-up where we can all stay together,' Helen suggested, looking round, willing the others to feel a spark of enthusiasm.

Saskia snorted.

'Another unused church, which happens to have five empty retail units and space for a café? Come off it. I think you've been spending too long reading fairytales to Megan. Life's not like that, at least not where I'm concerned. You might have a dream life, but for some of us it's one long slog.'

If this was a dream life, Helen thought, she would hate to know what a nightmare one felt like. She turned away, and went to open up Crazy Little Things. She gazed round at the books, the buttons, the brightly coloured skeins of wool and embroidery threads hanging like semi-precious necklaces, and at her crazy patchwork items that she had spent hours perfecting, even when the retail price barely covered the cost of the materials. This shop had been a true labour of love: she had poured herself into it. And in return, it had saved her. Now it was her turn to save it.

By the time the christening arrived the following Sunday, Helen was no further forward. She had reluctantly accepted that they couldn't stay in St Andrew's, though her heart trembled every time she pictured having to pack up and leave. She was working on the idea of recreating St Andrew's somewhere else, but an alternative location had been impossible to find so far. She had swallowed her pride

47

and spoken to Miriam Priestley again, to see what larger units might be available, that could be divided up into smaller stalls. She'd even gone to look at a couple, sneaking out without a word to the others so she didn't raise hope that was doomed to be unfulfilled. The rent and renovation costs had proved prohibitively expensive; and it was hard to imagine the patrons of Kevin's Klassy Kebabs moving seamlessly next door to spend money on crafts.

So the search for new premises went on, and the worry grew about how she would afford to live in the New Year. She could sew at home, and did, through the night on too many occasions, but the income from her crazy patchwork commissions wasn't enough to survive on, even though she claimed every benefit and credit she could; she needed the profit from the retail trade, not to mention the advertising it provided for her artistic pieces. Managing her finances was already a precarious walk across a tightrope; without Crazy Little Things, it would be a painful plunge into ruin.

The only good thing to be said about the whole business with St Andrew's was that it had stopped Helen dwelling on the prospect of seeing Daniel again at the christening. Not even the sight of him striding into church, wearing a perfectly tailored grey suit and a beautiful Australian, could make her spirits sink much lower than they had been all week. And at least they chose to sit on the opposite side of the church, slightly further back from her, so if she kept her eyes firmly fixed ahead, and resisted the urge to turn round, she could almost pretend they weren't there at all.

This plan proved a great success until the time came for the godparents to be called forward, and for the rest of the congregation to gather round the font. Helen took a place next to Anita's brother, the other godparent. And then Daniel stood next to her.

'This side of the font is for *godparents*,' she said to him, in a low voice, shrinking back from any potential physical contact. His aftershave invaded her nostrils, and she took several short sniffs, not recognising the musky scent. It wasn't the smell she associated with her Daniel, and the unfamiliarity jarred.

He didn't even look at her.

'I know.'

'But you're not...'

'I am.' He continued to gaze ahead, the public smile on his face at odds with the tone of his voice. 'Not as surprising a choice as you, am I?'

Helen looked at Anita, who flashed her an apologetic smile, and bent down to straighten Sophie's christening gown. The rest of the service raced by, and Helen heard nothing of it except the rumble of Daniel's deep voice at her side. She could have been vowing to take on the devil single-handed in a bare knuckle fight for all she knew. She smiled, and moved her lips at the right time, but it was impossible to concentrate, especially when the baby was passed along the row, and ended with Daniel. She saw him, a baby girl in his arms, and there was only one thought: that could have been Megan. That was what he would have looked like holding their daughter. She stared at him, emotions roiling, struck as never before by the reality of what she had done, to him and to all of them.

When the service was over, the guests crossed the graveyard to the church hall, where drinks and a buffet were being served. Helen decided to have one drink then leave, but her route to the door was cut off every time she tried to make her escape. And then, as she finally spotted a gap, Tasha of all people accosted her.

'Did you survive your soaking the other day?' she asked, her easy smile dwarfing the polite one that Helen had quickly dug out. 'I only thought as we were driving away that we could have given you a lift, but Danny said...'

'What did I say?'

Daniel appeared, and slung his arm round Tasha's shoulders. His other hand held an almost empty wine glass. He smiled down at Tasha and ignored Helen. She wondered why he had bothered coming over, if her presence was so abhorrent. Perhaps Tasha's attraction was strong enough to overcome anything else. And who could blame him? She was gorgeous, and apparently nice as well. She really did have it all. All including Daniel, Helen thought, as he bent and kissed Tasha. Helen turned away, searching for anything to scrub that image from her head, and caught Sally's anxious gaze. Sally came over, dragging Craig with her.

'That's another gorgeous bag,' Tasha said, indicating the crazy patchwork clutch tucked under

50

Helen's arm. 'You make me so jealous. I've never been creative, or good with my hands.'

'I'd have to disagree with you there,' Daniel said, smiling at her. Helen recognised the smile: it was one he used to save for her. She dug her teeth into her lip, hoping physical pain would overwhelm the emotional one. It was ridiculous; she couldn't have expected that he would never smile that way at anyone else. She'd had over four years to accept the idea. But seeing him do it was something else entirely. She glanced at Sally again.

'Is it one of your new lines?' Sally asked, reading and reacting to the silent appeal. 'I haven't seen it before. I keep meaning to come to your shop to have a look round. I've not been for ages.'

'You'll have to come soon, then.' Sally's attempt at distraction had merely sent Helen leaping from one painful thought to another. 'I'm closing the week before Christmas.'

Hearing the words aloud didn't make it any more real.

'Closing?' Sally repeated. 'For good? Why? I thought you were happy at St Andrew's.'

'St Andrew's?' Daniel's gaze fell on Helen at last. 'You have a shop in St Andrew's?'

'Yes.' She knew why that had provoked a response. They'd discovered the craft centre together: caught in the rain one day, they had run in, seeking shelter, and as the heavy oak doors banged shut behind them, they had fallen silent, recognising that this was somewhere special. They had browsed round

51

the shops, and enjoyed tea and cakes at Joan's, and for the first time Helen had felt a spark of ambition and purpose, a potential answer to the question that she hadn't until that moment known she was asking. She had shared with Daniel her idea that one day she might have a shop there. He had laughed, and said she was far too lazy ever to do it.

'So you have what you always wanted,' he said now.

There was no possible reply to that, not with him standing so near, with his arm around another woman.

'Why are you closing?' Sally asked again.

'I have to. The council has given us all notice to leave. We have three months, then St Andrew's will be sold.'

'Can they do that? Craig, can't you take a look and see if there's any loophole?'

'It's not my area, but I'll look over the contract if you like.' Craig was a personal injury lawyer.

'Thanks, but it would do no good. The deal is done. The new owners move in at Christmas.'

'But how will you manage with...' Sally trailed off, looking as if she'd noticed the minefield ahead in the nick of time. Her eyes flicked between Helen and Daniel. 'It seems such a shame. How long have you been there?'

'Over three years.'

'Three years?' Daniel repeated. 'It must be the longest commitment you've ever made. I'm amazed you lasted so long before giving up.'

52

His charming smile swept round, making clear it was a joke, but it pointedly excluded Helen.

'It wasn't my decision. The council have forced this on us. I'm not giving up. I love my work.'

'Love? So you do know that word?'

The rest of the room fell away, leaving Helen and Daniel staring at each other, shocked by this unexpected outburst and the rich seam of bitterness it exposed. It was all too much for Helen. She couldn't keep on doing this, having her heart fill with love when she saw him, only for him to squeeze it dry with every cutting word or hostile look. She would have to leave, and avoid their mutual friends until she was sure he was out of the country again. But if this was the last time she was going to meet him, there was something she had to do, though every drop of blood running through her veins was urging her not to.

'Can we have a word?' she asked. He slowly raised one eyebrow. She had forgotten how much it annoyed her when he did that.

'What about?'

'In private.'

'I don't have anything to say to you, in private or not.'

'Fine. You can listen to what I want to say.'

Tasha stroked Daniel's arm.

'No worries, Danny, you two must have loads to catch up on. I'll go with Craig and Sally for some cake.'

The other three wandered away, leaving Helen alone with Daniel.

'Well?'

'Not here, outside.'

Helen turned and marched out of the church hall, and into the graveyard. She pulled her cardigan tight around her as a chill autumn wind blew across the tombstones. She heard a crunch behind her. Daniel waited, saying nothing. This was her moment. She needed to do it now. But something about him – the lowered eyebrows, the crossed arms, the narrowed lips – killed the words before they reached the back of her throat.

'I want this to stop,' she said, stalling for time. 'I've got the message loud and clear. You hate me...'

'No, I don't.'

'What?'

'I don't hate you. It was all a long time ago. I don't feel anything for you.'

She heard his words, but his eyes said something different.

'So stop all the sniping, and the little digs. Not for me,' she said quickly, as his mouth began to open. 'Do it for your friends. Our friends. If we run into each other again before you go back...'

'I'm not going anywhere.'

'What?'

'I've moved back to England.' Cold blue eyes held hers. 'Why are you looking so shocked about that? It was always the plan. Four or five years out there to earn the big money, and then back here to settle down. Nothing's changed.'

Except, as they looked at each other, they both

54

knew that it had. Everything had changed. He was meant to be settling down with Helen. Instead...

'And Tasha?' She couldn't stop the question.

'Tasha has moved with me.' He smiled at her, though it wasn't a pleasant smile. 'After six months together, she was willing to travel across the world to be with me. That's my definition of love.'

And there was Helen's perfect opening to tell him. Tell him what her definition of love was. Explain that sometimes love could mean choosing *not* to travel across the world with someone, but to let go. And she opened her mouth, but there was a second's hesitation before she could bring herself to take the plunge, and he walked away.

CHAPTER 5

Who would have thought so much could go wrong in the space of a week, Helen reflected the next day, as she made sandwiches for lunch, while keeping an eye on Megan, who was playing in the sand pit which half filled the minuscule garden at the back of the house. Eight days ago she'd been paddling along quite placidly in the shallows at home and at work. Now it felt as if she'd been caught up in a riptide, and dragged out to sea with little idea of where she was heading.

The only consolation was that worrying about one problem gave her some temporary respite from the other. After the encounter with Daniel yesterday, today she was determined to focus on work. Monday was supposed to be her day off, but with a deadline looming for completing a crazy patchwork throw, ordered as a wedding present, she was having to use every spare minute she had. Luckily Megan could be occupied for decent spells sorting buttons and beads, and pretending to help.

The doorbell rang, and after checking Megan was settled, Helen went to answer it. Daniel was standing on the doorstep, looking sober, serious, and as handsome as ever. He held an envelope, which he was tapping against his leg.

'What are you doing here?' she gasped, clutching the door handle.

'I could ask you the same. Not quite the life you're accustomed to, is it? I would have put money on you not knowing that terraced houses exist.'

'It was convenient,' she said, with a shrug. She wasn't going to justify where she lived to him. How dare he come and sneer? She'd moved into this tiny mews house on a modern estate before Megan was born, when it was all she could afford to rent. It was close to a good nursery and a well-rated school, and that had been more important than underfloor heating and ensuite bathrooms. She glanced over her shoulder, anxious about leaving Megan outside – and more anxious that she might wander inside. 'Who told you where I was? And what do you want?'

'I came to give you this.' He held out the envelope. 'Craig gave me your address.'

'What is it?'

'What I owe you.' He waved the envelope at her. Curiosity getting the better of her, she took it and opened it. There was a cheque inside, payable to her, for fifteen thousand pounds. Helen stared at the paper in her hand, trying to make sense of it.

'What's this for?'

'It's your share of the proceeds of the house. When it was sold, all the money went into my account. I'd have given it to you before, if I'd known where you were. Or if you were still alive.'

Helen risked another look behind her. The front door opened straight into the living room; from there, there was a direct line of sight through the kitchen and into the garden.

57

'Am I interrupting something?'

'Of course not!' Helen thrust the cheque back at him. 'I don't want this. You don't owe me anything.'

'Take it. You'll need it if you're looking for new shop premises.'

Helen hardly knew whether he was patronising her or if, at last, a glimmer of the Daniel she loved had broken through. The cheque was still in her hand, held out to him, but she saw that his attention had changed. He was gazing past her shoulder, into the room beyond. Helen turned. Megan was standing in the kitchen doorway. It was a cold day; she was muffled up in a coat and scarf, a hat covering most of her hair; but Helen was so familiar with every stitch of her face, that the truth seemed blindingly obvious. Was he seeing it? Her eyes travelled back from daughter to father.

'Babysitting again?'

'I...' She stopped. Could he not see the truth? She couldn't say it. She really couldn't say it, not with Megan right behind them. Not when she could imagine the depth of his hatred when she did.

'Mummy, can I have my lunch now?'

Objectively, it was fascinating to see the play of emotion flow across Daniel's face. It started with a frown of confusion, then his eyes widened as comprehension took shape. Finally he looked straight at Helen and, for a moment, there was no hatred, no coldness, only the most profound pain. Then it was gone, replaced by a blank expression which was almost worse. He walked away, and got back into his car.

58

Helen closed the front door, strode over to Megan, and scooped her up into a desperate hug. Hands trembling, she took off the hat, unwrapped the scarf and unzipped her coat, until a mini-Daniel emerged from under the layers. Helen kissed the top of Megan's hair, hair the exact colour and texture of his.

'Pop upstairs and wash your hands, then you can have your lunch,' she said, trying to still the wobble in her voice. 'And use the soap!'

Megan had reached the top of the stairs when there was a savage banging on the front door. Helen opened it again.

'Who was he?' Daniel demanded. 'Do I know him? How long was it going on for?'

'What? Who are you talking about?'

Daniel pushed past her into the living room. It was a mess: scraps of richly coloured fabric and luscious embroidery silks were scattered round the chair in the corner where she did her sewing. But she suspected he hadn't even noticed the state of the room. He was gazing round, seeing nothing.

'Are you still with him?' There was a noise upstairs as Megan came out of the bathroom. Daniel's head whipped round. 'Is he here now?'

'There's no one here except me and Megan. There's never been anyone else.'

'Megan?' Daniel's voice had gone quiet. 'You had an affair, had another man's child, and called it Megan? How could you?'

It had been *their* name. When they'd speculated about the future – their future after Hong Kong – they

59

had imagined their children, Megan and Archie. But surely, surely not. Surely he didn't think that she'd cheated on him, had a child, and used their name? Did he honestly think so little of her that he believed she could do that?

'I didn't have an affair,' she said, desperate now that he should know the truth, and unable to get the words out fast enough. 'Megan's...'

On cue, Megan skipped down the stairs.

'Mummy, I can't hang the towel up.' She stopped when she saw Daniel, and hovered on the bottom stair, looking up at him with curious blue eyes. Identical blue eyes stared back at her. Helen wasn't sure if Daniel was still breathing. And it was no wonder he was so transfixed. She had always known that Megan looked like him, but seeing them together for the first time was incredible. He must have felt like one of his childhood photographs had come to life in front of him.

There was a horrible silence. Daniel looked from Megan to Helen, his eyes glazed with utter incomprehension.

'Is...'

'Yes,' she interrupted quickly, not wanting him to say it in front of Megan. 'Yes, she is.'

He stared at Helen, eyes drilling into hers, as they had done on so many other, happier occasions, as if he wanted to know every part of her.

'What was it, Nell? What did I do to you to deserve this?'

She couldn't help herself. She reached out and

touched his arm, feeling the tension in his muscles.

'Dan...'

He jerked away and stormed out, slamming the door behind him.

CHAPTER 6

Three days passed, and Helen heard nothing from Daniel. She tensed every time the door of St Andrew's opened, and every time she heard a car drive past her house – which, living on a busy estate, was quite often. But there was no contact from him. These three days of silence were worse than all the years of guilt and worry that had gone before.

'Are you okay?' Fiona asked, as Helen ran into St Andrew's on Friday morning, ten minutes after opening time. 'I was just asking the others whether we should call you.' She peered at Helen. 'If you don't mind me saying, you do look tired.'

'So much for the artfully applied make-up,' Helen said, laughing.

'You've done a good job,' Fiona replied, putting her hand on Helen's arm. 'But I can tell a disguise when I see one. You can't kid a kidder.'

Helen took her hand and squeezed it. She knew that Fiona had had to conceal more than the marks of insomnia in the past.

'I haven't been sleeping well,' she said, sliding back the glass door to open up the front of her shop. Each shop had been built using glass partitions, so that none of the features of the building were covered up. Helen's was one of the larger units, and the whole of the front panel could be pushed to the side.

'I'm not surprised.' Fiona sighed. 'It's preying on my mind too. The time until Christmas is going to fly by.'

'Have you thought about what you're going to do?' Helen asked, dragging her thoughts back to St Andrew's and the problems she faced at work. Not that she'd forgotten; but the situation with Daniel had stolen all her focus this week.

'No, I don't see what I can do. I can't afford a shop in town and, anyway, I don't want to be on my own. We're like a little family here, aren't we? I wouldn't last five minutes by myself. You're probably the only one who could survive outside St Andrew's.'

'I'm sure that's not true,' Helen said, but she had a horrible suspicion it might be. Fiona, Malcolm and Ron didn't have the drive needed to set up anywhere else, and even Saskia was showing surprisingly little motivation to plan her future. Helen resigned herself to another night spent looking at rentable property, and whether there was any prospect of them staying together. The responsibility for all of them had fallen on her by default. She had walked past an empty retail unit in the shopping centre the other day, which had seemed the right size, but she had recoiled against moving from St Andrew's to somewhere so soulless. There had to be a solution. She just needed to find it.

***

Friday lunchtimes were always busy, and Helen was happily helping choose some buttons for a knitted cardigan when she noticed a man loitering round the display of crazy patchwork pieces. She did have a few regular male customers, but they were normally of a certain age, and carrying oilcloth tote bags. This man was on quite the opposite end of the scale: tall, early thirties, with shaggy tawny brown hair, and not a bag in sight.

Helen kept an eye on him while she completed the button sale. He was picking up virtually every item and inspecting it before moving on to the next one. What on earth was he doing? He didn't look like a thief: he was definitely more suited to the romantic lead than a starring role on Crimewatch; but he didn't look like a crafter either. Checking that no one else needed her help, she wandered over to the crazy patchwork display.

'Hello,' she said, displaying her best customer friendly smile. 'Can I help? Are you looking for anything in particular?'

He looked up with a smile that started off polite and slowly grew as he regarded Helen.

'This is fantastic work,' he said. 'I've never seen anything like it before.'

'I should hope not. I designed it all.'

'So *you're* Helen?'

She nodded. Her name was all over the display and on every price tag, so it hadn't taken much deduction to work that out. Why then was he looking so surprised? Surprised and pleased: but that made no sense.

'Sorry,' he said, twisting a teddy bear round in his hand. 'I didn't expect...' He smiled as Helen rescued the bear and put it back on the table. 'Do you do all this yourself?'

'Yes. A friend helps out in the shop sometimes, but I do all the sewing myself.'

'You're very talented.'

'Thanks. I know. But it's always good to hear someone else say so.'

He laughed, and loose curls quivered around his face.

'Is it all done by hand?'

'All the decorative stitches, but with the stitches that hold the pieces together, see here...' She pointed to a cushion, and he nodded. 'It depends on what the item is. That teddy bear you were torturing was done mainly on the sewing machine. It's part of the Christmas range, when I try to make some small, quick items to keep the shop filled up.' She stopped, and smiled. 'Sorry, I didn't mean to rattle on. Push my button and I can go on for hours.'

'Is that so?' Sherry brown eyes held her gaze. 'I'll have to remember that.'

Was he *flirting*? The eye contact and the cheeky grin all suggested he was. That was a first. She'd never had a customer flirt with her before – thank God, considering most of them were ladies, and the

65

others – well, they probably didn't even know what flirting was. But was he a customer? He hadn't shown much sign of buying anything yet. In fact, he was showing more interest in *her* than in her work.

'If you're interested in a Christmas gift,' she went on, determined to ignore his continuing grin, and get back to the safe subject of business, 'I've got some more things that I haven't had chance to set out yet.' She bent down, and rummaged in her bag before pulling out a rectangular piece of crazy patchwork, created from scraps of fabric in various shades of pink, sewn together with a glittering metallic thread. Tiny embroidered flowers were scattered amongst the patches.

'If you're looking for a present for the special woman in your life,' she said, holding it out to him, 'what about this Kindle sleeve? I can do it in different sizes, to fit a phone, or iPad or laptop. Or,' she added hurriedly, realising she was making a big assumption, 'I have some in shades of blue if it's a special man you're buying for.'

'There's no one special. But if there was, I'd definitely be going for the pink.' He smiled, and Helen put down the Kindle sleeve. 'Will you be busy in the run-up to Christmas?'

'I hope so.' More than he could know. She needed to be busy, needed every penny she could earn, especially as life after Christmas was looking so uncertain.

'Is that when you get most of your sales?'

'It certainly increases then. But I have a loyal

band of followers who come all year round.'

'Do you ever put on demonstrations, show how it's done?'

'I'd love to! And to have a sewing circle, and classes, and seasonal workshops, but there's simply no room here.' She stopped, smiling. 'I did warn you about that button.' Helen looked round, checking what the other customers were up to, if she had any left. How had she become so distracted by this man? A coachload of visitors could have arrived without her noticing. 'I'd better go and serve some customers. Thanks for looking.'

She turned away, but he spoke again.

'Hold on, I am a customer.'

'I knew you wouldn't resist the Kindle sleeve. It was the sparkly flowers, wasn't it?'

He laughed. 'Actually, I'd prefer this.'

He picked up a scarf from the counter in front of him. It was one of the simpler pieces, made from scraps of woollen fabric in beautiful shades of brown and heathery green, joined together by a plain herringbone stitch and without any extra embellishments. It was one of Helen's favourite items, and she had never understood why it hadn't sold in almost twelve months. He wrapped it round his neck, and smiled. 'What do you think?'

She thought that if she put a picture of him wearing it in the shop, she'd sell hundreds of them. The colours in the scarf drew out an extraordinary warmth in his eyes: a warmth which was undoubtedly radiating towards her. She felt it like a flush along her skin.

'It's a perfect choice,' Helen said, smiling back. 'It could have been made for you. You can't possibly not buy it. The till is right over here...'

Laughing, he followed her, paid for the scarf and left. Saskia hurried over as soon as the doors of St Andrew's closed behind him.

'Who was that?' she demanded.

'Who?' Though there could hardly be any doubt who she meant.

'That hot man, of course. You're never going to tell me he sews.'

'Not that I know of. Although,' Helen added, pulling her eyes away from the doors at last and turning to Saskia, 'what if he does? Sewing is the new knitting. Lots of cool and stylish people sew now.' She only hoped Saskia wouldn't ask her to name one.

'If you say so.' Saskia was clearly unconvinced. 'What was all the flirting about?'

'Did you think he was flirting?' So she hadn't imagined it! And though Helen wasn't interested in finding a man – wasn't interested in any man after Daniel – it was the first time since having Megan, since her appearance had changed, that she had noticed a man pay her attention. The kickstart it gave her confidence was worth a thousand times more than the profit on the scarf.

'Not him, you! You were all over him!'

'No I wasn't!' Saskia had this all wrong. How could she have been flirting with him, when her

68

heart still longed for Daniel? 'I was being charming to a customer, that's all.'

'Next time you feel like not flirting with a totally gorgeous man, can you please send him my way? The only decent men to ever come to my shop are buying presents for wives or girlfriends. It's so depressing.'

The afternoon was quiet, which suited Helen. She was expecting a lady at the end of the day, who wanted her to sew a family tree, inset with photographs, for her mother's eightieth birthday. Helen loved the idea, and had already drawn a few sketches and gathered together some fabric samples. She was making further small improvements when she heard the click of purposeful heels across the wooden church floor. Thinking her customer might have arrived early, Helen glanced up and saw Valerie Blake.

It certainly looked as if Valerie meant business. She was wearing an immaculate navy wool coat, buttoned to the neck, polished navy court shoes, and her handbag swung from her arm as if she were the Queen. The outfit was formidable enough; the expression of grim determination on her face was terrifying.

Valerie stalked up to Helen, who waited in her shop, paralysed by foreboding, a tug of war raging in her stomach.

'May we have a word?'

'Of course.'

Valerie looked round.

'Is there anywhere private we can speak?'

'No, here's fine.'

'Very well. It's about these lies you've been telling my son.'

Helen flinched, and tightened her grip on the counter in front of her. But what had she expected? An eager request to meet her granddaughter?

'I haven't told him any lies. I didn't want to tell him anything.'

'And what about this child?'

'Megan,' Helen snapped. 'Her name is Megan.'

Valerie shook her head, as if the name was irrelevant.

'Haven't you done him enough damage without this? Why did you have to tell him such a thing?'

'Because he saw her. And because it's true.'

'I can see why it would suit you to say so. You've had plenty of time to rue what you gave up with him. And now you see him return, handsome as ever, rich and successful, and you think you can snare him in this stale old trap.' Valerie paused for breath, a flush of pink showing through her powdered cheeks. 'I will not let you do it.' She enunciated every word with cold clarity. 'How much do you want?'

'What?' Helen thought she must have misheard. Surely Valerie wasn't offering her money? But yes – she opened the clasp of her handbag, and pulled out her chequebook.

'How much will it take to convince you to tell him the truth? Hundreds? Thousands?' Valerie put

70

the chequebook down on the counter, and uncapped a fountain pen. She stood poised, ready to write. 'You must have a price. Whatever it is, I'll pay it. Nothing is more important than Daniel. I want you to leave him alone.'

The hand gripping the fountain pen was trembling. The sight took away the offence of Valerie's words, and left Helen feeling nothing but pity. Valerie was a mother, protecting her child in the only way she knew how. Helen understood all too well, and she couldn't hate her for it.

'I don't want your money,' she said. She reached behind the curtain at the back of the shop, and grabbed her handbag. She drew out an envelope and handed it to Valerie. 'Here. It's the cheque Dan gave me. I've torn it into pieces.' Valerie glanced inside the envelope, frowning. 'I don't want anything, from either of you. If I had wanted to trap him, I'd have done it a long time ago, not now, not when I've struggled for four years on my own. I would have been quite happy to keep Megan a secret from him for ever, if he hadn't come back. But he saw her, and he asked, and I wasn't going to lie. He is her father.'

'We'll see about that.' Valerie opened her handbag again, and withdrew a Waitrose sandwich bag. There was a dark sliver of hair inside it. She placed it down on the counter. 'If you're so confident about who the father is, you won't mind agreeing to a DNA test, will you?'

'Yes, I will mind! I'm not putting Megan through

71

a DNA test to prove that she is part of a family I'd rather she had nothing to do with!'

'It's a non-invasive test. All we need is a sample of her hair. Or are you having second thoughts now about your paternity claim?'

Oh, she was infuriating! That glint of anticipated triumph in her eyes was unbearable.

'Your hair may not be a strong enough match,' Helen said, pushing the Waitrose bag back across the counter to Valerie.

'Probably not. But this is a sample of Daniel's hair.'

Helen snatched up the bag and examined the clump of hair. There was no doubt about it, now she could see it up close. It was Daniel's hair. So he was a party to this DNA plan. He had seen Megan, heard Helen tell him that he was Megan's father, but he still didn't believe it. He needed proof. And this dart, that he hadn't even been brave enough to throw himself, plunged straight into her heart with a pain that flowed through her blood.

'No,' she said, hearing her voice come out as little more than a whisper. 'No. I won't agree to a DNA test. But not because there's any doubt about Daniel being Megan's father,' she said, as a triumphant smile began to ascend Valerie's face. 'It's because if he has to demand scientific proof, if the evidence of his eyes and his heart aren't enough, he doesn't deserve to have any part of her.' Helen held the bag out to Valerie. 'So you can give him this back, and tell him to stay away from us. I would rather Megan had no father at all than him.'

Valerie opened her mouth, but for once she was unable to find a suitable reply. She took her sandwich bag, folded it, and tucked it into her handbag.

'We clearly have nothing more to say,' she announced at last. 'You'll stay away from Daniel?'

'Gladly.'

Valerie nodded, and fastening the clasp of her bag with a click of finality, she turned to leave. Helen hesitated, one thought chasing round her head. Should she do it? Would it seem vindictive? But she had to. Valerie had acted as a mother; but she was also a grandmother. She had to know.

'Valerie?' As she turned back, with an expression of surprised enquiry, Helen grabbed her phone. She scrolled through and found the picture she wanted. 'Here. I took this picture of Megan last weekend.'

She held out her phone. Valerie stared at her, uncertain and unmoving. Then her eyes pulled away from Helen's, and flicked down to the phone. She blinked, and her hand came forward and snatched it off Helen. She held it close to her face, studying the picture. At last she dropped the phone onto the counter, and her hand flew up to her chest.

'Oh...' she moaned. Her eyes met Helen's again, and this time there was no hostility, no triumph, only recognition.

'Are you okay?' Helen touched Valerie's arm. The last thing she needed was for her to have a heart attack in the shop. But the words seemed to shock her back into life. Valerie nodded, and with one last glance at the phone, turned and walked out of St Andrew's.

74

CHAPTER 7

'Admit it, you wanted to give her a slap, didn't you?'

'Surprisingly not.' Helen laughed at Kirsty's disbelieving expression. 'Granny bashing isn't my thing.' She grimaced at her own words. Valerie Blake was possibly the world's least granny-like granny. 'Not even a verbal slapping.'

'She would have deserved it. Spiteful old trout. Fancy offering to pay you to stay away!'

'I know! As if I haven't spent the last four years trying to do exactly that! Perhaps I should have asked for the arrears.'

Smiling, Helen poured the last of the wine between her glass and Kirsty's. Their monthly night out, when Ben looked after all the children while they went for a meal and drinks, couldn't have come at a more perfect time. Delicious Italian food, accompanied by delectable Italian wine, had done a better job than another sleepless night in relieving the emotions stirred by Valerie's visit the day before. Although seeing Valerie hadn't been the worst of it. Valerie had never had a good opinion of her. It was the disbelief from Daniel that was so hard to stomach. Her smile faded.

'Hey, come on,' Kirsty said, squeezing Helen's hand. 'So Daniel's proved himself an idiot. You warned me not to expect a happy-ever-after.'

'I know. It seems I'm not great at taking my own advice.'

'Seriously? You expected that one day you'd end up back together?'

'I guess that makes me the bigger idiot, doesn't it?'

Helen drank some more wine, wishing they could stretch to another bottle. But a dozen bottles wouldn't drown out the pain of knowing that Daniel didn't trust her. How could his feelings for her be so slight, that he could believe she would lie about something so serious?

'I didn't expect to ever see him again. But it was always possible that I would. And so of course I thought about us getting back together. The idea was always there: every birthday and Christmas, every Mothers' Day or Fathers' Day...' Every night, she could have added; in the early days at least.

'Is that why you didn't take it further with Simon? I always wondered.'

'One of the reasons.' Helen's smile revived. Kirsty had persuaded her to go on a blind date with Simon about eighteen months after Megan's arrival. It was the first and last date she had been on since Daniel: the attempt to move on had failed, as every second had felt like a betrayal. 'But it was more that I simply didn't fancy him.'

'So if a seriously drop-dead gorgeous man showed you some interest, are you now open to offers?'

'Like that's ever going to happen!' Helen laughed; though as she did, an image whisked through her mind of the man in her shop yesterday. She swept it away.

'But what would you say if I told you that a

gorgeous man has been staring at you for the last few minutes?'

'I'd say you obviously had more than your half share of that bottle of wine.'

'That scarf round his neck looks very familiar. Isn't it one of yours?'

Helen spun round.

'Seriously?' Kirsty tutted in despair. 'You turn for a scarf, but not for a hot man? We really must start going out more.'

Helen wasn't listening. She was gazing across the restaurant, at a party who were taking their places at a large table. It *was* her scarf, and it was wrapped round the neck of the man who had bought it from her yesterday. In fact, he was unwrapping it, and smiling at her as he did. She couldn't stop an answering smile springing to her lips. She'd suspected he had felt obliged to make a purchase, and had grabbed the nearest thing. But if that was the case, he would hardly have chosen to wear it in public, and when he could have had no way of knowing he would see her. He must genuinely have liked it. So she continued to smile, and as she did, he began to cross the room.

'I think he's heading this way!' Kirsty hissed.

There was no doubt about it. He was heading their way, and his path brought him straight to their table.

'Hello again,' he said, the scarf still in his hand.

'Hello. Great scarf.'

'Isn't it?' The man laughed. Soft curls caressed the edge of his face. 'It's been admired all day. All

77

my friends want one.'

'I hope you told them where to find me. Or why don't you give them all one for Christmas? I might consider a discount for a bulk order.'

Helen glanced across at the rest of his group. There were three or four other men, and two swishy long-haired girls. She ran her fingers through her own shoulder-length hair, wishing she could still rustle up a swish. It had made sense to cut it off when Megan was born and personal grooming had come well down on a long list of new priorities. She wondered if she should start growing it back. Perhaps she would ask Kirsty later.

'I tried to look you up on the Internet, to see what other designs you had, but your website is very limited.'

'Limited?' Helen laughed. 'It's only one page, with the St Andrew's address on. I set it up when I first opened there, and haven't touched it since. It's on my to-do list, to make more of it. I didn't expect anyone to look at it.'

'I promise I wasn't looking in a stalkerish way.' He grinned, revealing a flash of dimples. 'I really did want to see more of your work. And I suppose I should admit I have a professional interest.'

'You sew?' Helen hadn't expected that. A hollow feeling settled in her stomach, and her cheeks ached with the effort of keeping her smile in place. So his questions yesterday had been about her work, after all. Had he only been interested in stealing her designs?

78

He laughed.

'No, I'm a web designer. You should have a better showcase for what you do.'

'I know.' Helen smiled with renewed brightness. 'I've been thinking about that lately. Time and money have always been the issue, but I do need to look into it. I suppose a good website soon pays for itself.'

'It should do. Perhaps I can help you out.'

A piercing whistle sliced through the restaurant.

'Hey, birthday boy! Are you actually planning to join us tonight?'

The man half turned and waved a hand in acknowledgement. He brushed the curls from his face as he offered Helen a quick smile.

'I'd better go...'

'It's your birthday?'

'It's tomorrow, but Saturday was a better night to go out.' He tossed the scarf about in his hands. 'Are you here for a meal? Perhaps we could have a drink later?'

'We came early. We've already finished. Sorry.' The sorry was automatic; Helen wasn't sure if it was genuine. She didn't want to analyse her feelings, or explore why her lips wouldn't stay down, or why when this man looked at her, heat spread from her scalp to her toes. She could sense that Kirsty was showering her with disapproving looks. Then came a disapproving kick under the table.

'We can order another bottle,' Kirsty said, when the looks and the kick failed to have the desired effect. 'We're not in any hurry.'

'Yes, we are.' Helen sent her a surreptitious glare. 'Ben will be expecting you home soon.'

'You can stay. We don't mind keeping hold of…'

'No need for that,' Helen said decisively, and returned the kick under the table perhaps more forcibly than Kirsty deserved. 'I need an early night. I'm going to have to work all day tomorrow.' She smiled at the man, who was hovering by the table. 'Have a great birthday. But please treat that scarf a little more gently, won't you? All my work is a little piece of me. I can feel every one of those twists.'

'Sorry!' He laughed, straightened out the scarf and laid it over his upright palms. 'There. From now on I'll treat it like the rare and precious thing it is.' Again, his eyes lingered on Helen's. She kicked her shoes off under the table and wiggled her toes, trying to cool down. 'It was great to see you again. Let me know if you decide you want help with your website.'

With a final smile, he disappeared to the far side of the restaurant to join his friends. Helen watched as he took a seat in the middle of them all, laughing and shaking his head at whatever they were saying to him. He hung the scarf carefully over the back of his chair.

'Hello?' Kirsty poked Helen's arm. Helen pulled her attention back to her own table. 'Who was that?'

'It was…' Helen laughed. 'Do you know, I've no idea. He never told me his name.' So he couldn't have meant it about helping with the website, could he? How was she supposed to contact him if she was interested? Interested in the offer of website help, that was, not in anything else. Not in that offer of a drink.

She wasn't likely to ever see him again, was she?

'You both seemed very pally for people who don't know each other. Where did you meet him before? And how did he get your scarf?'

'He bought it yesterday.'

'In St Andrew's?' Kirsty shook her head. 'Why don't I ever get customers like that on a Saturday?'

'You shouldn't be looking,' Helen pointed out. 'You're married.'

'They don't gouge your eyes out as you walk back down the aisle, you know.' Kirsty looked at Helen, a big grin on her face. 'I've never seen you flirt before.'

'I wasn't flirting!'

'Oh no?' Kirsty pretended to run her fingers through her hair, tilted her head and fluttered her eyelashes. 'Oh, do be gentle with me,' she fluted. 'When you touch that scarf it's like your hands are all over my body...'

Helen burst out laughing.

'I don't speak like that.'

'Yes, you do, you posh Southerner.'

'And I certainly didn't say that.'

'Your body language did.'

Helen shook her head, but it was harder to ignore Kirsty than Saskia. Had she been flirting? It had been second nature once, but in those days her confidence in how she looked, and who she was, had been watertight. That confidence had leaked away now. Even so, her skin tingled as fragments of her old self surfaced, stirring up a memory from the depths of the past. Fun. She had enjoyed the conversation with the

81

man, and had felt invigorated in a way she hadn't done for years. And at once she was swamped with guilt for having fun that didn't include Megan, and for flirting with a man that wasn't Daniel.

'Do you think I should grow my hair again?' She hunched her shoulders up to her ears and pulled her hair forward to show Kirsty what it would look like longer.

'Stop that!' Kirsty giggled. 'He's still looking over. You don't want him to think you're weird. I think he actually fancies you. You should contact him, ask him to work on your website.' Kirsty winked. 'There's a euphemism if ever I've heard one.'

'I don't have his number. And I certainly can't afford to pay him.'

'Perhaps he'll accept sexual favours in payment.'

'He doesn't look like the kind of man who'd be turned on by stretchmarks and saggy boobs, does he?' Helen smiled, and finished her wine. 'I've forgotten what sexual favours are.' She stood up. 'Shall we go? I think Ben might prefer to hear your sexual fantasies than me.'

'Okay, but don't forget to give your admirer a wave, will you?'

Helen put her coat on, and walked towards the door. She wasn't going to look his way. She almost reached the door without looking his way. And then she couldn't help it; her head turned. He was watching her. He smiled, and raised his hand. She smiled in return, and ignoring Kirsty's excited prod, waved back.

It felt like Groundhog Day when Helen walked into St Andrew's on Tuesday morning. The other shop owners were collected at the base of the pulpit, with letters in their hands. The only difference was that this time they didn't look miserable. They were chatting and gesticulating in a decidedly animated way.

'We've all had letters,' Malcolm said, with a surprising lack of gloom.

'Here is yours.' Fiona, her cheeks flushed pink, held out an envelope to Helen. It was white, which was a good start. A brown envelope always meant bad news; council letters came in brown envelopes. Bad news could also be hidden in a white wrapper, but at least there was a *chance* it might be good news. And surely the others wouldn't be watching her so eagerly if she was about to be dealt another blow?

The envelope was addressed to her personally – not simply as the owner of Crazy Little Things – and was handwritten, in a bold black hand. The postmark was local. It was all most intriguing.

'For God's sake, Helen,' Saskia said, snatching the envelope out of her hand. 'You're not Sherlock Holmes, inspecting for clues.' She ripped it open, and gave the letter to Helen. 'Here. Read the damn thing. We might have found somewhere to move to.'

'Have you? I don't believe it! I was up until two drawing up plans for how a place in the shopping centre might work for us.' Not well, had been her eventual conclusion, before she'd fallen asleep in her

83

chair; but it had seemed to be the only option, and Helen had come in today, armed with her plans, ready to convince the others that it was worth a look. She felt a ridiculous shaft of disappointment that after all her efforts, it might not be her who saved the St Andrew's community. 'What have you found? I thought I'd checked everywhere.'

'I've not found it. We've been offered a place.' Saskia flapped a hand at the letter. 'Read it for yourself.'

Helen skimmed through the letter. It was from someone called Joel Markham, who wanted to meet her to discuss the possibility of her moving her business into an empty unit at his craft centre. A newly converted barn – the words made Helen's heart race – was available which could offer places to the occupants of St Andrew's. He suggested coming to St Andrew's – this afternoon! – to show them his plans for...

'Oh damn,' Helen said. Her heart abruptly stopped racing when she reached the name of the location. She should have known this was too good to be true. 'I thought it sounded suspiciously easy.'

'What's the matter?' Fiona's face was now flushed with anxiety. 'Is your letter not the same as ours? This man – this...' she glanced down at her letter, still clutched in her hand, 'Joel Markham, has offered us the chance of a unit in a craft centre. We assumed yours would say the same thing.'

'It does.'

'Then what's the problem?' Saskia demanded. 'It

84

sounds perfect. I know I haven't had much luck finding somewhere myself, and I assume none of you lot has.'

There was a Mexican wave of shaking heads.

'I haven't really looked,' Ron confessed, with a cheery smile. Helen inwardly rolled her eyes, even more so when Malcolm added that he hadn't bothered either, assuming that it would be a lost cause.

'There's still my place in the shopping centre,' Helen said, but for once she had some sympathy with the scowl which blew across Saskia's face. The shopping centre was unappealing at the best of times. It could never hold its own in a beauty parade against a barn conversion. 'Think of the passing trade we would have there.'

It was the best argument she had, and Helen saw a brief flicker of acknowledgement on some faces.

'But what do you have against the craft centre?' Fiona asked. 'Have you heard of this man? Is he not what he seems?'

'I've never heard of him, but I know about Church Farm Galleries. It's been around for years. It was once the only place to go in Lancashire for arts and crafts, and quite a number of famous artists started off showing their work there. But those days are long gone. I went to have a look at a space at Church Farm before I took the unit here. It was terribly rundown, and there were hardly any artists left. Visitor numbers had plummeted, but they were still charging a fortune in rent on the back of their previous reputation.'

A gloomy silence fell over the group.

'That's that then,' Malcolm said at last, with glum satisfaction. 'Back to being snookered, unless the shopping centre is a goer, and I can't say I'm keen on the idea. It doesn't sound like this place is an option. I can barely afford what I'm paying here. I can't pay more for somewhere on its last legs.'

'Have any of you been to Church Farm recently?' Joan interrupted. It was the first time she'd spoken. Helen had noticed before that she didn't tend to get involved in discussions about their future. Helen had struggled to know what to do about her. Finding premises that could be divided into five individual units was hard enough; finding one with facilities for a café as well appeared impossible. Joan didn't have a letter in her hand now, unlike the others. Was she not wanted?

'I've not been since I opened here,' Helen admitted. After her initial visit, she hadn't considered it as competition. The others all shook their heads as well.

'I've been a few times in the last year. I live fairly close,' Joan explained. 'There's a new manager. The place is coming to life again. Why don't you at least listen to what he has to say?'

'I'm game,' Saskia agreed. 'What's there to lose? We can always say no.'

'And we can look at your plans for the shopping centre too,' Fiona said to Helen. 'This is good news, isn't it? Yesterday we had nowhere, and now we have two options to choose from. You will come, won't you? We need you there.'

All eyes turned to Helen.

'Fine,' she said, bowing to the inevitable as the weight of the others' dependence settled heavily on her. 'What time is he coming, two? I'll be here, as long as there aren't any customers.'

But it wasn't a customer who threatened to jeopardise Helen's attendance at the meeting. The doors of St Andrew's burst open at lunchtime, and Daniel Blake walked in.

CHAPTER 8

Helen watched, on an emotional carousel of surprise, apprehension and bubbling anger, as Daniel strode towards her shop. How dare he come here, breaching her sanctuary, after what he'd sent Valerie to suggest? Had her response not been clear enough? Or did he flatter himself that he would be able to persuade her, where Valerie had failed? She had always given in to him in the past; but it wasn't going to happen this time.

He stood outside Crazy Little Things for a moment, taking it all in. Helen waited, her stomach clenching in tight spasms, trying to judge from his face what he was thinking, and what he intended. Eventually his gaze settled on her.

'You've done this?' he said, and he couldn't keep the note of surprise from his voice. 'It looks great.'

'Thanks.' She didn't smile, or make any movement to suggest that he was welcome, but a treacherous flush crept over her neck at his compliment. She straightened some embroidery kits on the shelf next to her, in an effort to pull herself together. How could she still care what he thought, after what he had done?

'Isn't that the lamp we had in our house?'

Helen followed his gaze. In the darkest corner of the shop, she had displayed a reading lamp with a crazy patchwork lampshade. It was the best place to show off the effect formed by a marriage of thin satin and silk scraps, which the light shone through like stained glass, and thick, rich remnants that created a cosy glow. It had probably been one of her bestselling pieces of the last three years. This was the original, and he was right: it had been in the living room of their house. It had suited their old cottage perfectly, and had provided the romantic lighting for many a night in. She chewed the inside of her cheek, painfully aware that the cottage and the nights in belonged to someone else now.

'I only kept the things I made,' Helen said. 'The rest is still in storage. I posted the keys for the storage unit to Valerie years ago. It's all there, you can check.'

'It doesn't matter.' He frowned at her. 'You could have had it all.'

The irony in that sentence seemed to pass him by.

'What do you want, Daniel?' Helen asked, retreating behind her counter. 'I don't think we have anything more to say to each other, do you? Or was it not enough that you sent your mother to insult me? Did you decide to come and have a go yourself, see the reaction first-hand?'

'I didn't send her anywhere,' he said, coming into the shop and standing at the side of the counter so that she was trapped. Her breath quickened at his proximity, at the remembered bulk of him, in a place she had never expected him to be. 'I didn't know anything about the DNA test until last night.'

'She had some of your hair!'

He dismissed this with a shrug.

'She said there was a patch the barber had missed. I had no idea what she was planning. You have to believe me, Nell. I don't need any test.'

Helen stepped back and leant against the rear wall. She wanted to believe him, but was that just her heart speaking, seeing only the best in him, as it always had?

'Is everything all right, Helen?' Malcolm hovered in the open doorway. He looked an unlikely protector: his spindly frame was dwarfed by Daniel, and unless he knew how to watercolour Daniel to death, the paintbrush clutched in his hand wouldn't have been much use in a fight.

'Everything's fine,' Helen reassured him. 'This is just someone I used to know.'

Malcolm looked at Daniel curiously, and Helen saw a hint of recognition flash across his face. It was inevitable, she supposed: anyone who had seen Megan could hardly fail to spot the connection. Malcolm frowned, puzzling it over, and pottered back across to his shop.

'Someone you used to know?' Daniel shot at her, as soon as Malcolm had left. The determinedly reasonable tone he had used earlier was gone. 'Is that all?'

'What more do you want?'

'How about Megan's father, for a start?'

'That's not a start, that's well across the finishing line and on to the winner's podium.'

'And isn't that where I should be? Isn't that my place?'

'You don't have a place.'

'For God's sake!' Daniel's hand crashed down onto the counter. 'Did you actually mean it? You'd rather she had no father than me? I told you the paternity test was nothing to do with me.'

'Fine. I believe you. That was all Valerie's idea.' Helen picked up a spool of thread which was about to roll off the counter, and passed it from hand to hand. 'So who are you going to blame for the indifference? You've known for a week. Where have you been?'

'Thinking. Trying to understand it. Trying to understand how you could have done it. Don't you dare question *my* behaviour.' He took a great, shuddering breath. 'What the hell did you expect? If there are rules for how I'm meant to feel in this situation I wish someone would tell me what they are.'

His face could have been a piece of crazy patchwork, scraps of despair jostling alongside anger, hurt and confusion. It was too painful to look. Helen glanced away, and saw Fiona loitering anxiously behind the glass partition separating their shops. Helen knew that raised voices still unsettled her, and mentally kicked herself for letting things go so far.

'I think you'd better go,' she said to Daniel, and walked towards him, as if to shoo him out.

'No.' He blocked her way so she had to stop, centimetres from him, so close that she could see how the years they had been apart had marked their passing with new lines at the corner of his eyes and

91

mouth. 'I need to know why. I need to know everything.'

'Not here. Come round…'

'No,' he interrupted. 'Now. Christ, Nell, you owe me that.'

Helen couldn't deny it. An explanation was the least she owed him, but he had picked the worst possible moment to demand it.

'I have a meeting at two.'

'And that's more important?'

That was unfair. Of course nothing was more important than Megan. But trying to keep her business afloat was all about Megan too. How could she choose between them? Helen glanced at her watch. Perhaps she wouldn't need to choose. There was almost an hour before Joel Markham was due. She could be back by then. She doubted her conversation with Daniel would last that long, or that she would survive an hour in his company, feeling the force of his hatred rather than his love. So she nodded at Daniel, picked up her coat and bag, and went over to Fiona.

'Would you mind keeping an eye on the shop for a while? I need to go out.'

'Of course. Are you…' Fiona faltered, but her eyes pursued the question. Helen squeezed her arm.

'He's perfectly safe,' she whispered. Physically, at least, Helen added silently. She was quite certain he was planning a verbal attack, but hadn't she been preparing for exactly that for years? And didn't she deserve it?

'You are still coming to the meeting about Church Farm, aren't you? Remember the owner is going to be here at two.'

Helen nodded.

'I'll be back.'

She followed Daniel out of the church and on to the main road. He looked around, and gestured towards the pub a hundred yards away.

'Pub?' he said. He looked down the hill towards the town centre. 'Or…'

'The pub's fine,' she said. He wouldn't think so when he went in, she knew that, and even now she could see a frown of doubt creasing his brow as they drew nearer. It was a traditional spit and sawdust place, where layers of dirt had been polished into the furniture, and where years of smoke still appeared to hang in the air. Helen had ventured in once, and never again, which was exactly why it was perfect now. She didn't want to pollute anywhere she liked with the memory of the conversation that was about to happen.

Daniel hesitated on the threshold, until Helen pushed him on. He went to the bar and ordered a pint and a vodka and tonic, without even asking what she wanted: despite everything, the spectre of their old relationship swirled close around them.

They sat down at a table whose highly varnished surface had been engraved by customers' glasses over many years. Overlapping circles filled the table like a baffling series of Venn diagrams.

'This place is awful,' Daniel said.

93

'I know. It seemed appropriate.'

'As a place to discuss our daughter?'

Helen's eyes flew to meet his. Hearing him say it... The intimacy of hearing him describe Megan in that way... She gulped her vodka, almost inhaling the liquid in her haste to drown the ache his words had produced.

'What did you want to discuss?' she asked, when he continued to stare at his pint, saying nothing.

'I don't know.' He looked up. 'I don't know what I'm meant to know. I don't know what to ask. Where do I start catching up four years?' He leant forward. 'Is she four? When was she born?'

'September 3rd. So yes, she's four.'

'Does she go to school?'

'She just missed the cut-off for this year. She'll go next September.'

'So where is she now?'

'Nursery.'

'All day?'

'Yes, all day, four days a week. I have to work.' Helen waited, wondering if he would dare to disapprove, but though his fingers tightened round his glass, he didn't react.

'And is she...' He faltered, as if he wasn't sure how to ask it. 'Healthy? Normal?'

'Yes. She reached all the developmental milestones on time.'

'What the hell does that mean?' Daniel picked up a beer mat and turned it in his hand, tapping each edge on the table. 'Spare me the jargon. Don't forget I haven't had chance to become familiar with it.'

And she'd thought it had been going so well! She should have known better.

'She's exactly as she should be.' But then Helen pictured Megan, and smiled. 'No, she's amazing.'

'I want to meet her.'

'Okay.' She'd anticipated this, and knew she couldn't refuse, even though the terror of what that might lead to had balled in her throat so she couldn't swallow it down. 'But it has to be low key.'

'She doesn't know who I am?' The tap of the beer mat against the table increased to a definite bang.

'No.' Helen twisted her glass round and round on the table. 'Come for coffee on Sunday afternoon. She won't think there's anything unusual about that.'

'Won't she?' The beer mat slapped down on the table. 'You often have men round, do you?'

'I didn't mean...'

'How many fathers has she known? Or do you call them uncles?'

Helen pushed back her chair, the legs screeching noisily across the flagged floor.

'I don't have to listen to this,' she said, and picking up her bag, turned to go.

'Why, Nell? Why did you do it?'

She glanced back. He'd spoken softly, but she knew she hadn't misheard. His eyes were on hers, imploring her to tell the truth, make him understand. And though she'd rehearsed every possible situation in her head over the years, nothing could have prepared her for what it would actually feel like to

95

have to look him in the face and explain why she had hidden his daughter from him. It was a physical pain, deep in her chest, as if someone was laboriously carving her heart with a plastic knife. Her lips refused to move. What had seemed the sensible, the best choice at the time, now made no sense at all.

'What you've done is unforgivable,' he said, when she didn't speak. That stirred her to life. She'd thought the same thing, many times, but the familiarity of the accusation didn't make it any easier to hear from him.

'I'm not asking your forgiveness. I haven't done anything I need you to forgive me for.'

One eyebrow raised slowly. He had always done it, when he thought Helen had said something particularly stupid. How had she forgotten that?

'You've kept my child from me for four years!'

'I could have had an abortion and you would never have known anything about it!'

'Yes, of course, and you have form for that, don't you?'

Helen sank down, her hand covering her mouth. She couldn't believe he had thrown that at her. She'd had an abortion before, when she was nineteen. The pregnancy had been an accident, in a relationship that barely lasted a month, and it had been the hardest decision of her life – at the time. Daniel was the only person she had ever told about it. Though she had tried to put it out of her mind, it had been impossible to put it out of her heart. It was the one regret which dwarfed all others. Every day with Megan had shown

96

her what she had lost.

'So why didn't you?' Daniel ploughed on, relentlessly prodding at the wound he had opened. 'What was so different this time?'

Did he really need to ask? She must have been very convincing at Craig's party when she'd denied her feelings. But she couldn't do it now. She didn't have the energy left to dissemble.

'Everything was different,' she replied, gazing at him though she knew he would see the tears threatening to spill. 'The baby was yours. Ours. I could never have got rid of it.'

'So now you're claiming you did love me, after all? I can't believe anything you say, can I? Because if you had truly loved me, you couldn't have done this me. Keeping the fact I had a daughter a secret co never be described as an act of love.'

'Letting you have Hong Kong was. You ad there. I could tell that every time we spoke. A you sent me that email…' It had arrived, wi timing, two days before Helen had discove pregnant. 'You said how lucky we were second chance, after having to leave your father died. You said that part that there would be another phone home, but surely lightning coul Helen still had the email, though heart. 'There was no way I second bolt of lightning.'

He slammed back in his

'How is any of that re

the situations. You could have had the baby in Hong Kong.'

'On a six–month visa?'

'You could have stayed permanently if we'd married. I told you it would make the arrangements easier.'

'Yes, you were very thorough in pointing out the practical advantages.' There was a bitter taste in Helen's mouth all over again. It had been the least romantic proposal she could have imagined. He hadn't mentioned one word of love. When she was so deeply in love with him, how could she ever have accepted that? 'You had every detail worked out. Five years in Hong Kong, then back home ready to have a family. How can you deny it? You didn't want a baby four years ago.'

'It would have been different once it had actually happened.'

'Would it?' Helen drank some vodka, and smiled t him sadly. 'Are you sure about that? Because I have very clear memory of the scare we had, not long 'r we left London. The relief on your face when the gnancy test proved negative...' She took a deep th, fighting to disguise her feelings, just as she 'ad to do at the time. Because his relief wasn't all 'membered. She also had a clear recollection, as is the sensation of the smooth glass now in her of how unexpectedly, and unequivocally inted she had felt. That absent blue line had everything.

aid that any other result would have been a

98

disaster, and that we had been spared having to make a tricky decision,' she continued, not stumbling over a single word as she knew them so well. 'As far as I could see, nothing had changed a year later. With the job in Hong Kong, it would have been a bigger disaster. So I spared you the tricky decision, and let you have the life you'd planned.'

And let herself have the life she'd begun to crave. The truth stabbed her in the gut, so sharply she could no longer ignore it.

'You think I would have wanted you to get rid of the baby, one that actually existed?'

'Yes. I think you would have considered it.' And that had been enough. She couldn't have taken the risk of what he might have asked her to do – or what he might, ultimately, have persuaded her to do.

'No. We would have made it work.'

That was exactly what Helen didn't want to hear. If she didn't have the conviction of her own decision, where did that leave her? She glanced at her watch. It was already a couple of minutes after two. She finished her drink quickly and stood up.

'I have to go. If you want to meet Megan, you can come for coffee, Sunday afternoon, on strict condition that there's no fuss and no mention of her father.'

'We haven't finished.'

'Yes we have.' She picked up her bag. 'There's no point going over the same ground. You know what I did, and why I did it. It's up to you what you decide to do now. But make sure you're certain what you want. Because this isn't one of your business deals,

99

where you can take a punt and sell up if it doesn't work out. Megan is the most precious thing in the world. So if you start this, and then get fed up of playing daddy, then *I* will never forgive *you*.'

Helen left the pub, and half ran down the road to St Andrew's, still trembling from the encounter with Daniel, and the fact she had stood up to him in a way she had never managed in the past. She burst through the door, for all the world like a late bride, and hurried down the aisle to where she could see the others huddled round a laptop set on a table in Joan's coffee shop. But she slowed as she drew nearer to them. She'd expected to see a stranger with them. She'd expected to see Joel Markham. But the only person with them was a handsome man wearing her scarf.

CHAPTER 9

'At last!' Saskia grumbled, as Helen halted in confusion at the sight of the scarf man. What was he doing here? And where was Joel Markham? 'Thanks for tearing yourself away from lunch with your boyfriend. Talk about priorities...'

'He's not my boyfriend, he's...' She stopped. She didn't want to get into all that right now, especially not with the scarf man smiling at her and listening to every word. She smoothed her hair, taming the wind-tousled strands. 'I'm only a few minutes late, and this Markham guy isn't here yet, is he? Do I have time to pop to the loo first?'

'Helen!' Saskia was sending Helen a frown so deep she could have used it to grow potatoes. '*This* is Joel Markham.' Saskia pointed at scarf man. He was still smiling at Helen, with a smile so warm it produced a melting sensation deep in her bones.

'Feel free to go to the loo,' he said, his smile broadening into a grin which lured out the dimples. 'I wouldn't want to be responsible for any accidents. This parquet floor looks original.'

'How can you be Joel Markham?' Helen stared at him, thoroughly bewildered. He had told her that he was a web designer when they met on Saturday night. She hadn't been so drunk – or so distracted by the unusual attention of a handsome man – to have got that wrong. How had he become the owner of a craft

101

gallery since then? The melting sensation stopped, replaced by an embarrassed flush creeping over her chest as she realised how badly she might have misinterpreted this situation.

'My parents are Mr and Mrs Markham, and they named me Joel.' He laughed. 'Isn't that the normal way?'

'But you came in here last week and bought my scarf.'

'I did.' He touched the scarf round his neck, a gentle stroke with two fingers that Helen could have sworn she felt herself. 'Wouldn't you have sold it to me if you'd known my name? Don't you serve Joels? I'm sure there must be an -ism against that.'

'Can we get on now you've eventually shown up?' Saskia asked. 'Joel was showing us a virtual tour of Church Farm. It looks fantastic,' she gushed, her irritated frown at Helen transposing seamlessly into a flirtatious smile as she turned to Joel. Everyone switched their attention back to the laptop. Helen didn't move.

'How did you find out St Andrew's was closing?' she said, her brain still stubbornly refusing to take this in. 'It hasn't been publicised yet. I didn't tell you last week.'

Joel looked up from the laptop and regarded Helen. He let go of the mouse and pushed a curl back behind his ear. It immediately sprang back, though he appeared not to notice.

'I already knew.' His eyes moved away from her too quickly. He was hiding something. Just like he

102

had been hiding something last week, Helen suddenly realised. How stupid was she? All those questions he'd asked about her work, and how busy she was. He hadn't been interested in *her*. It had been about the business after all, and how many customers she might bring to his gallery if she moved there. On Saturday night too, had he been trying to soften her up, so she would be more likely to agree? Her stomach sank into her shoes, and she took a step back, as if to distance herself from Joel, and from what, egged on by Kirsty, she had allowed herself to believe. She had thought he found her attractive and, though she wanted nothing from it, she hadn't understood until this moment how great a boost that had given her confidence. That boost had just been punctured, and humiliation crawled over her skin. How could she have been such an idiot?

'How could you know?' she pressed him, blind to anything but herself, Joel, and an overwhelming sense of disappointment. 'The only people who knew were us, the new buyers, and the council.' Her eyes widened. 'That's it, isn't it? You were tipped off by the council. What do you do, give them a bung in a brown paper bag in return for details of failing businesses?' She swung her handbag down onto the nearest table, vaguely aware that she was being irrational, and that it wasn't his fault she had read too much into his behaviour, but unable to stop. 'What are you, some kind of retail ambulance-chaser?'

'It's not like that at all,' Joel replied. He wasn't

smiling now, but his eyes were on Helen's and he spoke with slow deliberation. 'I heard St Andrew's was closing down, and that some talented people were looking for a new place to show their work. I've got four new units to fill, and so it seemed a perfect...'

'Four?' Helen interrupted, hands on hips. 'There are five of us who need new shops, plus Joan and her café. Is that why you've been snooping round, asking so many questions? What's the plan, that you cherrypick the most profitable and offer them your new units? That's not going to work. I wouldn't leave one or two of us behind, and I don't think anyone else would either.'

'Speak for yourself,' Saskia muttered, glancing round, eyes narrowed, until she gave a nod of satisfaction. After Helen's, her jewellery shop and Fiona's stationery were probably the busiest. The men were the weakest links at St Andrew's.

'But I thought Ron was retiring.' Joel turned to Joan with a puzzled expression.

'Of course he's not!' Helen snapped. 'Did you think you could get rid of him because he's the eldest? And you're pensioning off Joan as well, are you?'

'Helen...' Joan began, but Helen didn't let her finish.

'I'm having no part in this,' she carried on. 'I don't like your style of doing business. I won't take one of your units.'

There was a shocked silence, and then everyone started speaking at once.

104

'Perhaps you need some time to think about it?' Fiona suggested.

'You can't do this!' Saskia hissed. 'What about us?'

'We're snookered, then,' Malcolm concluded with grim relish.

'No, we're not,' Helen said, and reaching into her bag she pulled out the plans she had worked on overnight for the space in the shopping centre. She spread the paper out on the table, pinned down by a sugar bowl and a bud vase holding a single carnation. 'We still have this option. It's one large shop, and we won't have the money to make individual units, but I've worked out how we might divide it up.' She pointed down at the graph paper, where groups of squares had been coloured in to represent each artist. Below that, she'd sketched an impression of how it might look. 'I've given you one of the window spaces, Malcolm, because your paintings will have more visual pull than our small pieces. And Ron, you can have the other window for your dolls' houses...'

Helen stopped, struggling to maintain any degree of enthusiasm when no one was showing interest. Or rather, no one from St Andrew's was showing interest. Joel had somehow found his way next to her and was leaning forward, his hands resting on the table, studying the plans. The pose emphasised his strong shoulders. He twisted his head and grinned up at Helen.

'This is great.' One long finger pointed to a trail of footprints she'd drawn on the plan, leading to

105

another unit. 'What do the footprints mean?'

'It's the route to the nearest available space that could be used as a café,' Helen said, her anger faltering under his apparent appreciation of her hard work. She turned to Joan. 'I'm sorry, there's no permission to use the main space for catering. This is the best I could do. It's only five shops away, so we'd be practically neighbours still. Don't think I'm trying to push you out,' she added, with a swift glance at Joel, who was still standing beside her, watching her with amusement. 'It may not sound as appealing as a barn conversion, but this way we can all stay together.'

'You're a good girl,' Ron said, squeezing Helen's hand. 'But you don't need to worry about me. I decided a while ago to retire at the end of the year. My hands aren't as nimble as they were, and the fine detail in the dolls' houses is too much for me now. I discussed it with Joan, and we decided to retire together.'

A pink flush lit up his wrinkled cheeks; a matching shade lay on Joan's face. If Helen had any doubts over what he meant, their expressions removed them. How had she failed to notice the most exciting thing ever to have happened at St Andrew's?

'I can't believe you've managed to keep this secret.' Helen smiled, and gave Ron a hug. 'I'm so happy for you both.' She kissed Joan, though it meant having to lean closer to Joel Markham, so close 'that for a moment she imagined she felt his breath whisper across her cheek. 'I should have known all those

106

delicious cakes would be winning some man's heart.'

'The offer to teach you to make them still stands!' Joan laughed. The happy sparkle in her eye made her look twenty years younger. Helen strained to keep her smile in place, while her stomach writhed with unstoppable envy. Everything in her life was changing, but none of it was for the better, or not for her. She thought she'd been doing good, fighting to save what they had at St Andrew's, but all the time people had been quietly working out their own happiness without her.

'This is all very convenient for you, isn't it?' Helen said, tossing a bitter look in the direction of Joel Markham. It wasn't his fault, she knew that very well, but her lingering sense of humiliation made him a natural target. 'Or are you going to claim that you knew about this development as well?'

'Yes, I did.' The grin was back, the dimples in all their glory. It was mesmerising, and all the more infuriating because of that.

'How could you possibly have known? I work here and hadn't spotted it. Do you have a mole here or something?'

'It's me,' Joan said. 'I told him.'

'Last week? I didn't see him go to the café. And why would you tell a stranger before us?'

'He's not a stranger,' Joan said. 'Maybe sometimes a little strange...' She looked at Joel with obvious affection. 'Joel is my nephew. My sister's youngest.'

'How can he be your nephew?' Helen caught Joel's eyes laughing at her. 'And I don't need another genealogy lesson from you, before you offer. Why did you keep it a secret? Why all the mystery with the letters and this meeting?'

'That was my fault,' Joan admitted. 'I hoped you would feel that he was inviting you to Church Farm on merit, not as a favour to me. And I wanted you to judge the offer objectively, not look kindly on him because he's my nephew.' She smiled at Helen. 'I seem to have got it wrong. I never thought that you would look on him so *un*kindly.'

'Not all of us have,' Saskia pointed out, edging closer to Joel. He was still watching Helen, his hands in his pockets, shoulders tensed forward.

'You told me you were a web designer,' she said.

'I am. I had my own business in Bristol for five years.'

'So what are you doing in charge of a rundown craft gallery? Did the business fail?'

'No. I sold my stake in it twelve months ago and moved back up here. For personal reasons,' he added, a cloud blowing over his face. Helen waited, but he didn't elaborate. 'I've taken over Church Farm for my dad. It was left to him by my uncle. And it isn't rundown.' Joel smiled, and his shoulders relaxed. 'It's up and coming. Let me show you the video and you can see for yourself. Then you can compare it to the place you've found.'

Helen hesitated. Everyone was watching her expectantly.

'It's only a few minutes long,' Fiona encouraged her. 'You'll be pleasantly surprised. I think it must have changed a lot since you were there.'

'For the better, I hope,' Helen muttered, but she let herself be pushed forward until she was standing in front of the laptop. Joel bent down to click the mouse, brushing against Helen's arm as he did. An unexpected shiver ran through her. She kept her eyes firmly on the computer screen, watching what was undoubtedly a very slick advert for Church Farm. Joel commentated as it played, showing how the gallery had looked a year ago, when he'd taken over, and all the work he had done since then, repairing the buildings that had been allowed to decay, sprucing up the communal areas, and finally showing the extra barn that he'd renovated and in which he had the four spare units that could be taken by the St Andrew's residents. The barn looked fantastic, with exposed stone walls, a flagged floor, and huge oak doors and beams. Helen felt a prickle of excitement that had nothing to do with Joel's continued presence beside her. The barn had character and warmth. It was the sort of place she would love to work, and she knew her customers would enjoy visiting. It was a million times better than the shopping centre option. But still...

'It all looks very impressive,' Helen conceded. Joel smiled in pleasure. 'But we all know that some careful dressing, skilfully applied make-up, flattering lighting and camera trickery can make anything look good. How can we know this is real?'

'Come and have a look. I was going to suggest it anyway. What about on Monday, when you're closed here?'

Everyone agreed, except Helen, who hesitated as she wondered what to do. She did want to see Church Farm; but Monday was her day with Megan. Nursery might take her for half a day, but she didn't want to do it. They had little enough time together. She glanced at Joel, who was watching her.

'Will you have your daughter?'

Helen nodded, slightly unnerved that he should know so much about her, when she barely knew anything about him.

He smiled. 'Bring her. It's safe – all the building work is finished. She can try out the play area and meet the animals. I'm trying to make Church Farm more family friendly, so she can tell me how I'm doing.'

'That's a lovely idea, isn't it, Helen?' Fiona smiled encouragingly at Helen. Saskia was glaring at her, defying her to refuse.

'Okay,' Helen agreed. She had no choice, that was clear. 'I'll come. And in the meantime, everyone can go and visit the shopping centre. No promises,' she told Joel. 'It's a look, that's all.'

'Understood. I can't promise not to do everything I can to persuade you, though.'

The grin was impossible to resist. Helen's lips began to curl up, and she was helpless to stop it. The doors of St Andrew's opened and she saw with relief one of her customers walk in. She grabbed her plans and hurried away, glad of the chance to bury herself in zips and fasteners.

Out of the corner of her eye, as she was serving, she saw the others drift back to their shops, and assumed the meeting was over and Joel had gone. She finished helping the customer, and tidied away the rejected zips.

'Helen.'

Joel was leaning in the entrance to the shop. He was on his way out: the laptop was stowed away in a leather satchel, and her scarf was wrapped snugly round his neck. It still suited him; but it no longer suited her to see him wearing it. She had thought he liked it – thought he liked her. According to Kirsty and Saskia, she had flirted with him over it. A fresh bucketload of embarrassment tipped over her head and trickled down her spine as she looked at the scarf now.

'I want my scarf back.'

'What?' His fingers stroked the scarf with a gentleness that made her skin tingle. 'I bought it.'

'I'll give you the money back.' She opened the till. There wasn't enough cash in there to repay him; it had been a quiet morning. She reached for her purse. There wasn't enough cash in there either. 'I'll let you have it on Monday,' she said throwing the purse back down.

'No. I don't want your money.'

'Except you do, don't you?' Helen's voice had taken on a queer, high pitch that she couldn't control. 'You want my money from renting one of your empty retail units. You were never a genuine customer. You were checking out my business, to see if I could add any value to Church Farm, that's all.'

'That's why I came initially.' Joel took a few steps into the shop. 'It's not why I bought the scarf. Everything I said was true. I love your work. I love this scarf.' He put down his bag. 'Look, I'm sorry I didn't tell you who I was last week. Auntie Joan asked me not to, but I wasn't comfortable with it. I don't blame you for being cross back there. I would have been too. I hate secrets.' He pushed a curl behind his ear. 'I would have told you on Saturday night if you'd stayed for a drink.'

'I thought there must have been a reason why you asked.' The words slipped out before she could stop them.

'There was a much simpler reason than that.' The cheeky smile flashed up. Helen's breathing quickened. 'What if I ask you for a drink now? You know who I am. There's no hidden agenda.'

'No.' And in case that wasn't emphatic enough, Helen shook her head and took a couple of steps back until her hands found the comfort of the wall behind her. 'Buying me a drink isn't going to make me like Church Farm any better. I've agreed to come on Monday. I'll make my mind up then.'

Joel laughed softly.

'I was hoping the drink might make you like *me* better. It has nothing to do with Church Farm.'

Helen let her fingers spread out against the cool stone wall. Was he asking her out? On a date? Or was she reading too much into it? She felt a faint flutter inside her, as the girl she used to be struggled to breathe again. The old Helen wouldn't have hesitated, when propositioned by a gorgeous man. The old Helen would probably have asked him out herself last week. But she wasn't that person anymore. She had left all that behind, the moment she had decided to raise Megan on her own. She had put away the old life, and made herself into a better person; a mother and a father; a Beefeater guarding the most precious jewel. She couldn't be distracted by dating. And then there was Daniel. There would always be Daniel.

'I'm sorry,' she said, more gently than she had spoken before. 'It wouldn't be a good idea. There's too much going on at the moment.'

'Bad timing?'

She nodded, relieved.

'Not to worry.' He grinned. 'That means it wasn't about me. The great thing about timing is that it's always changing.' He picked up the bag, and winked at Helen. 'And Monday is a whole new week.'

'I told you he fancied you,' Kirsty crowed, when Helen ran into her at nursery later that day. Helen had whispered a truncated account of the day's events while they waited for their children. Out of everything, Kirsty had homed in on this one point. 'Tell him you've changed your mind. I'll look after Megan.'

'I haven't changed my mind. And I still think he's trying to butter me up so I take on his unit.'

'A man who looked like that could cover me in any food substance he chose!' Kirsty grinned. 'Has he

113

invited anyone else from St Andrew's out for a drink?'

'Not that I know of.' It hadn't truthfully crossed Helen's mind. Perhaps he had issued the invitation to all of them, so they could get to know him better before deciding whether to move to Church Farm. Perhaps she'd jumped to the wrong conclusion – and not for the first time where he was concerned. Were they all at the pub now, talking business? Had she imagined the whole dating undercurrent, and let it tow her wildly off course? But then she remembered the wink. She hadn't imagined that. She groaned.

'I am definitely staying single from now on,' she said, retrieving Megan's coat and bag from her peg. 'It's too complicated. Either men have changed since I last dated, or I've forgotten everything I used to know about them.'

'What do you mean, *staying* single? I've never known you as anything else. You're so wholesome, it's hard to give credit to all those wild tales about your past and all the men you went out with.'

'You have to believe at least one of them.' Helen smiled, and waved Megan's coat at Kirsty. 'What more proof do you need? But all that was before I had Megan.'

'You must have read very different pre-natal books from me. Mine didn't say I had to transform into a born-again virgin after the birth.'

Helen's smile faded a little.

'But you have Ben. You can make decisions together. I can't even be a proper single parent and make decisions on my own. There's constantly been that risk that one day Daniel would come back and judge how well I've done without him. So everything has been about Megan, making her the best she could possibly be. I have to prove that she's come to no harm through what I did, through his absence. Every decision has involved thinking what he would want, or what he would do.'

'Oh Helen.' Kirsty squeezed her arm. 'You've been torturing yourself like this for four years? How were you ever going to have a date, if you were only doing what *he* would have done? Unless it was with a hot blond Australian perhaps.'

Helen laughed, and crouched down as the door opened at last and Megan hurtled out towards her.

'Hello, my lovely girl,' she whispered, pulling Megan into a cuddle, which was enthusiastically returned. She drew away, and bundled Megan into her coat. Kirsty was doing the same with Jenny and Tommy.

'At least now you're free,' Kirsty said.

'What?' Helen picked Megan up, and held her close, feeling the softness of her hair against her cheek. She blew on her ear and Megan giggled. It was the best sound in the world.

'No more guilt.' Kirsty raised her eyebrows pointedly in Megan's direction as she fastened Tommy's jacket. 'Nothing to prove. He's here and he can share the decisions. You're free to make your own choices about what you do. Or who you date.'

Would Daniel want to interfere, and make decisions about Megan? It was all Helen could think

115

about as she drove home. It was one thing for her to consider what he would want, quite another for him to be constantly around, telling her. And how far might he take it? A say in important choices? Regular access? Custody, even? Her stomach writhed with worry. How could she bear that? It had been her greatest fear over the years; the one reason above all others why she had continued to keep her secret, ignoring every surge of guilt. Daniel was intelligent, sensible, well-off; he had embraced the respectability that ran through his veins where Helen had spent years rebelling against hers. Despite her efforts to reinvent herself, if it came to a contest between her and Daniel, how could she possibly win? Helen looked in the rear-view mirror at Megan's precious little face, and felt as if a whole box of needles had been jabbed into her heart.

CHAPTER 10

Daniel was late, Megan had turned into a mini monster, and Helen was stressed. Sunday afternoon wasn't supposed to go like this.

By three o'clock, Helen had decided he wasn't going to come. She stopped arguing with Megan about changing out of her stained Disney Princess dress, and plastic mules that moulted feathers everywhere she went; let her bring down a plastic tub of dolls; and of course, the moment the tub was empty, and the contents scattered across the carpet, the doorbell rang.

Megan didn't even look up. Helen froze, then, when the bell rang again, got up off the floor and hurried over to the door. She opened it, and there was Daniel. Why did her heart jolt, when she wasn't expecting anyone else? Perhaps because, until then, she hadn't been sure he would come, or if she wanted him to come. And perhaps because it was clear from the smart jeans and jacket, and the faint tang of that unfamiliar aftershave, that he had made an effort with his appearance. For his daughter, she reminded herself swiftly. He had dressed up for meeting his daughter, not her. She must remember that.

'Hello.' He didn't smile, and Helen could see the nugget of anxiety lurking behind his eyes. 'Sorry, I didn't mean to be so late but something came up...'

Something more important than Megan? The silent

117

question hovered between them, but Helen let it float away. She was determined they wouldn't row in front of Megan.

'It's not a problem.' She opened the door wider and stepped back. 'We've made rather a mess while we were waiting. Watch where you walk.'

He stepped in, glanced at the floor and then his gaze was drawn irresistibly to Megan.

'I'm not here to judge how tidy you are.'

Though he would: he wouldn't be able to resist. There had been perpetual conflict between his tidiness and her relaxed approach to housework. If only he had been here half an hour ago when she had made sure the house would meet his exacting standards! Now it looked like a plastic factory had exploded over the floor. At least he was prepared to pretend not to notice.

Helen looked round the door behind him.

'Are you on your own?'

'Yes.' He looked away from Megan, briefly. 'We thought it would be better, this time.'

Helen shut the door, winded by all he had conveyed with that sentence. By 'we' she assumed he meant him and Tasha; had they discussed, on their own, what might be best for Helen's child? And what about that 'this time' he had so lightly slipped in? He was presuming he would be able to see Megan again, and that Tasha would meet her too, perhaps even on their own. Helen wasn't prepared for that. It was proving hard enough to accept that Daniel might have a place in Megan's life; but Tasha, as well? It felt about a million steps too far.

Helen picked her way across the toy-strewn carpet to where Megan was sitting on the floor. She stroked Megan's hair, though whether she was offering reassurance or taking it was debatable.

'Megan, this is Daniel,' she said. 'He's...' Oh God, how was she meant to describe him now? She couldn't risk him flaring up as he had at St Andrew's but she could hardly blurt out who he really was, either.

'He's a friend of mine,' she concluded, aware of how inadequate that was even before she noticed the flick of his eyebrow.

Megan stared at Daniel impassively, then turned her attention back to the doll in her hand, with the cutting dismissal only children can get away with. Helen winced, and her eyes darted to Daniel, to see how he reacted. He was watching Megan, wide eyed, transfixed.

'Coffee?' Helen asked, wondering if this afternoon was going to be a disaster, and if it was, whether that would be a good or bad result.

'Thanks, black, no...'

'I remember.' Did he think she could have forgotten any detail about him? She gestured at the chair, which she had cleared of her sewing. The room was only big enough for one chair and a small sofa. 'Sit down and I'll make it. Megan, why don't you show Daniel your dolls?'

Amazingly, given the mood she had been in half an hour ago, Megan obediently stood up and

119

approached Daniel. She proffered her doll to him in silence, and Helen retreated to the kitchen, leaving the door open.

'Does she have a name?' she heard Daniel ask.

'Barbie,' Megan replied. Daniel bent down and picked up another doll off the floor.

'And this one?'

'Barbie.' They were all Barbie. The plastic blonde dolls were Megan's favourites. Like father, like daughter, Helen thought, with a rueful smile.

'What about this one?' Helen heard amusement in Daniel's voice. 'Let me guess… Josephine?'

'No!' Megan squealed. 'It's Barbie!'

'I know I'm going to get this one right. She looks like… Jemima.'

'No! It's Barbie!' Helen thought she heard a tiny giggle, but when she looked through the open doorway, Megan was crouched down, picking up yet another doll. She took it over to Daniel.

'Guess this one!'

Helen watched as he took it off her, and studied it carefully, a frown of enormous concentration on his face.

'Lulu?'

'No!'

'Fifi?'

'No!'

'Mabel? Gloria? Trixie? Twinkle? Jane?'

And then it happened. Megan erupted into giggles. She managed to spit out, 'It's Barbie!' before collapsing to the floor in near hysterics. Helen,

120

hovering in the doorway with a jar of coffee in her hand, saw the utter enchantment creep over Daniel's face. He looked up and smiled at her, the first genuine, warm smile he had thrown at her since they had met up again. And there was no doubting why. He was thinking, as she was, what a wonderful being they had made together, and her heart exploded with pride to read that message written so clearly on his face. But she was also thinking that here in front of her lay the truth of what she had done, to Daniel and to Megan, and it lanced her with a pain that almost made her faint. She had deprived them both of moments like this. She had never felt so uncertain of whether she had done the right thing.

The afternoon passed more easily than Helen had ever imagined it could. Megan wasn't a shy child, and showed no hesitation in talking to Daniel, and pulling him down onto the floor to help with a jigsaw. Helen watched from the sofa, feeling oddly left out, and not liking the sensation. Could Megan somehow know who Daniel was? Perhaps she was too young to observe the resemblance between them; but was there some deeper bond that drew her to him? And if there was, would it stretch and weaken the bond between Megan and Helen? But as this thought was tormenting her, Megan yawned, and abandoning Daniel without a word, she climbed on Helen's knee and snuggled against her.

'She's had a long day,' Helen apologised, wrapping her arms round Megan. 'There was a birthday party this morning.'

'I wish I'd got here earlier. Craig took forever over lunch, you know what he's like...'

He stopped abruptly, perhaps conscious that it had once been Helen accompanying him to lunch, not Tasha. Helen supposed she would have to get used to seeing less of that group now he was back. Yet another aspect of her life that was changing. It was beginning to feel that this house, the least favourite thing in her life, was the only constant. And her love for Megan, of course, she thought, bending down to brush an idle kiss on the top of her head. As she did, an expression of helpless envy swept over Daniel's face.

'Can I come again?' He stood reluctantly, his eyes shifting from Megan to Helen.

'Yes. Give me a ring when you're free.'

'You'd better let me have your number.'

Helen eased Megan onto the other sofa cushion, stood up and found a scrap of paper to write her number on. She handed it to him, then went over to the cupboard under the stairs and opened the door. She pulled out a wicker basket and held it out to Daniel.

'What's this? A picnic?'

'It's things I've saved for you.' She peered over at Megan; her eyes were closed, and her head had drooped onto her chest. 'A hospital name tag, first shoe, a lock of hair from the first cut, photos and DVDs of every birthday and Christmas...'

He took the basket. 'And you think this makes up for missing all those things?'

'Nothing can do that.'

'No, it can't.' He looked over at Megan, and his face hardened. 'I won't miss anything else.'

Helen's phone rang late that evening. It was after eleven; Megan had been in bed for hours, but Helen would be working into the early morning to meet the deadline for the family-tree patchwork she was creating.

'Why is my name not on the birth certificate?'

So much for the entente cordiale of the afternoon: the hostility was loud and clear in Daniel's voice again.

'I couldn't put you on.'

'Couldn't or wouldn't? Is this all part of the plan to keep me out of Megan's life? Pretend I don't even exist? You thought of everything, didn't you?'

'It wasn't like that.' Her voice was husky with tiredness, and with the pressure of a sob caught in her throat. How could he think she would act so vindictively? Did he not know her at all? 'When I went to register the birth, I wanted to name you as the father, but I couldn't because you weren't there and we weren't married.'

'And whose fault was that?' He didn't wait for an answer, not that there was any she could give. 'Can we go back now? Get the birth certificate changed?'

'I don't know.'

'I'll ask Craig. He might be able to tell us the procedure. You will agree to change it, won't you?'

'If it's possible.' Helen hoped it was. She hated the

sight of the birth certificate, the empty space taunting her where the father's name should be. She didn't want Megan to have a blank father. She had been created in love. It mattered that she should know that. 'So you looked through the box.'

'Yes.' Even over the phone she heard the tremble in his breath. 'I've watched all the DVDs. She's fantastic. It looks like she's been happy.'

'I think she has.' She soaked up his words, and squeezed them out so that every last drop could quench the pain of the last four years. She had tried so hard to make Megan happy, and to show Daniel in films he might never have seen, that she was happy. His words unravelled the knot of anxiety she had carried for so long. 'I've done my best.'

'And...' He stopped, but the silence still screamed his apprehension. 'Has she ever asked about me? About her father?'

'She's never needed to. I've always told her that you love her a great deal, but have to work in another country. You've sent her cards and presents every Christmas and birthday.' Always the biggest and best present: the thing that Megan wanted most, or would love the best, had come from Daddy. It had been one of the ways in which Helen had tried to ease her guilt. It had been no more successful than the others.

'Am I supposed to say thank you?'

'No.' Helen still had her needle in her hand. Without even realising what she was doing, she jabbed the end into her knee, tiny pricks of discomfort hardly registering against the scale of the

124

pain in his voice.

'I want her to meet my family.'

'What?' Distracted, the needle poked too far into Helen's knee. 'It's too soon.'

'Is it?' he replied. 'I'd say it was four years too late.'

'I mean it's too soon to tell her who you are.'

'I want to spend more time with her. I want to get to know her. What did you think, that you might work up to telling her in six months' time?'

Six? Helen hadn't thought about timescales, but if she did, six months wasn't unreasonable, was it? And twelve months would be even better. It would give them all time to adapt, and for her to be sure that Daniel was serious about wanting to be involved. His anger was spurring him on now, his pride demanding that his position be acknowledged. He couldn't understand about the responsibility that came with it, or have any idea of the unwavering worry that went hand in hand with being a parent.

'It's too soon,' she repeated more firmly, determined that she had to stand up to him on this. 'I've said you can see her again. I'll let you know when I think it's the right time to tell her. I know her. It has to be my decision, Dan.'

'It's not my fault I don't know her, is it?' But he sounded resigned. 'She has a grandmother and an aunt who want to see her. Can they not meet her – as my family, if you won't let her know they're hers?'

'Perhaps we can talk about it in a few weeks...'

She thought she'd been vague enough to put him

125

off. She should have known better. He grabbed that word 'weeks' as soon as it left Helen's mouth, as if he had been waiting for it.

'Two weeks. Bring Megan for Sunday lunch at Mum's.'

'I...'

'Christ, Nell, I'm asking for one lunch with my daughter in four years. How can you deny me that?' And then, quiet but clear, she caught the words that she'd been dreading. 'It's not as if I'm asking for her to stay. Not yet.'

CHAPTER 11

Church Farm was set on the edge of the pretty Lancashire village of Crofters Fold, about twenty minutes' drive from Helen's house, and in character about as far away from her suburban estate as it was possible to be. At the heart of the village was a mismatched collection of old stone houses, much of the stone darkened by the effect of weather, time and industry. Green fields rolled away behind the clusters of buildings.

Helen paused at the crossroads in the centre of the village, taking in the butcher, the pub and the general store with post office. There were plenty of people about even in the middle of the morning, and a queue of mixed ages waited at the bus stop. The sunshine made anywhere appear cheerful, but Helen felt a definite sense of quiet prosperity and contentment here. First impressions were good, she acknowledged to herself, with a smile of growing anticipation.

At one corner of the crossroads, an old-fashioned black-and-white sign pointed the way to the nearest market towns. On another, a smart new tourist sign showed the direction of Church Farm. Helen turned that way and, after a few hundred metres, opposite a striking stone church with a pinnacle tower, drove into Church Farm and parked the car.

She hardly recognised the place from when she had last visited. Far from being rundown, it had the appearance of somewhere that was being continually spruced up. The car park was large, well laid out, and softened by trees and immaculate flowerbeds, still full of life and interest in October. If the car park was so well looked after, Helen could hardly wait to see the rest of it.

She led Megan past what was clearly the original farmhouse, a solid Georgian building, and entered a cobbled courtyard that was still bursting with colour from late-flowering dahlias and chrysanthemums. Former stable buildings and a vast barn formed the courtyard, and plaques outside provided a list of the shops that could be discovered inside each building. There was an eclectic mix of ladies' clothing, christening gowns, homemade toiletries, kitchen equipment, quirky gifts, children's toys...

'Helen!'

She spun round and saw Joel strolling round the corner of the stables into the courtyard. He was wearing jeans, a heathery brown jumper, and a wide smile. No scarf, she noticed, although perhaps it was unreasonable to expect him to wear it all the time.

'Sorry,' she said, though the smile which had sprung unbidden to her lips might have contradicted the word. 'Am I very late?'

'Yes, if you listen to Saskia.' Those cheeky dimples flashed up. 'I was glad to offer to look for you. But I don't mind if you were held up by admiring the shops. That's promising. What do you think? Not so rundown as you were expecting?'

'Not this area,' Helen conceded.

'So the shopping centre hasn't won yet?'

'No, I'll give you a chance to impress me.'

The dimples melted into a warm smile, and a warm look which went on for long enough for Helen to wonder if he had interpreted her words more flirtatiously than she had intended. Before she could decide how best to back pedal, she felt a tug on her hand. She looked down into a little face that was puckering into a frown scarily like her father's. It wasn't a good sign in either of them.

'Where are the animals?' Megan demanded. 'This isn't a farm.'

'I did try to tell you, sweetie, that it wasn't that sort of a farm.' Helen pulled an apologetic face at Joel. He crouched down in front of Megan.

'Hi, I'm Joel, and you must be Megan.' She gazed at him for a moment, then graciously nodded. 'Do you want to know a secret?' She hesitated, and nodded again. 'We do have animals. You can't have a farm without animals, can you?' Megan shook her head. 'And if your mummy agrees, we can have a look at some later. There's something very special I can show you.'

'Can we, Mummy?' Megan's voice had risen in excitement.

'Of course we can. If you're good while we look round the buildings first, okay?'

Joel led Helen out of the courtyard into a more open area of the original farmyard. On the right stood a substantial whitewashed building, with a sign over the door reading, 'The Feed Store'. The building opposite was smaller, with full glass windows running all across the front length.

'As you might guess, the Feed Store is where we have the café and the farm shop, and various small units selling artisan food and drink. Those are offices on the other side.'

A couple of young women with toddlers came round the corner from behind the offices.

'You start them young, don't you?'

Joel laughed.

'The play area and the animals are that way. I'll show you later.' He turned to the right, behind the Feed Store. 'This is the creative area. If you came before, you probably looked at a place in the Milking Parlour, here.'

They had reached an enormous, long building, painted a warm cream, with heritage green woodwork around the doors and windows. It didn't look at all like when Helen had last seen it.

'Wasn't it yellow?' she asked, trying to think back. The faded exterior had put her off before she'd even taken a step inside on her last visit. It hadn't looked the sort of place where great work would be produced or sold.

'Don't knock it, I once spent my school holidays painting that on. And it wasn't yellow, it was Sunshine Bouquet. Call yourself an artist, and you don't even know your basic colours...'

He rolled his eyes, and Helen laughed.

'So where is this fantastic new building you're trying to sell us? I hope you've not been inspired to paint this one.'

Helen stopped. They had strolled behind the Milking Parlour, and in front of her stood a small stone barn. The traditional arched entrance was filled with an oak-framed glass door, with matching oak windows along the side. The stone looked freshly sandblasted, and glowed in the sun. The farmyard ended here, and beyond the barn lay nothing but green fields speckled with sheep.

'Sheep!' Megan squeaked, trying to drag Helen over to the fence running round the fields so she could get a better look.

'This is the Hay Barn,' Joel said, glancing at Helen with a look that wavered somewhere between anxiety and pride. 'My first real contribution to Church Farm. And it's not yellow.'

'It's beautiful.' Helen felt a ripple of excitement. All thoughts of the shopping centre vanished. Imagine working here! Driving through the country lanes, taking inspiration from the colours of the seasons, being part of a growing community of artists... 'Can I look inside?'

'Of course.' Helen wondered if she was grinning as broadly as Joel. She couldn't help it. She loved St Andrew's, but something here tugged her heart in a way she hadn't expected.

Her grin faded as she followed Joel inside and

131

saw Saskia's scowling face. It was a temporary distraction from Saskia's bulging cleavage, which seemed determined to inspect the Hay Barn all by itself. Helen was half inclined to cover Megan's eyes.

'You decided to turn up, then,' Saskia said, her scowl deepening as she observed Joel standing close to Helen. Her gaze fell to Megan on Helen's other side, and she bit back whatever else she was planning to say.

Fiona and Malcolm were standing behind Saskia, and Helen could tell from their faces that they loved the Hay Barn already. And who could blame them? It was even better inside than out. Stone flags covered the floor, and restored oak beams had been left exposed in the vaulted roof space. A combination of sunlight and cleverly placed spotlights made the building seem spacious and intimate at the same time. It was perfect.

Megan let go of Helen's hand and ran over to hug Joan, who was hovering at the side of the barn with Ron.

'I didn't know you were going to be here,' Helen said, smiling at Joan. 'Have you changed your mind about retiring now you've seen this place?'

'Tempting, isn't it?' Joan laughed. 'Actually, I thought I'd better be here in case a peacekeeper was needed. I didn't know if you were planning giving our Joel a hard time again.'

'I can look after myself,' he protested, but he gave Joan an affectionate grin. 'Never mix business meetings and relatives,' he murmured, an easy smile floating across everyone before settling on Helen.

'We're both breaking that rule.' Helen smiled back, and stroked Megan's hair. 'But I promise I'm not planning to make any wild accusations against you today. Not unless you deserve them,' she added, unable to stop smiling.

'I think it's probably safe to leave you to it then.' Joan turned from Joel to Helen with a satisfied nod. 'Shall we go to the café, Ron?' He nodded. 'Would you like us to take Megan for a drink while you have a look round here? Are you thirsty, Megan, love?'

Megan nodded and took hold of Joan's hand before Helen could even open her mouth to answer.

'And a biscuit?' Megan asked hopefully.

'Try the gingerbread sheep,' Joel suggested. 'They're the best.'

Megan happily wandered off with Joan and Ron. Helen watched her go, and faced Joel again.

'So what's the plan? How are you going to divide the space?'

At the moment the interior of the barn lay empty, with no defined shops. Helen gazed round, her head buzzing with ideas about how it could be used. 'Are you going to have glass partitions between the units?' she asked, giving Joel no time to respond. 'It would work brilliantly here, so none of the character of the barn is lost, and you can keep as much of this light as possible. It can help sales too, because while a customer is in one shop, something next door might catch their eye. Sorry, I'm rattling on, aren't I?'

'And I haven't even pushed your button.' Helen smiled at Joel's reminder of their first meeting. 'I haven't decided what to do, but the glass partitions did look effective at St Andrew's. I thought the space could probably be divided so that one shop ran along each wall, although the one next to the door would end up smaller.'

'I'll have that one.' Saskia's voice made Helen start; she had been so caught up in the barn, and Joel, that she had forgotten the others were there. 'I only need a small shop. I don't want to pay for dead space.'

'My cards don't take up much room either,' Fiona said apologetically, as Helen began to pace round the barn. 'Even half a wall might be too much for me.'

Helen reached the far end of the barn, where light flooded in through a huge round window. The long side wall was probably double the size of her current shop and though she would welcome more room, and had already mentally filled it with extra stock, three quarters of the space would easily be enough. She looked round the end space again, picturing how her idea might work, and walked back towards the others. Joel met her halfway.

'I think you're missing an opportunity,' she said, the words tumbling out in her enthusiasm. 'You could still have four good-sized shops in here without using that end wall under the porthole

134

window. If you leave that empty, you could use the space for workshops, demonstrations, lectures, classes, temporary exhibitions... Anything!' she concluded, waving her arms around as if to scoop up a thousand more ideas. 'You could offer it to all the artists, not just those in the Hay Barn, and because it's at the furthest end of the site, anyone who attends would have to pass all the other buildings first, and may be enticed in to buy something. It could be brilliant!'

She could see in her mind exactly how it could be – see herself holding workshops there, as she had always wanted to do – and her stomach fizzed with all the possibilities before her. And perhaps because of the man before her too: because Joel mirrored the enthusiasm she felt, and he was studying her with a look of wonder that was more flattering than any compliment she'd ever been given.

'Will you do it?' he asked.

'Do what?'

'Draw up a plan of how you think the Hay Barn should be divided, like the one you did for the shopping centre unit.'

'But it's your project...'

'I know. But you have the vision for how to complete it. I need that. I need you.'

He needed her? When had anyone other than Megan needed her? When had anyone ever thought she could make a valuable contribution? Helen's head swam; it was intoxicating.

'I'd love to,' she said, drinking in Joel's delighted

smile to sustain her high. Then she heard Malcolm cough, and the spell was broken. She took a step back. She couldn't let herself be seduced; this had to be a decision of the head, not the heart. 'It doesn't mean I've decided to come here.'

'Fair enough.' Joel turned an amused smile on her. 'I'll pay you to draw up some plans, then you're under no obligation.'

'Talking of money, it must have cost a few bob to do all this,' Malcolm said, gesturing round at the barn. 'This is top-quality work. Have you paid for it all?'

'Malcolm!' Fiona nudged him. 'You can't ask that!'

'Ask what you want. I don't have any secrets.' Joel smiled, and returned to the rest of the group, followed by Helen. 'I managed to get a small grant but the rest was my money.'

'You must be loaded if you could afford this.' Saskia edged nearer Joel.

'Not any more.' He laughed, and moved towards Malcolm. 'I've invested some of the proceeds from the sale of my business into Church Farm.'

'So you're confident it's going to be a success?' Helen asked.

'Of course.' His smile grew as he looked at her again. 'But to be honest, I'd have done it anyway. My grandparents started Church Farm. My mum and dad met here, when Mum was a potter in the Milking Parlour in the early seventies. It's a special place for my parents and I'd do anything to bring it back to the glory days that they remember.'

His eyes didn't leave Helen's as he spoke. His enthusiasm, his passion, seemed to flow straight into her, reigniting that fizz.

'What a lovely family history,' Fiona said. 'I can't speak for anyone else, but I'd love to be part of it.'

'Depends on the price,' Malcolm said. He rocked back and forwards on his heels. 'Helen warned us about the inflated rent being charged here.'

'Inflated rent?' Joel repeated, eyebrows raised as he regarded Helen. 'I thought there weren't going to be any more wild accusations?'

She thought he looked amused, rather than cross, but all the same she cringed with embarrassment, especially now she had heard why he was so determined to make Church Farm a success.

'That was based on when I came before.' She offered Joel an apologetic smile. He accepted it, and returned it with interest. 'But I can't imagine you'd improve the place to this extent and then lower the price.'

He studied her for a moment.

'I'll offer you the first year's rent for ten percent less than you're paying at St Andrew's. And a three-month trial period, terminable on two weeks' notice.'

'Does that apply to all of us?' Saskia demanded.

'Yes.'

'Then you can have me. I want a space by the door. Anyone object?'

No one dared.

'I might take a night or two to think it over, if that's okay,' Fiona said, twisting her hands together. 'It's a big step.'

'Take as long as you need. I didn't expect any of you to decide today. Come back at another time and see how busy we can get. It can be packed at weekends, especially when the Farmers' Market is on. And you should check out Helen's option in the shopping centre, to be sure this is where you want to be.'

'Have you ever been there?' Saskia asked. 'It's a dive. God knows why Helen thought we'd want to move there. If it doesn't sell for a pound, no one's interested.'

'I thought it was the only option,' Helen said, but her heart wasn't in her defence. She'd known it was never going to happen as soon as she'd clapped eyes on the Hay Barn, and she couldn't mourn the loss, especially as she was buzzing with ideas for what to do here.

'Are there other artists here?' Malcolm asked. 'Will we be scrapping for customers?'

Helen had a sudden image of Malcolm duelling other artists with his paintbrush, and struggled to hide her smile. Joel caught her eye and his lips twitched.

'There are two other artists. But,' he continued over Malcolm's groan, 'one specialises in wildlife, and the other creates whimsical paintings and murals for children's bedrooms. She's fantastic,' he added to Helen. 'You should have a look for Megan.'

'Does anyone else sell sewing accessories or patchwork?' Helen could have kicked herself for not asking before. It should have been her first question, if she hadn't been distracted by the warm stone and the warmer smiles.

'No, but we do have two ladies who knit. Contemporary stuff, not tea cosies and bed socks,' he explained, as Saskia pulled her face. 'We're going to supply them with wool from our sheep. Perhaps they can put on a spinning demonstration in here if we're having an exhibition space.'

They spent some more time looking round the Hay Barn. Fiona and Malcolm were deep in discussion, pointing around, apparently deciding where they would prefer to go. Helen paced the floor, trying to gauge the size and scribbling notes on the back of a receipt for later.

'Do you need a tape measure?' Joel asked, as Helen chewed on her pen, having lost count of the number of footsteps when Malcolm got in the way. 'Or I have the plans with the measurements on in my office.'

'That would be great, and much more accurate than this.' She waved the receipt at him, laughing. 'It's obvious that any shop would be bigger than the one I have now. So would you charge me ten percent less than I pay already, or what I would have been paying for somewhere this size?'

'Interesting question. Stay for lunch and I'll think it over.'

'I can't. I have Megan.' The words shot out as a

knee-jerk response.

'I was expecting her to have lunch, too.' He laughed. 'Surely you're not accusing me of starving children now?'

'She has a play date after lunch. We'll need to go soon.' It was a slightly twisted version of the truth, but he wasn't to know that. They weren't meeting Megan's friend until three, so there was plenty of time. But why had he asked? Was it to talk about Church Farm, or something else entirely? She hadn't forgotten that he had asked her out for a drink before, even though her head had been so full of Daniel over the weekend that she hadn't given it any thought. And she couldn't forget the odd fizz she had felt earlier, and that was bubbling away again now under the scrutiny of intense brown eyes. Lunch didn't seem a good idea at all.

'So Megan can have dates, but not you? That hardly seems fair.'

Helen shrugged, looking away across the barn.

'It doesn't need to be fair. I'm a mother.'

'I think you're allowed to be a woman too.'

He didn't push the point, and walked away. A few minutes later, Helen saw him laughing with Saskia. She wondered if he was asking her to lunch instead. There was no danger Saskia would refuse him; and why shouldn't he ask? They were both attractive, unattached, uncomplicated. It was an obvious match. Helen said a quiet goodbye to Malcolm and Fiona, and went to collect Megan.

'Helen!' Before she had even reached the Milking

Parlour, Joel caught her up. 'Where are you going?'

'To fetch Megan. I said we needed to go soon.' She carried on walking. He stayed at her side.

'You can't go yet. I promised to show her the animals.'

'I don't think there'll be time today.'

'But she'll think I lied.'

That drew Helen's eyes to his face. There was no smile, and faint frown lines had appeared between his brows. He was serious. He genuinely was concerned about what Helen's daughter thought of him, though she couldn't imagine why. She didn't reply, and he followed her into the Feed Store and through to the café. Megan was sitting quietly, entranced as Ron folded paper napkins into various origami shapes. A duck, a boat and a whale were already floating on the table, amidst a sea of gingerbread crumbs.

'Time to go, sweetie,' Helen said, kissing the top of Megan's head. 'Has she been good?'

'She always is,' Joan confirmed. 'And she certainly enjoyed the gingerbread sheep. No, put your money away,' she said, flapping her hand as Helen reached in her bag for her purse. 'I'm going to miss her when we leave St Andrew's. You know I'm always available to babysit, don't you? If you want to go out one night... with anyone...'

Joan was a truly terrible actress. Helen wasn't fooled by the innocent old-lady face. Could there be a doubt over which 'anyone' Joan thought she might like to go out with? She wheeled round to

141

scrutinise Joel suspiciously, wondering if he'd cooked this up with Joan, but he had bent down to admire the napkin creatures, an unexpected flush on his cheeks.

'Can we see the animals?' Megan asked, as Helen zipped her back into her coat.

'Not today, we don't have time now.'

'But I've been good! And he said I could!'

'And you saw all those lovely sheep, didn't you?' Not even Helen's jolliest voice and a big squeeze could dispel the storm clouds gathering on Megan's face.

'Why don't I show you the very special ones, and you can see the rest of the animals next time you come?' Joel glanced at Helen. 'They're in my office so you'll be passing on the way out anyway.'

'That's a good idea, isn't it?' Helen said brightly and, saying goodbye to Joan and Ron, she dragged a still-frowning Megan out of the Feed Store and across into the office building opposite. She was bracing herself for fish – and Megan's inevitable disappointment – when Joel stopped in front of a wooden door which had a sign on reading 'JAM Design'. He crouched down in front of Megan.

'We need to go in slowly and quietly so we don't scare them, okay?'

Megan nodded, her eyes wide in anticipation. Helen regarded the closed door with a rising sense of dread. Fish couldn't be scared, could they? So what else might a man keep in his office? Insects? Mice? Rats? God help her – snakes?

Helen's fears must have been engraved on her face, because Joel's lips were trembling in amusement as he finally opened the door to reveal a large office with a wooden floor and a picture window framing a view of fields and trees. There were two desks, one scattered with papers and the other holding a keyboard, two computer screens and a laptop. Shelves filled the wall behind this desk, and Helen was relieved to notice the lack of tanks or cages. She heard an excited squeak.

'Kittens,' Megan breathed. She was gripping Helen's hand tightly, and staring at a basket on the floor, in which lay a fluffy cat surrounded by four tiny kittens. Joel knelt down by the basket, and stroked the cat between the ears.

'She doesn't hate cats, does she?' he asked, when Megan didn't move. Helen laughed.

'She loves them. But she's never seen a real kitten.'

Smiling, Joel picked up a tortoiseshell kitten.

'Do you want to come and have a look?'

Megan nodded, and tiptoed over to Joel, having clearly taken his warning about being quiet rather too much to heart. She sat down on the floor next to him, and he held out the kitten so she could stroke it. Delight burst over her face as she touched the soft fur.

'Is this your cat?' Helen asked.

'It might be more accurate to say I'm her human.' Joel picked up the next kitten for Megan. 'She adopted me when I moved here.'

'Whether you wanted her or not?'

'She must have recognised me as a lonely cat lover. I used to have two, but...' His smile faded a notch. 'I lost them in a custody battle.'

'And now you have five!'

'Yes.' Joel grimaced, and picked up the next one for Megan. 'I didn't realise she hadn't been done.'

'How old are they?'

'Almost four weeks. Luckily I've found homes for three of them, when they're old enough to leave mum. But no one wants the runt.' He picked up the final kitten, a black one with white patches on both front paws, which was definitely smaller and sleepier than the others.

'Can we have it, Mummy?'

How had she not seen that coming? Joel mouthed 'sorry' at her, as Helen wondered what excuse she could possibly make. She loved cats, but a kitten would be too much to cope with on top of everything else at the moment.

'I don't think Joel wants us to take away his last kitten,' she said, passing the mantle firmly back to him. He obligingly picked it up.

'This little one is very special,' he told Megan, placing it carefully down in her lap. 'I think mummy cat will want it to stay with her so she can look after it herself, like your mummy looks after you.' He watched as Megan gently touched the kitten. 'Would you like to choose its name?'

'It's Mr Cat.'

'It's a girl, so perhaps Miss Cat...'

'No. It's Mr Cat, isn't it, Mummy?'

'Megan's favourite toy cat looks just like it, and is called Mr Cat,' Helen explained.

'Okay, Mr Cat it is.'

'Is Mr Cat mine now?'

'She can be your cat, but she'll live here with her mummy, agreed?' Megan nodded at Joel. 'You can visit her whenever you want, and if your mummy gives me her phone number I'll send you photos so you can see how she's growing. How does that sound?'

'Good,' Megan agreed.

Joel stood up and turned to Helen, his smile wide and dimples deep.

'You'd better let me have your number.'

Helen wrote her number on a post-it note and handed it to him. Joel watched her, still smiling.

'The answer,' he said, as she put the pen down, 'is that you can have the largest unit for ten percent less than you pay now for your small one. Tempted?'

'Maybe.'

'Is there anything else I can do to persuade you?'

'No. I need to work on the plans and see what space is available, and get some feedback from my customers, to find out if they would be happy to come here.'

'Don't forget I can help with your website. We can set up online sales.'

Helen laughed.

'Let me think about it, okay?' She looked across

at Megan, who was engrossed with the kittens. 'It won't affect the others, will it? Whatever I decide?'

'No. They'd still be welcome. But I want you.'

Helen's eyes were irresistibly drawn to his. He gazed back, his expression serious, but with a hint of amusement about his lips. And there was something else too, about the way he was looking at her, and the way that look was making her feel, which made Helen realise there was more at stake than she had anticipated. She had to decide whether her business would survive the move to Church Farm; and on first impressions from this morning, she had begun to think it might. But would *she* survive the frequent contact with Joel Markham?

CHAPTER 12

Daniel called round after work twice over the next week, and again on Sunday afternoon, arriving so early this time that they had barely finished lunch. He patiently played monotonous games of Snap, re-did the same old jigsaws, and inevitably had to join in 'guess the name of the doll' until Megan rolled around on the floor in giggles as he came up with ever more outlandish suggestions.

With each visit, Helen could see Daniel embroidering his mark on Megan, binding them together with tiny blanket stitches in a strong, almost invisible thread, that was part agony, part delight to witness. She sat in the kitchen sewing, hearing them talk, hearing them laugh and, as her needle jabbed in and out of the fabric, so the refrain poked relentlessly in her heart: is this how it might have been?

It was a relief, during the week, to let the solid doors of St Andrew's close behind her, shutting out all that was going on at home as she tried to focus on her work. A local independent school had commissioned her to create a metre-square wall hanging, based on a design by a Year 6 student, to celebrate the opening of a new junior school building. When the shop was quiet, she threw herself into sketching out ideas, putting together a mood board of the material she wanted to use, and embroidering some sample pieces of the school's crest to show how

147

it might look. Along with finishing off existing commissions and producing more items for the Christmas display, she was kept busy for most of the days, and often many hours of the night as well.

As customers came to Crazy Little Things, Helen canvassed opinions on a possible move to Church Farm. Quite a number of her regulars had heard of it, and thought it was a great place for her to move to. Some of the more elderly customers were thrilled to have a different outing to look forward to. Reaction wasn't so positive from the lunchtime shoppers, mainly younger sewers who worked all week and had commitments at the weekend: but they seemed keen on an online shop, and there was unanimous interest from all age groups about the possible workshops and classes that Helen put forward as ideas. If she could keep a decent proportion of existing customers, and attract new ones at Church Farm, she was optimistic that the move could work.

She hadn't given Joel a decision yet; she hadn't spoken to him since they had gone to view the Hay Barn. She had prepared plans for the interior, and drawn pictures of how it could look, and had carried them round with her for three days, uncertain what to do next. Should she deliver them to Church Farm? She knew Joel would like them, and could imagine the way he would smile if she showed them to him. And then she felt guilt burn her skin like a rash. How could she be thinking of another man's smile? Daniel might be long past returning her feelings, but she had never stopped loving him; he was the father of her child, in her thoughts every day, and the connection between them was irreplaceable. So she passed the plans to Joan to hand over, and tried to appear indifferent when an effusive text arrived, every word laced with a smile.

On Friday morning, two days before the Sunday lunch with the Blakes that Helen had been trying hard not to think about, her mobile phone rang as she was packing her bags, about to head off to the independent school to present her ideas for the wall hanging.

'Hello, is that Helen?'

Helen's bag dropped to the floor, skeins of thread rolling across the shop like colourful mice. She hadn't recognised the number, but there was no mistaking the voice. It was Valerie Blake; and it was the last thing she needed before an important meeting.

'Yes. Hello Valerie.'

There was a momentary pause, as if Valerie had been wrong-footed by Helen guessing her identity before she could announce herself.

'I thought we might have a word about Sunday.'

'Okay,' Helen replied cautiously. She could think of several words she'd like to hear, top of the list being 'cancelled'.

'I was thinking about a roast chicken for lunch, but I wondered if you'd let me know what Megan would like.' There was a slight stutter over Megan's name. 'Would she prefer something else? Sausages? Fish fingers?'

Helen took the phone from her ear, and stared at

it. Was this a trick? This was a Valerie she'd not come across before: hesitant, uncertain, polite.

'Helen?'

'She loves chicken. Don't do anything special.'

'And dessert? Would she like ice cream? Any flavour?'

'Strawberry's her favourite.'

'Good. I'll get some. Can you remember the way?'

'Vaguely...'

'I'll ask Daniel to send some directions. And Helen?'

'Yes?'

'I wanted you to know how much I'm looking forward to meeting my granddaughter.'

Valerie hung up, and Helen stared again at the now silent phone. That last line – it had been Valerie's way of apologising, she knew that. It didn't matter that it was indirect, that she hadn't actually used the word sorry. She had acknowledged Megan as her granddaughter. For Megan's sake, that meant a great deal.

'You're miles away,' Kirsty said, giving Helen a nudge. She had come in to mind the shop for a few hours while Helen attended her meeting. 'Surely that wasn't Valerie Blake on the phone? You're far too calm.'

'It was her.' Helen put her phone away, and started to collect the loose rolls of thread in a daze.

'What did she want? Has she found a new paternity test to try out?'

'No. She was offering to make Megan fish fingers

150

for lunch on Sunday.' She looked at Kirsty. 'She's going to get her some ice cream.'

Kirsty laughed.

'You said that as if she'd offered to import some exotic dragon fruit from Mexico. It's only ice cream. But it's nice of her to think of it, isn't it?'

'Yes, it is, and very unexpected. You've been spoilt with Ben's mum, because she's lovely. Not all mothers-in-law are like that.'

'Interesting that you still see her in the role of mother-in-law.' Kirsty grinned. 'Is that a hangover from the past, or hope for the future?'

'A definite hangover,' Helen said hurriedly, kicking herself for the mistake. 'And that's exactly what I'm expecting to have on Monday morning, after I spend Sunday night trying to obliterate the occasion, so don't be surprised if you're needed for a spot of emergency babysitting...'

Valerie Blake lived in a respectable Edwardian house on a quiet street of other detached houses in Knutsford. As Helen drove in through the gates, dread gnawing her stomach, she saw no sign that any changes had been made in the five years since she had last been here. The paintwork was immaculate, the curtains at each window tied back in perfect positions, and even the garden appeared tidy, as if no autumn leaves dared fall on Valerie Blake's land.

She held Megan's hand tightly as they approached the front door, mainly for her own comfort. Before she could ring the bell, the door swung open and

Daniel stood there, a broad smile covering his face as his eyes immediately sank to Megan's level.

'Hello Megan.' He bent down and inspected the small tote bag she was carrying, which had a plastic leg poking out of it. 'Is that Tallulah's leg I can see there?'

Megan giggled. Daniel's eyes rose to Helen, and his smile visibly dimmed.

'Come in.'

He stepped back, and Helen led Megan inside. She stopped as the familiar smell assailed her, of polish and pot pourri, and something else she had never been able to define. If respectability had a perfume, it would be bottled in Valerie's house. And there she was, lurking in the hall, the picture of an upstanding gentlewoman in her woollen suit, blouse and pearls.

Just as Daniel's had done, Valerie's eyes first dropped to Megan. A flush of colour rose above the collar of her blouse, and her mouth opened slightly, showing where the lipstick was almost worn away on the inner edges by anxious biting. Valerie looked from Megan to Daniel, but didn't speak.

'Mum, this is Megan.'

His words revived her. Valerie walked nearer to Megan, bent slightly and smiled.

'Hello Megan, I'm...' She faltered, and her eyes flicked to Helen anxiously. 'I'm Daniel's mother. Valerie.'

'Hello.'

Valerie looked thrilled to hear Megan's voice. Little did she know, Helen thought, that Megan had been bribed with the promise of a new Barbie to be on her best behaviour today. Then Valerie surprised Helen by taking her hand, and squeezing it so that her rings pressed uncomfortably against Helen's fingers.

'Thank you,' she said, in a low voice, as tears glistened in her eyes. 'She's lovely.'

Helen didn't know what to say. She'd never had physical contact with Valerie before; but she'd never met this Valerie before. She simply saw a grandmother, overawed to be meeting her grandchild for the first time. And reacting as a mother, Helen squeezed her hand back, and nodded. Externally the house might look the same, but there had been a change at the heart of it.

Valerie led the way into the living room. Tasha at once bounded up to them, looking impossibly shiny.

'Hello! You must be the famous Megan that Danny talks so much about!' The voice and smile insisted she was happy but her eyes didn't seem to have received the same message. Megan edged closer to Helen, and no wonder – she'd just been accosted by a hyperactive Barbie doll. Helen said hello, and turned to the other two people in the room. A tall, stocky man was standing in front of the fireplace, offering a kind smile. Daniel's sister Alex was sitting on the sofa, a hand over her mouth and tears in her eyes as she gazed at Megan.

'Hello Alex.'

Alex slowly lifted her head to regard Helen, and the expression in her eyes was impossible to misconstrue. It seemed that Alex hated Helen quite as

153

much as her brother did, and it was almost as painful for Helen to see. Alex was eight years younger than Daniel, nearer in age to Helen, and they had been as close as sisters. They had spent hours together, never running out of conversation. They had run out now. Alex turned back to Megan without speaking a word.

Valerie brought in a plastic box full of toys, and placed it in the middle of the room.

'It's a few things that Daniel and Alex used to play with. I've been saving them in case...' She stopped, and fingered her pearls. 'Everything has been cleaned.'

'That's very kind.' Helen smiled awkwardly at Valerie. This new Valerie was taking some getting used to. Part of her was still convinced it must be a trick, and was wondering what lay behind this transformation. It couldn't be real, could it?

'Look, Megan, here's a tea set,' Daniel said, unpacking the box. With a nudge of encouragement, Megan sat with him on the floor. 'Come on, Alex, you used to love this.' Alex joined them, having a tea party, and the resemblance between the three of them was remarkable. Valerie was transfixed, and didn't notice when sherry spilled from her glass over her trembling fingers. They laughed and joked, Daniel every inch the proud father, delighting in everything Megan did. He only glanced once at Helen, but it was enough. She knew what that look meant. *This is where she should be,* it said, *with her family. This is where she should always have been.* And how could Helen disagree?

Lunch was an awkward business. Daniel continued

154

to audition for Father of the Year – albeit an unacknowledged one – but the undercurrent of tension and hostility swirled around their feet. Helen didn't dare speak, other than to Megan, terrified of what explosion one wrong word might set off. Alex's fiancé, Phil, came into his own and tried his best to push forward a safe conversation. He was head of PE at a nearby boys' school and had a convenient stock of stories to tell between mouthfuls of roast chicken.

'Which school will Megan go to?'

Helen, busy cutting up a roast potato for Megan – one of the few tasks that Daniel hadn't managed to snatch from her – turned to him. It was the first time he had voluntarily spoken to her, and though his face was carefully neutral, she knew him well enough to detect the first signs of trouble in his voice.

'I'll be applying to St Brendan's.'

'St Brendan's?' There was a flash of the old Valerie. 'Is that a *Catholic* school?' She could hardly have sounded more disapproving.

'Yes. My family are Catholic.'

Though Helen wasn't, as she had proved often enough in the past. It wasn't the religious element that had inspired her to pick St Brendan's. She had pored over OFSTED reports before renting her house, to make sure she found the best state school she could in the area.

'But we both went to private schools.' Daniel's fingers tapped against his wineglass.

'I know.' And Helen knew what Daniel meant by that remark. When, in the past, they had discussed the imaginary Megan and Archie, those children who still should have been no more than a twinkle in the eye, they had agreed to educate them privately – nothing but the best for their children. And though in everything else she had tried her utmost to do what he would have wanted, it was simply impossible with schools. She could never afford a private school on her own.

She pushed Megan's plate back towards her. Daniel was watching Helen.

'We'll talk about this.'

He could talk all he wanted, but words wouldn't pay the school fees. It wasn't a conversation she was looking forward to, or would encourage.

'This weather is so dire, isn't it?' Tasha asked. Megan stared at her. As the afternoon wore on, she appeared to be increasingly fascinated by her, perhaps because of the strange accent or the Barbie looks. 'I can't wait to get home for Christmas and soak up the sun, can you, Danny?' She put a possessive hand on his arm.

'I can't go away for Christmas.'

'But Danny...' Helen noticed the hand increase its grip. 'When I said I'd come over here, we agreed to go back after Alex's wedding.'

'That was before.' He didn't say anything more, but his glance at Megan said enough. 'You can still go, Tash. See your family.'

While he stayed with *his* family, continued the unspoken conversation. He was choosing Megan over Tasha. Would this be a good time, Helen wondered,

156

to let him know that she would be visiting her family over Christmas, so he needn't change his plans on their account? She opened her mouth, but closed it again when Tasha looked at her. Her expression was pure dislike. And who could blame her? Helen, of all people, knew the pain of being without Daniel. All it needed now was for Phil to find something to hate her for, and she would have a clean sweep round the table.

By the time the apple crumble arrived for dessert, Megan's patience at sitting politely was wearing thin. Before Helen could stop her, she jumped down from her chair, ran round to Daniel, and waved a doll in front of him.

'Guess who this is?' she demanded, bouncing up and down at his side. 'Guess, Danny!'

Helen's breath caught. For a second, it had sounded like she'd said... But that was ridiculous, wasn't it? Except the others round the table were suspended in silence, staring at Megan. And Daniel's face... His whole heart was right there, for all to see. Helen's spoon clattered into her bowl, splattering cream onto Valerie's pristine tablecloth. She wasn't sure she could do this. She'd always thought that the moment of telling him would be the worst; that there could be only one way to go from there. But she'd been wrong. Every meeting brought fresh pain, new examples of how she had injured him, that kept the wound raw. It hurt more than she could ever have imagined it would.

Seeing that Megan was occupied with Daniel,

Helen excused herself and went to the bathroom. She leant her hands on the sink and stared at herself in the mirror. She looked entirely normal, perhaps a little tired around the eyes, but otherwise her ordinary self stared back. Nothing in her face suggested that she was the sort of person who would cause another so much suffering. But she was. She had. Her parents had spent years telling her what a bad person she was, and she had tried so hard to change. But this terrible thing she had done to Daniel could never be undone.

On her way back to the dining room, she called in to the kitchen for a glass of water. Valerie was there, making coffee.

'It will get easier,' Valerie said, as if continuing a conversation they had already started. She smiled at Helen, a sight so unexpected that a lump of emotion gathered in Helen's throat. 'He simply needs...'

'This is the wrong juice.' Daniel came in and banged a plastic tumbler down on the worktop. Some of the contents splashed out.

'Is it for Megan?' He nodded. 'She doesn't like fresh orange juice with bits in. She'll want orange cordial if you have it.'

Valerie opened a cupboard and brought out an unopened bottle of cordial. She passed it towards Daniel, but he was too preoccupied glaring at Helen to notice.

'How the hell was I supposed to know that?' he shouted. 'Perhaps if you'd had one degree of humanity and let me watch my daughter grow up –

let me know I *had* a daughter to watch grow up – I might have known what she liked to drink and not got it wrong!'

'Daniel! That's enough...'

He clearly disagreed with his mother.

'And perhaps,' he continued, 'I might even have heard her call me Daddy!'

It was the tremble in his voice that broke her. Helen began to cry, huge tears that fell faster than she could wipe them away, and sobs that almost choked her as she tried to swallow them down. She hadn't shed a tear since he had gone; but now she had no control over herself, as every dream she'd had that somehow they would get back together slid away down her cheeks.

'For God's sake!' Daniel's hand crashed down onto the worktop. 'Do you really think that's going to work? I'm the only one here who deserves any sympathy.'

With another wholly unexpected gesture, Valerie put her arm round Helen. The shock of it gave Helen the shot of strength that she needed to pull herself together and to fight back. She wiped away the remaining tears.

'You think you deserve sympathy for missing out on some things? Shall I tell you what you missed? You missed six months of agonising over whether the baby would be okay, and not damaged by what I'd done or not done before I knew I was pregnant. You missed the worst twenty-four hours of my life, when the baby stopped moving and I thought it had died; I

159

thought I'd lost you both. You weren't there for two exhausting days of labour, which I went through on my own. You missed every nappy change; every sleepless night when it always had to be my turn to get up; the months when she screamed with colic until I thought I would go insane; the impossible tantrums; the moments of absolute boredom when I would have given anything to have an adult to talk to. You can't just focus on the big-money moments you didn't get to see; there's been a whole load of crap ones you've been spared.' She took a breath, but there was more she had to say. 'Hong Kong – the whole idea of a new life and new adventure – was my dream as much as yours. I let it go, so you could still have it. Some people would actually think you've had the best of both worlds here. You had the years of enjoying life while someone else minded your child. And now you can swoop back in and start playing Daddy with all the horrible messy bits out of the way.'

Briefly, she wondered if she saw something warmer in his eyes, something battling the dislike he usually bestowed on her. His arm jerked in her direction then fell back.

'Christmas,' he said, and his voice still wasn't quite steady. 'I want her to know by Christmas.'

'That's only a couple of months…'

'You tell her or I will.'

Did he mean it? Would he really tell Megan who he was, even if Helen didn't want him to? She sighed. She couldn't take the risk, and he knew it.

'Daniel, go and check on Megan while Helen tidies

160

herself up.'

He left, and Valerie turned to Helen. Her expression was so severe that Helen feared the old Valerie was about to make her return. But as she handed over a box of tissues, her hands were shaking again.

'I'm sorry,' Valerie said. 'I'm sorry for the way I always behaved towards you. I never thought you were good enough for Daniel. I misjudged you.'

'You've been proved right. I've hurt him more deeply than you could ever have predicted.'

Valerie shook her head.

'He'll get over it. You did something wonderful for him. You've given him – all of us – the most precious gift, one that we never expected to have. I only wish you'd felt you could have told me, and maybe we could have worked something out. I will never forgive myself for that.'

It was the first murmur of support, and from the last person Helen would have expected to offer it. She shook aside the niggle of doubt over whether she deserved it, and absorbed the absolution. Perhaps it took the depth of the love they had both felt for Daniel to realise that he had needed Hong Kong and no other option would have made him happy. Valerie's words chipped away at the block of guilt Helen carried round; it would always be there, but perhaps the edges weren't quite so rough, weren't quite so likely to snag her every day.

When Megan showed signs of becoming restless, Helen made her excuses to go.

'Alex, wasn't there something you wanted to ask Helen?' Valerie prompted.

'Oh, yes.' Alex looked at Helen and spoke to her directly for the first time all day. 'You know I'm getting married in December? We wondered if Megan would like to be a flower girl.'

A flower girl at her aunt's wedding. It was such a normal, natural thing, how could Helen refuse?

'I'm sure she'd love to.' She squeezed Megan's hand, and smiled down at her. 'Do you want me to buy her a dress? Any particular colour?'

'The bridesmaids are wearing pale blue, but I doubt the bridal shop will be able to make another dress in time,' Alex said.

'Helen could, though, couldn't you?' Valerie fixed her with a steely look. 'If we can obtain the same fabric, you could make something better than the bridal shop.'

It wasn't a question, Helen realised: it was a statement – an order, even, but one she recognised as Valerie's way of showing her support.

'Yes, of course I could.' Although she hardly knew when she was going to fit that in on top of everything else. She smiled at Alex. 'If you come to the shop we can look through some patterns.'

They fixed a time, then Helen and Megan said goodbye and left. Despite the tears, despite the angry words from Daniel and awkwardness with the others, as the front door closed behind them, Helen's shoulders lifted. The visit had gone much better than she had feared. Valerie Blake had been a revelation.

162

Helen smiled down at Megan.

'Race you to the car!' she said. Megan set off at once, and Helen followed, letting Megan streak ahead as they reached the car. Laughing, she swept a giggling Megan into her arms and as she did, her eyes were drawn back to the house. Daniel was standing alone in the window, watching.

CHAPTER 13

Daniel telephoned early the next morning while Helen was still clearing away the breakfast.

'How is Megan?'

'Very well.' Better than Helen. Her head swirled with a fog of tiredness after a largely sleepless night.

'Has she mentioned yesterday? Did she enjoy it?'

'I think so.' Although when they arrived home, she'd been more interested in the cute photo Joel had sent of Mr Cat exploring his desk. True to his word, he was sending regular updates, often accompanied by a funny message for Helen. 'She's excited about being a flower girl.'

'Good. It's a family day. She should be there.'

Helen wondered where that left her. No one had actually clarified how it was going to work. Was she supposed to drop Megan off at the wedding, and pick her up later? She wasn't prepared to do that, but nor did she expect to be invited: it was too late to add extra guests, she imagined, and how would they ever explain her connection? Daniel's ex-girlfriend who had his baby but didn't tell him? It would certainly be a conversation piece, if nothing else.

'Are you free tomorrow morning?' Daniel cut into her thoughts.

'No, I'm working.'

'No appointments?'

'No, but...'

'Good. I've arranged for us to see a solicitor at ten, to sort out the birth certificate. Craig recommended her.'

Was this how it was going to be from now on? Daniel making the decisions, and ordering her about, because she was the mother of his child? It stirred uncomfortable memories of how their previous relationship had worked, memories that had been airbrushed out of the Daniel she had thought about for the last four years.

'You could have checked with me first,' she protested, banging the dishes into the sink with more venom than they deserved. 'It's all rather rushed, isn't it?'

'I'm sorry, do you think so? Four years to be named on my daughter's birth certificate sounds rather slow to me.'

She hated his sarcasm. She'd forgotten about that, too, and how often he used it against her. 'Fine. Text me the address and I'll be there.'

The solicitor was based in a large brick and glass office building in the centre of Manchester. It looked expensive, and terribly professional, and Helen felt completely out of her depth even before she had set foot inside. This looked like the sort of place where great deals might be done, and complex problems thrashed out: what had it got to do with her and Megan, and adding a name to a bit of paper?

She took the lift to the reception area on the fifth floor, and found Daniel already there. He was sitting on the leather chesterfield, wearing a dark suit and reading *The Times*, a half-drunk coffee in front of him. He fitted in perfectly with this environment, and Helen clutched her handbag tighter, feeling ridiculously incongruous in her red wool coat and homemade skirt.

Daniel stood up when he saw her.

'Hello.' He hovered, clearly caught in that awful moment of wondering whether to kiss her or not, and then sat down again. Helen sank onto the sofa opposite him, and let out the breath she'd been holding. She couldn't have coped with a polite kiss on the cheek, not when he was looking so devastating. There was something about him, all dressed up for work in his sober suits, that she had never been able to resist: the contrast, perhaps, between the formal appearance and what she knew he was like underneath. However hot the weather, he had always kept his tie on for when he came home, knowing how much she loved to tear it off...

'Mr Blake? Miss Walters?' A lady in navy trousers and a cream silk blouse approached, her hand outstretched. Helen sprang up, as if the leather beneath her was growing as warm as her thoughts. 'I'm Rachel Ward. Would you like to come through to the conference room?'

They followed her down a corridor to a characterless room containing a round table surrounded by four chairs. A notebook and pen lay in front of one of the chairs. There was a box of tissues in the middle of the table. It wasn't an encouraging sign.

'Now, I understand you want to discuss changing your daughter's birth certificate, is that right?'

'Yes.' Daniel smiled at her, slipping easily into the charming manner he did so well. 'I was abroad when she was born, and Helen says she was unable to have my name added as the father.'

Helen looked at him, eyes narrowed. He continued to smile, his attention focussed on the solicitor. Had she imagined the slight emphasis there on 'says'? Did he not believe her?

'I assume you weren't married at the time of the birth?' Rachel asked.

'No, and we're not now.'

Helen noticed how quick he was to point that out.

'Then Miss Walters is right. She could only register you as the father if you both signed the register together, or if she had a statutory declaration of parentage, or an order giving you parental responsibility. You didn't have either of those?'

Helen shook her head.

'But it is possible to change the birth certificate now, isn't it?' Daniel asked.

'Yes, you can complete an application for re-registration of the birth. I assume it is something you both agree on? I can't advise you both unless you're in agreement.'

'Helen?' She felt the word like a physical prod.

'Yes, I agree.'

'So, once the birth certificate is changed, will that mean I have the normal rights of a father?'

'Rights?' Helen stared at him. 'What rights?'

167

'To have a say in everything. To make decisions about Megan.'

'You mean parental responsibility?' Rachel uncapped her pen and made a note on the pad in front of her. Helen tried to read what she'd written, but the writing was too small. 'You will obtain that by re-registering the birth. It will give you the right to be involved in decisions about the child's education, and religion, consent to medical treatment, and on a practical level, sign school forms and things like that.'

'That's what I want.'

'Hold on,' Helen interrupted. This was going further and faster than she'd expected. 'We haven't talked about that. I thought we were only changing the birth certificate.'

Rachel sat back.

'I'm sorry, but if you don't agree on this I can't advise you both.'

'So I don't automatically have parental responsibility? Even though I'm the parent?' Daniel was still presenting the charming smile, but had started his finger-tapping thing.

'No, it's not that simple, unless you're married. You can only gain it by jointly registering the birth, or re-registering in your case, or if the mother signs an agreement, or if a parental responsibility order is made by the court.'

Helen gazed at the tissue box. She could feel Daniel's eyes on her.

'And if Helen doesn't agree? Is the court order a formality?'

'I don't know the specifics in your case, but the court will consider things such as your reasons for applying, the degree of attachment between the father and the child, the level of commitment shown by the father...'

Daniel's fingers thumped onto the arm of his chair.

'And what would the court make of the fact that I haven't had chance to show commitment because I didn't know she existed?'

Rachel jotted another note on her pad. It was illegible, but Helen could guess it didn't say anything good.

'It's fine, I agree that we'll re-register Megan's birth,' she said. She didn't want to go anywhere near a court, in case it could punish her by taking Megan away. And a piece of paper wasn't going to make much difference after all: if Daniel was determined to interfere, he would do it, paper or not.

'And what about her name?' Daniel's fingers had stilled for the time being. 'How do we go about changing that?'

'What's wrong with her name?' Helen turned to him. 'We agreed – Megan for a girl.'

'But the birth certificate says Megan Walters.' Daniel spoke slowly and flashed a smile at Rachel, as if to apologise that she had to listen to this. 'She should be Megan Blake.'

'No.' How could he even suggest it? Helen's voice rose several pitches. 'I want her to have the same name as me.'

'So do I.'

Rachel pushed back her chair.

'Would you like me to give you a few minutes alone?'

'No, there's no need for that,' Helen said, conscious that she sounded over-wrought in contrast to his measured tone. She wasn't paying anyone to have a cup of tea while she argued with Daniel. And there was no point arguing. She was never going to back down on this. 'Megan is staying as Walters. It's not negotiable.'

'But what if you get married? You wouldn't have the same name then.'

Oh, that stung – that he could so casually, so carelessly talk about her marrying someone else, without a single flicker of emotion. She stretched across the table for one of the tissues.

'I'm not planning to marry,' she said.

Daniel had started the finger drumming again.

'But you might,' he insisted. She supposed she ought to be flattered that despite how much he thought she'd changed, he still considered it possible that she might attract a man. Just not him. He looked at Rachel. 'What would happen if Helen married? Would Megan take the husband's name?'

'Not automatically, no.' Rachel appeared relieved to be back on familiar ground. 'Changing a child's surname is a profound step. If there's any dispute over it, the court will decide, considering what's in the best interests of the child. It's very difficult to put forward a cogent case for a change.'

Daniel let out a sigh of frustration, and Helen

tensed, waiting for him to push the point, but he didn't. The meeting ended without further surprises, but as they were leaving, before Rachel could open the door, Helen spoke. One question had been torturing her ever since Daniel's return. She had to know the answer.

'Can I ask one more question?'

'Of course.' Rachel smiled. Helen could sense Daniel's frown without needing to see it.

'Daniel's in a relationship, and I'm not. He's more financially secure too.' She clutched the tissue tightly in her hand. 'Does that make a difference? If he applied for custody, would that mean he'd win?'

Suddenly she felt a strong hand on her arm, pulling her round.

'Nell.' She caught her breath. There was the old Daniel, in the timbre of his voice and the warmth in his eyes. 'I'm not going to take her off you.'

She believed him; the truth was there in his face. But still she turned back to Rachel for the answer.

'It's the child's best interests that matter,' she replied. 'There's no presumption that a couple would be better than a single parent.'

They left the office in silence, until they reached the street.

'Where are you parked?' Daniel asked.

'The multi-storey over there.' She pointed. Daniel nodded.

'I'm the other way.' He didn't make any effort to move. 'Thanks for agreeing to that. The birth certificate and parental responsibility thing, I mean.'

Helen dug her nails into her palm, unable to reply. It was unbearable. He was thanking her for giving him something he should have had anyway. It was almost easier to deal with him shouting at her.

'I'm sorry if you've been worrying about custody. It's never crossed my mind. Megan belongs with you. You've done a fantastic job.'

Damn tears! Helen quickly wiped her eyes. What was wrong with her? He could probably count on one hand the number of times she had cried when they had been together. Now she couldn't stop.

'Perhaps when she knows who I am, we can talk about an overnight stay?' Helen gave a slight nod. She knew he was entitled to it, and that she had to let them have time together at some stage; how she would bear it was quite another matter. 'It's not just you, now. We're doing this together. So, truce?'

He offered his hand and his smile. It wasn't the smile he used to give her; she couldn't expect that; that smile belonged to Tasha now. But it was like seeing the first crocus burst through the hard earth of a winter-battered garden. She shook his hand, and he walked away, while she remained on the pavement, watching him go, her heart aching.

CHAPTER 14

Thursday was the day Helen and Alex had fixed for their meeting to discuss Megan's flower-girl dress and, despite the apparent truce with Daniel, Helen was dreading it. It had been awkward enough at Valerie's house, when the company had been diluted: how were they going to manage alone? Perhaps Alex would bring Valerie with her; strangely, Helen found herself hoping she would. But what if she brought Tasha? That unwelcome thought had Helen spinning round anxiously every time she heard the doors open.

But the first familiar visitor to St Andrew's that day wasn't Alex. Helen was trying to convince a new customer that she would be able to manage a cross-stitch cushion, and demonstrating how easy the stitch was on a spare piece of binca, when Joel walked in. She hadn't seen him or spoken to him since the visit to Church Farm, despite the regular messages about Mr Cat, and wasn't prepared for the sudden prickle of interest, or self-consciousness, that hit her.

Carrying on with her demonstration, she saw from the corner of her eye that Joel headed straight for Saskia's jewellery shop. Saskia was clearly expecting him, and now the reason for her glamorous, if skimpy, outfit became clear. Helen heard them laughing and talking as she closed the sale with her customer, and noticed that Joel was taking photographs of some of Saskia's displays.

Helen tidied away the binca and thread, and watched as Joel next popped across the aisle for a quick word with Malcolm. They seemed to be discussing the new piece Malcolm was painting – after thirty years of gentle landscapes, he had revealed a hidden passion for bold abstract designs. Helen loved them, and tried to work out how Joel was reacting. He was smiling, but that was nothing unusual; she was inclined to think his lips worked in the opposite way to other people's, so he had to make an effort to curve them down if he wanted to appear serious.

Joel finished with Malcolm, and zig-zagged back across the aisle to Fiona's shop, where he took more photographs. Helen cleared a space on the counter and set up her laptop and a couple of patterns ready to show Alex when she came in. He hadn't looked her way once since he arrived. Panic flooded her veins and made her heart race. What if he had changed his mind, or had grown tired of waiting and let the unit to someone else, just as she'd decided to take it? She had been planning to go to Church Farm with Megan on Monday, to tell him her decision and have another look. What if she'd left it too late, and he no longer wanted her?

Trying not to stare in too stalkerish a way, she waited until he had taken two paces out of Fiona's shop – in the direction of Joan, not Crazy Little Things, she noted with another flare of anxiety –

and stepped out into the aisle.

'Joel!'

He looked round, the smile already in place.

'Hello.' He took a step nearer, but didn't say anything more.

'I didn't know you were coming in today.'

'I needed to take some photos of Saskia's and Fiona's work. I'm putting a feature on the Church Farm website about the new occupants of the Hay Barn.'

'So I'm too late?' The panic fuelling her heart evaporated, leaving her numb. What was she going to do? She realised now how perfect the Hay Barn would be for her. Had she lost that as well as St Andrew's?

'Too late for what?' Joel looked confused, then his smile grew. 'You mean you've decided? You want to join us?'

'If there's still a space.'

'Of course there is!' He laughed. 'I told you it was yours if you wanted it. Your plans were fantastic. I've already ordered the glass partitions to go where you suggested. It's been torture not asking about your shop, but I thought I should leave you alone to decide without pressure.'

He was genuinely pleased. His whole face glowed with his smile. Helen felt an answering ripple of excitement, and wondered if she looked as happy as he did.

'Have you time for a coffee?' Joel asked, unfastening his scarf. 'I was about to go to Auntie

Joan's. We can talk through the details and then I could take some photos while I'm here.'

'I can't, I'm expecting someone in a few minutes.'

'Oh.' The smile dimmed a notch. 'I've got a meeting in Leeds for most of the day tomorrow. I know nights will be difficult for you, but is there any chance we could meet tomorrow night? I want to update the website as soon as I can. I could come round to yours if that's easier.'

'No, I should be able to pop out for an hour.' If she spoke very nicely to Kirsty. But it concerned Kirsty's job too: surely that would persuade her? Not that Kirsty would probably need much persuasion to facilitate Helen going out for a drink with an attractive man, even if it was strictly business. Which it was, wasn't it? She looked at Joel with sudden uncertainty. He winked.

'I knew I'd entice you out for that drink eventually.' Those dangerous dimples came out again. Helen glanced away, attacked by an unexpected palpitation. 'Do you mind if I get a couple of quick photos? I'll go as soon as your customer arrives.'

He followed Helen into Crazy Little Things and took photos of the crazy patchwork and of the shop, while Helen lurked, trying not to be caught herself. She was so busy watching him that she didn't even notice the sound she'd been waiting for all morning, and she jumped when she saw Alex hesitating in the doorway.

'Am I too early?' Alex asked, regarding Joel curiously.

'No, come in.' Helen turned to Joel. 'Have you taken enough for today?'

'Yes. It's going to look great.' He packed away his camera. 'I'll show you a mock-up before it goes live, but that won't be for a few days.' His smile stretched over Helen and Alex as he squeezed past them to get to the door. 'I'll text you about tomorrow night.'

Helen nodded, and watched as Joel crossed back over to Malcolm's shop. He said something, and within seconds Malcolm was shaking his hand. Helen smiled. It looked like the Hay Barn was now full.

'Who was that?' Alex gave Helen a penetrating stare, horribly reminiscent of her brother.

'Joel owns a craft gallery. St Andrew's is closing so we all need to move, and he has vacant units. He was taking photos for the website.' Helen shut up, wondering why she had felt compelled to give so much explanation. Alex was still studying Joel. She needed to be distracted. 'Have you managed to get any more of the fabric from the bridesmaids' dresses?'

'Yes, it won't be a problem.' At last Alex tore her eyes from Joel, and pulled out a small sample of pale blue material from her bag. Helen picked it up, admiring how the light shimmered over the surface.

'Megan is going to adore this,' she said, laughing. 'I know exactly what she's going to say.

It's the colour of Cinderella's dress. You do realise she'll want to wear her tiara and plastic glass slippers, don't you?'

Alex smiled awkwardly.

'You don't have to make a dress,' she said, fiddling with the handle of her bag. 'I know Mum railroaded you into it, but I won't mind if you back out. I can buy something instead.'

'I couldn't back out now I've seen the Cinderella fabric.' Helen smiled. 'And Valerie didn't railroad me. It was an obvious solution.'

Alex stared at Helen. Valerie's interference had never passed by with so little remark. The old Helen would have relished ranting about this, even to Valerie's daughter.

'I only had two patterns in stock,' Helen continued, picking them up off the counter and passing them to Alex. 'But I think they may be rather plain for this fabric.'

'I'm sure one of them would be fine...' Alex began.

'And then I found this!' Helen spun the laptop round and showed Alex the picture she'd found of a flower girl, in a simple puff-sleeved dress in pink satin overlaid with net. 'I can adapt it so the sleeves aren't quite so puffy, and make a round neck instead of the V. And look at this net!' She ducked under the counter and pulled out a roll of net studded with tiny beads. 'Tell me if you think it's too bling, but it will look gorgeous when the light sparkles on the beads, and Megan will think she's a

178

princess. Although obviously it's your day...'

Helen stopped. Alex wasn't speaking, simply looking at Helen as if she had two heads.

'You hate it, don't you?' Helen said. She hoped she didn't sound too wistful: she would have loved to see Megan in this dress.

'No, not at all.' Alex continued to look at her. 'It's you.'

'You hate me?' Helen had felt it at Valerie's, but to hear it out loud, from Alex, and here where she had always found sanctuary... It hurt more than she could have expected.

'No.' Alex fingered the netting. 'I tried to. I thought I should. But I can't. You're still you. But in some ways you've changed so much I hardly recognise you.'

'Dan has already made it plain quite how much I've changed for the worst over the last few years.'

'Really? That's not the impression...' Alex stopped, and there was an awkward silence.

'Did you never guess I was a natural mouse?' Helen dragged out a laugh, touching her hair ruefully.

'It's more than the hair. You seem so...' Alex waved her hand. 'I can't think of the right word.'

'If you're heading towards "mumsy", be warned that I have plenty of sharp implements to hand.'

Alex laughed, then covered her mouth guiltily. 'That's not it, or not all of it. You seem so settled, like whatever's going on around you, you have an untouchable core of contentment. You didn't have

179

that before. You were always so bound up with Dan, and what he wanted. Now you've become yourself.'

Was it true? Did Alex know her so well, even after all this time? Helen had been happy with Daniel, blissfully so, she would have said. But she had let her own life slide to fit in with his. It hadn't troubled her at first, when their relationship had been new, and she had had the whole of London to fill her days. But when they had moved to Lancashire, pulled up on Valerie's apron strings after Daniel's father died, Helen had been forced to re-evaluate her life, and had discovered she wanted – needed – more. Being Daniel Blake's partner had no longer been enough.

Hong Kong had come at a perfect time: she had thought that a new city and a new country would be the challenge she was looking for, and perhaps restore them to how they had been in London. But in the end, a thin blue line on a plastic stick soaked in urine had proved exactly what she needed. It was hard to believe she would ever have made it to St Andrew's when she was with Daniel, even if Hong Kong hadn't come along. It had taken Megan to give her the motivation to start a career, and to be herself. Perhaps the break from Daniel had been the best thing for both of them. But how could that be right, when she had mourned him for the last four years?

'Why did you do it?' Alex was looking at Helen, her expression more confused than condemnatory.

'How could you? He adored you, you must have known that, and I always thought it was mutual. He was absolutely frantic when he came back and couldn't find you. He almost decided to move back for good. It took us days to persuade him to return to Hong Kong.'

'Why?' Helen asked.

'Why what?'

'Why did you persuade him to go back?'

'Because it was what he wanted, what he needed.' Alex frowned. 'He had been so excited about the opportunity. It was what he'd been working towards for years. We didn't want him to ruin his life because of you.'

'And I felt exactly the same,' Helen said. Alex's words were like arnica for her soul. 'That's why I didn't tell him, and why I let him go. So he didn't ruin his life because of me.'

And perhaps, she was beginning to realise, so she didn't ruin hers because of him. But that thought was too new, too contrary, for Helen to give it head room yet.

Alex's eyes widened.

'Oh God,' she said. 'You still love him. But he's with Tasha...'

'I know. And I won't interfere with that. But he's never done anything to make me stop loving him. Feelings don't just vanish.'

'No, they don't.' Before she knew what was happening, Alex had come round the counter and was hugging Helen. 'I can't believe how much I've missed you. Whatever happens with Dan, can we be friends again?'

Helen nodded, tears the only answer she could make. How could she have dreaded today? She could hardly believe how her fortune had turned around, after it had all looked so bleak. The new shop premises, the truce with Daniel, the restored friendship with Alex... Only a few days ago this would have seemed impossible. Perhaps, at last, things were starting to go her way...

CHAPTER 15

'Are you sure you don't want me to cancel?' Helen asked for the umpteenth time as she hesitated by the front door. 'I feel awful dragging you out, especially when Tommy's not well.'

'He made it very loud and clear that he didn't want me,' Ben laughed. 'Our neighbours can vouch for that. Besides, Kirsty would probably kill me by the most painful means possible if I let you cancel your date.'

'It's not a date.'

Ben looked her up and down and grinned.

'You're dressed for a date, you smell like a date... The subtle distinction by which this *isn't* a date is lost on me.'

'I've overdone it, haven't I?' Helen glanced down. Her red wraparound dress and boots suddenly seemed way more vampish than when she'd emptied her wardrobe earlier. But Joel had sent her a text suggesting they meet in the bar of a smart gastro-pub midway between their houses. She could hardly turn up there in jeans on a Friday night. She'd dressed up for the venue, not for Joel, she reassured herself. 'Should I change?'

'No, you look fine. And if you change you'll definitely be late.' Ben checked his watch. 'Later.'

Helen let that 'fine' go. It wasn't a description a woman ever wanted to hear, even from a friend's husband. And she really didn't have time to change, especially when, despite the pile of clothes now on her bed, she had nothing else to wear. So she opened the front door, and walked straight into Daniel's raised fist.

'What are you doing here?' she asked, too surprised to be polite, as she clutched the door to stop herself falling over.

'Visiting.'

'Megan's in bed.'

'Visiting you. There are things we need to discuss.' He looked her over, very much as Ben had done, and his gaze dwelled on the boots. 'Are you going somewhere?'

'Out. I'm meeting someone. It's a business meeting.'

'Really?' There was a whole wealth of disbelief invested in the word. Daniel leaned forwards slightly. 'You're wearing your favourite perfume.'

Technically *his* favourite perfume, which he always bought her, but still – he remembered! For a moment Helen's heart soared, but the frown on his face sent it plummeting back down. He was looking past her now, and had clearly noticed Ben, who had settled down in the armchair with a newspaper. Daniel pushed past Helen, into the house.

'Who's this?'

Ben stood up and held out his hand, smiling.

'Hello, I'm Ben. I don't need to ask who you are. You're like peas in a pod.'

Daniel ignored the proffered hand, and turned to

Helen, who had closed the front door again.

'Is he your boyfriend?'

'Of course not. Ben is Kirsty's husband.'

Ben had returned to the chair. Daniel faced him.

'Are you involved in this business meeting?'

'Me?' Ben laughed. 'No, I'm no businessman. I'm the babysitter.'

'He's babysitting Megan?' Daniel's fingers tapped slowly against his thigh. 'Why didn't you ask me?'

Helen blinked up at him as if he were shining a spotlight in her face. How could she answer, when she hardly understood herself? It had simply seemed wrong, in ways she didn't want to explore, to use Daniel as a babysitter when she was going out with Joel: even when the meeting with Joel was absolutely not a date.

'It was supposed to be Kirsty,' she said instead. 'But Ben's just as good. He's used to children. Megan knows him.'

She could probably have phrased that better, she realised as soon as she saw the way Daniel's jaw clenched.

'And whose fault is it that she doesn't know me? That I'm not used to children?'

So much for the truce.

'I didn't mean it like that.'

'Didn't you? Then Ben can go home and I'll babysit.'

'But Megan thinks Ben is looking after her. If she wakes up she won't expect to find you here.'

There was a creak on the landing, and a sleepy

185

little figure in Hello Kitty pyjamas trailed down the stairs, Mr Cat clutched in a tight cuddle under one arm.

'Have you brought back more photos of Mr Cat?' Megan asked, aiming straight for Helen.

'I haven't been out yet, sweetheart,' Helen replied, picking Megan up and kissing her cheek. She smelt deliciously warm and sleepy. 'I'll be on my way soon.' Although she was running so late now, it would be a miracle if Joel was still there when she arrived. 'Come on, I'll put you back to bed first.'

'Danny's here,' Megan said, as Helen carried her to the stairs.

'Yes, he is. He's come to visit.'

'But I'm asleep.'

'I know. Isn't he a silly billy?'

Megan giggled, and Helen hugged her tighter as she took her back to her bedroom and laid her in bed.

'Can I have a story?'

'You've already had three!' Helen pulled the duvet up to Megan's chin, and perched on the edge of the bed. She stroked the hair away from her face. 'You should be asleep, and I should be out.'

'Let me do it.' Daniel leaned against the doorway. He hadn't been upstairs before, and he hadn't been invited up now. Helen's heart pounded at the invasion. He seemed overpoweringly male in this pink environment. 'Let me read a story and put her to bed. Please.'

It wasn't the 'please' that persuaded her: it was the look on his face, the desperate desire to do something that most fathers would have done hundreds of times by now, without having to ask permission first. How could she refuse?

'Would you like Daniel to read you a story?' she asked Megan.

'Will he do the voices?' Megan whispered loudly.

'I'm sure he will.' Helen glanced at Daniel. He was smiling. It was such an ordinary, everyday scene: a family scene. But it wasn't ordinary in this house.

Helen bent down and kissed Megan.

'Be good. Only one story. I'll be back soon.' She crossed over to the door, and Daniel stepped forward to let her pass. 'I won't be long. Ring if you have any problems.'

He nodded, but he wasn't listening, she could tell. He had eyes only for Megan. His attention was solely on her, and he didn't even notice when Helen left the room.

The bar was busy, and for an awful moment Helen thought that Joel had gone. Then, as she squeezed through the happy Friday crowd, peering round and over bodies, she spotted him at a small table in the corner. A barely touched pint was sitting on the table in front of him, and he was bent over a folded newspaper, twirling a pen in his hand. Helen's stomach fluttered in relief as she hurried over to him.

'I'm so sorry,' she said, as she reached his table and dropped her bag onto the dark oak settle opposite him. 'I know I'm horribly late. I didn't think you'd still be here.'

187

She stopped. Joel had stood up, and was smiling at her with pleasure that he made no effort to hide, as if she had made his day simply by being there. It was a long time since anyone had looked at her like that. She smiled back.

'I don't mind waiting,' he said. 'Although nursing a pint is harder work than you'd think. And I've had to fight off several pretenders with designs on that settle.' Helen laughed. 'Can I get you a drink?'

'White wine, please. Just a small one.'

He headed to the bar. He was dressed up, Helen noticed: smarter trousers than the jeans she'd seen him in before, and a fresh cream shirt. Was it for her benefit? At least she didn't feel so over-dressed as she took off her coat and revealed the red dress. She sat down and pulled the newspaper over to her side of the table.

A few minutes later Joel returned with her drink.

'Thanks.' She looked up and caught his gaze sliding back up to her face. He flashed her an unapologetic grin.

'You can't wear a dress like that and not expect to be admired.' He sat down. 'You look gorgeous.'

Helen took a sip of wine, not meeting his eyes. Her old self would have expected such a compliment as a matter of course; now she didn't know what to do with it. So she ignored it and changed the subject.

'You're clever,' she said, indicating the crossword that he had almost completed in the newspaper. 'I wouldn't have known a quarter of these.'

'Blimey,' Joel replied, sitting back and shaking his

head. 'Where do I start with that? I could be offended that I compliment your appearance, and you can only praise my brain. But I think that note of surprise in the accusation of cleverness might be even more wounding.'

'I didn't mean...' She spotted his grin, and laughed. 'Can you tell I don't get out much?'

'I can't imagine why not.' His eyes were soaking her in again, so intensely that Helen was sure her skin must be the same colour as her dress. 'Is it a nightmare to find good babysitters?'

'It can be.' And then two come along at once. But she wasn't going into all that. 'I don't try very often.'

'Really?' Joel picked up his pint. 'Now I am flattered.'

Helen drank more wine. It wasn't going to last long at this rate.

'Obviously I made a special effort to come out tonight,' she said. His smile widened. 'It's business, after all.'

He had an attractive laugh, deep and bubbly. It was the sort of laugh you wanted to draw out again and again.

'That's put me back in my place, hasn't it?' He opened a bag on the seat beside him and brought out an iPad, and a notebook and pen. 'We'd better talk business then. Have a look at the photos I took yesterday, and let me know if there are any you'd like on the website.'

He pushed the iPad over to her, and she swiped through the photographs of her work and shop. They were good: he had brought out the colour and vibrancy of her crazy patchwork and made it look…

'It looks so professional.'

She didn't realise she'd spoken out loud until she heard his laugh.

'It is professional. It's incredible. I don't know why you've been hidden away in St Andrew's for so long. You could have a much bigger market. Auntie Joan told me you were good, but I never expected anything like I found. I'm kicking myself that I didn't come sooner. She's been raving about you since I moved back from Bristol. About your work,' he corrected himself, with a charming flush of self-consciousness.

'It's okay,' Helen laughed, though it was always thrilling to hear her work admired, when it had taken her years to believe it was good enough to sell. 'You can cut down on the extravagant praise now. I've agreed to come to Church Farm. I'm not going to change my mind.'

'It's genuine praise.' He certainly looked serious, for once. 'And it's not just my opinion. I emailed some of the photos to my sister last night. She works for a magazine in London, and sets up photoshoots of interiors that we're all meant to aspire to. She loved it. She said I should snap you up.' He grinned. 'In a business sense, of course.'

'Consider me snapped. Professionally speaking.' Helen grinned back. She was enjoying herself, and her whole body felt lighter with the novelty of it. When had she last chatted like this, had fun like this, with a man? Not since the early days with Daniel. And then

190

a slug of guilt kicked in.

Joel must have noticed the shadows drift across her face.

'Is everything okay? Am I pushing too much? Aren't you ready for all this?'

Helen began to shake her head, then realised he was talking about work.

'It's what I've wanted for ages,' she gabbled, covering her embarrassment. 'I've all sorts of ideas about new projects. I'd love to open a shop on Etsy and to be able to take on commissions beyond the north-west. But I didn't have the time when Megan was younger. Or the computer skills,' she added, with a smile.

'Lucky you know someone who does.'

'Oh, I wasn't suggesting...'

'I know you weren't, but I'm offering. Seriously, it will be a doddle to set you up with a new website.'

'I can't afford to pay you,' she admitted, sliding her glass around the table until some wine sloshed onto her hand. She licked it off, but became conscious of Joel watching her and stopped.

'I was never planning to charge you.'

'Then what do you get out of it?'

'Interesting question.' She watched as he opened his notebook and wrote down ETSY??? Then he looked up, dimples dancing in his cheeks. 'What are you offering?'

Her stomach somersaulted in a way she remembered from long ago.

'I'll barter you for any three items from the shop.

191

You can get started on your Christmas presents! And,' she added, laughing at his disappointed expression, 'I'll buy you a drink now. I think I can stretch to that.'

'If that's the best offer I'm going to get...' He held out his hand. 'I accept.'

Helen took his hand and they shook on the deal. His hand was strong, but smaller than Daniel's; his long fingers wrapped comfortably round hers. It felt a good fit. She felt suddenly hot. She let go.

'I'll fetch those drinks.'

When she came back to the table, with a large glass of iced water for herself, Joel was poring over the iPad again.

'This is a website I created a couple of years ago for an independent bookshop near Bristol. It has a link for online sales.'

He passed over the iPad and Helen spent a few minutes flicking through the pages.

'It's fantastic,' she said, looking up at last. 'Now I think you're even cleverer. But you've made a very stupid deal with me. This is worth a lot more than three pieces of crazy patchwork.'

'And a drink,' he replied, raising his glass to her. 'Don't forget that.'

'Even with the drink it's a wholly uneven deal. I'll let you out of it.'

'Too late, we've shaken on it. And look,' he added, leaning across the table and pointing to the bottom of the webpage. 'I'm not so stupid. My name will be on the website, too, so it's all good advertising.'

Helen looked where he was pointing.

'But that's not you. I thought you were JAM Design.'

'I am now. That was the name of the company I had before.'

'So you're not getting any benefit now from designing this site?'

'No.' He sat back, his upper arm resting on the back of the settle, and teased a strand of hair above his ear. 'It can't be helped. I couldn't carry on with the old company.'

'Couldn't you?' The unexpected chink of vulnerability was fascinating. 'Why not?'

Joel made a slight grimace.

'Do I have to go there?'

'No. But as my business is now linked to one of yours, I'd like to know if there's anything I should be worried about. You didn't go bust, did you?'

'The business didn't. The relationship behind it did.'

'Oh!' This was even more fascinating. Helen leaned forward. 'What happened?'

'Nothing that you need be worried about on that score either,' he said, with a quick smile, which disappeared as fast as it arrived.

'So you're divorced?'

'Never married.' His eyes, usually so bright, seemed to dull. 'I came close, but there turned out to be a large impediment which I'd known nothing about. Our relationship was based on lies. She wasn't the person I thought she was.'

Helen was dying to know more, but it was clear from his expression that he wasn't going to tell her.

'What about you? You're not with Megan's dad?'

'No. We'll always be connected, because of Megan. But we haven't been romantically involved for a long time. He has a new partner.' She sat back and crossed her legs. 'Beautiful, blonde, Australian. The dream girlfriend.'

'Not mine.' His smile was like a floodlight again, shining on Helen and brightening her darkest corners. She felt a fizzing sensation, immediately flattened by a surge of panic. What was happening? Why did her lips keep smiling at him whether she wanted them to or not? She reached across the table and grabbed his notebook and pen.

'Back to business,' she said, wagging the pen at him. 'Stop distracting me.'

'Me?' He tried an innocent expression, but couldn't hide the laughter in his eyes. 'What have I done?'

Helen wished she knew. Because she couldn't deny that he did *something* to her; but it was a something she simply wasn't ready to face.

CHAPTER 16

Helen let herself in at the front door, and stopped dead. It wasn't the sight of Daniel that sent shock racing through her nerves – his car was outside, after all – it was the familiarity of coming home from a night out and seeing him: the footprints of their past lingering in the sand, that the tide hadn't quite washed away.

He was sprawled in her chair, his shoes off, watching *Newsnight* with the volume turned down so low he must barely be able to hear it. One of her mugs was sitting on the table at his side, evidence that he'd been through her kitchen. This house had always been a Daniel-free zone; there had been no memories of him here to plague her. Now it felt as if he'd sprayed his presence in every corner.

She closed the door and unzipped her boots, conscious of his silent scrutiny as she padded across to the sofa and sat down.

'Did Megan get off to sleep?'

His face softened at once.

'Yes. I've checked her a few times and she's fine.'

'Did Ben not stay?'

'For a while, but he didn't want to be out late when his son was ill.'

Perhaps she was feeling overly sensitive, but his words slapped her like a rebuke.

'I'm sorry I'm later than I expected. Don't let me keep you.'

195

He didn't move.

'Where have you been?'

'The Thresher's Arms. It's a pub about five miles away.'

Daniel's eyebrows slowly rose.

'I thought it was a business meeting.'

'It was.' Helen refused to say any more. He had never quizzed her like a possessive husband in the past, and he certainly had no right to do so now. And yet, absurdly, she felt another spasm of guilt, as if she had been cheating on him. Which was ridiculous, because all she'd done was have a drink with Joel – a drink stretching from one hour to two without her noticing – and been kissed on the cheek by Joel when he'd walked her back to her car... She curled her legs underneath her, wondering how just the memory of a chaste kiss could make her heart skitter. She flicked a glance at Daniel. He was staring at her, a frown darkening his brow.

'I've been thinking about what the solicitor said, about my right to a say in Megan's education,' he said, when it became clear that Helen wasn't going to volunteer any more information about her evening. 'I want her to be privately educated. It's what would have happened under normal circumstances. There's a private school about thirty minutes from here which has great inspection reports and exam results. It's called Broadholme.'

Helen knew the one. It was the school she was designing the crazy-patchwork mural for. It was a beautiful school, and of course it had crossed her mind how lovely it would be to see Megan there. But it wasn't an option, and he must realise that. So why did he have to embarrass her by making her spell it out?

'I can't afford it.'

'Really? Then I'll pay.'

Helen sighed, and shook her head.

'You say that now. Have you any idea how much we're talking about for fourteen years' education? It's not only the school fees: there's the uniform, the equipment, the trips... You can't promise to pay for it all. What if you have more children in the future? I can't start Megan at a school that she may have to leave when the money runs out.'

Daniel's fingers were drumming with a steady thud on his knee.

'My bonus in the last year alone could pay for her entire school career, and any other children.'

'Well, aren't you the lucky one?' Helen replied, with ill-disguised bitterness. She knew he had hoped to make serious money in Hong Kong, but hadn't realised it was on the scale this suggested. He had never consulted her over financial arrangements. 'To have all that money – money you wouldn't have had if I'd held you back here with a baby.'

'Maybe. But it should have been my choice which I wanted most, shouldn't it?'

It was too much, it really was: for him to sit there in the chair she was still paying for, boasting about how rich he was, and fooling himself that he would have been happy to live like this. She dashed away a tear.

'And you would have wanted this, would you?' she asked, waving her hand around. 'The shoe-box house on the family-friendly estate? You'll have noticed the shortage of space, the lack of designer furniture and top of the range conveniences.'

'We wouldn't have lived here.' He shrugged. 'And even if we had, it wouldn't have mattered. Because we would have been together. I would have had Megan.'

They were never going to agree: not when she had made her decision at the time, based on love, and he was making his in hindsight, based on grievance. Helen stood up.

'I think you'd better go. It's getting late.'

'There's an Open Morning at Broadholme tomorrow. Will you come and look?'

He gripped the chair as if he had no intention of moving until she agreed. She didn't have the strength to challenge him. She never had done.

'Fine. But no pressure, okay?'

Daniel nodded, and rose. He took his coat off the post at the foot of the stairs, and Helen hovered, ready to open the front door.

'Thanks for tonight,' he said, and a smile paid a brief visit to his lips. Then, before she could guess what he planned, he leaned across and kissed her cheek, the opposite one to the cheek Joel had chosen. She breathed in, expecting the familiar smell of Daniel, but it wasn't there; he was wearing that new aftershave again, and it jarred rather than soothed. He left, and she leaned against the front door, listening to his car drive away. Two kisses in one night, both from handsome men, both entirely unexpected; and one had made her heart dance, the other had left it aching.

Daniel turned up to collect them early on Saturday morning. He looked the perfect affluent father, but it was irritating the way his eyes skimmed over Helen and Megan as if checking they were appropriately dressed. What had he expected, that they'd be wearing something run up from an old pair of curtains? And why would it matter if they were? But he had nothing to worry about. Not even Valerie could have made any criticism of how respectable they appeared. After last night's revelation of how much money he'd made in their years apart, Helen had been determined to make an effort today. She wasn't having him look down on her, or think she was too poor to dress Megan well.

'Is Tasha not coming?' she asked, as he led them out to his car. She was thankful for her coat given the chill of the look he threw at her.

'It's none of her business.'

She'd hit a nerve there, clearly. She hoped he hadn't used that line on Tasha. What relationship could thrive after a snub like that? And it wouldn't make Tasha any fonder of Helen and Megan either, would it? She didn't particularly care what Tasha thought of her; but if Megan was ever going to stay with Daniel – and her heart still reared at the very idea – she didn't want Tasha to be unpleasant to her.

If she was honest, she didn't want Tasha and Megan to be close, either: but there had to be a happy medium, hadn't there?

Daniel's shiny new BMW was immaculately clean inside and out, and still had the new car smell. Megan stared at it wide eyed, and it was hardly surprising; in comparison, Helen's red Renault Clio, unwashed for months inside or out and with the lingering smell of travel sick defying the best efforts of the air freshener, was about as appealing as a ride in a wheelie bin. A brand new childseat was fastened in the back of the BMW.

'Is it okay?' Daniel asked as he opened the door. 'It was recommended by *Which?* as the safest seat available.'

'It's fine, but you could have borrowed the one from my car. You didn't need to buy one.'

'I'll need it in future though, won't I?'

That threat – or so Helen felt it – hung over them for the entire ride to school. Broadholme was a magnificent stone stately home, which had been run as an increasingly successful independent school for the last thirty years. The main house was now solely occupied by the senior school, the boys' division and girls' division each having a wing, with communal facilities in the centre. A new home for the primary section of the school had opened in September, in a modern stone and glass building which both complemented and contrasted with the original house. Helen, Daniel and Megan joined the crowd of other parents heading towards the primary school, some with children who could barely walk, she was surprised to see.

Junior-school prefects were giving tours of the school to the visiting parents and prospective pupils. Helen had only seen a few of the rooms on her two previous visits, and it was hard now not to be impressed by the facilities available: spacious classrooms considering the small class sizes, dedicated music, art and ICT rooms, and a library that made Helen long to sink down onto a beanbag and revisit some childhood classics. And it was impossible to ignore Megan's reaction. From the dressing-up and role-play areas in the Reception room, to the Lego tables in the older rooms, she was touching and joining in with everything with eager enthusiasm that was both a delight and despair to witness. How could Helen not want her to come to a school like this? And the satisfied look that Daniel kept shooting at her was asking exactly the same question.

Perhaps if she had enough money to pay for the entire school career of several children, it would be as easy a decision for her as it was for him. She might want to see Megan here, but the financial implications were terrifying. She fingered the school summer dress, which was hanging up in a display of uniform in the hall. Thirty-eight pounds for one dress, which would only be worn for one term! And it wasn't even that well made, she noted with a critical eye, inspecting the wonky hem. She could do a better job herself for a fraction of the price.

'Helen? I thought it was you.' Helen turned and

saw the junior school headmistress, Mrs King, smiling at her warmly. 'I didn't know you were interested in Broadholme. Are you looking for your daughter?'

'Yes, this is Megan,' Helen replied, pulling Megan forward. 'Megan, this is Mrs King, the headmistress. Say hello.'

'Hello,' Megan said, to Helen's relief.

'Have you enjoyed looking round the school, Megan?' Mrs King asked. Megan nodded. 'What did you like best?'

'The princess dresses.'

'Ah yes,' Mrs King smiled. 'The Reception class have a lot of fun with the dressing-up box.' She looked up and her eyes fell on Daniel, standing behind Megan. 'Goodness me,' she said, holding out her hand. 'You must be Megan's father. The resemblance is remarkable.'

Helen stared at Daniel in silent horror, goosebumps raging up and down her skin, her lungs frozen so thickly she thought she might never breathe again. And the Daniel she had loved so much lifted her with an answering look of unequivocal support. He shook hands with Mrs King, and drew her to one side, leaving Helen to deal with Megan.

What should she say? She'd been thinking about how to break the news: she'd even Googled 'how to tell a child who their father is' and had been terrified by countless tales of children traumatised by not having been told the truth about their parentage. She had resolved that they would have to tell Megan soon. But here? Now? She wasn't prepared for it.

But when she looked down at Megan, bracing herself for awkward questions, confusion, even a tantrum, there was nothing. Megan was busy picking her nose and watching some other children playing with percussion instruments at the far side of the hall. If she'd heard what Mrs King said, and if she'd understood it, she wasn't showing any signs.

'Are you okay?' Helen asked, crouching down in front of her and gently extracting the finger from the nose.

Megan nodded.

'Can I play with the drums?'

'Perhaps later.'

She stood up and glanced back at Daniel and Mrs King. Daniel's fingers were twitching. Helen led Megan over.

'We're too late,' Daniel said. 'We should have applied last year.'

He said 'we'. They both knew what he really meant.

'I'm almost at the end of interviews for next September's intake,' Mrs King explained. 'Applications were due in by spring.'

'Spring?' Helen repeated. The surge of disappointment made her wishes all too clear. She wanted Megan to come to this school; she would have sacrificed anything to pay for it. She wasn't giving up yet. 'That simply wasn't possible. Daniel has had to work in the Far East for the last few years,' she said in a low voice that she hoped Megan couldn't hear. 'It's only recently become clear that he's going to

203

settle in this country, so we could make a decision about Megan's education.'

'Yes, I see,' Mrs King nodded. 'There's always a little leeway for families who move into the area after applications have closed and in other exceptional circumstances and, of course, you do already have links to the school.' She smiled, and Helen could have sworn she caught a slight wink. 'Take one of the application forms to fill in. Would you be able to bring Megan for an interview on Monday lunchtime? It's short notice but interviews end this week so we can make the offers in December.'

'That will be fine, won't it, Helen?' Daniel asked.

'Yes. But what do you mean by an interview? She's never done anything like that before.'

'It's very informal,' Mrs King assured her. 'It's not really about asking questions at all. We might ask her to do puzzles or a jigsaw, or draw a picture, and see how well she can follow instructions. It's nothing to be anxious about.'

Easy for her to say, Helen thought, knowing she was doomed to a sleepless couple of nights worrying about this now. Megan might be keen on jigsaws, but her willingness to follow instructions was as variable as the direction of the wind. But she thanked Mrs King, picked up one of the application packs, and let Megan lead her over to the drums.

'You didn't mention you had links to the school,' Daniel murmured, as they stood together, watching Megan bang away on a lollipop drum.

'It's a slight exaggeration. I'm working with Year 6

to create a crazy patchwork wall hanging to commemorate the opening of this new building.'

'You've obviously impressed the headmistress. Well done. Megan wouldn't have got the interview without you.' He smiled at her, and for once there was no edge to it, no side: he was pleased with her, that was all. 'How was Megan earlier? Did she hear what Mrs King said?'

'I don't think she can have done. She didn't mention it, and seemed perfectly normal. But,' she carried on, though it took an effort to say the words, 'we will have to tell her. Soon.'

'Can we do it together? Please, Nell, I...'

'Yes,' she interrupted, cutting him off as Megan abandoned the drum and headed their way. 'I think that would be best. Let's get the interview out of the way first.'

He nodded, and they watched as Megan approached. She squeezed between them and took Helen's hand. Then she looked up at Daniel, and without saying a word, put her other hand in his.

CHAPTER 17

The interview at Broadholme went well, as far as Helen could tell from Megan's excited chatter afterwards, although there was so much about princesses and cats that it was hard to tell where the account of the interview ended and normal conversation began. Megan's enthusiasm exacerbated Helen's concerns about paying the fees if she were offered a place. She had been seduced by the school on Saturday. Now, with the bright reality of a morning after, she was realising that the consequence of having her head so effectively turned might prove very expensive.

Daniel had offered to pay, of course, but Helen felt uncomfortable about accepting. That had been the way of her old life, living off an allowance from her father and later letting Daniel pay for everything. It was the easy option – but did she really want to go back to that? She had supported Megan for four years on her own, scrambling for every penny, and she was proud of the independence she had found. But how could she let her pride deny Megan something so advantageous to her? Hadn't she already denied Megan enough for one lifetime?

As the drive home from Broadholme took them within a couple of minutes of Church Farm, Helen decided to call in with a box of crazy patchwork items. Joel had offered to create a window display near the entrance to advertise the new shops opening in the New Year, and hopefully whet the appetites of visitors. She couldn't remember how large the window was, so had packed a selection of items, including a handbag, a cushion, a few hanging hearts and one of the new Kindle sleeves, hoping that a combination of these should be enough alongside the work of the others from St Andrew's.

Her plan had been simply to dump the box with Joel and leave him to it; it would be even better if he was out, and she could abandon her delivery outside his office. The memory of the kiss on the cheek and how unsettled it had made her feel had troubled her over the weekend, even with the distraction of Broadholme, and she thought it would be best all round if she could avoid him today. But she was out of luck. As she rounded the corner from the first courtyard, she saw him walk out of the office building and head straight across toward the Feed Store.

She didn't move or call out but somehow, even so, he turned his head in her direction.

'Hello, you two.' His face lit up. 'I didn't know you were coming here today. Are you staying for lunch?'

'Actually, I'm just...'

Joel cut her off before she could complete the denial.

'You can't leave me to have a miserable lunch on my own,' he said, his grin about as far from a picture of misery as it was possible to be. He bent down to

Megan. 'I bet you're hungry, aren't you?'

Megan nodded and looked up at Helen hopefully.

'Can I have a gingerbread sheep?'

Helen laughed.

'I'm outnumbered, aren't I? Okay, we can have lunch, but can I leave this box with you first? It's a few pieces you might be able to use for the window display.'

Joel took the box and peered inside.

'Fantastic, this will look great. My sister's visiting at the weekend so she's going to do the window as she has a much more creative eye than I do. I'll put this in the office and meet you in the café.'

He jogged across to the office building. Helen stared after him until she felt an impatient tug on her hand and hauled her attention back to her daughter and away from Joel's bottom, giving herself a mental slap in the process. This was business – and Joel's bottom was strictly none of hers.

She took Megan into the Feed Store, inhaling the rich mix of smells, from coffee to Greek dips, which bombarded her nose as she walked to the café at the end. But when she opened the doors to the café, she stopped in surprise. It was full.

'Is there a problem?' Joel asked, coming up behind Helen.

'There's only one table left, and it's reserved.'

'Lucky you're with me, because that's my table. I've had to start reserving one, as we're packed almost every lunch time now.'

'Should you be taking up a table that could be

used by a paying customer?'

'I am a paying customer.' He led them over to the table, and removed the reserved sign. 'There are no perks to being in charge.'

'Aren't there?' Helen glanced at him as she unfastened Megan's coat and pulled out a chair for her. 'I wouldn't stand for that if I were you. I'd have to negotiate some benefits, at least from the fabulous shops in here.'

'You've convinced me.' Joel handed round menus, grinning. 'We'll talk another time about what benefits you can offer.'

Lunch arrived quickly and was delicious: huge bowls of steaming vegetable soup with hunks of crusty granary bread and homemade butter. Megan's cheese sandwich and the coveted gingerbread sheep were delivered in a special box designed to resemble a cowshed. It was no wonder the café was full if the food was this good. Helen was heartened to see so many visitors who might be tempted to wander up as far as the Hay Barn when it was open. For the first time in a long while, she had something to look forward to: she could see a future, not only a past.

'Are you on your way somewhere this afternoon?' Joel asked, pushing away his bowl at last. 'You're both looking very smart.'

'We've been to school,' Megan said, glancing up from her colouring book.

'Have you?' Joel smiled at Helen. 'Is this because you can't do crosswords? Did you think you needed to go back and start again?'

209

Helen laughed and picked up the last piece of bread.

'We weren't having lessons. Megan had an interview at Broadholme.'

'The private school?' She nodded, noticing a tiny frown twitch along Joel's brow. 'Have you won the lottery or something since the day you told me you couldn't afford to improve your website?'

'No, of course not, nothing's changed,' Helen replied, spreading the same piece of butter round and round the bread. 'Except...' She put the knife down, reluctant to say more but not wanting to lie. 'It wouldn't be me paying.'

'Ah. Very generous.' Joel sat back. 'Won't that make it difficult when you have other children, though? If you can't afford to send them to the same school?'

'Other children?' Helen stared at him, as if he had started speaking Swahili. 'What other children?'

'Come on, you're only young...'

'I'm thirty.'

'Two years younger than me. That's still young. Don't you think it's likely you might meet someone and have more children? You must have thought about it.'

'I haven't.'

His expression was sceptical, but it was the truth, or a simplified version of it. Any wish that Megan needn't be an only child, the stirrings of envy when Kirsty had given birth to Tommy, had been swiftly quashed. She was everything to Megan, and Megan was everything to her. She couldn't have risked Megan suffering in any way; and she had never met a man who had made her even think about other children. But as she stared at Joel, and those lovely brown eyes gazed straight back at her, she wondered...

Helen's mobile phone rang.

'It's Danny!' Megan said. It was: she must have recognised the D when the name flashed up. Helen cut off the call, almost knocking the phone to the floor in her haste. Moments later it rang again.

'Mummy! Talk to Danny!'

With an apologetic glance at Joel - who was regarding her far too curiously - Helen picked up the phone.

'Helen? Are you still at Broadholme? I've been waiting to hear from you for the last hour.'

'We're out for lunch.'

'Are you?' There was a significant pause. 'How did the interview go?'

'Well, as far as I can tell.'

'Was there no feedback from Mrs King?'

'She said Megan had been fine, and not to worry.'

'Not to worry in what sense? That she'll get the place? Or that she handled the interview without a problem?'

'I've no idea.' Helen heard a loud sigh at the other end of the line. 'Excuse me a moment,' she said to Joel, and got up and wandered a few steps away to the window. 'Dan, don't get too set on this. I've already told you I can't afford...'

'Who are you with?'

'What?'

'You said excuse me. Are you with someone?'

'Lots of people. I'm in a busy café.'

'Hmm.' Daniel didn't press the point. 'Don't worry about the money. I spoke to the school treasurer this morning. All the fees can be paid upfront. In fact there's a discount for doing that.'

'You can't do that without telling me!'

'I can. I have parental responsibility now. And I'm telling you in advance what I plan to do. Better than four years after the event, isn't it?'

Helen hung up, but stayed where she was, staring out of the window. He was never going to let it drop, was he? Every disagreement they had was going to end with him hurling a fistful of guilt at her again – as if she wasn't drenched in it already. But before she could return to the table, he called back.

'Sorry. I shouldn't have said that. I'm not trying to take over, Nell. I'm trying to help, but it's going to take me a while to figure out how to do it. Bear with me, okay?'

'Okay.' The unexpected warmth in his voice was unbearable. Helen rested her cheek against her phone.

'I have the money from the house sale that's yours. I owe you thousands in child maintenance payments for the last four years. If you add it up, most of the money for the school fees would be yours. I'm hardly contributing at all.'

She hadn't thought about it like that, and it did make it seem more palatable. She'd ripped up his cheque before, even though there were a thousand ways she could have used the money; but she could never refuse it being spent on Megan in this way.

'You don't owe me any maintenance,' she said.

'I do, and we need to discuss how much I should give you going forward. I'll call round one night and we can sort it out.'

Helen returned to the table, struggling to disguise her heartache with a smile for Megan. Joel had a pencil in his hand, and Megan's colouring book in front of him.

'You'll be careful not to go outside the lines, won't you?' Helen said, sitting back down. Joel laughed.

'I've been trying to draw a cat.' He pushed the book over to Helen. He had managed a tolerable picture of a cat, standing up against a scratching post. His eyes roved over her face. 'Everything okay?'

She nodded, and was glad when he didn't ask anything more. The conversation with Daniel had killed her pleasure over the lunch. She had enjoyed herself too much, and now the guilt was kicking in like a bad dose of indigestion.

'We should get going,' she said, rubbing Megan's arm. 'Joel will need to get back to work.'

'But I haven't seen Mr Cat yet and he promised.'

Joel shrugged as he caught Helen's questioning glance.

'Who wouldn't rather play with a kitten than do some work?'

He insisted on paying for lunch, then took them over to his office where Megan squealed with delight

213

at seeing Mr Cat again, even more so when the kitten was brave enough to climb on her when she sat down cross-legged next to the basket.

'She'll never want to go home now,' Helen said, watching Megan copy Joel in gently stroking the kitten. He smiled up at her.

'Who would? I didn't realise how much I missed it here until I came back from Bristol. I can't imagine ever leaving again. What about you? You didn't pick up those posh vowels round here. Do you think you might be tempted back down south?'

'Not to live, no. My life is here now.'

'Good.'

The heat of Joel's smile was overwhelming. To distract him, Helen picked up a paper from his desk.

'What's this? A Christmas market at Church Farm?'

Joel wandered over to her.

'It's a new idea I thought we'd try this year. We'll decorate the whole place with lights and trees, have mince pies and carols, and bring in some extra stalls alongside the regular shops. There's been a great response.'

'Can we come?'

'Of course you can. There will be activities for children, and we're even hoping that a special visitor may put in an appearance.'

Helen laughed.

'I didn't mean that. I meant the St Andrew's group. Could we have stalls? I'd have to ask the others, but it's on a Sunday so St Andrew's would be closed, and it would be a great opportunity to meet the other artists here and make some extra money before Christmas...'

She trailed off. Joel was smiling at her, his head tilted to the side, flecks of gold lighting his brown eyes.

'You're incredible,' he said.

'Am I?' Embarrassment washed over her, and she dropped her eyes to the leaflet in her hand. 'You don't know me.'

'I know what Auntie Joan has told me. I've seen the way you are with Megan. And the way you fight for the group at St Andrew's. You're always thinking about other people.'

'Not many people would recognise that version of me.' She didn't recognise it herself. She was certain that Daniel wouldn't agree with it.

'Then perhaps they don't see what I see.'

Helen shook her head, and fiddled with the paper on the desk.

'Perhaps you haven't yet seen what they have,' she replied, looking behind him at Megan, who was still engrossed with Mr Cat.

'I can't believe there's anything bad.' He was laughing, and Helen pushed her lips up into a smile, but it didn't filter below the surface.

'Joel, don't...'

'What?' He flashed her a grin. 'I think all my friends are incredible, don't you?'

'Friends?'

He was close to her, and she saw humour and

215

something else shifting across his eyes.

'It's a start, isn't it?'

The start of what, Helen wondered, even as she felt a flicker of a response deep inside her, a response to the way he was looking at her. A relationship? It simply wasn't possible. She might find Joel attractive, she might enjoy his company, but it wasn't enough. Because how could she ever contemplate a new relationship when her heart couldn't accept the end of the old one?

'We're snookered,' was Malcolm's reaction when Helen suggested to the group at St Andrew's that they could all take up a stall at the Church Farm Christmas market. 'It's less than three weeks away. I can't have enough new work ready for then. It's too short notice.'

Helen had anticipated this reaction, and had already telephoned Fiona to talk her round to the idea. Fiona was well known as the most cautious in the group, and if she was prepared to support an idea the men tended to pay attention. Fiona offered to keep an eye on Malcolm's shop as well as her own for a few days if he needed time to produce more of the abstract work he was determined to sell at Church Farm, and with a combined effort they eventually wore him down. It helped that Ron decided he would like to take on a stall, to see if he could shift some of the remaining model houses and furniture before he retired.

'Don't expect me to dress up!' was Malcolm's final verdict.

216

Saskia was enthusiastic about the plan, but it was tempered with a sulky air that it had been Helen who first mentioned the market.

'When did you hear about it?' she asked, as Helen handed out a pile of flyers for each shop, and for each table in the café.

'On Monday. I saw a poster at Church Farm.'

'What were you doing at Church Farm?'

'I needed to deliver some of my work for the window display.'

'And you saw Joel?' The piercing look in Saskia's eyes was at odds with her attempt to sound casual.

'Yes, I ran into him.'

Saskia tossed her hair and snatched the leaflets from Helen.

'Strange he didn't mention the market when I was there on Sunday,' she said. 'But I suppose we had more to talk about than business.'

With a satisfied smile, Saskia marched back to her jewellery shop. A few moments later she was sellotaping leaflets to the glass door panels. Helen exchanged a smile with Fiona, and returned to Crazy Little Things, where she busied herself with rearranging displays that didn't need arranging, and with not thinking about what Joel and Saskia had been up to on Sunday, and whether Saskia was incredible too.

Although Helen remained convinced that joining the Christmas market was a good idea, it was an extra layer of stress that she could happily have managed without. With the pressure of making more gift-sized items, as well as working on the Broadholme mural, several smaller commissions and Megan's flower-girl dress, she was barely averaging four hours' sleep each night. The inevitable happened. Helen fell asleep at the kitchen table one evening while Daniel played with Megan in the living room.

Megan laughed and shook her awake, but her neck had stiffened up. It was a familiar problem, from the hours she spent bending over her sewing, and Daniel knew it. He knew what to do about it too. After the briefest hesitation, he walked round the table to stand behind her.

'You need a massage.'

'No!' That was absolutely the last thing in the world she needed from him. How could he even offer? Did he not remember where his massages had inevitably led? She could feel his frown boring into her back.

'Come on, Nell, you know it helps.'

But she stood up, moved away, and wouldn't let him. It might help her neck, but feeling his hands on her, giving her the tender massage as he had so often and so well in the past, certainly wouldn't help any other part of her.

One night, when Helen was reading Megan a bedtime story and wondering which one of them would fall asleep first, the doorbell rang. Helen ran downstairs, assuming it could only be Daniel, though it was late for him to call, but the man on the doorstep was a stranger – although, when he stepped into the light shining from the door, there was a vague familiarity about his face.

'Helen Walters?'

She nodded, clutching the door tightly and ready to throw herself at him if he tried to get past her and anywhere near Megan. But he made no move to come in, and merely waved an envelope at her. She looked down at it, puzzled.

'Sorry, you don't remember me, do you?' The man smiled, a nervous smile. 'John Arkwright. I'm your landlord. This is my house.'

Helen felt the creep of foreboding across her skin. Her landlord, making an unexpected visit, with an envelope for her: was she being paranoid to think this could only end badly?

'I'm sorry to call so late, but I wanted to give you this as soon as possible.' He thrust the envelope at her hand so she had no choice but to take it. 'My contract in Canada has been terminated, so we're moving back here. We need the house. I have to give you two months' notice, so you're okay to stay for Christmas.'

With these words of purported comfort he smiled, not so nervously now, and was gone. Helen closed the door and opened the envelope. The paper inside confirmed what she had been told: she had two more months before she had to leave the house she'd rented for the last four years – the only home Megan had ever known. The last stone in the protective wall she had built round them had been kicked away.

She stared at the paper in her hand for a long while, and then sank to the floor, feeling the tide of emotion swirl over her head, pushing her down. It was simply too much to bear, on top of everything else. She had never loved the house, but it had been theirs: the place she had spent the first night on her own with Megan, wide awake with helpless terror over how she could do this by herself; and the place where she had finally found the strength and determination to start her business and have responsibilities. She had grown up in this house as much as Megan.

And the thought of having to look for somewhere else at this time of year, and to deal with moving house as well as moving business premises... Helen wasn't sure she could summon the energy, physically or emotionally. Two months would vanish, especially with Christmas in the middle. Was it even legal to give her so little notice, after four years of being the perfect tenant, looking after the house as if it were her own, and always paying the rent on time whatever sacrifices it had cost?

There was one person who would surely know the answer, she realised, with a revival of spirits. Craig was a solicitor: he should be able to tell her whether she could argue against this notice or not. She dialled his number, wondering as she did why she hadn't seen Sally and Craig for so long. Invitations to Sunday lunch had dried up, and she hadn't spoken to Sally or Anita for weeks.

Sally answered the call at the point where Helen had resigned herself to hearing the answering machine.

'Hi Sally, how are you?' There was no audible

220

response, only an uncomfortable silence which floated down the phone and lapped over the edges. 'Is Craig at home? I've had a visit from my landlord and wondered if I could ask his advice on my tenancy.'

'You have a bloody nerve.'

Helen couldn't have been more surprised if the phone had grown teeth and bitten her.

'I'm sorry?' she said, wondering if she could have imagined the venom in Sally's voice.

'You're not, though, are you? Not from what I've heard. You keep trying to justify what you've done. But there can't be any justification for it, not for how you treated Daniel. How could you not tell him about Megan? What did he ever do to you except adore you, and look after you so you never had to lift a finger yourself? And you thank him by stealing his daughter...'

'Sally...' Helen tried to interrupt, but it was no good. Sally had clearly become a fully paid up member of the Hate Helen club and was determined to give her maiden speech.

'And as if that weren't bad enough, you made us complicit in your grubby secret. You lied to us. You said that Megan had nothing to do with Daniel, and we believed you, despite the evidence of our eyes. We felt sorry for you, losing Daniel and then getting into trouble with someone else on the rebound. How do you think it makes us feel, knowing that if we hadn't trusted you, we could have told him about Megan? We ignored our suspicions, because we would never have thought someone could be so *evil*.'

Sally took a deep breath. Helen thought about hanging up, but she couldn't move the phone away from her ear. Hearing herself abused, when deep down she felt she deserved it, was curiously addictive.

'You fooled us all, reinventing yourself as the perfect mother, when all the time you've been the same lazy, selfish bitch you always were. God, you must have laughed at the way we all ran around trying to help you. And you're still expecting us to do it! Well we won't, and that goes for Anita and Dave too.'

'It wasn't...' But Helen was wasting her breath even trying to start an explanation. Sally wasn't done yet.

'And don't think for a second that you're going to get back with Daniel, not if we can do anything to prevent it. We never told you, because we wanted to spare your feelings, but he had the time of his life over the last few years without you. He'd never sounded so happy. There's no way we're going to let you drag him back down.'

CHAPTER 18

Helen looked at her watch again, but it still told her the same thing. Daniel was late, even later than he'd been when she'd looked at it one minute ago, two minutes ago, three minutes ago... She couldn't stop. Checking her watch had become a nervous tic.

Megan was sitting on the sofa, dressed in her best Cinderella outfit, watching cartoons with no idea that the lovely afternoon she'd been losing sleep over for days – ever since Daniel had told her about the tickets to see *Disney Princesses on Ice* – was about to turn into a disaster. Unless he arrived in the next few minutes, they were never going to make it to Manchester on time. Where the hell was he?

Helen's phone rang as she was asking herself that question for what seemed the hundredth time. Seeing Daniel's name flash up, she turned up the volume on the television, went into the kitchen and closed the door. She was anticipating a conversation it would be better for Megan not to hear.

'Nell, I'm sorry, I'm not going to make it back.' He sounded rough, his voice dry and gravelly as if he'd had too much to drink. It didn't engender Helen's sympathy.

'Back?' she hissed, trying to keep her voice down despite a rampant urge to shout. 'What do you mean, back? Where are you?'

'York.' The word slipped out on a sigh.

'York? What are you doing in York?'

'I brought Tasha for a couple of days.' He didn't need to say any more. Helen knew exactly what they would have been doing in York, because he had done them with her. He'd taken her to York for a weekend, after they'd moved north, because she had never been, and he had said it was a magical place and shouldn't be missed. So they had spent two beautiful sunny days walking the city walls, having lunch overlooking the river, taking afternoon tea at Betty's, and wandering down The Shambles and the cobbled shopping streets in the heart of the city. She still had a bracelet he'd bought her there, stowed safely away at the back of the drawer, where toddler fingers couldn't reach. Perhaps Tasha had a matching bracelet now.

'And you're still in York?' she asked, casting the memory adrift now it had lost all value, and focusing on the reality presented by her watch. 'Even though we're supposed to be in Manchester in a little over an hour and you have the tickets?'

'Yes.' His voice sank, as if he was trying not to be heard. 'Look, we had a bad night, things got heated, we drank too much, and overslept...'

'Until after lunch? That's quite some hangover.'

'Tash isn't feeling great today, so what did you expect me to do, walk out and bloody leave her?'

'Yes!' If Megan's happiness was at stake, that was exactly what she expected him to do. 'Or how about not arranging a couple of days away when you've already made plans, and made promises that you can't now keep?'

224

'I know it wasn't perfect timing, but things have been awkward recently and Sally suggested...'

Helen stopped listening. She didn't want to hear about whatever problems he was having with Tasha, or how his – formerly their – friends were rallying round trying to shore up the breach. She leant against the French doors, and felt the chill of the glass seep through her cheek and into her bones.

'How is Megan? Is she going to be very upset?'

'What do you think? You saw how excited she was when you told her you'd bought the tickets. She's been counting down the sleeps since then. She's been ready in her princess dress since seven this morning. So yes, I imagine she is going to be upset when I tell her we're not going. How could you do this to her? You can't forget about her because you've had a row with your girlfriend and feel like getting drunk.'

'It wasn't like...'

'I don't care,' she interrupted. She didn't want to hear any more excuses. She had spent years nurturing the memory of him as the perfect man, and he had just shattered that into smithereens. Where did she go from here? 'There's been nothing but stress and aggravation since you came back. We were better off without you.'

'Don't say that...'

But she had said it, and she cut the call before she was tempted to say anything more. Life as a single parent had never been easy but the mistakes had been all hers, and she had dealt with the consequences. She wasn't prepared now for the resentment she felt, the

225

pure anger, that Daniel could do something which would hurt Megan, and that she would have to deal with the consequences of that too. She had always wondered if she had deprived Megan of half the love that she was entitled to. Perhaps she had rather spared her half the pain and disappointment.

Daniel called round unexpectedly but not unsurprisingly the next morning, carrying an apologetic air and a large Toys R Us bag loaded with princess and Barbie dolls for Megan. Megan was thrilled, and any lingering traces of disappointment over the day before were swiftly swept away with the pile of plastic packaging. It was as if the tears of yesterday had never happened, which was good, of course; but it was galling to see him buy the smile it had taken Helen an afternoon of love to achieve.

Helen retreated to the kitchen and left them to play. She could have done with using the time to sew, but she needed to prepare the special Sunday lunch she had promised Megan as part of her effort to cheer her up yesterday. The chicken was already roasting, the potatoes and carrots were peeled, and now she had to make jam sponge and custard for dessert.

'Something smells good.' Helen jumped, and flour bounced from the sieve in her hand and floated back down all over the work surface. Daniel was standing in the kitchen doorway, though she had been so lost in her thoughts that she hadn't noticed him approach. 'You don't always have to hide in the kitchen.'

'You don't come to see me.'

He didn't deny it – how could he? – but foolishly

Helen felt a pang that he didn't, that not even the anger of yesterday could wholly prevent. She dampened a piece of kitchen towel and wiped up the flour.

'I'm sure there are games the three of us could play.'

'Happy Families? As I'm sure you'll be the first to point out, it's a little too late for that.'

'How many times do I have to say I'm sorry about yesterday? It won't happen again. Can't we move on?'

'Yes, because you're the expert in forgiving and forgetting, aren't you?' Helen hurled the kitchen towel into the bin and let the lid bang shut with a satisfying thud.

'I'm trying.' Daniel looked at Megan. 'But the more time I spend with her, the more I realise how much time I missed.' He turned back to Helen. 'Can we tell her?'

'Not today.' She was running out of time, she knew, and yet she still hesitated. 'Not when she will be upset about yesterday.' It was a convenient excuse, though Daniel nodded and seemed resigned to her answer. Telling Megan, acknowledging Daniel's identity, was a final step she wasn't ready to take. It was harder than she'd anticipated to let someone else in, and to learn to share Megan.

'I've never seen you cook,' Daniel said, as Helen mixed the sponge ingredients. 'Was Waitrose closed?'

'I've had to learn.'

'You'll tell me you do housework next.'

'Sometimes.' She smiled at him, at the shared old

joke about how useless she was at domestic tasks. 'It turns out that I was lazy, not incompetent.'

'So what are you making?'

'Jam sponge. It's Megan's favourite.'

'Is it?' His smile was delighted. 'It used to be mine.'

'Hardly surprising, when she is so wholly a mini-you,' Helen replied, putting the potatoes on to boil. She took the chicken out of the oven: perfect golden skin, and a delicious smell permeating through the house. Daniel was close behind her, peering into the roasting dish.

'She has some of your mannerisms. The way she tilts her head when she's thinking, and her eyes widen in surprise when she laughs, just like yours do.'

Helen faced him. He was only a few inches behind her. She hadn't noticed any of those things in Megan; she saw only reminders of him. Did Daniel look at Megan and see only reminders of her? And if he did, were they good things that he treasured, or bad ones that he wished he could ignore? She didn't dare to ask.

'Do you want to stay for lunch?' It slipped out, quite unplanned.

'Yes.' He answered without hesitation.

'Won't Tasha mind?' Helen backtracked, regretting her impulsive offer.

'She's gone shopping.'

'Feeling better, then?'

'Yes.' He opened his mouth as if to carry on, but stopped and went back into the living room to play

228

with Megan. Helen made the lunch, taking special care to make it perfect, and called to Megan to wash her hands when it was almost ready. As Megan made her way upstairs, Daniel returned to the kitchen.

'Shall I set the table?' Without waiting for a reply, he moved round Helen and opened the cutlery drawer.

'What's this?' His tone was sharp. 'Are you moving? Are you taking Megan away? Is this because of yesterday?'

He waved a stack of papers at Helen. She knew what they were without needing to look. They were estate agents' details for potential houses to rent. She'd hidden them in the cutlery drawer, away from Megan's prying eyes, but not, it seemed, far enough away from her father's.

'I've no choice. My landlord wants the house back. I'm looking for somewhere else in this area.' Looking, but not finding, so far. She now realised that she had been exceptionally lucky with her current house, and that she had been paying below the market rate for some time. It was proving impossible to find a house for the same rent in what she would consider a good-enough area for Megan, especially if she wanted even a small patch of grass. And that was before she'd worked out how she was ever going to afford a deposit, and Christmas presents, and moving costs, as well as all the expense involved in relocating the business to Church Farm.

'When do you have to move out?'

'A couple of weeks after Christmas.'

'So soon?' Daniel frowned. 'Surely you need more notice than that? Have you spoken to Craig? He could take a look at the tenancy agreement.'

'No, there's no need to bother him.'

'He won't mind.' Daniel already had his phone out. 'I'll call him now.'

'Don't.' Helen reached out and put her hand over his. He stared at her, shocked either by her touch or her sternness, or a combination of both.

'Why not?'

'I've tried. He won't help.'

'Rubbish. Of course he will. I'll speak to him now.'

She tightened her hand on his.

'Don't ring. I don't want you begging for me. Sally made it perfectly plain…'

'Sally?' Daniel's lips narrowed. 'What did Sally say?'

'Nothing.'

'Nell.' He twisted his hand so he was holding hers. 'Tell me.'

Helen shrugged, pretending she was entirely unaffected by his touch, and by the concern in his eyes.

'I've not to contact her or Anita again,' she blurted out, unable to stop herself when he was acting like her old Daniel. 'They don't approve of the way I've treated you. It's fine.' She puffed out a tiny smile. 'It's not as if she's the first to think what she said, is it? It's not as if I don't deserve it.'

He squeezed her hand, fleetingly.

'Come and stay with me.'

'With you?' Helen pulled her hand away. 'With you and Tasha?'

'There's plenty of room. We have three bedrooms we never go in.'

Helen backed away and gave the carrots a quite unnecessary stir. She didn't want to hear anything that involved Daniel, Tasha and bedrooms.

'You can't have discussed this with Tasha.'

'She won't mind.'

Tasha wouldn't mind? Wouldn't mind Daniel inviting his ex-girlfriend and their child to live in the house she had crossed the world to share with him? Of course Tasha would mind, and Daniel's drumming fingers confirmed that he knew it too.

'It would never work.'

'It would. I'd be able to see Megan every day.'

Oh, that hurt. Once again he'd prodded the wound that shouldn't even still exist. He wanted Megan to move in with him. Helen was simply a necessary appendage, the handle on the teapot. When would she ever learn? She shook her head, as the words were stuck in her throat.

'Think about it, at least as a temporary solution, if you can't find another house in time.'

'Why do you want another house?' Megan had come in without either of them noticing, and her face was already puckered, expecting to be upset. Helen had no choice but to tell her that they needed to move, and despite her best efforts to turn it into an adventure, Megan cried, screamed, and refused to go anywhere. Daniel hadn't seen this side of childhood before and watched helplessly as Helen soothed Megan until the tantrum passed away. Helen wondered if he would be quite so keen for them to move in now he'd seen that parenting wasn't all bedtime stories and giggles.

Lunch was delayed, and not as perfect as Helen had hoped, although Daniel managed two bowls of jam sponge. While Helen was making coffee, he took his phone out again. For an awful moment she hesitated, milk bottle in hand, fearing that he had decided to contact Craig after all.

'*Princesses on Ice* is in Liverpool next Sunday afternoon. I've found tickets on the Internet. Shall I book them?'

'No,' Helen replied, pouring the milk and trying to ignore Megan's excited face. 'There's a Christmas market on next Sunday.'

Daniel looked up, frowning.

'There are hundreds of Christmas markets on at this time of year. Surely you can go to another one? This is more important than shopping.'

Helen slapped a coffee mug down in front of him.

'It's not shopping, it's working. I've taken a stall there.'

Daniel's frown deepened, and his index finger tapped a steady beat against the back of his phone. Helen could guess what was coming.

'Who's looking after Megan while you work?'

'Kirsty is helping out on the stall, so between us and Ben we can...'

'You'll pass her round between you? No. I'll look

232

after her. You can spend the day with me, can't you, Megan?' He smiled at her. Who could resist that smile? Megan nodded. 'We'll go to visit Gr...' He stopped short. 'Valerie and Alex. You remember them, don't you?'

Megan nodded again. Daniel picked up his coffee, and looked at Helen with cast-iron determination. Dare to deny me now, he was saying: and how could she, when Megan thought she would be spending the day with him? He had broken a promise yesterday. How could she force him into breaking another? But the idea of him taking Megan to his house, of him playing families with Tasha... It turned her blood cold.

'You can bring her to the market,' Helen countered, cradling her coffee mug between her hands. 'There are activities for children and a Santa's grotto. She'll enjoy it.'

They glared at each other, until eventually he nodded. Helen was unclear which of them had won, if either of them. Daniel turned his attention to his phone again.

'Birmingham, in two weeks' time, on the Saturday. You don't work then, do you?'

'No. But it's a long way...'

'Good.' He tapped the phone. 'I've bought the tickets.' He smiled at Megan. 'We're going.'

CHAPTER 19

The Christmas market at Church Farm was magical: Helen could think of no other word for it. Even early in the morning, with stalls and gazebos being erected in the courtyard, and manic people rushing round carrying bags and boxes of goods to sell, Helen felt a buzz of excitement at being part of this. There was a genuine sense of community between everyone working there, like there had been at St Andrew's but on a much larger scale. Each time she came, she felt more certain that this was going to work. Perhaps, after all, she was ready to leave St Andrew's, however much she had loved it there, ready to try something new, something bigger and brighter. She felt she belonged here.

Each building had been decorated with miniature Christmas trees, high up near the roofline, and their tiny white lights were already sparkling, and would look even better as the afternoon darkened. One large tree stood in the centre of the first courtyard, and the florist who owned one of the shops had produced huge garlands and displays of holly and ivy which marked a path, drawing visitors round the whole of Church Farm. Catering stalls were being set up in the space between the offices and the Feed Store and already the air was suffused with the aroma of mulled wine and roasting chestnuts. All it needed was snow to make it picture perfect but, thankfully from the point of view of sales, none was forecast and the sky was a crisp winter blue with not a cloud to be seen.

Tables had been set up in the Hay Barn for the St Andrew's group. Helen had persuaded the others that to make a good first impression they should decorate their stalls in a subtle and sophisticated Christmas style. Tinsel and plastic ornaments were banned, to Fiona's disappointment. Helen had brought matching crisp white cloths to cover every table, and on each one she stood a white ceramic pitcher in which she'd arranged some branches dripping with lush red berries. With Kirsty's help, she strung rows of bright white fairy lights from beam to beam over the top of the stalls. It was her own contribution to the magic, and even Malcolm agreed when she'd finished that it 'didn't look too shabby'.

Helen left Kirsty to start setting up the stall, and helped Ron and Malcolm carry in their items, as they were by far the biggest. Ron had one exquisite Victorian townhouse left to sell, which had to be wheeled in on a trolley. By the time he had arranged furniture and figures in every room, it looked worthy of a museum, never mind a Christmas market. Malcolm had brought a couple of his usual landscapes, but his stall mainly featured the new abstract pieces he had produced recently.

'These are fantastic,' Helen said, as she unwrapped a group of pictures labelled *New Beginnings I, II and III*, all based around different

235

shades of red. 'Red is absolutely my favourite colour.'

'Well, we'll see if they sell, that will be the test of how good they are,' Malcolm replied, but another shade of red was creeping up his neck, confirming Helen's suspicion that he was secretly pleased with his work.

'I'm sure they will. I can't believe you didn't try this style before.'

Malcolm shrugged.

'I dabbled, but I could never find the pluck to bring them into St Andrew's. I've done the landscapes for so long. It's what I know best, and it was easy to get to thinking that's all I know. Moving here has given me a leg up out of the rut I was in. It's a new beginning for all of us, isn't it?'

There was an anxious wait for customers after the official opening time. As the Hay Barn was at the furthest point of Church Farm, there was bound to be a delay before anyone reached them, even if crowds had flooded in on the dot of opening. After fifteen minutes of staring at each other, unnecessarily tweaking their stalls, and exchanging smiles that tried to hide apprehension, Kirsty was sent out to recce the situation and see if there were any visitors at all. She was soon back, bathed in a smile of relief, to report that the crowds were pouring in, and hot on her heels came the first visitors to the Hay Barn.

It was the start of a busy morning, helped by the fact that a small choir had been booked to perform

236

Christmas carols and songs right outside the entrance to the Hay Barn. They drew visitors to the barn, and each time a performance ended, there was a surge inside. By the end of the first two hours, Helen had already seen Malcolm sell one of his paintings, and had restocked her own stall: the fabric Christmas tree decorations were selling brilliantly well. She had also acquired some names on her contact list for people who might be interested in classes and workshops to be held in the tantalising empty space at the head of the barn. It was going better than she had ever hoped.

Ben and the children arrived not long after the market opened, and whisked Kirsty away to explore. She came back bursting with enthusiasm.

'I'm going to be as fat as a pig when we're working here,' she said. 'Have you seen those shops inside the Feed Store? Any extra money I make from working on Mondays will be spent in there before I can make it home.'

Kirsty had agreed to work in the shop on Monday as well as Saturday when they moved, for a trial period; Helen needed to be sure that there were enough sales to justify the extra wages that she could barely afford.

'How is it going round the rest of the market?' Helen asked. She hadn't managed to pop out for so much as a loo break yet. 'Are people still arriving?'

'Loads,' Kirsty nodded. 'Although it's reached that time where the catering stalls are distracting a lot of people.'

Having said that, they were then distracted themselves by a group of ladies who were flatteringly impressed with Helen's work and between them bought a cushion, two Kindle sleeves and a crazy patchwork clutch bag.

'You're going to be opening branches of Crazy Little Things all across the country if this rate of sales continues,' Kirsty said, as Helen rummaged under the table for more items to fill the gaps. 'You'll have to employ a team of seamstresses to keep up with demand.'

'I hardly think I need to put an advert in the Job Centre just yet.' It was a lovely thought, but also a slightly worrying one. The idea of someone else carrying out sewing for her was as strange as someone else looking after Megan. Which reminded her – as if she could have forgotten – where was Megan?

'Have you seen Megan wandering round?' she asked Kirsty.

'No, but it is very busy at the moment. I'm not sure I would have spotted her, especially as I've never met Daniel.'

'You'd definitely know him if you saw him. Surely Ben told you how similar they are? You'll see for yourself at the wedding, if you don't meet him today.'

'Oh yes, the wedding.' There was no mistaking Kirsty's awkward tone, or the shifty expression on her face. 'I meant to have a word with you about that.'

'Don't tell me you're standing me up?' Helen plastered on a smile as a couple stopped to browse at the stall. She had received an unexpected invitation to Alex's wedding, and Kirsty had agreed to be her plus one. She'd already sent back the RSVP with her name on. How embarrassing was it going to be if she had to retract that, admit that she couldn't even convince a friend to accompany her, never mind a date? How humiliating was that going to look in front of Daniel? And oh, how she hated herself for even caring what he thought.

'I really am sorry.' Kirsty looked it too: if she bit her lip much more she'd make a hole in it. 'I know what an ordeal this is going to be for you, but I've no choice. Ben's mum has invited herself up for that weekend, for turkey and tinsel. Apparently it's the only weekend she can fit us in.'

'Don't worry,' Helen replied, squeezing Kirsty's arm. 'Family first, even if they are outlaws, that's the way it goes. I'm sure I can manage to attend a wedding on my own. And I'll have Megan there, anyway.'

'No, you need to have a date.' Kirsty's face brightened in a way that made Helen's heart sink. 'Leave it with me. I made this mess so it's the least I can do to sort it out.'

'Please not a blind date,' Helen said, but she was interrupted by a customer and by the time she had made the sale, Kirsty seemed to have forgotten the subject.

Shortly afterwards, while Helen was explaining

239

the details of some of the workshops she was planning to a pair of elderly sisters who appeared willing to join anything to get them out of the house, she noticed Joel enter the Hay Barn, an attractive woman at his side. It was clear Saskia had seen him too, as her face creased into a frown which flicked immediately to a smile as he made his way towards her stall near the entrance.

Helen was still engaged with the sisters when Joel approached her stall, and he started chatting to Kirsty. It took the old ladies forever to decide what their email address was so they could be added to the mailing list, and the debate over whether it was a '.com' or '.co.uk' could have gone on all afternoon if Helen hadn't promised to try both. At last they shuffled off to inspect Fiona's stall, and Helen was able to turn to Joel.

'That sounded fun.' He grinned, and Helen's eyes were drawn from the very attractive scarf round his neck, to the very attractive set of his lips. She returned the smile.

'I may need to consider streaming my classes like they do at school if they join, or they'll hold everyone up.' She laughed. 'I always assume that elderly ladies can sew already, and darn socks and make proper pastry. Is that terribly ageist?'

'Don't forget knitting. They can all knit as well, can't they? It's practically the law.' The woman at Joel's side smiled and held out her hand to Helen. 'Hi, I'm Joel's sister, Liz. You can only be Helen. Good to meet you at last. I love your work.'

240

'Thanks. I love people who love my work. I love people who buy my work even more. Can I tempt you?'

'I think you can. You must be irresistible to my family.' Liz laughed and tweaked the scarf round Joel's neck, making his cheeks darken. 'That wreath would look perfect in my flat. The colours are gorgeous. Did you make that as well?'

'I made everything here.' Helen pulled down the wreath and passed it to Liz for her to examine. 'That was actually very simple. You know how you make pom-poms as a child, wrapping the wool round and round the cardboard circles? The wreath is the same idea, but on a larger scale, and without cutting it apart at the end. Then I sew the felt flowers on. It's so simple even Megan helped with wrapping the wool round the card.' Helen grinned. 'I shouldn't have admitted that, should I? Child labour is never a good advertising feature. But it is technically still a Walters creation.'

'Where is Megan?' Joel asked, as Liz admired the wreath. 'I thought you'd have brought her.'

'She's coming later.'

'Good. I thought I might have been too late, as I've not had chance to come round until now. I've brought her a special ticket for Santa's Grotto.'

'A special ticket?' Helen took the piece of card Joel held out. 'What does this do?'

'It will mean she can avoid the queue. Hand it in at the side door, not at the front.'

'I didn't know there were VIP tickets available,'

Kirsty interrupted, peering at the ticket over Helen's shoulder. 'Is that a perk for stallholders?'

'Well...' Joel fiddled with his scarf. 'I suppose it could be. I could get you one if you want...'

'You're alright, we've already done the grotto.' Kirsty looked from Joel to Helen, and in an awful moment of clarity, Helen knew exactly what was coming next. She shook her head, but Kirsty paid her no notice whatsoever. 'Joel, are you doing anything two weeks yesterday?'

'I don't think so.' He appeared understandably confused at the way the conversation had jumped. Liz was standing by, wreath and purse in hand, looking fascinated.

'Kirsty, don't...'

But Kirsty took as little notice of Helen's voice as she had of the shaking head.

'Great! I was supposed to be Helen's plus one at a wedding but my mother-in-law has screwed up the plan and now I can't go. I promised Helen I'd find a replacement. You'd be perfect!'

'Would I?' Joel looked at Helen, eyebrows lightly raised, and a smile waltzing round his lips.

'You don't have to,' Helen began, shifting slightly to dig her heel into Kirsty's foot in what she hoped was a painful thrust.

'I'd love to. Whose wedding is it?'

'Ah...' There was an awkward question. How could she tell Joel before Megan? 'A family friend,' she finished. That wasn't entirely untrue, was it? 'Have you decided to take the wreath?' she asked

242

Liz, trying to kill the conversation. Sadly it survived.

'Email me the details and your address and I'll pick you up,' Joel said. His dimples were out. Helen supposed it wouldn't be too bad to turn up at the wedding with him. And it would probably have been too late to cancel Kirsty's place now, wouldn't it? It would save Alex the stress and bother of having an empty space on a table too. By the time Helen had taken Liz's money, she had pretty well convinced herself that taking Joel to the wedding was entirely in Alex's best interests.

It was well after two before Megan finally arrived, by which time Helen had already sent three increasingly frantic text messages to Daniel wondering, asking and finally demanding to know where they were. And then, at one of the busiest moments of the day, when the choir had finished another performance and the audience had flooded into the Hay Barn, Helen spotted them through the crowd. Daniel, Megan and Tasha, strolling in together, smiling together, and looking every inch the perfect family together. Helen stared, and forgot to breathe.

'Jesus,' she heard Kirsty say close to her ear.

'Not quite,' Helen replied. 'Just Daniel.'

'And his mum needed a paternity test? Seriously?'

'Not once she'd seen Megan.'

'He's gorgeous. Is it wrong to say that when he looks so like Megan?'

243

'It's probably more wrong for me to think it.'

Helen passed over a crazy patchwork tissue box to an interested customer, and watched as Tasha pointed something out to Daniel on Saskia's stall. Was it the display of rings? Helen couldn't see past the other customers, but as she was focussing that way, Saskia caught her eye, and gave a slight tilt of the head in Daniel's direction, an open question on her face. It wasn't a question Helen planned to give Saskia an answer to any time soon.

'Mummy!' At last the crowd shifted and Megan saw Helen. Pulling free from Daniel's hand – Helen could see now, with a whoosh of relief, that she hadn't been holding Tasha's – Megan ran over, and crawled under the table to reach Helen.

'Mummy! I've been to Danny's house and I ate some cheese and Valerie was there and his garden is big and he said I can have a swing...'

Laughing, Helen scooped Megan into her arms and kissed her.

'She did eat more than cheese.' Daniel had followed Megan, and was standing on the opposite side of the stall.

'And the swing?'

He shrugged.

'Why not? There's plenty of space.'

Unlike in her garden, Helen thought – her garden for a few more weeks, at least. She would love to have given Megan a swing – or even a garden she could properly run round. Once again Daniel was swooping in and easily providing Megan with exactly what she wanted, and what Helen couldn't give her. Helen buried her face in Megan's hair to hide her irritation. When she looked up, Tasha was at Daniel's side.

'Hello,' Helen said. Her impeccable upbringing came to her aid, and she was able to find a smile. 'Has she behaved?'

'I think so.' Tasha manoeuvred her lips into a poor imitation of one. What did that mean, Helen wondered? Had Megan been naughty? Or had Tasha not noticed whether she had or not?

'She's been an absolute pleasure.' Valerie Blake appeared from behind Daniel. Helen hadn't realised she was here, and bizarrely felt relieved that she was. 'She ate most of her lunch and enjoyed exploring Daniel's house.' Valerie gave Helen a significant look. Helen understood it. Valerie was reassuring her that Megan had managed without her; that the first of what would have to be many visits to Daniel's house had gone well. It was what she wanted to hear; but the relief was tempered with a sting of pain, as if one of the bonds that tied Megan to her had snapped.

'Can I see Santa now?' Megan wriggled in Helen's arms.

'I need to speak to someone first, and then we can go, okay?' Helen had arranged to go through her crazy patchwork portfolio with a couple who lived too far away to come in during the week. They had appeared to be seriously interested in a piece for the reception area of their new office

245

building; but judging by Megan's cross face, it wasn't okay at all.

'I'll take her,' Daniel said.

'Thanks, but I'd like to.'

'So would I. And I haven't had chance before now.'

Of course he hadn't, and that had been her fault, as his raised eyebrow and pointed tone stated so eloquently. They stared at each other, battling it out, but how could she ever win when her guilty feelings gave him the ultimate trump card? Megan was already sliding down out of Helen's grasp – metaphorically as well as physically, Helen couldn't help thinking.

'Fine. You take her.' Helen thrust the special ticket at Daniel. 'She has a VIP ticket. Take it to the side door of the grotto and she won't need to queue.'

Megan crawled back under the table and took Daniel's hand. He smiled down at her, his whole heart on display. Tasha had noticed too, and a ripple of sadness washed across her face. Valerie leaned over the stall and squeezed Helen's empty hand.

Helen watched the four of them walk away, until she realised that Kirsty was studying her.

'So that's Daniel,' Kirsty said, in a neutral tone that was hard to gauge.

'Yes. So, what's the verdict?'

'Older than I thought he would be. Late thirties, is he? But very handsome. I can see why he would catch your eye.' Kirsty straightened the display of Kindle sleeves as a customer walked away. 'He's quite domineering, isn't he?'

'Domineering?' Helen repeated. How had Kirsty reached that conclusion from a few minutes' encounter? 'He's trying to adjust, that's all.'

'And he does that by bossing you about, does he?'

'He wasn't...'

'Of course he was! I can't believe you took it. You wouldn't have stood that from anyone else. You can't feel guilty for the rest of your life, you know. And you can't let him make you feel like that, either.'

Easy for Kirsty to say, Helen thought, and she turned away as she saw her couple approaching. The meeting went well, and she had arranged to prepare some preliminary sketches when Megan came dashing back in, looking like she might burst with excitement at any moment.

'Mummy!' she squealed, crawling under the table again and almost sending the stall flying. 'Look what Santa gave me! A Hello Kitty rucksack!'

She waved the rucksack at Helen.

'That's lovely, isn't it?' she agreed. 'Santa must know how much you like Hello Kitty, mustn't he?'

'Jenny didn't get that,' Kirsty said, inspecting the rucksack. 'All she got was a colouring book and some felt tips.'

'Perhaps Santa knows how much she loves

247

colouring?' Helen suggested. Kirsty grinned.

'Or perhaps Santa's little helper arranged for a special present as well as a special ticket.'

Helen dismissed the idea, but now Kirsty had planted it, she couldn't dislodge it from her head. Had Joel arranged for Megan to receive a different present from the other children? When she managed to escape from the stall, and took Megan outside to watch a candlelit procession through Church Farm, complete with a real reindeer, she looked around at the other children but didn't see another backpack like Megan's. Perhaps it was true – and if it was, she needed to thank Joel, but there was no sign of him amongst the crowds.

Daniel took Megan home again after the procession, as Helen still had to man the stall for another half hour and then tidy up. The choir had gone, and most of the visitors were making their way home too. Helen left Kirsty in charge and headed off to search for Joel. She toured the whole of Church Farm, and had reached the conclusion that he must have gone home, when she noticed the light on in his office. There was no reply to her knock, and she peered round the door. Joel was sitting in the chair behind his desk, so she walked in.

It was only when Helen was in front of him that she noticed he was asleep. Under the bright office light, she saw now what she had missed when they had met in the Hay Barn earlier: shadows of exhaustion ringed his eyes, and tiny frown lines left their mark between his eyebrows. An unexpected swell of tenderness rushed through her.

Slipping out again, she went over to the Feed Store and bought a coffee. She left it on his desk, in case he woke up, and was on her way out of the office, quietly she thought, when she heard him speak.

'Helen.'

His voice was husky with tiredness, but as she turned round his smile was automatic: only half a smile, though, as if it didn't have the energy to spread up to his eyes.

'I'm sorry,' she said, taking a few steps back towards him. 'I didn't mean to wake you. I've brought you a coffee.'

'Thanks. Is it too late to claim that I actually wasn't asleep at all?'

'You've been well and truly caught.' Joel stood up and stretched. His shirt rose above his belt, exposing a patch of taut flesh. 'Don't worry, your secret is safe,' Helen said quickly, forcing her gaze back up to his face. 'I won't tell all the hardworking stall holders out there that the fat cat landlord has nothing else to do but sleep.'

'Fat cat landlord!' He laughed, and sat down again. Helen drew nearer, irresistibly pulled forward, and sat on the edge of the desk next to his. 'I can't be too offended by that, coming from someone who likes cats.'

'Megan likes cats,' Helen corrected him.

'And your smile is as big as hers when you look at those kittens.'

'Okay, Sherlock, I can't deny it's an inherited passion. I'm a confirmed cat-woman.'

'Now that's quite an image to wake up to.'

And there it came, the full-dimpled cheeky grin, strong enough to overcome any degree of tiredness. It acted like a magnet, pulling Helen's lips into an answering smile every time.

'Talking of Megan,' she said, swinging her legs backwards and forwards, 'did you arrange for her to get a special present from Santa? A Hello Kitty rucksack?'

'Did she like it?'

'She adores it. Shall I take that as a yes?'

'A partial yes.' Joel drank some of his coffee. 'Liz chose it. I thought she'd have a better idea of what girls like. What *little* girls like,' he clarified, laughing at the unspoken comment on Helen's face.

'It was a lovely thought. Thanks. You must have had more than enough on your hands arranging the market.'

'Do you think it went well?' It was no polite question: as Joel looked at Helen, there was a twist of anxiety in his eyes.

'Yes, it must have done. It looks fabulous, and I was so busy I could hardly leave the stall all day. Even Malcolm was seen to smile this afternoon, and I can think of no greater endorsement. Surely you're not doubting the success of Church Farm? You've always seemed so confident about it.'

'If I'm not, who else will be?' He leaned back in his chair, playing with the curl that fell over his ear.

'Planning and organising this market was a lot more stressful than I expected. It's taken more time and money than I could spare, and it could all have been for nothing if the weather had been worse, or if no one had come.'

'Did you have no one to help? What about Liz?'

'There was only a limited amount she could do when she lives in London. My other sister, Ruth, is a potter and lives on the Scottish coast near Oban. She has no organisational skills at all; her idea of helping with the market was to send down a crate of pots to sell. And Mum and Dad have the enthusiasm but not the energy these days.'

'And your friends?'

'They've been here today, but they all have their own jobs to do.'

'So do you.'

'Yes, and I'm finding that doing two jobs at once seems to involve at least four times as much work. But I have to do it.' His fingers rubbed a slow streak across his forehead. 'Church Farm isn't only about my parents' past. It's their future too, their pension pot. If I screw up, they have nothing.'

Helen moved across and perched on Joel's desk, in front of him.

'You won't screw up. You've done a fantastic job today.' She reached out and pulled his hand away from the curl he was torturing again. His hand closed round hers so briefly that she might have thought she'd imagined it, but for the ripple that rolled from her fingers through every limb.

'You should have called me. I'd have helped. Friends, remember?'

'I remember. But you have enough on.' He slowly studied her face. 'You already look like you're having too many sleepless nights.'

'Says the man whose eyes are surrounded by so many shadows it's a wonder they don't need a torch to see out.'

'We make a good pair, don't we?'

It wasn't said flirtatiously; and his smile was warm, not suggestive. But there was something in the way Joel looked at her, a look of understanding and of tenderness that stretched like a cord between them, which reached inside Helen and teased into life a response that she had never known with any man before. And long after she had picked up Megan and returned home, the feelings were still there, faint but clinging on to life.

CHAPTER 20

After the perfect conditions of the Christmas market day, the weather grew progressively colder and cloudier, until on Friday the first flakes of snow began to fall. Megan thought it was thrilling, having no concept of the danger this weather posed to the planned trip to *Disney on Ice* the next day.

Helen phoned Daniel when she brought Megan home from nursery at the end of the day.

'Have you seen the weather?' she asked. 'It's snowing.'

'Is it?' She heard movement, as if he was getting up to look out of the window. 'Are you sure? It isn't snowing in Manchester.'

'The forecast is for even more tomorrow, and the Midlands might be the worst affected. The BBC has issued an amber warning.'

'It will be a precaution. They always predict the worst now so they don't get caught out.'

'But we don't want to get caught in bad weather so far from home.'

Daniel laughed.

'When have you ever let the weather stop you doing what you want?'

Since she'd become a mother, she could have said, but she could tell he wasn't giving her his full attention. And *Disney on Ice* was hardly something she wanted to do. It was entirely Daniel's plan: he had told her to leave all the arrangements to him.

'You know how important tomorrow is,' he continued. 'We're not cancelling it unless the car is buried ten feet under a snowdrift.'

Helen hung up. She was still uneasy about the weather, but she'd known even before she had spoken to Daniel that there was no way he would change the plan. He had decided – and she had agreed – that this would be the weekend they told Megan who he was. They would have the day out together on Saturday, then he would come over on Sunday morning and they would tell her. It had been inevitable since the Christmas market. He had loved having Megan for the day, and wanted it to happen more often. He could hardly have been plainer: either they both spoke to Megan, or he did it himself. Helen's time had run out.

By Saturday morning, a couple of inches of snow lay on the ground. Daniel arrived earlier than expected.

'The main roads are fine,' he said, before Helen had even asked. 'It's only the side streets where the snow has stuck. And the sun's out – it will soon melt.'

'But the forecast...'

'We're going,' he interrupted. He glanced over at Megan, resplendent in her Cinderella dress, who was busy packing dolls into her Hello Kitty rucksack. 'I'm not letting her down again.'

By the time they reached Birmingham, another inch of snow had fallen and the flakes were becoming heavier all the time. They stopped for lunch and, though Daniel was trying to make the best of it, his fingers tapped relentlessly on the table as he looked out of the window. He only relaxed when they arrived at the Arena and Megan was sitting in her seat, happily waving the flashing plastic wand he had bought her from the souvenir stand. Helen could tell what he was thinking: he had promised Megan that he would take her to *Disney on Ice*, and here she was – job done. Helen wondered if she was the only one to spare a thought for how they were ever going to get home.

It was dark when the show finished, and as soon as they stepped outside they realised their problem. Snow had fallen heavily throughout the performance, and even the main roads were now covered. The cars had carved out two grooves in each direction, and were crawling along, tail to bumper. It was going to take them hours to make it home. Daniel checked the travel news on his phone, and Helen could see from the drumming fingers that the news wasn't good.

'One lane of the M6 is closed because of the snow,' he told her, 'and there's already a four-mile queue heading north. We'll have to try a different route.'

'Are you sure?' Helen clutched Megan's hand. 'If the motorway is bad, won't the minor roads be even worse?'

'It's probably lorries blocking the M6. I'm sure we'll find a quieter route.'

They piled back into his BMW, and Daniel set the sat nav to find a route avoiding the M6. Their progress was slow but steady at first, as they crawled along with all the other cars, and Megan didn't stop chattering about the Disney Princesses, and flashing her wand. But when Daniel followed the sat nav's instructions to turn off the main road, the traffic thinned out, and the marked tracks in the road became harder to follow. And then Daniel turned left, the car skidded, and came to a halt at a 45° angle towards the kerb.

Daniel tried rocking the car backwards and forwards, and pulling on the steering wheel, but it was no good. They were completely stuck. Megan was silent, and Helen could see her wide, terrified eyes shining from an eerie fluorescent face as the wand continued to flash on and off.

'Bloody rear-wheel drive,' Daniel said, thumping the steering wheel. 'It's useless in the snow.'

Helen bit back the obvious response. It wouldn't help to row in front of Megan. But really, it was beyond irritating. Had he not listened to a word she'd said about the amber weather warning? Could he not have accepted, just for once, that she might have been right?

'Do you have a shovel?' she asked instead, but without much hope. Did they even have snow in Hong Kong and Australia? He was bound to be out of practice for an English winter.

'No.' He leaned over and rummaged down by Helen's feet. He pulled up an ice scraper. 'I have this. I'll have to see if I can dig us out.'

Daniel put on his coat and went outside. Helen

could see him trying to shift the snow with the tiny ice scraper. He might as well have been using a spoon; and the snow was still falling so heavily, any progress he made would soon be covered over.

'What's Danny doing?' Megan asked, as a dark shape crouched down at the side of the window next to her.

'He's trying to clear the snow away from the wheels so that the car can move,' Helen replied, reaching over to the back of the car and stroking Megan's foot.

'I don't like it,' Megan said, and she started to cry, quietly at first and then with increasing volume, despite Helen's efforts to comfort her. It was clearly loud enough to be heard outside. Daniel yanked open her door, making Megan scream.

'What's the matter with her?' he asked, staring at Helen.

'She's tired and hungry,' she replied. 'Probably freezing too,' she added, gesturing at the open door, through which snow was drifting in.

Daniel closed the door, and opened Helen's instead.

'Haven't you brought any food?' he asked.

'Only snacks, and she's already eaten those. You said we would be stopping for supper on the way home.'

'I didn't know this was going to happen!'

'I warned you about the amber forecast.'

'Then you should have brought some food!'

He slammed the door shut. Helen stared at it,

257

open-mouthed. Was this how it always went, being part of a two-parent family? Bickering, blaming and passing responsibility to the other? She'd never seen Kirsty and Ben behave like this, but perhaps behind closed doors they were the same. Perhaps: but somehow she doubted it.

Helen's door opened again.

'Can you move to the driver's seat? Keep in first; try to edge forward while I push.'

They tried this for five minutes, but the car wasn't going anywhere. Eventually Daniel opened the door again. Despite the cold night, his brow glistened with sweat, and he was breathing hard.

'This isn't working.'

There was no arguing with that.

'Don't you have breakdown cover?' Helen suggested. In the light reflected from the car she could see the sarcastic lift of his eyebrows.

'I think they may be rather busy tonight, don't you?'

'Can we catch a train back to Manchester?'

'From where? Can you see a station?'

Of course she couldn't. She couldn't see any buildings at all, and no other cars had passed since they had stopped.

'What ideas do you have?' Helen asked. 'You told me to leave the arrangements to you. So what do you propose?'

Daniel's hand was thudding on the roof of the car.

'There was a small town half a mile back. We'll have to go there. There might be a hotel.'

'A hotel?' Was he serious? 'You think we're going to stay overnight?'

'There's no option. You said yourself that Megan was tired. It's either that or sleep in the car, and I don't think any of us want that.'

Helen didn't especially want to spend the night in a hotel with Daniel either, but he was already unfastening Megan.

'I'll carry Megan so we can walk faster.'

They trudged through the deepening snow back towards civilisation. It was too dark to see much of Daniel's face, but Helen could tell from the brooding quality of his silence that he wasn't happy. He had wanted this day to be perfect, and instead it could hardly have turned out worse. Was he changing his mind about telling Megan who he was tomorrow? Might he be changing his mind about being involved at all? She tried to interpret his thoughts but it was impossible to work out what he was thinking. If he was thinking at all: Helen was so cold she wasn't sure her brain was still functioning.

At last they reached the outskirts of the town. Only the occasional 4x4 was still on the road; other cars and vans had been abandoned by the kerb. Helen hadn't taken much notice of the place when they had driven through, but now she saw it, her hopes were low of finding a hotel. But Daniel suddenly shouted out as if he'd spotted an oasis in the desert.

'There's a B&B over there.' His finger pointed at a detached red-brick building squeezed in between a launderette and a row of terraced houses. It became obvious as they approached that it had passed its glory days some time ago, and that was judging it in the flattering glow of the street lamp. Helen could readily imagine what it would look like in the morning. But a tatty sign in the window said 'Vacancies'. It was all the adornment needed to make the place look beautiful.

Daniel rang the doorbell and eventually a well-built lady in her sixties answered. She was resplendent in baggy cord trousers, a polo necked jumper and padded navy bodywarmer which made her appear even bulkier than she already was.

'Bless you,' she said, casting a smile over them that was as warm as a blast from a heat lamp. 'Come inside and let's shut that cold air out. Look at this poor little mite, she looks perishing. We need to get you warmed up, don't we?' The woman reached out and tickled Megan's cheek. 'Is it a room you're after? I've had a few surprise arrivals already tonight who can't make it home, but you're in luck, I've got the one room left and it's the family room, so it will be just the job, won't it?'

'One room?' Helen began, as the front door was closed and locked behind her. 'That's...'

'Perfect.' Daniel interrupted. 'We'll take it.'

Helen stared at him. What was he thinking? How could it possibly be perfect for the three of them to be sharing one room? But he looked back at her with an uncompromising expression.

'Is there anywhere nearby we can find something to eat?' he asked the lady, who now introduced herself as Mrs Kirkbride.

'Oh, you don't need to worry about that,' she replied cheerfully. 'I've had a pot of stew on the go since the weather turned bad this afternoon. I was expecting trouble. It happens every year. Those blasted sat navs send people this way to avoid the M6, but the road can be lethal up ahead, as I guess you've discovered!' She laughed. 'I'll show you the room, and then you can come down to the dining room when you're ready. And I'll fetch you some of my Dennis' socks,' she added, pointing down at Daniel's feet. 'You'll perish in those wet ones. How are your pants?'

'They'll be fine,' he said hastily. He shot a look at Helen, a flicker of alarm, followed up with a smile. For a moment it was as if the last five years had never happened, and they were united in a shared sense of how ridiculous this situation was. The woman was trying to strip Daniel of his clothes and he hadn't even made it past the floral-carpeted hall yet. Helen smiled back.

'Is there a shop nearby where I could buy a few things?' Daniel asked as Mrs Kirkbride led them up two flights of stairs to an attic room at the top of the house.

'There's a lovely big Tesco on the way in to town. You'll be able to get your basics there. It's open late so you've time to have your tea first. I'll lend you my Dennis' wellies when you go.' She swung the door open with a flourish. 'And here's your room. You'll be nice and snug up here.'

Helen led Megan into the room. It felt more like walking into a greenhouse than a bedroom: there was a riot of unmatched flowers on the carpet, the walls and the curtains, and a vase of plastic carnations bloomed on the dressing table. There was one small single bed tucked away in a corner under a steeply sloping roof. The only other bed was a double. Helen absorbed this with a creeping sense of uncertainty. How was this going to work? Where would they all sleep?

'A bunny!' Megan squealed, and ran over and sat down on the single bed, grabbing the toy rabbit that was propped against the pillow. Her answer to the sleeping conundrum was clear. But that only left... No. That simply wasn't possible. She couldn't do it, couldn't bear an illusion of the past when their circumstances were now so different. Helen turned to Daniel. She saw his eyes flick round the room, but his face was impenetrable.

'It's perfect, thanks,' he said to Mrs Kirkbride.

Helen stared. Perfect? For the second time in ten minutes? This was politeness run mad. Sharing a room was not perfect. And as for sharing a bed... It was the most imperfect situation she could imagine.

'Dan...'

He spoke over her.

'Is there a bathroom?'

'Yes, next door. Technically anyone can use it, but no one else knows it's up here. All the benefits of an en-suite without the price!' Mrs Kirkbride beamed. 'Is ten minutes enough for you all to spend a penny? I'll

262

have your tea ready then if you want to come down.'

She left and closed the door behind her. Daniel swung round to Helen.

'What choice is there?' he said, though she hadn't spoken. 'It might not be the five-star standard you expect, but it's warm and dry.'

'Life hasn't been five star for some considerable time, or hadn't you noticed?' she shot back. She gestured at the room. 'It's not the lack of stars that bothers me. It's the lack of beds.'

'Megan's chosen her bed. We'll have to take this one.' He waved at the double.

'No!' Helen took a step back. 'You'll have to go in the single.'

'Don't be ridiculous. I'm too big, and I'd crack my head on the ceiling. Megan wants it.'

'This bed's mine,' Megan said, in a tone that Helen knew well was one nudge away from a full-blown tantrum.

'I'm sure we're grown up enough to share a bed. We've managed it before.'

He avoided Helen's eye. How could he so carelessly, so dismissively, refer to their past like that? It made her pull herself together. She couldn't let him see that the idea bothered her, when it was clearly a matter of no consequence to him. So she shrugged as if it were unimportant where they slept, gathered Megan, and took her to the bathroom.

Mrs Kirkbride's stew was delicious, but Megan was visibly drooping by the time they had finished. Daniel passed on the offer of apple pie and, kitted out in Dennis' coat, socks and wellingtons, headed out to buy provisions at Tesco. Barely an hour had gone by before he knocked on the attic room door. He staggered in, laden with four Bags for Life.

'The snow's stopped,' he said, dropping the bags at the foot of the double bed. 'We shouldn't have too many problems tomorrow.'

'That's a relief,' Helen said. 'You look like you've bought enough to last a week.'

'It's essential stuff.' He unloaded the first bag. 'Toothbrushes, toothpaste, deodorant, nightwear...' He was dividing everything in three piles on the bed. He didn't look at Helen as he added a packet of ladies' knickers to what was clearly her pile. Size 8 knickers, she noted, the size she used to be. He clearly hadn't paid her much attention since his return to England.

Helen took Megan to the bathroom and helped her change for bed into her new pyjamas. Daniel had bought a book for a bedtime story, but she fell asleep before he was halfway through reading it. He came back over and perched on the double bed. Helen was sitting on it with her feet up; she had gravitated to 'her' side of the bed without having given it any conscious thought.

'I brought you these to read,' Daniel said, and reaching into the final bag he pulled out three thick glossy magazines. Helen stroked the cover of the first magazine, her fingers gliding across the shiny surface. She used to love these magazines, poring over the adverts to decide what to buy, but it had been a long time since she'd had either the time or the money to spare for them. Tears pricked her eyes at the realisation that Daniel had thought to buy them for her, and had remembered her favourites.

'And I smuggled these past Mrs Kirkbride,' he continued. 'I was sure the bottles were clanking all the way up the stairs.' He drew out a bottle of vodka and a bottle of tonic. 'Can we manage without ice and lemon?'

Helen would happily have drunk the vodka neat to see her through this ordeal.

'We've no glasses.' Would swigging from the bottle be too desperate? Swigging from a shared bottle would certainly be too intimate. Helen's eyes fell on the hospitality tray, and she padded across the room. 'Will coffee cups do?'

They sat on the bed, as far apart as they could be, in a silence which the vodka gradually helped smooth from awkward to comfortable. Helen flicked through the magazines, and snapshot memories of her old life scrolled through her head with every turn of the page. Once this news about the latest fashion, hairstyles and cosmetics had seemed important, but it bore no relation to her life now. The little girl snuffling in the corner had changed her too much – had changed everything. Helen tossed the magazines aside.

'Finished them already?' Daniel looked up from his paper. 'I should have bought more.'

'It's hard to concentrate,' Helen said, reaching over to the bedside table and picking up her cup of vodka. 'This isn't how I was supposed to be spending the evening.'

'Did you have plans?' Daniel put down his newspaper. 'Did you have a date?'

'No,' she replied quickly, sensing the frown starting, and fearing there would be a cross-examination about the babysitting arrangements. 'I needed the time to work. I can fit in six or seven hours after Megan has gone to bed.'

'Six or seven hours? When do you sleep?'

'When the work's done.' Or when she nodded off in her chair, needle in hand. Some nights she never made it into bed at all. She decided not to tell him that. She couldn't risk him thinking she might be too tired to look after Megan properly.

'I don't understand. Why do you have to do that?'

Helen shrugged.

'The same reason as everyone else. I need to earn money.'

'No, you don't.' Daniel shifted so he was turned towards her. 'You never worked before. Your parents...'

'I haven't taken anything from my parents since Megan was born.'

'Why not?'

'I don't want to discuss it.' Helen drew her legs up under her. Daniel studied her, fingers drumming steadily against his cup.

'We haven't sorted out the maintenance yet. Have you any idea how much? A thousand a month?'

'No!' Helen waved her hand at him. 'Don't be silly.'

'What? Isn't it enough? Two thousand? Three?'

'I can manage.'

'Working into the early hours of the morning isn't managing, it's struggling. Take the money, and you can give up work again.'

'I don't want to give up. I love my job. We're surviving, and we're not dependent on anyone else.' Helen sipped her vodka, resolutely looking away from Daniel. She was never going to let him know, directly or indirectly, how close they had come to not surviving on a couple of occasions. She had pulled them back from the brink, and the realisation of her own ability had astonished her. But she could sense his eyes on her, and inevitably she turned towards Daniel.

'Has it been very tough, on your own?'

Helen hadn't expected that, nor the sympathy that was creeping into his eyes.

'Yes.'

'Were you really on your own for the birth?'

'Apart from the medical staff.'

'Why? There must have been someone. Your mother...'

'Certainly not her.' Helen had drunk enough vodka to make the truth easier than concocting a lie. 'It was your place. No one else could take it.'

'Nell...'

He reached out and put a tentative hand on her shoulder.

'Don't pity me, Dan. You, of all people, have no cause to pity me. I chose to do it alone. I can hardly complain about it now.'

Helen went to the bathroom, needing some time to herself, and away from Daniel's scrutiny. His sympathy, the three of them being together, the vodka... It was a lethal combination. Every time they were together, she had to close her mind to thoughts of how different it might have been, how if she had acted differently, this could have been real. Now the alcohol had opened the floodgates to all those thoughts and they crashed in, wave on wave. And yet... She looked at herself in the bathroom mirror, seeing the melting remains of her make-up, the weathered hair, and the tiredness glazing her eyes. She felt the customary ache that any thought of Daniel produced: but was it slightly dulled? Perhaps it was the vodka, or the familiarity of seeing him more often; perhaps it was something else entirely, but for once she felt that the edge had been taken off the pain. It hadn't gone away, but it was bearable.

'What are we going to do about Christmas?' Daniel asked, when Helen returned to the bedroom. Her drink had been refilled in her absence. She wandered over to Megan, looked down for a few moments on her beautiful girl, sleeping soundly, and went back to sit on the bed.

'We're going to my parents' house. We do every year.'

'Even though you won't accept their financial help?'

'It's better than being on our own. And Adam and Jane will be there.'

'Why don't you come to my house this year?'

That would be cosy, Helen thought, reaching out for her cup. Daniel and Tasha, Helen and Megan, all sitting down to Christmas lunch together. She was fairly certain he couldn't have run this idea past Tasha before suggesting it.

'What does Tasha think about that?'

'She won't be there. She's going back to Australia for Christmas.'

Helen looked at Daniel, trying to read from his face the lines missing from his words. Had he even mentioned this plan to Tasha? Was this a secret Christmas dinner, for the three of them? For so many reasons, she recoiled at the thought of it. She shook her head.

'Megan loves playing with Adam's boys. It's good for her to spend Christmas with other children.'

'Fine. I'll come with you to your parents' house.'

'You can't do that!'

'Why not? They're hardly short of space, and I don't think they'll mind, do you?'

Of course they wouldn't. They had adored Daniel. When Helen started a relationship with him they had been proud of her for probably the first time in her life. They would be thrilled to hear that he was back, and to learn that he hadn't abandoned Helen when she was pregnant, as she had let them believe.

'What about presents?' Daniel pressed on. 'We may as well sort it out now. What can we get for Megan?'

'I've been saving for a bicycle.'

'Great idea. Let me know how much it is and

I'll send you half.'

Why was she finding this so difficult, Helen wondered? Christmas was always a financial minefield, and now this year half of it was being paid for by someone else. She should be relieved, pleased even. But it was one thing for her to write 'love from Daddy' on a few presents, and quite another for Daddy to be here, asserting his will in every aspect of their lives. She began to see what she had never appreciated at the time: how entirely Daniel had led their past relationship. She had been a spoiled rich girl when they met, idly drifting through life, and she had let him sweep her along the road he chose. Now he seemed to assume they would fall into those roles again. And though she had found her own feet, and had no intention of being swept off them again, when he tried to push through his own way, echoes of the past and her feelings of guilt made it hard to withstand him.

Helen picked up a magazine again and turned the pages blindly, to stop the conversation. After a while she felt a nudge against her arm, and realised drowsily that she was nodding off.

'Go to bed,' Daniel said. 'Make the most of the unexpected night off.'

Helen nodded, grabbed her Tesco pile and headed to the bathroom. She changed into her pyjamas, thankful, even though they were rather tight, that he had bought any nightwear at all: she hadn't wasted time with it when they had lived together, given how quickly it would have come off. She wiped away her make-up with some reluctance, wincing at the thought of Daniel seeing her naked older face tomorrow, brushed her teeth, and hurried back to the bedroom. She dashed into bed almost before Daniel could raise his head from the newspaper, lying as near to the edge as she could without risking falling out.

After what seemed like a momentous pause, Daniel rose from the bed and went to the bathroom. Helen hadn't known how thin the wall was: she could hear every sound he made, and the familiarity of it made her throat burn with suppressed tears. He came back into the room, and though she was clutching the duvet tightly so that it covered most of her head, she heard him as he stripped off his clothes, item by item. And then, what she had never expected to happen again: Daniel Blake climbed into bed with her.

CHAPTER 21

As Helen waded back into consciousness, she became aware of a persistent niggle that something wasn't right. She was too comfortable to pursue it at first, until at last her eyes opened and she noticed three things. The first was Megan, standing at the side of the bed.

'Mummy! Mummy!' she repeated crossly. 'I'm talking to you!'

The second thing Helen noticed was that she wasn't at home: the bright light shining in through the thin floral curtains on the opposite wall reminded her where she was, and who she was with. And that led on to the third thing, which should probably have been the first, if she'd been alert enough to process it. The duvet was now pushed down as far as her waist; and Daniel, who should have been on the far side of the bed, was right up behind her, his chest pressed against her back, his legs knotted with hers. His breath was warm in her hair, and his arm was slung across her body. His hand had found its way inside her pyjama top, and was resting on her skin, no more than a finger's width away from her breast. She hoped he hadn't noticed her saggy stomach; and then decided that perhaps that was the least of her concerns.

She tried to sit up, but was too firmly pinned down. Her movement roused Daniel, and his hand slid speculatively over her, in a way she knew so well. She rolled onto her back to try to dislodge him, and saw the moment his eyes opened. He looked at his arm, still on Helen, as if wondering whether it really belonged to him, and if so, why it was there. He looked at Helen, as if somehow she had enticed his arm to lie over her. And only then, when they had recognised the incomprehension in each other's eyes, did he at last draw his hand away.

'Danny had his arm on you.' Helen sat up and faced Megan. Her expression revealed nothing: she was stating a fact, that was all.

'He was keeping warm, like you do when you cuddle Mr Cat,' Helen replied, then wondered if it might have been better to say nothing. Cuddling was quite the wrong image.

'I'm hot.' Megan did look hot: her hair was sticking round the edges of her face. The heating must be on full, to compensate for the cold outside. 'You need pyjamas if you're cold.'

Helen was momentarily confused, until she saw that Megan's gaze was directed at Daniel. Helen turned back to him. He was sitting up in bed, his chest bare, the sheets pooled – thank goodness – below his waist. How had she not noticed his lack of clothes before? Had he been in bed like that all night? Was he *naked*? Helen wasn't waiting to find out. She leapt from the bed – taking care not to disturb the sheets – picked up their clothes, and whisked Megan off to get dressed.

The dining room was set out for breakfast, with

273

Tupperware boxes of muesli and cereal, and jugs of fruit juice laid out on a table along one wall. A menu on the table offered a selection of hot food cooked to order, and Mrs Kirkbride soon bustled in to offer tea or coffee.

'Did you all sleep well?' she asked, notebook poised to write down the order. 'I knew you'd be cosy up there in the eaves.'

Cosy? That was one word for it. Helen's eyes flickered over Daniel, noting the stubble darkening his chin. His eyes were fixed firmly on his muesli. He'd hardly spoken to her since they'd woken up, and they hadn't managed to make eye contact yet. Perhaps he was feeling guilty about Tasha – not that there was any reason why he should. Anyway, if he was feeling guilty, it was entirely his own fault, and there was no need to take it out on her. Her arms had stayed exactly where they should.

Lost in thought, Helen wasn't aware how much time had passed until Mrs Kirkbride placed a plate of scrambled eggs under her nose.

'That's no protection against this cold weather,' she laughed. 'You should all be on the full English.' She placed an overflowing plate in front of Daniel, and walked round to Megan, with a small plate of eggs, sausage and bacon. She ruffled Megan's hair. 'You be a good girl now, and eat all that up for your mummy and daddy, won't you?'

She walked away with a jaunty stride. Helen froze, fork in her hand, watching Megan. They had got away with it once before. Was there any chance that

274

she hadn't heard again? Daniel put down his knife and fork, waiting.

'Are you my daddy?'

Helen exchanged a look with Daniel, but the helplessness was evident in every line of his face. This wasn't the way he had planned it, and now he didn't know what to do. It was down to Helen to sort this out. She put her arm round Megan and pulled her close, kissing the top of her hair.

'Yes, he is, sweetheart. Daniel is your daddy. Is that okay?'

She didn't know why she asked that. What if Megan said no? But she didn't. Megan nodded, and picked up her fork. She looked across the table at Daniel. Helen wasn't sure if he was still breathing, as he waited for some reaction.

'I don't want a sausage. Do you want it?'

And that was it. Megan reacted to the biggest news of her life by offering her newly found father a sausage. Daniel's gaze slid over to Helen in wary confusion. She gave a shrug, and carried on with her breakfast. Though she watched Megan carefully throughout the meal, there was no sign that she was bothered by the revelation at all.

After breakfast Daniel went out to meet the breakdown company who had arrived to free his car. Helen packed up their belongings and sat on the bed with Megan until he came back. Megan was lying stretched out on her tummy, colouring a frog in a vivid shade of pink.

'Where will Danny live?' she suddenly asked.

275

Helen looked down at her anxiously. Megan hadn't paused in her colouring, and the tip of her tongue was poking out between her lips as she concentrated.

'What do you mean, sweetheart?'

'Now he's my daddy, will he be going away again?'

'No, he won't.' Helen wriggled down the bed and lay next to Megan, giving her a cuddle. It had never crossed her mind that Megan might be so used to 'Daddy' living in another country, she would assume that was normal. 'He'll be staying here, so you'll be able to see him just like you do now.'

'We don't have a bedroom for him.'

'He won't live with us.' Helen leaned over and kissed Megan's cheek, glad that Daniel wasn't around to hear and interfere with this. 'Dan... Daddy –' she corrected herself, the word feeling foreign on her tongue – 'has his own house, where he lives with Tasha. You went there last weekend, remember?' Megan nodded. Helen forced herself to go on. 'And you'll visit him there again, and sometimes you might sleep there too.'

'With you?'

Helen hesitated, and Megan glanced up. Her eyes were wide and trusting.

'No,' Helen admitted, tightening her squeeze, as unhappiness tightened its squeeze on her heart. She forced her lips to smile though it was the last thing they wanted to do. 'It will just be you, and Daddy and Tasha, but only if you want to.'

276

'Will he have the swing then?'

'I'm sure he will if we ask him.'

'Okay.' Megan smiled and turned back to her colouring. Helen watched, biting her lip until it hurt, and wondered how she could ever bear to let her go.

'So he's never mentioned the groping?' Kirsty asked.

'No. And it wasn't groping.'

'It was the closest you've come to a good grope for years, so I'd make the most of the memory if I were you.'

Helen laughed, and started constructing another cardboard box. Kirsty had come over to St Andrew's for the afternoon to help Helen go through the stock to decide what was worth taking to Church Farm. Anything too old was going to go in a pre-Christmas sale. The sale pile was already looking alarmingly large.

'Honestly, you're making it sound much more thrilling than it was.'

'Seriously? No thrill? Has he lost his touch?'

Helen turned away from Kirsty's sceptical expression, and taped the bottom of the box for extra support. Her first concern after the weekend's drama had been Megan and how she was reacting to Daniel's new status. It had been a couple of days before Helen had been reassured enough to let her mind dwell on other events, and particularly how she had felt to have Daniel's hand on her again. She couldn't deny it any longer. The truth was that she had felt nothing. Perhaps it was because she knew he had a girlfriend; although there had been enough evidence in her past to establish that her body and her brain didn't always see eye to eye in those circumstances. Perhaps it was simply that she was older, and less susceptible to desire; perhaps it had been a response to Megan's presence in the room. She couldn't explain it. Once Daniel had only needed to look at her to lure her into bed; last weekend his hand on her naked skin had elicited no reaction. Could it be her? Had it been so long since she'd felt the touch of a man that her body had forgotten what to do?

'Has he avoided you this week, so he can't be tempted again?' Kirsty carried on, when Helen refused to answer her last question.

'He took us out for a pizza last night.' Helen looked up. 'Megan has been offered a place at Broadholme. Daniel is delighted.'

'Oh, that's brilliant. Well done.'

'It has nothing to do with me.' Helen laughed. 'She didn't inherit her brains from me, and it won't be my money paying for her to go.'

'But you do want her to go, don't you? You're not letting him bully you?'

'Of course not.' Helen threw some cotton bobbins into the basket, ready for the sale. Why had she ever bought so much emerald green? 'I know Megan will love it there. And Olivia from nursery has been offered a place too, so there'll be a familiar face. It's more than she would have had at St Brendan's.'

'Did Tasha join you for the pizza?'

'No, she was busy.'

'On a Wednesday night? Doing what? Did he not invite her?'

'I didn't ask.'

'Wanted him all to yourself, did you?' Kirsty grinned and waved her hands at Helen. 'Hoping for a bit more wandering hand action...'

Helen smiled, but that wasn't the reason at all. It was almost the opposite: she hadn't asked, because she hadn't wanted Daniel to think she had any interest in the state of his relationship, or that she was imagining that one accidental grope was going to lead somewhere. And it suited her for Tasha to be absent. She had no choice but to share Megan with Daniel; it was much harder to share her with another woman. What if Daniel married Tasha, and Megan called *her* Mummy too? The very idea filled Helen with such jealousy that she hardly recognised herself.

'Didn't you go viewing a house this week?' Kirsty asked, as she lifted down a plastic box full of sewing patterns. She pulled a face as she picked out the first one. Helen could hardly blame her. In her first rush of enthusiasm for opening a shop, she had made some shocking decisions on stock purchases, desperate to fill the shelves. Their failure to sell had proved an expensive education.

'It wasn't suitable,' she replied, taking the pattern from Kirsty and adding it to the bargain pile, though she'd be amazed if she could give it away. 'It had been freshly painted, but the damp was coming through already. I should have known there was a reason why I could afford something that size.'

'How much longer have you got to find somewhere?'

'Five weeks. It will fly by, won't it? But now I'm wondering whether to try looking somewhere else. From next September, my life will be between Church Farm and Broadholme. Perhaps I should see what's available over there?'

'Worth a look,' Kirsty agreed. She smiled. 'And if you can't find anywhere, you've always got the offer of a very interesting ménage à quatre!'

'That's never going to happen.' Helen laughed. 'Can you imagine? It would be like the whole house was carpeted with eggshells.'

'I think you've been incredibly lucky the way it's gone,' Kirsty replied, sellotaping up a battered package. 'Jenny says Megan is always talking about her daddy at nursery. She seems happy. And you must admit that Daniel could have been a lot madder about finding he had a daughter he didn't know existed. His interference, I suppose, is better than indifference or worse.'

A noise in the shop made Helen spin round. Saskia was standing behind the curtain. Helen wondered how long she'd been there, and how much she had heard.

'Sorry to interrupt,' Saskia said, smiling. If she had heard any of the conversation, she wasn't giving it away. 'I wanted to check whether Kirsty is coming to the Christmas meal. I need to confirm numbers with the restaurant.'

'Yes, Ben can babysit so I'm in. Can everyone else make it?'

'Everyone except Malcolm. He's wavering.'

'Is he?' Helen said. 'He does this every year, but always turns up in the end. He can't miss the meal this year. It's supposed to be a special one to mark the end of St Andrew's. I'll go and speak to him.'

She checked that Malcolm had no customers, and went into his shop. He had marked down the price on many of his paintings, she noticed, and had put up a display of his new abstract pieces in one corner. *New Beginnings II* and *III* were hanging on the wall.

'Have you sold *New Beginnings I*?' Helen asked. It had been her favourite, and while she could never have afforded to buy it, she had selfishly hoped it would remain unsold so she could gaze at it across the Hay Barn.

'Someone reserved it at that Christmas market,' Malcolm replied, putting down his paintbrush. 'A woman. She's never been in here before.'

'That's fantastic! It shows moving to Church Farm will bring you a whole new group of customers.'

'I'm snookered if it doesn't. My regulars are getting on a bit. I've lost two good customers this year.'

'Perhaps you could offer to visit them if they're too old to get out,' Helen suggested.

'A door-to-door salesman? Not likely. Besides, they're not too old, they're too dead, and I'm not planning on visiting them there any time soon.' Malcolm smiled, apparently cheered by his morbid joke. 'Anyway, what's Saskia said now to send you flying over here? Nothing offensive, was it? There

281

seems to have been a bit of friction between you two lately.'

'Has there?' Helen hadn't noticed anything, or not more than usual, and certainly didn't think she'd been behaving differently with Saskia. Perhaps she had been distracted, and not paid Saskia enough attention? She knew Saskia could be insecure and had never quite got over being made redundant from a job at which she thought she'd excelled. Helen vowed to try harder, and glanced across to Crazy Little Things. Saskia and Kirsty were deep in conversation.

'I've come to persuade you to join us for the Christmas meal,' Helen said, turning back to Malcolm. 'It's our last St Andrew's night out. You have to be there. And don't forget,' she added, as Malcolm opened his mouth to utter what she was sure would be an excuse, 'that this year we're also celebrating Ron's and Joan's retirement and their new life together. You've worked with them for years. You can't miss out on giving them a good send off.'

'Steady on,' Malcolm replied, almost smiling. 'I'll have to check with the missus, but I daresay we'll come. Anything to avoid another dose of the hard sell. Heaven help us all at Church Farm with you and that Joel fellow organising us. Once you two get together, there won't be a moment's peace...'

282

CHAPTER 22

Helen opened the front door, and the smile which was already shaping her lips in anticipation stopped in its tracks. Joel was standing on the step, wearing a well-fitted charcoal suit and shiny shoes. She had never seen him in a suit before, only in casual clothes. His hair had escaped the smartening process, and stubborn curls caressed his ears. He looked stunning. Helen felt well and truly stunned.

'You're wearing a tie,' she said, when her brain staggered into motion again and she recovered the capacity to speak.

'I am.' Joel fingered his tie, which was decorated with splashes of red. 'Isn't that what you wear for weddings? Is this the point where you remember to tell me that there's a dress code, and it's not this?'

'No, it's just...' She laughed, unable to drag her eyes from him. 'It's silly, but I have a thing about men in ties.'

The smile that had been playing over Joel's lips – lovely wide lips, Helen noticed, as if seeing them for the first time – paused.

'A thing in that you like them, or hate them?'

'Love them. It's the thought of taking them off...'

'God help me, then, taking you to a wedding where there'll be loads of men in ties.' Joel grinned. 'Is this the real reason Kirsty backed out? Was she afraid she couldn't handle you?'

'Do you think you can?'

'I'd be more than happy to try.' The dimples deepened, and Helen laughed. 'But if you make me wait out here much longer it might be a very icy experience.'

Helen stepped aside and Joel came in. He leaned forward and kissed her cheek. It wasn't an icy experience at all. In fact, Helen felt decidedly hot. Her body seemed suddenly to have remembered in tiny detail how to react to a man, and the presence of Megan in the room behind her wasn't having any sort of dampening effect.

'You look beautiful,' Joel said as he drew back. Corroboration of his words was etched all over his face.

'What, in this old thing?' Smiling, Helen indicated her dress. It was an old one, a pre-Megan dress that she had loved so much she couldn't let it go. It had beckoned at her from the wardrobe when she had been wondering what to wear to the wedding, and luckily it had been a loose enough style that with only a few minor adjustments it fitted her post-child figure. Feeling the luxurious silk slide against her skin was like rediscovering something of her old self.

'Especially in that old thing,' Joel said. His eyes roamed over the cream silk, adorned with bold red flowers, and continued past her bare knees and down her legs. She hadn't worn so short a skirt for years, even though her legs were as slim as they had ever been, and considerably more toned, with all the running round after Megan. Joel's smile widened as his eyes landed on her red shoes. 'We co-ordinate well, don't we?'

The same thought had crossed Helen's mind when she had seen his tie. They could hardly have planned their outfits better if they had discussed them in advance. It was subtle enough to establish a connection, without being twee.

They smiled at each other, assessing.

'Mummy!' An impatient little voice floated between them. 'Can I move yet?'

Helen turned round. Megan had been confined to the sofa for the last fifteen minutes, ever since she'd put her flower-girl dress on, so she could stay clean and as uncreased as possible.

'Okay, come and put your shoes on.'

Megan rolled off the sofa and ran over. She smiled at Joel.

'Do I look as beautiful as Mummy?'

Trying to hold back his smile, Joel nodded.

'Yes, you do. Just like a little princess.'

Megan pushed her feet into her shoes, and Helen crouched down to fasten the buckles.

'My shoes are more sparkly.'

'They are very sparkly. Do you think your mummy should have worn shoes like that?'

Megan giggled.

'Her feet are too big.'

Helen wrapped Megan in a furry white bolero and pulled on her own jacket.

'Would you mind carrying the carseat?' she asked Joel.

'Sure.' He picked it up and watched as Helen grabbed a large bag. 'Did you also forget to tell me we're staying overnight?'

'You can never travel light with a child.' She gave the bag a rueful look. 'It rather ruins the attempt to look elegant, doesn't it?'

Joel regarded the pair of them, standing hand in hand in front of him, and shook his head.

'You look lovelier than ever.'

The journey to the church where Alex was to be married took almost an hour, but the time flew by. Megan loved being so high up in Joel's 4x4, and provided a commentary on what she could see all the way there. They laughed and chatted like... Helen reined in her thoughts before they could reach the finishing post. *A family* had been the words galloping through her brain, but that couldn't be right, could it? It was nerves, she told herself, making her confused, that was all.

Helen recognised the church as soon as she saw it, though the name hadn't rung any bells: she had been here before for the funeral of Daniel's father. And as she walked in through the doors, with Joel brushing against her arm on one side and Megan holding her hand on the other, and saw the faces of the other guests turn to inspect the new arrivals, she realised that it was more than the building that was familiar. How could she have been so stupid, that this hadn't occurred to her before? Alex's family

286

was Daniel's family. She had met many of these people during her time as Daniel's girlfriend, even if only briefly. They may or may not recognise her; but they would recognise Megan; they would have heard what Helen had done. The whole day had suddenly taken on a new, nightmarish hue.

As they shuffled into a pew on the bride's side of the church, Helen felt the puzzled glances flicker over her, pass on to Megan, then return to her. Was she imagining the hostile vibes? And could Joel detect them? For the first time she wished that Kirsty was with her instead. Kirsty could have supported her through this. She looked at Joel as they sat down. He smiled warmly back. Would his smile be warm if he knew? *He mustn't find out.* The thought came fast and shocked her. Why did she care so much?

Helen's mobile phone buzzed. Joel nudged her arm.

'You're supposed to switch that off!' he murmured, smiling. 'The bride must be about to arrive.'

'She is. That's my signal.' She checked the message. It was from Daniel, letting her know they were arriving at the church. He had wanted Megan to get ready at Valerie's house, and travel in with them, but Helen had refused. 'I need to take Megan to the back of the church.'

She led Megan to the door, and waited with the bridesmaids until Alex and Daniel arrived. Helen kissed Megan for luck, handed her over to two of

287

the bridesmaids, and slipped back to her seat. She turned and stood with the rest of the congregation as the bridal party walked up the aisle. Her eyes were solely on Megan, to see how she was managing with this new experience. Judging from her excited smile, she was loving it.

As Alex and Daniel drew level with their pew, Helen felt movement behind her.

'When you said it was the wedding of a family friend,' Joel said quietly in her ear, 'was the emphasis more on family than friend? Whose wedding is this?'

Helen turned her head. Joel's face was still close to hers.

'The bride is Megan's aunt.'

'And I'm guessing that's not the father of the bride walking her down the aisle? Father of the flower girl?'

Helen nodded.

'I see.'

Helen saw Joel's gaze fixed on Daniel. Daniel was wearing the full wedding regalia of dark tail coat, grey trousers and waistcoat, and a blue cravat to match the bridesmaids. The formality of the clothes suited him; he looked handsome, Helen had noticed that at once. But what did Joel see, and what was he thinking? His face, usually so sunny and easy to read, now may as well have been covered in hieroglyphics for all the sense she could make of it.

The wedding reception was taking place at a

hotel a few miles away, and the weather was so cold that after the service many of the guests took a quick snap of the bride and groom and headed straight there. Helen would have been happy to do the same, but Megan was whisked away to join the formal photographs that were being taken outside the church.

'You should have told me,' Joel said, as the number of guests diminished. Helen understood at once what he meant.

'I'm sorry,' she said. 'It wasn't deliberate. I wasn't keeping it a secret. It's... awkward.'

It was an inadequate word, but she didn't have time to think of a better one, in her haste to reassure Joel.

'So that's Megan's dad,' he continued, watching as another family group was arranged. 'They're alike, aren't they?'

'Yes.'

'And is the dream girlfriend still around?'

'Yes, she's over there, by the old lady in the wheelchair.'

'Hmm.' Joel's gaze swivelled towards Tasha. She was wrapped up in a long cream wool coat, and looked thoroughly miserable. 'She doesn't look like she's enjoying the dream today.' He reached out and gently brushed his fingers against Helen's. 'It can't be easy for you either, being stuck out on the fringe, with people you were once close to.'

'It doesn't matter. I'm only here for Megan.'

'And I'm here for you. Friends, remember?' His

289

fingers were still touching hers, and that feather-light contact was warming Helen's entire body. 'How can I help if you don't tell me what's going on?'

'Mummy! Did you see me?' Megan ran up and clutched Helen's hand, pulling her attention away from Joel. 'I'm in lots of photos.'

'I know, and you'll look very beautiful in them.' Helen stroked Megan's hair, noticing that she had brought a line of attendants with her: Daniel, followed by Tasha and Valerie, with Alex and Phil bringing up the rear.

'Am I still as beautiful as Mummy?' Megan asked Joel. He laughed.

'Just as beautiful, and twice as sparkly.'

Daniel looked Joel up and down silently.

'Where's Kirsty?' he asked, his eyes boring into Helen.

'At home.'

'Your plus one is Kirsty. It said so on the RSVP. It says so on the table plan, and on the place card next to yours.'

'Sorry. There was a change of plan. I've come with Joel.' Helen smiled at Alex. 'I would have told you, but I guessed it was too late to change anything.'

'I should have brought a name badge,' Joel said. 'I promise not to mind if you call me Kirsty by mistake.'

Alex laughed.

'You're not Kirsty.' Megan giggled. 'You're Joel!

290

Daddy, don't call him Kirsty!'

Judging by his expression, and the clouds of hostility hovering over him, Kirsty was not the name Daniel was currently christening Joel in his head. Even the 'Daddy' didn't seem to soften him.

'Haven't we been lucky with the weather?' Valerie said, in an obvious bid to disperse the clouds. 'After all the snow last weekend, I was worried that some of the guests might not make it. Either that, or be stranded here once they'd arrived. We don't want any more adventures like yours last weekend, do we, Megan? It must have been very cold for you all out in the snow.'

'I cuddled Mr Cat to keep warm.'

'Did you?' Valerie smiled down at Megan. 'That was very sensible.'

'And Daddy cuddled Mummy.'

They were never to hear whether Valerie thought that was very sensible too. A heavy pause followed Megan's announcement, which was broken by a noise from Tasha which could equally have been a sob or a snort of rage. She stormed away into the graveyard. Daniel, prodded into action by his mother, followed her.

'Phil, you must introduce me to your grandparents before the meal,' Valerie said, and drew Alex and Phil off with her. Helen looked at Joel. He seemed wholly engrossed with the cars turning round on the narrow lane outside the church.

'It wasn't quite how that sounded,' Helen told

291

him. 'Daniel's car became stuck in the snow on the way back from Birmingham and we had to book into a B&B...'

'You don't need to explain.' Joel turned back to her. He wasn't smiling, and disappointment hung like voile over his face. 'It's one of the chief rules of friendship. Never judge.'

'There was only one family room left, and we had to share a bed,' Helen ploughed on, determined to make her confession. There was plenty he might judge her for, but not this, not when she was entirely blameless. 'Neither of us chose it. When I woke up, Daniel's arm was over me. He must have been dreaming about Tasha.' Joel's eyebrows twitched, as if he wasn't as convinced of this as Helen. 'Tasha will understand,' she added. 'Nothing happened. Megan was in the same room all night.'

'Is that the only reason why nothing happened?'

'No, of course not. We were both horrified. We haven't been together for years.'

They stood in the cold churchyard, looking at each other. Slowly a smile began to curl Joel's lips, a semi-skimmed version of his usual smile, but Helen had never been so glad to see it.

'Kirsty knew what she was doing, missing this, didn't she? Come on, let's go and see what trouble you can cause at the reception.'

Helen was very grateful that Alex had placed her, Megan and Joel on a table of friends, not family, and a good distance away from the top table. There were a couple of other children with them, and Megan instantly made friends with a girl in the next seat, who was a year or two older. All the children had been given activity packs to amuse them through the meal.

The other girl's mother leaned across and introduced herself as Debbie.

'How old is she?' Debbie asked, nodding at Megan. 'Three? Four?'

'She was four in September.'

'Just started school then?'

'No, she was a couple of days too young, so she'll go next September.'

'Make the most of this last year,' Debbie smiled. 'They're never the same once they start school. It's the beginning of the end.'

'Is it?' Helen didn't know whether to laugh or be alarmed. 'In what way?'

'They stop being so entirely yours. School and friends begin to assert their influence. They learn to be independent and less in need of their mothers.' Debbie laughed. 'It's tough. I have two teenagers at home. I couldn't stand becoming redundant, and persuaded Paddy to start again with these two. Perhaps you'll need to do the same,' she added, with a wink and a gesture at Joel. 'Or maybe you'll enjoy having more time together again!'

Helen was too dazed to correct the assumption. She looked down at Megan and felt a chill at the prospect of the baby years coming to a close. She'd never thought about the future, other than in practical terms of deciding which school to choose. But it was true: Megan was growing up, and slowly she would come to need Helen less than she did now. What would Helen do then? She was never going to need less of Megan. She had nothing – no one – to fill the chasm that time would stretch between them.

Alex had organised a crèche to run throughout the reception, and when the meal was over, one of the helpers came to gather up any children who wanted to avoid the speeches. Helen had expected Megan to stay with her, but as soon as her new friend announced her intention to go to the crèche, Megan was desperate to go too, and happily wandered away without a backward glance. It was a painful confirmation of all that Debbie had said.

Daniel gave the first speech, and was suitably complimentary about the bride and groom. He held the audience effortlessly with a mix of authority and charm.

'You all know, or realise, that I'm standing here in the shoes of the man who ought to have given Alex away,' he concluded, letting his hand rest momentarily on Alex's shoulder. 'But although our father isn't with us today, I know what he would have wanted to say. He would have been delighted to welcome Phil as a new member of our family...' For a second, he hesitated. 'And to wish them many happy years of marriage, and that together they can experience the utter joy –' and here his voice

definitely wobbled, '– of having their own children.'
He paused and, without needing to search the
room, his eyes darted straight to Helen. She wasn't
close enough to see their expression. The pause
lengthened, and one table applauded. Alex reached
for Daniel's hand.

'To the bride and groom, Alex and Phil!' he
concluded.

The guests all rose to join the toast.

'Great speech,' Joel murmured, leaning towards
Helen. She nodded, and took a large gulp of
champagne.

When the speeches were over, the guests started
to mingle. Helen was rising to go and check on
Megan when Joel put out a hand to stop her.

'I heard what Debbie was saying to you earlier,
about how Megan will change when she starts school.
Don't take it too much to heart. You looked as though
she'd convinced you the world was about to end.'

'Mine will.'

Her face must have reflected her misery, because
Joel reached out and gently swept his fingers across
her bare arm. The tickling sensation was so acute it
was almost painful.

'She's going to need you for a long time yet.'

'I know.' Helen moved her arm away and topped
up her glass. 'But when she doesn't, what will I
have then?'

'A great business? An incredible talent?' He
smiled. 'Are you fishing for compliments? Because I
can think of plenty more if you are.'

Helen smiled back, and turned in her seat so her knees were touching Joel's.

'The business might not be so great by then if it doesn't work out at Church Farm.'

'Of course it's going to work out. We'll make sure it does.' That 'we' made Helen's heart float several inches higher in her chest. 'Next week do you want to make a start on your new website? I've had some ideas of how it might look, but we need to go over it together.'

'Are you sure you have time? I know how busy you are, and there's no hurry. It's been terrible for so long, I'm sure a few more weeks won't matter.'

'There is a hurry. Don't forget our deal. We have to sort it out before Christmas, so I can choose my three gifts from your shop.'

Helen laughed and, on impulse, she stretched across and kissed his cheek. His skin was warm and smelt deliciously woody. 'Thanks, Joel.'

'Helen.' Helen felt herself yanked back by the sudden sound of Daniel's voice. He was standing on the other side of the table, frowning. All the other guests at their table had gone. 'Where's Megan?'

'She's at the crèche.'

'Why did you send her there?' His frown expanded to a scowl. Helen caught a movement behind her as Joel's arm stretched out across the back of her chair. 'If you wanted to get rid of her, you could have brought her to me.'

'I would never get rid of her. You know that very well.'

'Do I? It seems to me that I'm the last to know everything.' His eyes swept over Joel's arm.

Helen stood up. She didn't want to have this row in front of Joel. She didn't want to row at all. She couldn't think of anything she had done to make Daniel so annoyed with her today. Perhaps Tasha had been giving him a hard time since Megan's little revelation earlier, but that was hardly Helen's fault; she hadn't wanted Megan to disclose that any more than he had. But if his mood was as dark as his face suggested, who knew what he might go on to say next, and what further revelations Joel might hear? She couldn't risk it.

'I'm going to check on Megan now,' she said.

'I'm coming.'

'There's no...'

'Yes, there is.'

Daniel walked towards the doors. Helen turned to Joel, who was standing behind her. He smiled, though there was confusion and concern in his eyes.

'Everything okay?' he asked. Helen nodded.

'I won't be long. I'll see if she wants to stay or come back out.'

She hurried after Daniel and caught up with him at the door of the room which had been turned into a crèche. All the children were sitting on the floor while an entertainer wrestled with a puppet of a hairy green frog. Megan was in fits of giggles. One of the helpers came over.

'Have you come for Megan?' she asked. 'Do you want to take her?'

'Yes,' Daniel replied.

'Not if she's happy here,' Helen said. 'How has she been?'

'She's loving it, don't worry. We're doing party games and a disco after this.'

'She needs to come out. My family want to see her.'

Daniel went over to Megan and spoke to her. Helen couldn't hear the reply, but the way Megan emphatically shook her head was clear enough.

'She won't leave.' Daniel was frowning again. 'You'd better speak to her.'

Helen had a quick word with Megan and returned to Daniel.

'She's staying here. It's what she wants.'

'Some of my family haven't met her yet.'

'Daniel, she's four. Of course she'd rather enjoy a party than be passed around people she doesn't know.'

'And is this what you've taught her? That life is all about parties? And I was beginning to believe that you might have grown up at last. Why is it that she doesn't know my family? Remember that.'

Helen walked out. Remember? Even if her own conscience had let her forget, he wouldn't. He had called for a truce, but clearly his anger was so shallowly buried that even the slightest breeze would expose it. If he couldn't let it be at his sister's wedding, he never would. What had set him off today? Was it simply that she had brought Joel instead of Kirsty? Alex hadn't minded the change,

298

so why should he? Unless... No. He wasn't jealous, was he? Surely that was impossible?

She went into the ladies, and as she was washing her hands, she looked up and saw Tasha's face reflected in the mirror behind her. The contrast between them was stark. Despite Helen's skilfully applied make-up, despite the sadness radiating from Tasha, Helen could never compete with Tasha's freshness and her natural glow of health. Tasha was gorgeous. Of course it was impossible.

'Danny swears nothing happened in Birmingham,' Tasha said, catching Helen's eye in the mirror. 'Is that true?'

Helen picked up a paper towel and dried her hands. She turned and looked straight at Tasha.

'Yes.'

'Did you want it to? Do you want him back? I need to know, because if you do, I can't win. You have Megan.'

Was it really that simple, Helen wondered? Could she have Daniel back? Could Megan be the salve that brought them back together, and healed all the angry wounds between them? Wasn't that exactly what she had longed for over the years apart and hoped for since his return? But instead of a burst of happiness she felt... uncertain. She hesitated, though she couldn't put her finger on why she did. Perhaps it was because she had spent five years convincing herself that it could never happen. Perhaps it just felt wrong to celebrate the idea in front of his girlfriend, who had followed him across the world. Or perhaps... the memory of warm skin and a woody scent drifted through her mind.

'I'm not trying to take him back,' she told Tasha. It didn't answer the question, but then she didn't have an answer. She had no idea what she wanted; and the fact that she didn't know – that every nerve fibre didn't immediately cry out that of course she wanted Daniel back – confused her more than ever.

Helen went back to the reception. Daniel was on one side of the room, without Megan, she was relieved to see, charming some guests as if a cross word had never passed his lips. Joel was on the other side, in an animated conversation with two women. He looked over at her, and with a quick word to the ladies, headed across the room to join her.

'Is Megan having fun?' Helen nodded. Joel smiled. 'Good. Come with me and meet these ladies. One of them works for *Lancashire Life.* I'm trying to persuade her to carry a feature on Church Farm.'

'I'm not sure how I can help.'

'You can. I need you. Tell them your story, how you set up your business to support Megan and have survived despite the recession. Tell them about crazy patchwork, how fantastic it is, and how it can be a piece of art. Convince them that sewing isn't only for old ladies, and that it can appeal to gorgeous young women, too. Show them... What?' He stopped. 'Why are you looking at me like that?'

Helen had no idea what her face was doing. She was too dazzled by his words, and the passion with which he was speaking. Was that how Joel saw her? A successful businesswoman? A gorgeous young woman? An equal, who could offer him help? No one had ever described her the way he did. She wanted to be the Helen that Joel saw. And knowing he viewed her like that gave her confidence to be that Helen. So she let him take her hand and lead her over, and together they set out to prove that Church Farm deserved an article in *Lancashire Life*.

The discussion went well, and ended with the journalist taking Joel's number and promising to be in touch.

'If this happens, it will be amazing,' Joel said. Delight spilled onto every feature. 'You were brilliant.' He stepped towards Helen, rested his hand on her waist, and kissed her softly on the cheek. The woody scent of him embraced her senses again. 'Thanks.'

'Don't say thanks until you know if she rings.' Though Helen didn't doubt it. She felt the same delight as Joel, and the intoxicating buzz of a job done well. 'Or rather, see if she rings about the article, and not just to see *you* again.'

Joel laughed. He was standing so close that the sound vibrated down Helen's body. 'I'm only interested in her journalistic skills.' He looked over Helen's shoulder. 'The evening reception seems to have started. Thank God I can get this off now.'

301

He raised his hands to his tie. Helen skipped a breath.

'Don't.'

'Does it have to stay on? There are men arriving with no ties.'

'Let me. I have a special way.'

Her mouth was operating independently from her brain. She hadn't planned to say that but, now she had, she felt it had been inevitable since the moment she had first seen Joel on her doorstep.

'Now this I have to experience.' Joel smiled, and his hands fell back down to his side. Without breaking eye contact, and with her head so close to his that their breath mingled, Helen ran her fingers round his collar and drew off his tie, inch by teasing inch. She let the column of silk slither between her hands, and reached up to undo the top button.

'Promise me you're not going to offer to do that to anyone else here,' Joel said. His voice sounded odd, and his eyes glittered, the pupils wide and dark. 'There might be riots.'

Helen laughed, then realised that her fingers were automatically unfastening the second button too. She stopped, and took her hands away. Joel's eyes were still on hers.

'Sorry to interrupt,' Daniel said, sounding anything but. 'I need to speak to you, Helen.'

'Now?'

'Yes.'

'Is something wrong with Megan?'

302

He was already striding away, giving Helen no choice but to follow, after a quick apology to Joel. Daniel led her out of the reception room, but to her confusion, turned the opposite way from the crèche, then whirled round to confront her.

'What about Megan?' she asked, when all he did was glare at her, his breath heavy.

'So you do remember her? She's fine. I've checked.'

'What's all this about? What's the problem?'

'It's not Megan. It's him.'

'Who?'

'Joel.' Daniel spat the name. 'How far does his plus-one role stretch? Does he stay at your house? Does he stay when Megan is there?'

If he didn't look so furious, Helen would have laughed at how ridiculous this was.

'Of course not,' she said, trying to sound calm. 'He's never stayed. It isn't like that.'

'So you say. That's not what I saw. It's quite obvious from the way he looks at you what he wants.'

'Is it a crime to find me attractive? Don't be so hypocritical. Are you going to send Tasha off to a hotel if Megan ever stays at your house?'

'*When* she stays. It isn't the same. What sort of example are you setting Megan by having random men to stay over?'

Helen's hands flew up in frustration.

'For God's sake, Dan, will you listen to yourself? I've told you Joel has never stayed over. The only

303

man who has ever stayed in the house with us is Adam, and I hardly think you can object to her uncle visiting. How dare you suggest I'm corrupting her? I've given up everything to be the best mother I can for Megan. What more do you want from me? Christ, I've not had sex for five years, not since the morning you left...'

Helen caught a sound and saw Joel emerge into the corridor. She could tell from his expression that he'd heard at least the last part of the conversation. Daniel didn't notice, and Joel turned and went back to the reception.

'You're planning on changing that tonight, aren't you?' Daniel ploughed on. 'The thing with the tie...'

'No! But what business is it of yours if I did?'

'It's my business if it affects Megan. She's still getting used to me. I don't want you to confuse her by introducing another man.'

And there was the truth of it. How could Helen have been so stupid, even for a second, to think that Daniel might have been jealous because of her? It was Megan's affection he was concerned about, her feelings he was jealous over, not Helen's. How could she blame him, when she had felt exactly the same about Tasha? She shook her head, sadness taking over from the anger.

'Don't you understand, Dan? Don't you see why there hasn't been anyone else for five years? Megan only has one father. I wouldn't let anyone take your place while you were away. Now you're back, no

304

one can. Whatever happens in my life in the future, that won't change. She's yours. She'll always be yours.'

Daniel looked as if he was about to say something more, but Helen didn't wait to listen. She went to the crèche, promised Megan a final fifteen minutes, and returned to the reception to tell Joel they were almost ready to go. He approached as soon as she stepped foot in the room.

'Friendly hug?' he asked. Surprised, she nodded, and he pulled her into him, wrapping strong arms round her as he held her to his chest. It was innocent and brief, and reached way down inside her. It was the closest contact she'd had with another person, other than Megan, for so long. Her family weren't huggers. Daniel had never embraced her in so chaste a way. But everything she tried to offer Megan in a hug – affection, comfort, support – she felt flowing from Joel.

'So,' he said, letting her go before she was ready for the hug to end. 'The elephant in the room. Five years? You know I believed you that nothing happened last weekend. You didn't need to go to such lengths to convince me.'

'It doesn't make me desperate.'

He laughed. 'I never thought you were. But five years? A slight exaggeration, surely? I mean, Megan's only four.'

Helen shrugged, and slid her eyes away from his.

'Perhaps,' she said. 'I told you we've not been together for a long time. Daniel's been away. He

305

only came back recently. It's all... strange.'

Joel touched her chin and gently turned her face back to meet his.

'Have I said before how amazing you are?' he asked. 'You've been on your own for so long, and still you're forgiving enough to get involved in all this, and let him be close to Megan. I've never met anyone so incredible.'

If Helen was ever going to tell him the truth, here was the moment. The door was open, the way ahead well lit and clearly signposted. But did she have to take it? A lovely, kind, handsome man was smiling at her, and telling her she was amazing; and it was such a long time since she had felt like this. She couldn't know how he would react if she told him everything; perhaps he would understand. But there was always the risk that he might not. She didn't want to take the risk. She wanted to hold on to this feeling, to revel in it, for a few moments more. So she said nothing, and the door slammed shut.

CHAPTER 23

First thing on Monday morning, Helen began a fresh tour of the estate agents and lettings companies, investigating whether there might be a better supply of rental properties around Church Farm or Broadholme. She was an amazing, incredible businesswoman, she reminded herself, still glowing from Joel's words. She could do this.

By the time she had dragged a complaining Megan into the sixth or seventh office, where she was offered a flat above a betting shop or a rundown mid-terraced house with a backyard and not even a blade of grass to fasten a swing to, her confidence was ready to fizzle out. Everything was too big, too small, too expensive, or simply too horrible to consider. And then she saw it, on the corner of the desk, almost hidden by the agent's elbow: a picture of the perfect stone cottage.

'What's this?' she asked, leaning over the desk and whisking away the sheet of paper. 'Pleasant View Cottage, Crofters Fold', she read. The same village as Church Farm! Surely that had to be some sort of fate? She turned the paper over, but there were no other details. 'Is this available for rent?'

'It will be,' the agent said, trying to regain the paper without any success. 'It's a new instruction. We haven't taken interior pictures yet, or discussed the rental price with the owner.'

'Can I see it?' Helen studied the photograph. It didn't look a large house, but based on what she had been shown so far today, it would probably end up outside her price range. Still, it looked friendly and welcoming, and it appealed to her in a way that no other property had since her search began. She couldn't not see it.

'Leave me your details and I'll get in touch with the owner, to see if they're accepting viewings yet.'

'Can you ring them now? I'm off work today. It would be a perfect time to view. And think how impressed the owner would be if you found them a tenant before the place was even on the market!'

Laughing, the agent tried calling the owner, but there was no answer. Helen extracted a promise that he would keep trying and reluctantly left, sneaking the photograph of the cottage out with her. She took Megan to a nearby café for lunch, intending to pop back in to see the agent on her return to the car, but such tactics proved unnecessary. He phoned her while she was still in the café, confirming that she could view the cottage that afternoon. Helen left at once.

If Helen had been infatuated with the picture, it was love at first sight as soon as she saw the cottage. She parked her car on the lane outside, and gazed out of the window in silent admiration. The left hand of a pair of mirror-image semi-detached cottages, bark-coloured stone walls rose with reassuring solidity to meet a slate roof. Helen couldn't find a fault. The low stone wall at the front of the cottage, the well-stocked front garden promising discoveries of colour as the seasons passed, the porch covering the front door... It was perfect. If only the garden had room for a swing...

She dragged Megan up the front path, but before she could ring the bell the door opened and Joel stepped out, smiling.

'What are you doing here?' she asked.

'I was told there was a demanding woman who insisted on viewing the cottage today, and wouldn't take no for an answer.' He grinned, amused not annoyed, but Helen cringed all the same. Perhaps she had been rather insistent.

'So this is your house?' She was sure the agent had mentioned a retired couple – when she had let him speak.

'No, it belongs to Church Farm, and so my parents. These used to be agricultural workers' cottages. My parents are out for the day so couldn't do the viewing.'

'I'm sorry, I didn't mean to drag you away from work. You should have said no.'

'Jimmy was concerned you might stage a sit-in at his office if I did. And he kindly pointed out that I'm never likely to have such a gorgeous woman so desperate to see me again. He's an old friend,' Joel explained, laughing.

'And it just turned out to be me,' Helen said, scuffing at some moss on the York stone path, not looking up.

'Yes. When he mentioned your name, I knew he wasn't exaggerating for the first time in his life. And now you've distracted me from my sales pitch. My parents would not be happy.' He leaned forward and kissed her cheek, warm lips against her cold skin. 'Welcome to Pleasant View Cottage. Find it okay?'

'Yes,' Helen replied, determined to concentrate on the assets of the house, not the man on the doorstep. 'I hadn't even noticed this lane before. Where does it go?'

'There are two other houses further on, and a working farm at the end. It's a quiet lane, and you'll see more tractors going up and down than cars. Although,' he added, bending down to speak to Megan, 'in spring and summer you can watch the cows parading along here to move between the field and the farm.'

Megan looked at Helen with excited eyes. The mention of passing cows had clearly won her support for this house.

'Why the name?' Helen asked. A high hedge ran along the side of the lane opposite the cottages. 'Was that hedge not here when they chose it?'

Joel laughed. 'When you've been round the back, you won't need to ask. What do you want to see first? House or garden?'

'House,' she said firmly, fearing that if she was seduced by the garden at the outset she might be tempted to overlook all manner of horrors inside.

'Wander round by yourselves,' Joel said, standing back.

Helen needn't have worried. The inside was as perfect as the outside. There was a hall from which

310

stairs led up to two double bedrooms and a new white bathroom. Downstairs there was a living room with a wood-burning stove, and a large dining-kitchen stretched across the back of the house. Off the kitchen another door opened to... Helen gasped.

'This used to be the bathroom,' Joel said, coming up behind her. 'We had it moved upstairs into the smallest bedroom. So this can be a study, or utility, or...'

'A sewing room,' Helen finished. 'This would be a fantastic sewing room.' She stepped forward, picturing instantly how the room would be set up, with storage shelves on one wall, and a table for her sewing machine under the window. Although perhaps that wouldn't be the most productive idea, she thought, as she gazed out of the window. How would she ever keep her eyes off that view?

'Can we go out to the garden?' She couldn't wait any longer, and Joel opened the French doors in the kitchen. Megan didn't hesitate. She took one look at the expanse of flat lawn rolling a good thirty metres ahead of them, squealed, and set off running down the grass to the fence at the far end, her plaits flying out from beneath her hat. Helen couldn't blame her. She felt like doing the same herself – and then she thought, why not? So she ran after Megan – without the squeal – and caught her in a hug as they reached the fence. Megan giggled, her cheeks flushed pink and her eyes shimmering with happiness. Helen kissed her, inhaling her simple joy, and vowed on the spot that they had to rent this house, whatever it cost. She would take in alterations, sew every hour of the night until her fingers bled, do anything to make this happiness last.

'Don't scare the animals, will you?' Joel joined them, laughing. Both Helen and Megan stared over the fence. The land on the other side sloped down in a patchwork of fields, meadows and woods and into a valley, before the hills rose again in the distance. In the valley, a reservoir sparkled silver in the winter sun.

'Sheep!' Megan said, climbing up onto the fence for a better look. Helen noticed for the first time a group of sheep huddling together on the far side of the field. She felt Joel move behind her.

'What do you think of the view?' he asked. 'Pleasant enough?'

'Yes.' Pleasant hardly covered it. 'It's absolutely beautiful.'

She turned and smiled at him. The wind was ruffling the curls round his face. The view wasn't bad in this direction either.

'Wow,' she said, as her gaze fell on the back of the cottages. 'Look at the house next door!'

The cottages had been identical from the front. Helen now saw that the one attached to hers – she was thinking of it that way already – had a modern aluminium and glass extension wrapped across the back and round to the side where Helen's sewing room was in the other cottage. It opened up the whole of the downstairs to make the most of the view.

'Do your parents own that one as well?' she asked.

'Yes. It's already rented out.'

'Oh God.' Helen laughed. 'I knew there had to be a catch. Don't tell me it's the family from hell next door. A dozen noisy dogs, all-night parties, teenage boys ogling out of the window...'

'No dogs, no all night parties, and no teenage boys. I live there.' His smile grew cheeky. 'I can't promise not to ogle though.'

'*You* live there?' Helen pointed at the neighbouring cottage, as if there could be any doubt where he meant. 'Next door?'

'Yes. Is that a problem?'

Was it? Helen couldn't decide. Would this bind their lives too closely together? Would it be awkward to live side by side, aware of every coming and going, seeing him bring girlfriends home... That idea gave her an uncomfortable twinge. Daniel wouldn't like it, she was certain. She watched as Megan jumped down from the fence, climbed straight back up, and launched herself off again. She was the only one who mattered. Helen caught her.

'What do you think, Megan?' she asked, hoisting her up so their faces were level. 'Would you like to live here?'

Megan nodded.

'I can have a swing,' she said. Helen smiled and kissed her. She could have a swing if Helen could find the money. And thinking of money... Could this really be within her budget? Not everyone would like the rural setting, but the house was so much better than anything she had seen. She had been entirely

313

seduced, and if the rent was too high she would be devastated.

'Do you know how much your parents will charge for rent?' she asked Joel, nibbling the inside of her cheek and bracing herself for the answer.

'I spoke to them earlier. They'll take the same as I pay. £400 a month.'

'Seriously?' It was less than she was paying now, and well below the market rate.

'Yes. You get a discount as a gallery tenant, and Jimmy has waived any agency fees as he didn't actually introduce you to the property before you snatched it off his desk.'

'That's fantastic. Will you let your parents know that I'll definitely take it?'

'With pleasure.'

His warm smile washed over her, and Helen felt tears prick her eyes and tickle the back of her nose. She buried her face in a cuddle with Megan. She hadn't appreciated until now quite how stressed she had been about finding somewhere to live. The relief was dizzying. And beyond the relief lurked an unexpected sense of pride. She had faced a crisis, and found a solution, without help from her father, her brother or Daniel. She was an amazing, incredible businesswoman. She whispered Joel's words to herself. Perhaps it was time to start believing it.

The doors had closed on St Andrew's for the final time as a shopping destination. The shops stood empty, waiting to be ripped out. The entire contents of Crazy Little Things had been packed away in boxes and was now sitting in a van outside Helen's house, waiting to go to Church Farm the next day, where it would be stored until the Hay Barn opened in the New Year. Helen was desperately trying to focus on the practical arrangements, to keep the emotion at bay.

Malcolm was the first to threaten her mascara, when they all met up at a town centre restaurant to celebrate Christmas and the end of St Andrew's.

'Fourteen years I had that shop,' he said, and for once Helen forgave him his air of gloom. 'It got me through some bad times.'

Helen reached out and squeezed his hand. His son had suffered brain damage at birth as a result of a botched delivery, and had died in his late teens. Malcolm had given up his job and become a painter after that.

'You'll do brilliantly at Church Farm,' she assured him. 'A fresh start will revitalise all of us.'

'I thought we were snookered when we had that letter about St Andrew's closing. Thought I'd have to retire. I'm not sure what our Brenda would have made of that.' He cast a fond look at his wife Brenda, who was talking to Joan. Helen had seen them together often enough to know that Brenda would have been thrilled to see more of Malcolm. 'That young man has given us all a lifeline. I'd have been proud if our Jamie had grown up like him.'

'What young man?'

Malcolm was too choked to speak, and nodded his

315

head in the direction of the entrance to the restaurant. Joel had walked in, with Saskia at his side. They were laughing. Joel looked delicious. Saskia looked delighted. Delighted, and very smug. She immediately sought out Helen and smiled. Helen didn't know what to make of that smile. Was it a friendly greeting, or was there a hint of triumph? Helen shook the thought from her head. Surely Saskia could only feel triumphant if there was some competition between them? And there wasn't. They weren't competing over anything – or anyone. Or Helen hadn't thought they were.

'I didn't know Santa's little helper was coming tonight,' Kirsty whispered in Helen's ear.

'Neither did I.' But why should she have known? He didn't have to tell her if he was having a date with Saskia. And Saskia was certainly dressed for a date. Her bodycon dress barely covered her breasts and her bottom. Helen glanced down at herself. She was wearing the dress she had made for Craig's party several months ago. Though she knew that Saskia was at least three years older than her, and though she had felt confident in her appearance when she left the house, she now wondered whether in fact she looked dull and – the dreaded word – mumsy.

'You look totally hot,' Kirsty whispered, reading Helen's mind. 'So does he. I can see why you wouldn't mind him filling your stocking.'

'Kirsty!' Helen laughed. 'I've never said that.'

'Not in words, maybe, but your face is saying it loud and clear.'

Was it? Helen tried to channel a neutral

expression, but she caught Joel's eye for the first time, and his smile openly grew. It was impossible not to smile back at those dimples.

'Hmm,' Kirsty murmured. 'That settles it. He has a special smile for you. He doesn't dimple me. I wonder what other parts of his body react in a special way to you.'

'Stop it!' Helen reached for her glass, laughing, and tried to ignore the *Carry On* winks Kirsty was sending her way.

'You two sound full of the Christmas spirit already,' Joel said. He crouched down between Helen and Kirsty, his hand resting on the back of Helen's chair. 'How many bottles behind am I?'

'It's a Christmas party. It's against the rules to count,' Helen replied. 'And surely you know that ladies are only ever jolly, not drunk.'

'You're drinking tonight?' He took the glass from Helen's hand and had a sip, grimacing as he tasted the vodka. Helen felt a pang. Daniel loved vodka almost as much as she did. They had bonded over a bottle of Konik's Tail on the night they had met. 'Not driving, then?'

'No. Another unbreakable rule. Taxis are essential expenditure for a Christmas party.'

'I wish I'd known. I'd have worn a tie again.'

The combination of the look in his eyes, the smile and the vodka was deadly. Helen looked at Kirsty for rescue.

'Do you want to sit down?' Kirsty asked Joel. 'I can move.'

That wasn't the response Helen had been hoping for. Joel looked tempted for a second.

'Better not,' he said, his grin turning rueful. 'Bad form not to sit with a date, isn't it? And she already looks ready to box my ears for turning up late.'

So it was a date! Helen looked at Saskia. She was stealing glances their way, but Helen would have put money on her wanting to spank Joel's bottom rather than box his ears. And perhaps she'd be doing just that later. Helen took a large gulp of vodka, feeling abruptly sober.

'I'll catch you later,' Joel said, and briefly Helen thought his fingers brushed her shoulder. He went round the table, in the opposite direction to Saskia, and greeted Joan with a kiss and a hug. Joan shook her head at him, and tapped her watch. Joel laughed and took the empty seat next to his aunt.

'Interesting,' Kirsty whispered, as the menus were finally handed round.

Helen ignored her, and picked up the conversation with Malcolm again, but Kirsty was not easily deterred when she was on a mission, and tonight she seemed determined to make Helen her mission.

'Shall we move around between courses?' she suggested, as the plates were cleared from the starters. She stood up. 'Every other person, grab your cutlery and glass, and move two spaces along.' The amazing thing about Kirsty was that she was such a force of nature, no one thought to disobey. The relevant people started to move. Kirsty and Malcolm collided behind Helen. 'Anti-clockwise!' Kirsty bellowed.

Everyone obligingly moved the opposite way. Helen looked round, making a quick calculation. She was about to be joined by Saskia for the main course, Ron's daughter for dessert, and Joel for coffee.

'Good plan, isn't it?' Kirsty said in Helen's ear, as she settled herself down on Helen's right. 'You can thank me later.'

Only if she survived the next course, Helen reflected, as she watched Saskia sit down reluctantly beside her. Judging by her expression, Saskia had worked out all the next moves too, and she hadn't planned on lingering over coffee with Ron.

'That's a great dress,' Helen said, determined to make an effort.

'Thanks.' Saskia smiled. 'I'm lucky I have the figure for it. Everything is still in the right place.' Her gaze flicked briefly over Helen. 'Where is Megan tonight?'

'At home. My brother has come up to help move everything to the Hay Barn, so he's babysitting. You probably saw him at St Andrew's this afternoon.'

'Yes, I did. I haven't seen any of your family before. Don't you get on?'

'They live a long way away,' Helen replied, forking in a large mouthful of risotto to excuse not saying more.

'You're from Surrey, aren't you?' Helen nodded. 'What brought you up here? A man? Megan's father? You never mention him.'

'There's nothing to say. We're not together anymore.'

319

'What happened?'

Helen stared at Saskia. Why the sudden interest in her history?

'We drifted apart.' With the help of an aeroplane, but she was hardly going to admit that to Saskia.

'Did you?' Something about Saskia's tone made Helen look at her sharply, but her smile was sympathetic. 'And do you still see much of him? I suppose you have to, for Megan?'

'Yes.' Helen grabbed her glass of wine, and tried to turn to Kirsty, but Saskia reached out and touched her arm.

'Is there no chance of the two of you getting back together? It would be the ideal solution for Megan, surely?'

'No. He has a new partner now.'

Helen turned in her seat, and talked across the table to Joan. After about five minutes, as Helen pushed her empty plate away, she felt Saskia lean in towards her.

'Are you dating at the moment?' she asked. 'We never have chance to discuss it at St Andrew's.'

This wasn't true: they had hours without customers, but Helen had never felt inclined to discuss her private life with Saskia. She didn't now. She might be making the most of her night out, but she wasn't *that* drunk.

'No.'

'It's tough, isn't it, trying to find a man who wants commitment.'

Helen made a discouraging noise. It had no effect.

320

'Most of the ones I meet don't even seem interested in having their own children, never mind taking on someone else's cast offs. I'd never thought about how much harder it must be for you, until the other day.'

'What do you mean?' Helen asked, unable to stop herself.

Saskia smiled.

'I'm probably not meant to repeat it...' She glanced round, and her eyes lingered on Joel. She leaned closer to Helen, and lowered her voice. 'Someone told me that he'd backed away from a potential relationship, because he couldn't stand the way the child was always tagging along. Awful, isn't it? But you know what men are like. They think there's no freedom and spontaneity left when children are around. But why should it matter if you have to rush off straight after pudding tonight? Don't let it get you down. I'm sure there are some men out there who wouldn't mind at all. You'll find one, one day.'

Intentionally or not, Saskia's words plunged straight into the heel of Helen's newly awoken confidence and deflated it. She looked across at Joel, hoping for a smile to revive her, but he was busy talking to Malcolm's wife. He had hardly glanced her way all night, though she had been conscious of his every move. Through the thickening haze of alcohol clogging her head, she replayed Saskia's words, and recalled the significant glance Saskia had given Joel before making her

321

revelation. Had she been talking about *Joel*? Was Joel the person who had backed away from a relationship because of a child? And if so, had Helen been the other half of the relationship, and Megan the cast-off child? Stung by the apparent betrayal, she dashed to the bathroom, wishing she could stay there through the next two courses.

By the time she emerged, the next shuffle had taken place, and although she was still next to Saskia, Malcolm was regaling her with a gloomy tale across the table, leaving Helen to talk to Ron's daughter. And then, almost before the final spoon was down, Kirsty was on her feet, urging on the final move. Joel took the seat next to Helen, and angled it towards her. His smile was so open and innocent that Helen felt a surge of relief and wondered how she could have doubted him.

'Are you staying for coffee?' he asked, as the waiter approached to take their orders. 'Don't tell me that now I'm finally here, you have to rush off?'

'No, I'm staying.' She needed the coffee, after drinking far more than usual following the conversation with Saskia. The echo of Saskia's words in Joel's question was an unfortunate coincidence that she decided to ignore.

'Great. Where's Megan tonight? I'm amazed she didn't want to tag along.'

Helen stared at Joel. One echo was a coincidence, two was proof. How could his smile still seem so attractive, his eyes so full of warmth?

'We're not tied together,' she snapped, furious

322

with herself as much as him. 'Life doesn't end when you have a child. I can still be free and spontaneous. I could stay out all night if I wanted.'

Helen ordered a cappuccino and another vodka. Joel was giving her an amused smile.

'Are you going to?'

'Going to what?'

'Stay out all night.'

'No. I'm just making the point that I could.'

'Right. That's good to know. I'll bear it in mind.'

'I don't mean with you.'

'Ah. Is it important that I know you can stay out all night with people who aren't me?'

'Yes, if it stops you making assumptions that single mothers are all dullards who have to be in bed by nine o'clock.'

'Dullards?' Joel laughed, then as he realised that Helen was serious, he leaned towards her, his smile fading. 'When have I ever said that?'

'I don't know. Your date has been at pains to pass the message on. Perhaps it was pillow talk? Perhaps it was when you were making her laugh with tales of me not having had sex for years?' Ignoring the coffee, Helen drank half the vodka in one long gulp. 'That's a shabby definition of friendship, Joel.'

There was a hitch in her voice, and she stopped, feeling weary of it all. The irony was, that all she wanted was to go home, curl up in bed, and be exactly the sort of dull person she had tried to argue she was not.

323

Joel grabbed her hand. Helen looked up into eyes which had turned from warm to hot. She had never seen him angry.

'Come outside,' he said. Tiny orange sparks seemed to flicker in his irises. 'We can't talk about this here.'

'No. What's the point?'

'Do you want me to explain the point in front of all these people?' He stood up, still holding her hand. 'Come with me.'

Helen let him lead her out of the restaurant, noticing Kirsty wink and give the thumbs up as she did. The few tables in the bar were full, but Joel found a quiet space near the door where they could stand and not be overheard.

'Tell me what I've done,' he demanded. 'Tell me what the hell I've done to be called a shabby friend, when frankly I'm struggling to see what more I could have done to try to help you. What's all that nonsense about being dull and going to bed at nine o'clock? What has Joan said?'

'Joan? Joan hasn't said anything.'

'But you said she'd been passing on messages.'

'Saskia, not Joan.'

'Saskia?' he repeated. The confusion in his face was genuine, Helen was convinced of it. In which case... What had she done now? She couldn't look away. 'She's not my date. Auntie Joan invited me. I arrived at the same time as Saskia, that's all.' He frowned. 'What has Saskia said to make you so worked up?'

324

'It's not important.'

'Yes it is.' He squeezed her hand, which for some reason he was still holding. 'I don't like secrets and I don't want any between us. Tell me.'

The sparks in his eyes had reduced to glowing embers.

'Something about single mothers having no freedom or spontaneity, and that no men want to date them...'

The words dissolved under Joel's gaze.

'You do know that's nonsense, don't you?' Joel asked. His voice was soft and slid over Helen. His face was so close to hers that she could see every one of his long, silky eyelashes curling up towards his brows. 'I would never say that, and certainly don't think that. Haven't you understood that by now? But why did it make you so upset to think that I had said it?'

How could Helen answer that when she had no idea herself? There wasn't a rational thought left in her head. There was nothing in her head except consciousness of Joel. As she hesitated, confused, wondering, she realised that his face was coming nearer. His eyes held hers. He was going to kiss her. And desire raged to life. She wanted him to kiss her. She wanted it so badly that she felt she might burst out of her skin. She hadn't wanted anything so much since... Her head jerked back. Since she had met Daniel. Daniel! Sense rushed back in, crushing the desire. How could she have forgotten him, even for a moment, when she had spent years clinging to his memory? Was she really ready to let those memories go?

'I can't do this,' she whispered, and ran back to the restaurant to collect her bag and coat, desperate to get home.

CHAPTER 24

'I feel like I've slipped back in time,' Adam said, laughing, as Helen crept through the door, shoes in her hand. 'Seeing you tiptoe home barefoot, steaming drunk. Please tell me this time you haven't left behind a posse of heartbroken men... Oh no,' he said, sitting up as he saw the faintest twitch of a reaction in her face, 'you haven't, have you?'

'Of course not.' Helen flopped down on the sofa, still in her coat, not even looking at what detritus she might be sitting on. An image of Joel, hurt, confused, apologetic, rolled like a wave into her mind, and back out again, leaving shells of guilt behind. He had asked her to stay; he had offered to leave; he had volunteered to accompany her home in the taxi, in place of Kirsty. 'I'm off men, you know that.'

'But you have that unmistakable air of Helen-in-lust about you. Come on, big brother is listening. Who is it?'

'No one.'

'Still?' Adam leaned forward. 'It has been five years, Helen. If you hadn't so categorically renounced the Catholic faith, I'd swear you've become a nun. I know what Daniel did was terrible, but I had hoped that as you'd invited him for Christmas, you'd managed to forgive him and move on... Oh crap. Don't tell me. The Helen-in-lust air is for him, isn't it?'

327

'No.' She leaned her head back and closed her eyes. 'Stop prying. Do something useful and make me a coffee.'

She heard him get up and move about in the kitchen. The kettle boiled and the spoon clinked against the side of the mugs: the sound of companionship, of not being alone. Somebody making a drink for her; why did it mean so much? Because it was so rare. The simplest things were the ones she missed the most.

She opened her eyes when the aroma of coffee assaulted her nostrils. She reached out to take it, but Adam whisked it away.

'No coffee unless you promise to tell me what's going on. I've had thirty years' practice of knowing when you're keeping a secret... Oh hell, what have I said now? Are you crying? You don't cry.' He stepped away awkwardly, dumped the mugs on the mantelpiece, and thrust a box of tissues at Helen. She grabbed a handful and wiped her face. He was right. She never cried in front of him. He was seven years older than her, and she had adored him from birth. From as early as she could remember, she had craved his attention, wanted him to be proud of her, to see her as cool not the soppy baby sister. No wonder he was scratching his head in bewilderment.

'Helen?' he asked, sitting down on the edge of the sofa. 'You're not pregnant, are you?'

That made her cry even more, although she did manage to shake her head. Adam leapt up and passed a mug of coffee to her.

'This is about Daniel, isn't it?' he said, the moment Helen's crying subsided to a volume where he could be heard over it. 'Tell me what he's done. It had better not be too bad. It's going to be hard enough to be civil to him over Christmas as it is.'

'He hasn't done anything.'

'Come on, Helen, that's what you said last time, even though the evidence of what he had done was visible to us all. Stop defending him. Has he upset Megan? She seems happy. She could hardly tell me enough about her precious daddy. Let's hope she never hears that he abandoned her before she was even born.'

'He didn't.'

'When he left you, he abandoned her, it's all the same thing.'

'He didn't leave me.'

'Why are you still propping him up on that pedestal? He never deserved it. Remember what he did, Helen.'

'He did nothing.' Helen looked at her brother. She adored him, as much as she ever had. The idea of losing his good opinion paralysed her with horror; telling him the truth was almost as difficult as telling Daniel. But she had to do it. She couldn't let him treat Daniel like this over Christmas; she couldn't let Megan pick up on any bad feeling towards him. So she forced her mouth to open and the words to trickle out. 'Daniel went to Hong Kong expecting me to follow him. I chose not to go. And I never told him I was pregnant.'

She waited, holding her breath, for the truth to filter into Adam's mind, to stain his features and colour the look in his eyes when they fell on her. But his reaction wasn't what she expected.

'Thank God,' he said, and sank into the chair. 'Thank God it was that way round.'

Helen didn't understand. Where was the hatred, the blame, the disapproval?

'Did you hear what I said?' she asked, when Adam leant his head back against the chair, eyes closed, and didn't speak. 'I didn't tell Daniel about the baby. He wasn't aware that Megan existed until a few months ago.'

'And how is he with her? Does he want her?'

'All the time,' Helen replied, puzzled by the odd question and the even odder way her brother was taking this news. 'He can't see her often enough. What did you expect?' It was a rhetorical question, but Helen saw a flicker of consciousness pass briefly over Adam's face. What was that about? 'Adam? What's going on? I thought you'd be outraged at what I did to Daniel. Most people are.'

'You should have told him. You don't need me to point that out. But his feelings aren't my concern. I've spent years worrying about you, and how you would ever trust a man again after his betrayal. And as for Megan – what might it have done to her to find out that her father rejected her? So on balance I'm not outraged, I'm relieved.'

'But I've kept them apart for Megan's whole life.' Helen had to keep on prodding the wound. There was

330

something wrong here: Adam's reaction was too simple. 'Megan could have grown up in a family, with two parents, like you and Jane.' And there it was – a flash of denial, expressed only by Adam's face in a series of rapid blinks. 'Adam? What aren't you telling me?'

He waited, studying her, and she could almost hear the clunk of the weights falling on each side of the scales, as in his mind he balanced the arguments, deliberating whether to say more. At last he sighed, and lifted his arms in a gesture of surrender.

'Remember when you came to stay with us, to say goodbye before Daniel left for Hong Kong? We were supposed to go out for a meal, but Sam was sick so we cancelled?'

'Yes.' Helen must have been in the early weeks of pregnancy then, but hadn't known it. She had felt nauseous on and off after that weekend, and they had laughingly blamed Sam. 'The curse of having children,' Helen remembered Daniel saying. How right he had been. 'I stayed at home with Jane and you went to the pub with Dan. What of it? Did something happen in the pub?'

'No. It was something he said.' Adam paused and drank some coffee. 'He was annoyed we'd had to cancel the restaurant, as it had received a good review in *The Times*. He said no offence to our boys, but as far as he could see, children had a knack of ruining adults' lives. He smiled as he said it,' Adam added, ever the fair man, but it was evident the smile hadn't convinced him. 'He told me that he wouldn't trade what I had with Jane for what the two of you were going to have in Hong Kong. He wanted a last few years of fun, and you were the perfect person to share that with.'

'You see! He loved me,' Helen interrupted, clutching at these words in the hope that the rest would fall away.

'I never doubted it. But he loved it the way it was. The *two* of you,' he repeated, with pointed emphasis. 'He was amazed that you'd made so little fuss about staying at home with Jane, because you would choose a night out over domesticity every time. He said...' Adam paused and looked at Helen, but she only nodded, encouraging him to carry on. 'He said that you'd joked about having children together in the future, but that unless they could be ordered from a glossy magazine and came with a team of nannies, you would never manage. You might be a perfect girlfriend, but he pitied any man who ended up having children with you. I'm sorry, Helen.'

'What are you trying to say, Adam?' But she hardly needed to hear his reply. She knew what he was about to say. Perhaps she had always known.

Adam looked at her, sympathy bleaching the deep blue of his eyes.

'I don't think there could ever have been a different outcome, Helen, from the moment you found you were pregnant. He wasn't ready for a baby, and he didn't want one with you. If you'd told him, he would have left you anyway.'

Adam drove the van to Church Farm the next day, and helped Helen carry the boxes to her shop in the Hay Barn. Helen hadn't been for a couple of weeks, and she couldn't believe the change when she walked in. The shops had been fitted out and looked ready for occupation. The sign she had designed was in place above hers: the name Crazy Little Things picked out in colourful stitched letters against a warm red background. She stood with her hand on the door, savouring the anticipation of going in and claiming this place as her own.

'Do you plan to open that door, or are you making handprints for artistic effect?' Adam asked, coming up behind her. 'I didn't realise a box of cotton could be so heavy. Couldn't you have taken one of the shops near the entrance?'

'You must have the books.' Helen opened the door. 'The shops near the entrance are all full. And none of them look like this.' She waved her arms round. 'Look at those beams.' She gazed upwards at the oak beams that ran across the top of her shop and over to the other side of the barn. She loved those beams, and the arched barn door, and the window letting light spill in over the empty area at the end where she would soon be holding lessons and hosting sewing groups. She had loved St Andrew's, too, but that was in the past: it had been exactly what she needed at the time, but now she was ready for a new start and a new challenge.

'This is excellent, Helen,' Adam said, putting down the box and walking round. 'I think this place will suit you better than St Andrew's. It should certainly be busier. You've done well to find it.'

Helen at once thought of Joel and how ungrateful she had been when he had first told them about Church Farm. It was hardly surprising he had been cross when she accused him of being a shabby friend. Without him, she wouldn't be here and wouldn't have a new shop to look forward to. And as it felt as if her entire relationship with Daniel, past and present, had disintegrated overnight, she needed the focus of her business to keep her going.

'Do you hope there's a prospect of me paying back your loan now I'm here?' Helen asked.

'It was a gift, not a loan, you know that,' Adam replied. 'And you also know that Mum and Dad would be more than happy...'

'No,' Helen interrupted. 'I won't take any kind of help from them, not after...' She stopped. It was still too upsetting to talk about, even to Adam. 'Shall we go for more boxes?'

They were only on their third return journey to the Hay Barn when Joel walked out of the office building in front of them. Adam carried on, oblivious. Helen stopped, wracked with awkwardness, and wondering how to react after what had happened – and almost happened – last night. But when Joel saw her, the smile that rose on his face was the normal, full-dimpled Joel smile.

'Hello,' he said, stepping forward and taking the

box from her arms. 'Why didn't you tell me you were here? I could have been helping.' He set off towards the Hay Barn.

'My brother's here to lend a hand,' Helen said, walking by his side. 'I didn't want to disturb you.'

'I was already disturbed wondering whether you were going to come,' he admitted. 'Don't worry, I'm not planning to pounce on you again. I didn't exactly plan it last night, either. I can't seem to help myself. But hey, I like you. I shouldn't have to apologise for that, should I?'

He tossed his cheeky grin to Helen, and she caught it and laughed. It was the first time she'd managed as much as a smile since her conversation with Adam the previous night. Adam heard her as they entered the Hay Barn, and looked up with obvious curiosity.

'Joel, this is my brother, Adam,' Helen said. 'Adam, this is Joel. He...'

'I know who he is,' Adam interrupted, coming forward and shaking Joel's hand. 'He runs Church Farm, is going to be your new neighbour, has a cat, and escorted you to Alex's wedding. I have heard the name once or twice.'

Had he? Helen thought she'd barely mentioned Joel to Adam. Obviously he had cropped up in conversation more than she realised. Adam was giving her an infuriating big brother look, which she chose to ignore. Joel was watching the two of them, amusement twitching at his lips. She couldn't look at those lips without remembering. How had a few hours so completely shaken her world?

335

'Shall we go for the rest of the boxes?' she asked, desperate to avoid any more embarrassing revelations. The last thing she wanted was for Adam to start repeating whatever it was she might have said about Joel.

'Joel and I can bring them,' Adam replied. 'You stay here. Someone should keep an eye on the stock.'

Annoyingly, that made sense, and Helen watched as they wandered off together. Every time they returned with more boxes, they were either deep in conversation or laughing. She busied herself with unpacking, determined to ignore them and whatever it was they found so amusing. Was it her? When she thought of some of the mortifying things Adam could reveal...

'What do you think of the shop now?' Joel came up behind her, making her jump. He laughed, and touched her arm to steady her. That almost made her jump again.

'I love it. The sign looks fantastic, doesn't it?' He nodded. 'I can't wait to move in. My first class is already full, thanks to the Christmas market.'

'The tables and chairs for the empty space should be arriving tomorrow. Will you be here? You can tell me how you want them arranged. One large table or smaller groups?'

'One large one, I think. But I won't be here. When we've finished unloading the boxes, Adam's driving us down to my parents' for Christmas.'

'So you're away over Christmas?' Joel's disappointment was evident. 'Until when?'

336

'Boxing Day.' It was long enough. Church Farm had proved a perfect excuse for her to come home as soon as possible. Daniel was driving them back, as Helen wouldn't have her car. With an effort, she dragged her mind away from Daniel. She wasn't ready to think about him yet, or process what Adam's revelations might mean.

'I suppose you can't stay away long. Daniel will want to see Megan, won't he?'

'Yes. Actually,' Helen continued, conscious of Adam lurking in the background, 'he wanted to see her on Christmas Day, so he's going to my parents' as well.'

'With his girlfriend?'

'No. She's in Australia.' Helen watched as Joel digested this, and the smile vanished as he reached the obvious conclusion. Something forced her to carry on, to chase away the cloud and restore the smile. 'She's coming back in the New Year. We're not together.' She settled on the truth, or half of it. 'It's the first Christmas he's been around. I didn't feel I could say no.'

'I suppose not.' The smile did flicker back, but not as brightly as Helen had hoped. She wondered if he was remembering that she had proved herself more than capable of saying no to him, as recently as last night. Perhaps he had realised that she wasn't so amazing after all. She'd never deserved the description, but now, as she saw a hint of doubt shadowing his eyes for the first time, she missed it.

'It's for Megan,' she said, hardly understanding

why it was so essential that she reassure him, but knowing that she had to try. 'It will make her happy. That's all that matters.'

Joel looked across at her silently, and at last his smile revived.

'Wait there a minute,' he said. 'I have something for Megan.' Smiling, he jogged out of the Hay Barn and returned a couple of minutes later carrying two paper carrier bags with rope handles. He held one out to Helen.

'It's a Christmas present for Megan,' he said, with uncharacteristic diffidence. 'I hope you don't mind.'

'Of course not, that's lovely of you.' Helen peeped in the bag, and saw a neatly wrapped present in sparkly Christmas paper, full of cavorting fairies. 'Thanks, Joel.' She hesitated, wondering whether to add a thank-you kiss, or whether that was a bad idea after last night.

'And this one's for you,' Joel continued, holding out the other bag. Helen took it, their fingers brushing. She looked inside, and saw another immaculately wrapped present, in glossy red paper. There was no hesitation this time. She leaned forward and pressed her lips to his cheek. His woody scent curled round her senses, like the ribbon circling the gift, and for a second, as her eyes caught his, the feeling she'd had last night roared inside her again and she wanted to shift her head a fraction until her lips met his. It was the effect of the Christmas present, she told herself, stepping back. She wasn't used to such kindnesses, or such interest from handsome men.

The attention was as intoxicating as the first drink after years of abstinence.

Pulling open one of the boxes she had placed on the shop counter, Helen lifted out a present.

'I've brought one for you,' she said, offering it to Joel, awash with sudden nerves. 'It isn't much...' It really wasn't much: a crazy patchwork cushion to go on his office chair, that she'd made for him in similar fabrics and colours as his scarf. The look he gave her, the undoubted surprise and pleasure that flooded his face, was more than the gift deserved.

Joel kissed her cheek, his hand lingering on her arm, wished them both a Merry Christmas, and went back to work. Helen watched him go, until she heard Adam laugh.

'Now I know I've regressed fifteen years,' he said. 'The two of you are acting like a pair of teenagers. Although more innocent teenagers than you were the first time around. How long has this been going on?'

'Nothing is going on.'

'If I had a pound for every time I'd heard you say that...'

'You'd be a millionaire?' Helen finished for him, laughing. 'You mean you're not already?'

'Not quite there yet.'

'Well, let's hope I can make a success of being here, repay your loan and tip you over that edge.'

Helen picked up the two gift bags from Joel. 'Shall we go? Megan's Christmas party should be over by now.'

Adam nodded.

'I like him, if you're interested,' he said, as they left Crazy Little Things, and Helen locked the door. 'He seems a good sort. Reliable.'

'Is that meant to be a recommendation? You don't make him sound very sexy,' Helen said.

'Only you can judge that.' Adam looked at her. 'Was Joel at dinner last night by any chance?' Helen nodded. 'I see.' Adam smiled, the infuriating big-brother smile. 'That explains everything. I knew I wasn't mistaken about that look...'

CHAPTER 25

Christmas turned out to be full of surprises. The first was that Daniel arrived on Christmas Eve bearing not only gifts, but his mother. Valerie had been due to have Christmas lunch with a friend, but the friend had been hospitalised with a broken hip, leaving Valerie on her own. Daniel had contacted Helen's mother before he set off, to ask if she could accommodate one extra. No one had thought to tell Helen.

She could hardly blame others, of course, for keeping secrets, when she had held on to such an enormous one herself. No one dared mention it, but the oxygen around the house seemed laced with disapproval and disappointment; thicker disapproval than in previous years, which Helen had scarcely thought possible.

Helen only endured Christmas with her parents for Megan's sake, and chiefly so that Megan could spend time with her cousins and enjoy the illusion of a family Christmas. She had been worried this year that Megan might start to notice that Adam's boys, with their married parents and baptism certificates, received a great deal more time and attention from their grandparents than she did. Valerie was a revelation and swept away any such anxiety. She doted on Megan and, amazingly, given Helen's historic view of Valerie, the feeling appeared mutual.

Megan adored having a grandmother who wanted to spend time with her, and Helen could imagine what Daniel was thinking every time he looked from his mother and daughter to Helen. It was another offence to add to Helen's charge sheet. She had deprived Megan of a grandmother as well as a father.

Or had she? Helen couldn't push Adam's words out of her head, especially now Daniel was here in front of her. He was acting as if nothing had happened – and of course, in his world, nothing had. He was blatantly thrilled to be here with Megan, and apparently enthusiastic about meeting Helen's parents again, which was exactly how she would have expected him to behave. Helen watched carefully when he greeted Adam, and there was no hint of consciousness, or of memory that the conversation Adam had reported had ever taken place. Helen looked out for any sign that he was judging her, and finding her a disastrous mother, but there was none. So was he an amazing actor, or had Adam got it wrong? She didn't know what to believe.

Valerie had brought a gingerbread-making kit with her, and spent Christmas Eve afternoon showing Megan how to make edible Christmas decorations. At first Helen hovered, unused to having anyone else take responsibility for Megan, especially in this house, but Valerie sent her away.

'Have a rest for a couple of hours, Helen,' she said, helping Megan sieve the flour, and seeming unconcerned that most of it was going over the arm of her twinset. 'Daniel told me how hard you've had to work in the run up to Christmas. Tomorrow will be a busy day. Take a break and let me look after Megan.'

Helen wandered into the drawing room. Adam had taken the boys outside to play football. Daniel was marooned amongst the chintz with Helen's mother Christine, and Jane. When Helen came in he looked like a prisoner who had seen the key brought in on a tray. He stood up.

'Fancy a walk?' he asked, turning desperate eyes on Helen. 'I could do with stretching my legs after the drive.'

'What a splendid idea!' Christine said, loudly enough to drown out the beginning of Helen's refusal. 'Do take Daniel out, Helen. You look like some exercise would do you good. Daniel may not remember the way, it's been such a long time since he was here.'

Only the prospect of Christine's blatant matchmaking if they stayed in the house could have persuaded Helen to agree. She fetched her coat.

'Pub?' Daniel asked, as they crunched their way down the gravel drive. She nodded, and he led the way to the village pub, a quarter of a mile down the road, their habitual bolt-hole from Helen's parents. Helen found a booth near the log burner while Daniel went to the bar for drinks. She sat back, and let the memories wash over her. It was impossible to hold them back. They had been here so often before, that nothing needed to be said. He knew which drinks to buy; she knew where he preferred

343

to sit. It was easy, familiar. These memories were real, she would have sworn to it. How could Adam be right in suggesting the past had been a sham? They had sat at this table and discussed Megan and Archie. Wouldn't she have known if it had been a joke?

Daniel sat down, and slid Helen's vodka and tonic across the table.

'This place hasn't changed at all,' he said, looking round.

'Neither have my parents,' Helen responded. 'I'm sorry for anything they say over the next few days, or anything that's been said already. I wish they still believed you abandoned me. It would have been marginally less awkward.'

'Not for me. Why hasn't Megan been baptised?'

Helen looked at her watch.

'You've been here three hours and they've brainwashed you already.' She picked up her glass and took a long sip, savouring the indulgence of vodka in the afternoon. 'Why do you care? You're not a Catholic.'

'Surely she should have been baptised, or christened, whatever you want to call it, by now? It should have happened when she was a baby.'

It hadn't happened because he wasn't there. She'd thought it a good reason. Did he see it as evidence that she was a terrible mother?

'Do you think, to celebrate the season of peace and goodwill, we could manage one drink without a row?'

Daniel stared at her. 'Is that what you think? That we always argue?'

'We do. Now we're even arguing about whether we argue.'

He smiled at her then, and the years rolled away, and she had to grip her glass tightly to prevent herself reaching out to touch him, to convince herself that it really was her Daniel here, drinking with her as they had done so often before it all went wrong. Adam had misunderstood. She was sure of it.

'I don't want to argue with you, Nell,' he said, picking up his wine. 'Perhaps at first. It was a shock, I admit, and the last thing I would ever have expected. I didn't handle it well. But all that matters is Megan. We have to do what's best for her, don't you agree?'

'Of course.' Helen ignored the prickle of irritation that he should even feel the need to ask. What did he think she'd been doing for the last four years, but what was best for Megan? Daniel studied her and nodded, as if they had reached an understanding.

'So what's the plan for tomorrow?' he asked. 'How do we do the presents? I want to be there when she opens them.'

'The presents go under the tree tonight, when she's in bed. Everyone comes down in the morning and opens them together before breakfast. It will be early. She's very excited, and there's no way she'll stay in bed with presents in the house.'

Daniel smiled.

'I didn't expect anything else. She might look like me, but her character is entirely you.'

Was it? Perhaps she was too close to see it herself; or perhaps she had never wanted to see beyond the resemblance to Daniel.

'Is that a bad thing?' she asked, bracing herself for the answer with a long swallow of vodka.

'No.' He smiled. Helen thought he had smiled at her more often during the course of this drink than in all the weeks since they had met up again. 'Not at all.' And then came the killer line, which brushed all her doubts aside, and would go on to haunt her Christmas. 'I always imagined our Megan would be a miniature version of you. She's all I could have wished for.'

Helen had given Megan a bath, tucked her into bed, read *The Christmas Bear* three times, and was about to enter the drawing room to find Daniel and send him upstairs to say goodnight, when she heard his voice coming from the snug on the other side of the hall. She headed that way but stopped outside the door when she heard Adam say her name.

'I felt I had to apologise,' Adam was saying. 'When you telephoned, trying to find her... I shouldn't have said what I did. Called you what I did,' he corrected himself. 'I had no idea you didn't know.'

'How could you believe I'd abandon her? How could you think I was the sort of man who would do that?'

It was impossible to know who he meant, her or Megan. Emotions pounding in her head, Helen missed the next couple of exchanges.

346

'I don't deny I wanted to go to Hong Kong,' she heard Daniel say now, a familiar note of irritation in his voice. 'I don't see how you can be so sure I'd have put that first. We'll never know. I wasn't given the choice.'

'I don't agree with what she did, but I can't regret the outcome.' Adam's voice was suddenly close to the door. Helen stepped back, but he didn't come out. 'She's not the same Helen you left. The last few years have been the making of her. She was always too dependent on you. She's found herself now, learnt to make her own way, and she's much stronger. I'm so proud of her. You'd better not pull her back down again.'

'She can hardly be much further down.' Helen could imagine how furiously Daniel's fingers must be tapping. 'She sews through the night, looks exhausted from lack of sleep, and has to make her own clothes. Megan spends more time at nursery than with her mother. What have you all been doing to let her get in this state?'

And there was the eavesdropper's reward. Helen crept away, knowing that the scar from this wound was never going to fade. Never mind her brother's pride in her; never mind that Daniel had enough feeling left to be concerned about her. She had tried so hard to change when he had gone, to grow up and be a success; but it hadn't been enough. He looked at her life, what she thought she had achieved, and he didn't see anything amazing or incredible. All he saw was a complete and utter mess.

If Helen could freeze one moment in time and never let it go, it would have been the moment she opened the drawing-room door on Christmas morning, and saw Megan's face explode in a riot of disbelief, excitement and delight as her eyes fell on the pile of presents under the Christmas tree.

'He's been!' she squealed, and raced across the room, closely followed by her older cousins, who were pretending they were only excited to indulge Megan, and fooling no one. Helen glanced at Daniel, saw that he was smiling with the same enchanted expression she was sure was on her own face, and their eyes met. His appeared suspiciously moist. She knew, though family were surrounding them, that this wasn't a moment she could ever have shared with anyone else. No one but Daniel could understand exactly how her heart was lifting right now, because his was beating in perfect time with hers. For that fleeting moment, they were a proper family, relishing Christmas, and the last five years were forgotten.

Megan loved her presents, especially the bicycle, and appeared not to notice that presents this year were from Mummy and Daddy jointly. She was probably dazzled by the sheer volume of parcels addressed to her, as the contributions from the Blake family and friends had doubled the usual pile. Megan wasn't the only beneficiary. Adam, who always took on the role of chief distribution officer to ensure gifts were fairly passed round between the children, handed a parcel over to Helen.

'To Mummy with love from Megan,' he read out. 'Well done, Megan. Excellent writing.'

'I didn't write it,' Megan said, with all the weight of a four-year-old's scorn. She climbed onto Helen's knee and pointed at a messy row of Xs across the bottom of the gift tag. 'I did the kisses, Mummy.'

'And they are very lovely kisses,' Helen said, giving Megan one back, to hide her flustered feelings. She knew exactly who had written the card, and he was watching her now, expectantly. Though there was a present under the tree for Daniel, from her and Megan, somehow she hadn't expected this. She had never received a present from Megan before, not for Christmas, birthday or Mothers' Day. There had never been anyone to arrange it, and she hadn't honestly thought there was now. 'Do you want to help open it?'

Megan tore the wrapping off in seconds, revealing a small cardboard box.

'It's a key ring,' she blurted out, before Helen could open it, and everyone laughed.

'Bang goes the surprise,' Daniel said. But it was still a surprise, when the key ring was revealed. It was a thick silver fob, with a tiny thumb print in the centre, and Megan's name etched round it.

'That's my thumb,' Megan announced helpfully.

'It's beautiful,' Helen replied, giving her another kiss, not daring to do the same to the real donor of the gift. 'Thanks Dan. I love it.'

'There's something else,' he said, reaching under the tree, and ignoring Adam's disapproving face he

349

picked up an envelope and passed it to Helen. 'From me.'

Conscious of too many eyes focussed curiously on her, Helen opened the envelope and found a voucher for £200 for a spa she used to go to, in the days when they had been together, and when she had had nothing more pressing to do with her time than beautify herself for him.

'Thanks,' she said again, wondering if he thought that she looked so awful that it would take £200 to fix her. 'That's very generous.' Though when she would ever find time to go was anyone's guess.

'You deserve a treat. I know you always liked it there.' Daniel smiled. 'And I'll look after Megan whenever you want to go.'

Helen looked at him quickly, suspecting an ulterior motive in the gift, but his smile appeared genuine enough. She turned to Adam.

'Can you pass that one next?' she asked, pointing to a large rectangular package. 'I'm sorry, it's going to seem nothing now.'

Adam obligingly picked up the parcel, and read out the label. 'To Daniel, from Megan and Helen. Brief and to the point,' he commented with an amused smile, and gave the gift to Daniel. Daniel unfastened the paper and let it fall to the floor, until he had on his knee a photograph album. But it was no ordinary album. Helen had made a crazy patchwork cover for it, using snippets of fabric from Megan's old clothes. Inside she had created a scrapbook, with all her favourite photographs of

Megan, dated and labelled, as well as drawings and other items Megan had made at home or nursery. Items that Helen had treasured for years were in there, now entrusted to Daniel. She had agonised over whether to give this to him, fearing it might only remind him of what he had missed. But even if she'd had a million pounds to spend, she couldn't have found anything more valuable. She watched as he strolled through the pages, his face blank, hoping he understood the spirit in which it was given.

'Did you make that, Helen?' Christine asked, peering over at the album. 'What a clever idea. It looks quite professional. Do you sell these in your little shop?'

'Not with pictures of Megan in,' Helen retorted, irked by the way Christine still spoke to her as if she were a wayward child. She caught Valerie watching her.

'It's beautiful, Helen, like all your work. And the contents...' Valerie smiled, and swallowed down her emotion. 'What precious memories.'

Except they weren't memories for Daniel, and that fact seemed to suddenly strike Valerie. She put out her hand and lightly touched Daniel's shoulder. He looked up at Helen. She held her breath. Surely he wouldn't make a scene in front of Megan?

'It's fantastic,' he said, and his eyes were dragged irresistibly back to the photographs.

'That's me, Daddy,' Megan said, abandoning Helen to join Daniel, and sticking a finger on top of a picture of a laughing toddler. 'I did laugh when you were away,' she added, slinging an arm easily round his neck. 'But I laugh more now you're back.'

Daniel's glance flew to Helen, with an expression she found impossible to interpret. Adam found this an appropriate time to abandon his careful gift management, and distracted everyone with a swift division of the remaining presents. Chaos reigned for several minutes, as the adults expressed delight in the usual collection of chocolate, slippers, socks and toiletries. Daniel received an enormous pair of ski gloves from Tasha, and Helen opened a plum silk dressing gown from Kirsty. 'Just in case you have someone to impress in the morning next year!' read the card. Helen breathed a sigh of relief that Adam had stopped reading them all aloud.

Presents done, Megan's thoughts turned to breakfast, and Helen stood up to go and make it.

'Hang on,' Adam said, stretching under the tree. 'We've forgotten one. This is yours, I think.' He pulled out a thin parcel in glossy red paper. Helen recognised it at once. She'd assumed she must have left it at home. Now she wished she had. 'To Helen,' Adam began to read, the teasing smile known only to big brothers curving his lips. 'Hope you have an amazing Christmas. Look forward to ...'

'Thank you!' Helen interrupted, snatching the parcel from him to shut him up. Unfortunately the clumsy attempt to silence him drew all eyes to her.

'Open it, Mummy!' Megan cried, foiling Helen's plan to squirrel it away upstairs to open later. Helen carefully unwrapped the paper, and found a smaller

352

parcel in a layer of tissue. Inside that was a chunky cashmere scarf, in a cable knit pattern, and a beautiful shade of holly-berry red. As she opened it out, she found a handwritten note. 'I know it can't match the quality of the one you made, but I hope you love it as much as I love mine.' Smiling, Helen ran her fingers down the length of the scarf, revelling in the soft warm texture, and remembering the soft warmth of Joel's cheek. She loved it already. It was her favourite colour. How could she not? She wrapped it round her neck, wondering what Joel was doing now, and whether he was imagining her opening his present.

Looking up, she realised that everyone was still watching her. She smiled, and unwound the scarf again, letting the fabric trail through her fingers.

'Breakfast?' she asked. The response was a hubbub of voices, all except Daniel's. He was staring at Helen, a frown loud on his face, his fingers tapping at his leg, and he didn't say a word.

'Will you stay for one last drink?' Daniel asked, as Helen rose to follow Adam and Jane. It was almost midnight, and the children and grandparents had retired to bed hours ago, worn out by the early start and the hullaballoo of a family Christmas. The four of them had stayed up, drinking, pretending to watch television, and undoubtedly thinking how similar and yet how vastly different it was from all the other evenings they had spent together.

Helen had a fluttering suspicion that Adam was deliberately staying up to prevent her being alone

353

with Daniel, confirmed when he shot her a look of alarm when Daniel made his suggestion. Quite what he feared was lost on Helen, nor did she understand his whispered instruction to 'be careful and remember the scarf' after she agreed to another drink.

Daniel poured them both a glass of wine, and sat down on the sofa opposite Helen. His camera lay beside him on the sofa arm, and he picked it up and switched it on.

'There are some great shots here,' he said, a smile bursting to his lips as he reviewed the photos. The camera had hardly been out of his hand all day. 'Look.'

He leaned across and showed Helen a picture of Megan, absolute wonder on her face as she unwrapped her bike. He scrolled on, shot after shot of Megan, virtually every minute of Christmas captured. He paused as an image flashed up of Helen with Megan, both laughing as Helen tickled Megan to chase away the shock of the first tumble from the bike. She hadn't realised he'd been taking pictures of her.

'I'll send you copies,' he said, turning off the camera and sitting back down. He drank some of his wine, his finger drumming against the glass. 'Do you think she enjoyed the day?'

'Of course she did,' Helen replied, surprised he even needed to ask given the overwhelming photographic evidence he'd produced.

'As much as other Christmases?'

'More,' she said, and it was the honest answer, not

just the one she knew he was hoping to hear. 'She loved having you here. You can't doubt it.'

And nor could she, more's the pity. She offered him comfort at the sacrifice of her own. It had made Megan's day to have Daniel there. He was a more welcome visitor than Father Christmas. How was Helen ever to persuade her – and him, for that matter – that it was a one off? Tasha wouldn't be absent every year. Extended families might manage happy Christmases together in TV drama, but Helen had no intention of trying it.

'I love her,' Daniel said, the emotion raw on his face. His hand lifted in a slight flap of bewilderment. 'I wouldn't have believed I could feel this way. I want to be with her all the time.'

'I know.' What else could Helen say? She felt exactly the same. But their feelings were mutually exclusive. They couldn't both be with her. A chill of premonition spread through her, and she drank her wine, dreading where she realised this conversation was now heading.

'We need to arrange formal access,' Daniel said, the emotion now switched off. Helen understood. This was business. This had been his ulterior motive in inviting her to stay for a drink. Adam had been right to be alarmed. 'I'm sure we can agree something between us, and only involve lawyers as a last resort. I thought she could stay with you during the week, and spend weekends with me.'

'Every weekend?' Wine spilled over Helen's hand. 'No. That's not going to happen.' She had to put down her glass, her hand was shaking so much. 'How can you even ask that? I work in the week. We would only have Monday together, and not even that when school starts.'

'You don't have to work. Give up the shop, take Megan out of nursery, and you can have every day with her. I've spoken to Patrick, and he'd be happy to reinstate your allowance. With the maintenance payments I've offered, you'll be much better off than you are now. It will be more like the life you were used to.'

But the life she had been used to was with him, and he wasn't offering her that back. He was offering her less than she had now, if more than money was taken into account, and a seed of disappointment took root in her mind that he still didn't take her seriously. Perhaps if he had offered her this when he first came back, she would have agreed to it, to keep him happy, because it was what he wanted. It was the way their relationship had always worked. But since then, she had seen how other relationships worked, based on mutual support and encouragement; and she had begun to believe in herself, as someone who had skills and talent – as a successful businesswoman, even. She wasn't prepared to abandon four years of hard work. She had changed too much. She would rather be poor on her own money, than rich and idle on someone else's. And how dare he speak to her father to arrange this without consulting her?

'I won't give up work,' she said, determination sobering her up better than any amount of coffee. 'I want to support Megan. I want something to do when she's at school, and I want her to grow up and be proud of me. I'm good at it,' she added, remembering Joel's words, and his enthusiasm. 'I'm winning more and more commissions. I'm launching a new website, and I'm going to make a success of this.'

A twitch of the eyebrow was the only response. She couldn't tell what it meant, but it certainly didn't suggest pride, or admiration, or whatever else she might have hoped for.

'You're expecting too much,' Helen said, goaded into challenging him. 'It's too big a step to take her away from me for a whole weekend, when she's still so young, and you're still...' A relative stranger, she had been on the verge of saying, and how apt that would have been. Apt, but unhelpful to her cause, she realised in time to let the words die on her tongue.

'Very well,' Daniel replied, and his instant acquiescence made Helen suspect that she'd been played: he had demanded her worst-case scenario, so she would agree a compromise that he had really wanted all the time. 'We'll start slowly. I'll have her for the day every Sunday, and she'll sleep at my house every other Saturday night. We'll build up from there. Eventually I'll collect her from school on Friday, and take her there on Monday morning.'

This had turned into the least merry Christmas Helen could remember. Three nights without Megan? Was he serious? But he was, there was no mistaking the expression in his eyes, in no way dimmed by alcohol. She wished he had never come back. She wished Megan was still her secret. Tears of frustration rolled silently down her cheeks, and she didn't try to hide them. Daniel was so keen to give himself the role of victim. Let him see that he wasn't the only one hurting here.

He watched her for several seconds, saying nothing, revealing nothing. Then he crossed the room, sat beside her on the sofa, wound his arm round her back and pulled her to him. It was a clumsy move. They banged heads, and he had to slacken his grip so she could wriggle to rest her head on his shoulder, her tears dampening his shirt. The shock was almost enough to stop the flow. They simply didn't do this. Their relationship had been extreme, either rowing or making up, always when Helen had backed down. There had been no in-between, no gentleness, no hugs. Familiar as Daniel was, this felt wholly alien. Helen drew back.

'Sorry,' she said, stretching over the arm of the sofa to reach for a tissue. 'I can't take alcohol like I used to. Don't ever suggest a nightcap again.'

She regretted the words immediately. Did it sound like she was expecting more late nights together? His eyes settled on hers, navy blue in the light of the lamps.

'We've made a mess of things, haven't we?'

'You mean I have,' she replied flatly, wiping the residue of the tears from her eyes. The moment of empathy hadn't lasted long, she thought. 'Or do you simply mean I look a mess? I'm not a pretty crier. Perhaps that's why I never did it before.'

'You look as...' He stopped, leaned back against the sofa. 'I'm still getting used to the hair.'

'It can't be that much of a surprise. You knew I wasn't a natural blonde.'

'I like it,' he said, and smiled. 'But I wasn't talking about your looks. This situation is a mess. Neither of us has what we want.'

'No. But I chose to have the baby, and you did want to go to Hong Kong.' She looked at him. 'How was it? Honestly?'

His response was carefully weighed, as always, but in the end it was simple.

'Fantastic. Everything we hoped it would be.'

A flash of regret whisked across her face and he caught it. He leaned towards her, eyes roving over her face to read any other thoughts.

'Do you wish you'd come?'

It was the impossible question. How could she wish she'd gone, when that would mean unwishing Megan and the last four years? But she'd asked him to answer honestly, and she had to do the same.

'What do you think? I was twenty-five, no ties, no responsibilities, and was offered the chance of a lifetime to live in Hong Kong for a few years with...' She paused. The man she loved, she had been about to say, but it wasn't appropriate, was it? 'I wanted to go every bit as much as you. I'd been feeling restless here, and thought it would give us back what we had in London. But it would never have worked with a baby, we both know that. Only one of us could go, and it had to be you. And I can't regret my choice.

359

Megan has given me a million times more happiness than Hong Kong ever could.'

Daniel looked at her for a long time.

'It wasn't the same without you.'

Helen smiled, though his words were like jagged shards of glass piercing her heart.

'Bringing up Megan wasn't the same without you. But I suppose neither of us can say it would have been better together. How could we know?' She stood up, too tired, too drunk and too emotional to be having this conversation. 'There's nothing unusual about parents living apart. We'll work it out. We have to, for Megan.'

His answer was so late, and so quiet, that Helen was halfway through the door when it came, and she was sure she must have misheard him.

'We'll see.'

CHAPTER 26

Helen had one day after returning from Surrey to prepare her shop for the grand opening of the Hay Barn. Megan's nursery was still closed, so Daniel had offered to look after her for a couple of days, and Valerie would step in for the next two, when Daniel had returned to work. Helen had no idea how she would have managed without them.

Only Helen and Fiona were at the Hay Barn that day. Saskia and Malcolm had clearly been busy over Christmas, and Helen could see as she peered through their shop windows that they were ready for opening. Fiona's cards and invitations were made to order, so it was the work of no more than a couple of hours to set up her display of samples. Though she helped Helen for as long as she could, she was meeting friends for lunch and couldn't stay. By midday, Helen was on her own, with more than half the boxes still unpacked. She stared at the chaos that was her shop. It seemed an insurmountable task to make this ready for the morning.

'Will the boxes magically unpack themselves if you stare at them long enough?'

Helen spun round at the sound of Joel's voice, a smile on her lips already.

'Unpacking isn't the problem,' she said, drinking in the sight of the dimples and the curls. 'It's what to do with everything when it's unpacked.'

'Don't tell me the shop isn't big enough? You must be a phenomenal businesswoman if you need to expand before you've even opened.'

'Phenomenally messy.' Helen laughed, waving her hand around. 'I'm never going to open at this rate. The other shops look great. I'm letting the side down.'

'You could never do that. Saskia and Malcolm were here most of yesterday, and had help. Are you on your own?'

Helen nodded. 'Can you believe Megan would rather play Barbie than do some work here? I thought having a girl would guarantee me a free shop assistant. Something has gone terribly wrong.'

Joel laughed, his lovely deep burble, and moved closer.

'Will I do as your shop assistant for the day?'

'Seriously? You're willing to help?'

'If you think I can.'

'Look at the state of the place. If a monkey came offering assistance I'd be overjoyed at this point.'

'Are the hairy body and red bum prerequisites? If not, I'm all yours.' As Helen laughed, he continued. 'Sorry. I expect you're too posh to use the word bum. What should I have said? A scarlet derrière?'

'You forget I have a four-year-old. Bottoms and bodily functions are our main topics of conversation. Quite frankly, I'm so desperate I wouldn't care if your bum was neon green with pink polka dots.'

'For the record, it's not. I'm happy to help, but I can't offer my services for free.'

'No?'

'No. I'm good for nothing when I'm hungry. Have you eaten?' Helen shook her head. Food had never crossed her mind. 'Okay. The price of my help is that you come for lunch first.'

'I didn't think the café was open.'

'It's not. We can go back to my house. I'll make something.' He laughed when Helen hesitated. 'I promise I won't poison you. It wouldn't be in my interests, would it?'

Food poisoning seemed the least of the dangers in this situation.

'Worried about losing your rent?' she asked, trying to make light of it.

'I wasn't, but that's another good point. Are you coming?'

Of course she was. Her arm was already in her coat, and she pulled it on and wound the scarf round her neck. Joel watched.

'Great scarf.'

'Isn't it?'

'You really like it? You're not just keeping it here to throw on if I ever appear?'

'Didn't you believe the thank-you text?' She had sent him a text on Christmas morning, thanking him for the presents. It would have been rude not to, especially when he had already sent a message gushing over hers. Several more had followed. 'I love it.'

His smile was so wide it almost fell off the edges of his face. Helen locked the shop and followed him to his car, and he drove the short distance to Pleasant

363

View Cottage. Helen stared at her cottage in excitement. She couldn't wait to live here.

'When are you moving in, neighbour?' Joel asked, reading her thoughts easily. Helen shrugged.

'Your mum's been lovely. She said I can move in anytime, and she won't officially start charging rent until I stop paying it on my current house.' Helen suspected Joel's hand behind that. 'Now I'm working at Church Farm, it would be much easier to live here, but I need to wait for Adam to have a free weekend and then I'll hire a van. I'm sure I can persuade Ben to help, and I hope we can manage between us. Proper removal firms are too expensive.'

'Is Adam the only hold up?' Joel asked, as he unlocked his door and stood back to let Helen in. 'I know where we can get a van, and my friends can provide the muscle.'

'Why would they do that?' Helen followed Joel into a living room with a solid oak floor, two squashy brown leather sofas and a TV. She longed to throw some crazy patchwork at it to brighten it up.

'Does friendship mean something different down south?' Joel took off his jacket and threw it on the sofa. 'If I ask them to help, they'll do it for me. They don't need any other reason.' And he would do it for her, continued the unspoken line. 'How about Saturday?' Joel continued, taking Helen's coat and scarf and dumping them on top of his. 'Some friends are coming round anyway for New Year's Eve, so they may as well work for their supper. Kirsty runs your shop on Saturday, doesn't she?'

'I've no boxes,' Helen said, wondering if it was possible to pack the house by weekend.

'You'll have loads by the time we finish unpacking the shop this afternoon.'

Joel slid open the wall at the end of the living room to reveal the most incredible kitchen. The outside wall was formed from glass folding doors, as Helen had seen from the garden next door when she had viewed her house. Even on a winter's day, light drenched the room. A modern cherrywood kitchen filled one end, a long table stood in the centre and, at the other end, where the kitchen had been knocked through into what was her sewing room in the neighbouring cottage, a large L-shaped sofa in front of a log-burner begged to be sat on. Helen promptly sat down, gazing down the garden and to the view beyond.

'I could live in this room,' she said. By the looks of it, Joel did. There were more signs of life here than in the living room: pictures, a scattered newspaper, an abandoned mug, quirky pots which she guessed must be his mother's work.

'Glad you like it.' He grinned as he opened the fridge. 'But perhaps we should at least try one date before you move in... Joke,' he added, as Helen's face froze. 'Wow, I don't think you could look more horrified if you practised for a month. That hurt. I might have to poison your lunch after all now.' He pulled things out of the fridge: eggs, cheese, and a carton of orange juice. Helen went over to the kitchen. He looked at her and smiled, but there was a distinct horizon to the smile.

'It wasn't horror. You touched a nerve.' She hadn't planned to tell him this; she only knew she had to make the smile as bright as it was before. 'I met Daniel at a party, and pretty much moved in with him the same night.'

'Wow again. That must have been quite some connection. Or one hell of a party.' He laughed, and picked up a baguette from the worktop. 'I don't know whether to ask you to slice this, or leave it whole in case I need a weapon to force you out of the house after lunch.'

Helen snatched the baguette and hit him with it. It broke in two and flopped limply in its plastic packet.

'Oh God,' Joel cried, raising his arms and backing away. 'I've invited a mad baguette murderer home with me...'

Helen hadn't laughed so much for years. Lunch was over far too soon, and Joel drove her back to Church Farm, where they continued to unpack and fill the shelves ready for the morning. Even with his help, the job took longer than expected, and Helen had to ring Daniel to ask him to hold on to Megan for another hour.

'Does Megan ever stay with her dad overnight?' Joel asked, when at last the shop looked ready and they were loading flattened boxes into Helen's car. A flutter of anxiety attacked her. She'd had a great day. He wasn't going to spoil it by asking her on a date, was he?

'She hasn't done yet,' she replied, giving a box a

366

wholly unnecessary shove. 'We've agreed she'll stay over on alternate Saturdays, starting the weekend after next.' She gave Joel a look of such unfeigned bleakness that he reached out his arm and pulled her into a brief, comforting hug. It ended too soon.

'Liz has been an absolute star, and managed to blag a stand for Church Farm at a new craft and design show in London,' Joel explained. 'It's the first weekend in February, Friday to Sunday. I thought the fairest thing would be for different artists to exhibit each day. How would you and the rest of the Hay Barn feel about taking the Saturday?'

Even with the excitement of this news, Helen recognised a perverse flash of disappointment that he wasn't actually asking her on a date. It didn't last. A chance to exhibit in London! It was something she could only have dreamed of. Joel laughed.

'Can I assume by the size of your smile that you're interested?'

'Interested? Are you serious? I would love it. Are you sure?' she asked, her enthusiasm deflating. 'Other people have been at Church Farm longer than me. Don't they deserve the chance?'

'You deserve the chance,' he said. 'And it makes sense to push the Hay Barn as a unit, especially as it will have recently opened. I'll talk to the others this week, but can I count you in?'

'Definitely. Will we need to stay overnight, though, if we're only exhibiting on Saturday?'

'You'll have to catch the first train down, so it will be a long day. And there is something else as well.'

'What is it?' Was this the date? How could she refuse after what he'd just given her? And – the thought took her by surprise, as she regarded his smiling face – would she truly want to refuse?

'You know I mentioned that Liz works for magazines, setting up mock living rooms for celebrities to be interviewed in, or arranging rooms that we should all be aspiring to copy? She thinks some of your crazy patchwork would fit in perfectly. She'd like to see you…'

Helen couldn't wait for the end of the sentence.

'My patchwork could be in magazines? Proper glossies? With national circulation? Seriously?' Helen simply couldn't help herself. She stepped forward and threw her arms round Joel in a hug. A friendly hug, she thought, before his arms came up round her, and all thought disintegrated.

The launch of the Hay Barn was a great success. Helen had been focussed on Crazy Little Things and the transition from St Andrew's, and it had never crossed her mind how much work Joel was putting in behind the scenes. He had advertised on the website, on Facebook and Twitter, by leaflet dropping, and in the local newspapers, and the result was a turn out hardly less than they had seen at the Christmas market. It helped that so many people were off work for Christmas, and that many of the other stall holders had started a winter sale, but there was no doubt that Joel had made the day the success it proved to be.

Daniel brought Megan in to say hello, but Helen was too busy to do anything but show him the way to the soft-play area and the animals.

'Was that Megan's dad?' Saskia asked, as Helen returned to her shop.

'Yes, it was.' Helen hesitated in the doorway, reluctant so say more.

'We've seen a lot of him lately. I don't remember him calling at St Andrew's.'

'He's been working abroad.'

'You must be glad to have him back.' Saskia smiled in such a friendly way that Helen pushed down on the shoots of suspicion that had threatened to rise.

'For Megan, yes.'

'You make such a sweet family. He does that stern, sexy look to perfection, doesn't he? Don't your knees tremble with every frown?'

Helen laughed and went back into the shop. With a combination of loyal customers from St Andrew's and new visitors, by the time she put up the 'closed' sign she could count the day a huge success: she had taken as much money through the till as she'd sometimes done in a month at St Andrew's. It wouldn't last every day, and January and February were bound to be tough, especially if snow came, but she'd already filled up the first course she was planning to run, and had half the names she needed for the second. If Joel found time to help her set up online sales on her new website, and if she could maintain a steady number of crazy patchwork commissions, her income would comfortably improve on what she was used to. She wouldn't need any maintenance from Daniel. She would prove to him that her life wasn't the mess he thought it was.

Joel popped in as they were closing up to see if the day had gone well. Everyone was enthusiastic, in their own way, and Joel was showered with gratitude for giving them a new start after St Andrew's.

'But I miss Ron,' Malcolm said, always reluctant to sound too happy. 'There's no escape from female conversation now. I even overheard a conversation today about frowns that make the knees tremble – whatever that means.' He gave a wry smile in Helen's direction.

'Oh yes?' Joel followed the direction of Malcolm's smile and looked at Helen. His face wore the usual open smile, not a hint of a frown. 'Did I miss something interesting?'

'We were talking about Hel...'

'Did I see you sell some paintings today, Malcolm?' Helen asked, raising her voice and cutting off Saskia. 'That's a fantastic start, isn't it, with the one you sold at the Christmas market as well?'

'Better than expected,' he had to concede, 'although the sale at the Christmas market was different, because...' Joel dropped an enormous bunch of keys, and Malcolm stopped. 'Ah,' he murmured, having apparently lost his thread. 'We'll be snookered if we have another bad winter. I bet we won't see hide nor hair of anyone round here then.'

'Of course we will,' Helen replied, hearing that she

370

was using her cheery Megan voice but unable to stop it. 'My classes are proving popular. Why don't you do the same? What about lessons in watercolour painting?' she continued, warming to her theme. 'Art classes are always in demand. You could run them in the evenings, too, as I can't use the free space then. I had loads of enquiries about after-work activities. If Joel doesn't mind late-night opening.' Belatedly she glanced at Joel, to see what he made of the plan. He was smiling at her in amusement.

'You simply can't stop, can you? I think it's a great idea. And if your helpfulness stretches to volunteering as a life model,' he added, the cheeky grin targeted straight at Helen, 'you can sign me up as the first student.'

'How did the move go?' Kirsty asked, as Helen dropped her overnight bag in the hall late in the afternoon on New Year's Eve, and Megan raced off to play with Jenny.

'Exhausting,' Helen replied, kicking off her shoes and sinking onto the sofa. 'I'm in no hurry to do it again.'

'Aren't you?' Kirsty grinned. 'Did the sight of some hunky men rippling their muscles to your order not make it all worthwhile?'

'That's why it was so exhausting. My neck aches with swivelling from one side to the other, deciding which way to look.' Helen laughed. Four of Joel's male friends had come along to help in the end, to join him in the heavy work, and one had brought his girlfriend, who had helped Helen unpack and try to keep Megan out of the way. They had all been lovely, and didn't seem to mind giving up their Saturday to assist a stranger move house. They had laughed and joked all day, treated Joel with obvious affection, and teased him with a secret that somehow involved Helen but which no one chose to explain to her.

'Everything has worked out brilliantly, hasn't it?' Kirsty smiled. 'Santa's little helper does have the magic touch, doesn't he? Or haven't you found out yet?' she finished, with a dirty cackle.

'Is it safe to come in?' Ben asked, peering round the kitchen door. 'When I hear that filthy laugh I worry what might assault these delicate ears.'

'Nothing worse than you've heard before, I'm sure,' Helen said, rising and kissing him on the cheek. 'Is that a bottle of wine I can see behind you? I've two in my bag as well, so shall we make a start?'

'We wouldn't have minded if you'd decided to stay in your new house tonight,' Kirsty said, several hours and bottles later, when they'd eaten and sent the children up to bed. 'It sounds like you love the place already. You must have been tempted.'

'With a wild party going on next door? I can think of better introductions.'

'Wild party? Tell me again how to get there?' Kirsty laughed. 'I'm surprised you weren't invited.'

Helen drank some wine and didn't reply. Of course she'd been invited. Joel had it all worked out, offering to make up a camp bed for Megan in his spare room. Quite where Helen was supposed to sleep

372

hadn't been discussed. His friends had tried almost as hard to persuade her to stay, but the plan to spend New Year's Eve at Kirsty's had been in place so long that Helen had been firm in her refusal.

Her resolution had almost wavered when Joel had carried round a moving-in present for her. She hadn't expected anything: he had done more than enough in arranging the move. She certainly would never have expected what the gift turned out to be: Malcolm's painting, *New Beginnings I*. She had stared at it in silence, appreciating again the rich warm swirls of colour.

'Don't you like it?' Joel had asked, sudden uncertainty clouding his face. 'I thought red was your favourite colour. And Malcolm assured me…'

'I love it. I loved it as soon as he showed it to me. But he said a woman bought it.'

'Liz.' A faint flush of consciousness rose in Joel's cheeks. 'I sent her as my envoy so you didn't see me buy it.'

Helen had thought back.

'You didn't know I was going to move in here at the time of the Christmas market. You can't have bought it as a new house present then.'

'No. But that's not the only new beginning is it?' He had paused, a warm smile on his lips, and she had wondered what he was going to say. 'It's a new start for you at Church Farm. I want you to remember it. I hope it's the start of something special.'

As Helen had given him a thank-you kiss on the cheek, his hand had rested briefly on her waist, and…

'Ben, could you fetch one of Tommy's bibs?' Kirsty's loud voice shattered the memory. 'Helen is practically drooling. Who exactly are you thinking of right now?'

The bongs of Big Ben on the television saved Helen from having to reply. Amidst the kissing and the sound of fireworks exploding all around, Helen's phone beeped twice in quick succession. Champagne in one hand, Helen reached for her phone with the other.

'Someone's popular,' Kirsty said, trying to peer over Helen's shoulder. 'Two messages within seconds of midnight. Who got in first?'

'Joel,' Helen replied, smiling as she read his text. 'Closely followed by Daniel.'

'And does that reflect your order of preference?'

'Kirsty!' Helen laughed. 'Don't think because you've plied me with champagne I'm going to answer that.'

'Come on,' Kirsty replied, filling up Helen's glass. 'I've been waiting four long years to gossip about your love life. Give me something. I know,' she said, collapsing onto the sofa beside Helen. 'Imagine they'd both been here for dinner, and their car keys were in that bowl on the coffee table...'

Helen spluttered over her champagne.

'Dare I ask what sort of dinner parties you two have?'

'It's her favourite fantasy,' Ben said. 'Why do you think she's been trying to fix you up for four years? And she's only asking now out of pure self-interest, to see if you prefer the same man she does. On the up side,' he added, winking at Helen, 'in exchange you get all this.' He gestured up and down his body, and Helen burbled with laughter.

'To get back to the point,' Kirsty said, poking Ben to shut him up, 'we have both their car keys in the bowl. What does Daniel drive?'

'A BMW.'

'Smooth and rich,' Kirsty commented, not without a wrinkle of the nose. 'And Joel?'

'A Land Rover.'

'Rugged action man...'

'That's utter rubbish,' Ben protested. 'What does it say about me that I drive a crumb-filled Citroen Xsara?'

'Tell you later,' Kirsty murmured, squeezing his knee. 'Can we return to the question? Two sets of keys in the bowl. Which do you pick up?'

'Daniel has a girlfriend,' Helen protested, knocking back the champagne and half wishing she hadn't been so determined to come here tonight. Kirsty rolled her eyes.

'Okay, let's pretend that neither of them has a girlfriend, there's no other conceivable objection, and they both want you. Who do you choose?'

'It's impossible.' Helen shook her head. 'Daniel's so familiar. I've loved him for years. And Joel...' His smiling face filled her head, and she remembered the moment when she had removed his tie at the wedding, and when she had thought he was going to kiss her in the restaurant. Her blood pranced in her veins. 'I don't like this game,' she said. 'It's not as if I'm ever going to have to choose for real, is it?'

'Perhaps not. But you'll have to choose someone someday, unless you're planning to be on your own forever, and they're not bad options, are they?' Kirsty laughed. 'Or are you holding out for an Aston Martin key to fall into the bowl?'

Thankfully the subject dropped after that, and not long afterwards they went to bed. But Helen found it hard to sleep. The wine and the champagne had stimulated rather than tired her, and she thought of the year ahead and all the changes it already held: a new shop, new home, Megan starting school, learning to share Megan's time with Daniel... Everything was changing in all ways but one: she was still on her own. She lay in bed, trying not to listen to Kirsty and Ben having sex, and wondered if she would ever do that again. She heard Tommy whimper, and got up to see to him before he could interrupt his parents. She cuddled his sleepy warm body, inhaling his baby smell, and the knowledge that she might never again have a child of her own felt like a corkscrew spiralling slowly into her heart. She had thought that Megan was all she needed, that with Megan she had enough. So why now was she craving more?

CHAPTER 27

January rolled on, and a routine gradually fell into place. Helen worked at Church Farm on her usual days, plus Sunday when Megan was with Daniel. Keeping busy was the best way – the only way – to cope with her absence. After a couple of weeks, during which some members of the Hay Barn worked every day to keep their shops open, Joel pointed out that other artists ran reciprocal arrangements with neighbours: they would each take a different day off, trusting the other occupants to deal with any enquiries in their absence. They agreed to trial a similar arrangement in the Hay Barn, as they all knew each other's work so well. Helen closed Crazy Little Things on Wednesday, and found a huge benefit in being able to spend the day sewing.

It was agony dropping Megan off at Daniel's house for her to sleep over for the first time. She had decided to deliver Megan herself to extract every last minute they could be together. She regretted her decision as soon as she saw Tasha lurking in the hall behind Daniel, newly returned from Australia, and looking tanned and more gorgeous than ever. Her own skin seemed to dull as she looked at her. Imagining her putting Megan to bed and giving her a goodnight kiss was absolute torture. Helen refused to go in, and barely managed to hold herself together long enough to drive home. Joel found her sobbing in her car outside the cottages, and took her to his house for a comforting hug and cup of tea. Helen let Daniel collect Megan the next time.

The weekend of the craft fair in London arrived, and the group from the Hay Barn caught the first train from Manchester to London on the Saturday morning, laden down with as much stock as they could carry in bags and suitcases. Malcolm's larger canvases had been taken down the day before in a van owned by another artist. The fair was being held in a newly renovated mansion house, which was intended as a space for temporary fairs and exhibitions, and Joel met them outside and helped carry their bags up a magnificent sweeping staircase to the Church Farm area in a huge high-ceilinged room which must once have been a ballroom.

'Amazing, isn't it?' Joel put Helen's case down beside her. 'It was busy yesterday, and today should be even better. Liz knows some journalists who are coming, so keep an eye out.' He took a piece of paper out of his pocket and passed it to her. 'Here's her address for later. Sure you don't want me to pick you up? It's no trouble.'

'Of course not.' Liz had invited Helen to dinner at her house to discuss the crazy patchwork. Joel was staying with her, while the Hay Barn group were booked into a hotel. 'I lived in London for five years. I'm sure I can remember how the Tube works.'

'Get a taxi,' Joel began, but Saskia demanded his help and he hurried away.

Helen loved being able to focus entirely on her

378

crazy patchwork. She sold several pieces, was interviewed by a journalist for a possible article on up-and-coming artists, and was asked to submit designs for two potential large commissions. The day paid for itself many times over, and that wasn't even the best of it. As they were packing up, a lady whom Helen had seen hovering several times approached and asked if she would be interested in submitting a proposal for a book of crazy patchwork designs. She thought Helen and her work were hugely marketable. Helen felt drunk on happiness before her night out had even begun.

Liz lived with her partner John in a classic stucco-fronted building in Kensington, in a two-bedroom apartment divided over three floors.

'This place is gorgeous,' Helen said, as soon as Liz opened the front door.

'Wait until you see inside,' Liz replied, with a laughing wink. She lowered her voice. 'One of the many advantages of falling for a successful older man.'

'I heard that.' John appeared behind her. Joel had warned her there was an age gap: John was tall and silver haired, in his late fifties but still handsome. 'What she means is I'm so old that I bought this place before the property market in London exploded.' He smiled and kissed Helen on both cheeks. 'Let me take your coat and scarf. Joel's upstairs in the living room.'

Running footsteps were heard on the stairs.

'He was,' Liz corrected, exchanging a look and a

smile with John. Joel skidded to a halt in the hall, confronted by three amused faces. 'We were about to bring her up. There's no need to be impatient.'

'That's exactly the kind of comment I dashed down to prevent,' Joel replied, grinning at Helen. 'Can we stop the embarrassing big-sister act now?' He approached Helen and kissed her, wrapping her in his delicious woody scent as he did. 'I'd say you look beautiful, but it might set her off again.' His eyes still said it: she could read it loud and clear.

'Don't worry,' Helen replied, laughing. 'I'll say you look awful, and that will be the end of it.' Joel laughed, and led Helen upstairs. Of course he wasn't looking awful; quite the opposite. In a grey shirt, dark jeans and with hair still slightly damp from the shower, Helen was finding it hard to take her eyes off him.

The living room was a shrine to grown up, child-free living, all blond wooden floors and enormous neutral sofas on either side of a giant coffee table that looked more like a sculpture than a piece of furniture. Accepting a glass of perfectly chilled white wine, Helen couldn't help contrasting this life with hers.

'I know you're the expert in interior design,' she said, looking round, 'but do you know what this room needs? Some plastic toys sprouting out of the sofa, random crumbs and sticky fingerprints.'

'Don't even joke about it.' John laughed and gestured for Helen to sit down on one of the sofas. Joel sat down beside her. 'I have two daughters in their twenties. I'm seriously worried they may be banned from visiting if they ever dare to have babies.'

'I have it all worked out,' Liz replied. 'I know where to find industrial-sized rolls of plastic sheeting.'

'For the flat or the babies?' Joel grinned.

'The flat, obviously. As if I'd shrink wrap my step-grandchildren. Or my nephews and nieces,' she added, with a pointed look at Joel.

The evening rushed away in a pleasant haze of good food, wine and laughter. Helen relaxed in a way that she hadn't felt she could for years, knowing that Megan was safe, and that she was off duty for once. It was as if the evening had reminded her of who she was, and that a whole part of her still existed beyond being a mother. And for once she didn't feel guilty for thinking that way. She felt... exhilarated. And acutely conscious of Joel looking at her, listening to every word she said, being close, brushing against her... Every sense seemed more alive than normal.

'It's a long time since I've seen Joel smile so much,' Liz said, as she and Helen made coffee in the glossy white kitchen.

'Really? He smiles more than anyone I've ever met.'

'He used to,' Liz said, bending into a cupboard to pull out a designer set of coffee cups which Helen suspected had cost more than she earned in a week. 'All that business in Bristol knocked him badly. You know about that?'

'A little,' Helen replied, torn between curiosity and a sense that this was none of her business. 'He mentioned that he'd broken up with someone.'

381

'That's quite an understatement. You know he was on the point of proposing when he found out that Fliss was already married? Everything was planned: surprise weekend in Venice, best room in the best hotel, the most incredible ring, specially designed for her. She later claimed to be separated, but she'd still kept it a secret and Joel knew nothing about it until her husband turned up at the office two days before they were due to fly out. He was devastated. He took off, without a word to anyone. We were on the point of calling the police.' Liz laughed, as she set out the coffee tray. 'It sounds melodramatic now, but it was so unlike him. He's as honest and straightforward as they come. Never a day's worry since the day he was born, Mum has always said.' Liz smiled as she handed Helen a plate of chocolates to carry through. 'It's great to see him so happy now.'

'We're not...' Helen began.

'I know. Think about it though, won't you? The connection between you is obvious. And I know from bitter experience how tough it is to find a good bloke. You must be even more wary with Megan to consider. But have you seen how he dotes on those damn cats? Only imagine how he would be with children.'

Helen didn't need to imagine. She had seen how at ease he was with Megan. He would be a great father, given the chance. She felt a surge of anger at the unknown Fliss for hurting him; chased on its heels by a surge of relief that she had. Helen would never have met him otherwise, and where would she have been then? No job, no home and no Joel. And why, out of everything, did the latter seem the biggest potential loss?

'I promise I'll think about it.' Helen laughed. 'Is this a well-rehearsed sales pitch?'

'I've never done it before. I'm more likely to try to scare off the women I don't like, especially after Fliss. I mean, how could she have done that to him? Some women are toxic, and shouldn't be allowed near a man.' Liz hesitated, her back against the kitchen door, ready to push it open. She smiled. 'But I've never seen him look at anyone the way he looks at you. And as you give him the same look back, I can't believe you would ever hurt him.'

Over coffee, Liz studied Helen's portfolio, and made a list of the pieces she wanted Helen to make, specifying the colour schemes and theme of the decorative embroidery.

'I won't use it all,' she said, 'but if I have it to hand I can play about and see what works best. I'll be at Church Farm for Dad's birthday in five weeks, so could pick it up if you can manage that?'

Helen agreed, though it was a tight deadline with her normal work as well.

'Is it a special birthday?' she asked.

'Seventy,' Joel said. 'Not special, according to him, but we're going to make a fuss anyway, whether he likes it or not. There's even a rumour that Ruth may manage to find her way down from Scotland for the occasion.'

'Just make sure he's around that day. When my

383

father was sixty, my mother organised a huge surprise party for him. He never turned up. He'd flown out to Germany on business that morning and forgotten to tell her.'

'Were you hiding behind the sofa for days, waiting to shout surprise?' Joel asked, laughing.

'Not quite. We were in a hotel, so they had to kick us out eventually. It was still a great party.'

'It's not Patrick Walters, is it?' John said. Helen nodded. 'I remember hearing about that. It was at Claridges, wasn't it? I've thought all night you reminded me of someone. I met him a few years ago when our companies worked together. How is he? Didn't he receive a CBE a couple of years back?'

'Yes, for services to business and charity. He's sold his company, but still works at least as many hours as CEO of a Catholic aid agency.'

Helen became conscious of Joel staring at her. He looked puzzled.

'Your dad has a CBE? You never said you were that posh.'

'I'm not. And it wasn't a secret,' Helen rushed to assure him. 'It had nothing to do with me.' She laughed. 'I was definitely a hindrance, not a help to his success.'

Eventually Helen rose to go, reluctantly remembering that she was on an early train the next morning. John directed her to the best place to find a taxi, and Joel offered to come with her – to the taxi rank, she thought. But as he opened the door of the cab, and she turned, wondering how ever to thank him for today – for everything – he steered her into the taxi and jumped in behind.

'I thought you were staying with Liz,' she said, as he fastened his seatbelt.

'I am, but I'll sleep better once I've seen you walk safely through the doors of your hotel.'

Slightly drunk, slightly tired, and still totally exhilarated by the success of the day, Helen merely nodded. She leaned her head back, watching the lights of London race past the window, aware that Joel was watching her.

'Dinner was fun,' she said at last, rolling her head back to face him. 'This is how life used to be.'

'Fun?' She could see him smiling in the half light. 'Isn't it fun now?'

'Sometimes. With Megan. But not like this.' She waved her arm, hardly knowing herself what she meant by it. She saw him nod.

'How many times since Megan was born have you got away, and done something purely for yourself?'

'Never.'

'Exactly. You need more time to be Helen, the woman, not just Megan's mum. And no,' he added, smiling as she opened her mouth, 'that doesn't make you a bad mother. My mum took a fortnight's holiday by herself every year. She said it taught her to appreciate the other fifty weeks with us. She's the worlds' best mum. I'd say you come a close second.'

How could he know what she was thinking? Did he mean it? She wasn't even sure she cared. The taxi turned a sharp left, and Helen rolled towards Joel, her head landing on his shoulder. He lifted his arm and put it round her. She didn't move away.

They reached the hotel and got out of the taxi. Joel asked the driver to hang on, and turned back to Helen.

'Helen, tonight was great...'

'Yes, I said it was fun,' she gabbled, shivering with nerves as much as from the chill of the night air. 'And thanks so much for today...'

'No,' he interrupted, and he reached out and took her hand. 'I mean, being with you... at Liz's house together... It felt right.'

He pulled her towards him so their scarves were touching, and bent his head until his lips were close to hers and he was looking directly into her eyes, and she knew what had to happen next, and couldn't even have been certain which of them finally closed the gap. He kissed her with pure tenderness, his whole heart in his lips. Helen had never been kissed like that in her life. Her fingers threaded through his hair, and she was lost.

'Oi!' Helen was too dazed to recognise the noise as a voice at first. She felt Joel's kiss turn into a smile against her lips as he reluctantly pulled away. Glancing round, she caught a vaguely familiar figure darting into the hotel, then realised that the sound had come from the taxi driver, who was leaning out of the window, grinning.

'Oi, mate, are you getting a room or what? Only, the clock's still ticking and this is costing you.'

Joel's eyes repeated the question to Helen.

'You should go,' she said softly. 'Liz is expecting you back.'

He groaned.

'Do you have to think of other people, even now? Why can't you be selfish for once in your life?' He smiled, and stroked her hair, tidying it up. The tenderness was there again, trying to reach in and curl around her heart. 'I didn't think the night would end like that. Hoped, maybe, but then I've hoped for it ever since I first saw you in St Andrew's.'

The taxi driver gave a long beep of the horn. Joel kissed Helen again, and got in the cab. It waited until she was inside the hotel, and then drove away, but before it was even out of sight Helen's phone beeped. She read the text:

'Taxi driver thinks I'm an idiot to leave you. I am an idiot. Tomorrow night? Sleep well. J. x'

Sleep? Helen felt as if she'd just been woken up, like one of the princesses in Megan's stories, and in the most delicious way. How could she fall back to sleep after that? She felt more alive than she had done in years.

CHAPTER 28

Helen woke and stretched her arm out across the bed. She buried her face in the pillow as she felt the cold and empty patch beside her. So it was true. She had let Joel kiss her like that – but there had been nothing passive about it; *she* had kissed Joel like that – and then sent him away. *She* was the idiot.

She rolled over, trying to convince herself that it was better to regret nothing happening than something, and reached for her phone. Would he have sent a text yet? There was nothing, only a message from Daniel telling her what time he would drop Megan off. Helen sent a reply to him, and a good morning to Joel, and got up to meet the others for the train home.

She didn't hear from Joel all day. He had stayed behind in London for the last day of the fair, and she told herself he would be busy. But too busy to send even a hello? After last night?

'Is anything wrong?' Daniel asked, after she'd handed him Megan's strawberry milk instead of his coffee, and made him coffee with one sugar – which was how Joel took it – instead of none. 'You seem distracted.'

'Still thinking about yesterday,' she replied honestly.

'Did it go well?'

'It was amazing. I mean, the fair was amazing,' she

added, and then could have groaned at her stupidity when Daniel raised his eyebrow at her, because what else could she have meant? He didn't know there had been anything else, although her guilt was currently so pungent she was surprised he couldn't smell it on her. Helen dragged her mind back to the fair. 'Two potential commissions, a magazine feature, and I've been asked to draw up a proposal for a book!'

She stopped. Joel hadn't been around when she'd been approached about the book, and she'd forgotten to mention it to him. How could she not have told him? He would be thrilled for her. She'd send him a text when Daniel had gone. Or should she wait to tell him tonight? Her stomach spasmed at the thought of seeing Joel later.

Daniel's frown clawed her back to the present.

'Where will you find the time for all this extra work? You barely have much time with Megan as it is. That isn't a criticism,' he said, forestalling the argument that he must have guessed was on its way. 'Let me help. I don't understand. You were happy for me to support you before. I have even more obligation to do it now.'

Obligation. It was such an unattractive word.

'I don't want to be anyone's obligation,' Helen protested. 'And while we're talking about money, I don't need you to pay the school fees either.'

He leaned forward.

'You can't change your mind about Broadholme. I thought you'd accepted the place.'

'I have. But when I did, I spoke to Mrs King about

the fees, and she explained that I could apply for a bursary as I'm a single parent on a low income. Confirmation came through this week.'

'You're not a single parent.' Daniel's fingers tapped his mug so hard that his coffee almost sloshed out.

'Yes I am. It's not an attempt to exclude you, it simply means that I'm not in a relationship, and there's only one income coming into the house.'

'At the moment.'

'What do you mean?' Helen ran nervous fingers over her chin. Surely she hadn't missed the tell-tale signs of stubble rash?

Daniel smiled at her, and flicked a glance at Megan.

'Now's not the time. It can wait.' He was still smiling. Helen had no idea what was going on. 'What if we compromise? Give up the shop, but carry on with the crazy patchwork. Do the commissions, do the book, but fit it round Megan. Don't you want to spend more time with her before she goes to school?'

Of course she did, and it was unfair of him to ask. The compromise he suggested had been the Holy Grail when she had first opened Crazy Little Things: she had wanted to reach the point where she could support herself from crazy patchwork alone. The retail side had been a necessary evil to earn some money initially, but had seemed too much hard work to keep going forever. Now she wasn't sure. Apart from the practical point that the shop provided a showcase for her work, she loved working there, and dealing with the customers. She loved it even more so far at Church Farm, and the first two sessions of her sewing class had gone brilliantly well. Would she really want to give all that up?

'Promise you'll think about it?' Daniel asked, stretching across and stroking her hand with his finger. Helen jumped. What was he doing? 'Take as long as you need. You know I'm not going anywhere.'

Joel didn't reply to Helen's text telling him about the book. He didn't call round later, either. In fact, he didn't seem to return home at all. Helen looked out of the window so often her thighs began to ache with all the bobbing up and down. When ten o'clock came, she tried ringing, but his mobile was off or flat, and his landline went through to the answering machine. Helen went outside and looked at his cottage, which was in darkness. She rang the bell and knocked on the door, but there was no sign of life at all.

She looked again at the text he'd sent on Saturday night. It clearly referred to tomorrow night. Then she noticed the time and kicked herself. It had been sent after midnight, early on Sunday morning. He must have meant Monday night. But he didn't show up then either.

Helen left the shop three times on Tuesday morning to visit Joel's office, but it was locked up, and there was no sign that he had been there. His mobile was still off.

'Has anyone seen Joel?' she asked, with an attempt at nonchalance, when she returned to the Hay Barn for the third time. Only Saskia and Fiona were around, as it was Malcolm's day off.

'Not since Saturday,' Fiona replied. 'Have you tried the office?'

'He's not there.'

'Is there a problem with the shop? Isn't that typical on the day we don't have Malcolm!'

How Fiona thought Malcolm would be good in a crisis was lost on Helen.

'The shop's fine. I only wanted to talk to him about the website,' Helen improvised.

Saskia sidled out of her shop.

'He's staying down in London for a few days,' she said, smiling at Helen.

'With Liz? How do you know?'

'He sent me a text.'

'When?'

'Sunday afternoon. Didn't he tell you?' Saskia's smile grew broader. 'I think he had a last-minute change of heart about coming back.'

About coming back? Or about her? Helen wondered as she drifted back to the comforting embrace of Crazy Little Things. It must be her, mustn't it? Had she been no more than a drunken fumble, and now he was too embarrassed to face her? Had he only been interested in a one-night stand, while they were both drunk and away from home? His kiss hadn't felt like that. But how else could she interpret his continuing absence, and the fact that he was texting Saskia while ignoring Helen's calls?

Shortly before lunch on Friday, a woman came into the shop and looked round. She was vaguely familiar.

'Hello,' she said, catching Helen's eye. 'You don't remember me, do you?' She held out her hand. 'Lucinda, from *Lancashire Life*. We met at Alex's wedding. Didn't Joel tell you I was coming today?'

'No, I've not seen him for a few days.'

'That explains your blank look. I only fixed it up yesterday. Sorry it's such short notice, but we've had to pull a feature for legal reasons and when I mentioned Church Farm the editor agreed it would make an ideal filler. Do you mind if I take some photos?' Her camera was out of her bag before Helen had chance to nod in agreement.

'Is this the crazy patchwork you mentioned at the wedding?' Lucinda asked, snapping away. 'It's beautiful. Tell me how it's done again, and about yourself while I make some notes.'

Helen did, watching as Lucinda scribbled it all down.

'You will feature the other artists as well, won't you?' Helen asked. 'Malcolm and Fiona are here today. Saskia's on her day off but we can open her shop if you want photos, and there are all the other buildings as well.'

Lucinda laughed.

'Don't worry, Joel has given me the grand tour. I've seen all the other artists. You were the only one left.'

'Joel's here? I thought he was away.'

'He does look like he's been travelling, but that

393

rough, unkempt look is pretty appealing, if you know what I mean!' Lucinda laughed again, but Helen couldn't join in. Joel was here, but hadn't returned any of Helen's messages or calls. He hadn't told her Lucinda was coming, or asked for her help as he had at the wedding. He had provided a tour of Church Farm, and avoided the Hay Barn. How much more clearly did she need it spelling out?

For the rest of the day she looked out through the shop, through the huge Hay Barn doors, wondering if she would catch a glimpse of him. And then she did – she was sure it was him, the back of his head turned resolutely away from the Hay Barn. It was too much. She followed him to his office, knocked on the door and marched in.

Lucinda hadn't exaggerated about how he looked. His clothes were rumpled, tawny stubble covered his chin, and a paleness around his eyes suggested he needed sleep. But it was the eyes Helen noticed most, as they fixed on her as she barged through the door. Their expression was dead. With a jolt of shock, Helen realised it was the way Daniel had looked at her when he first came back. Seeing it from Joel was devastating. What had happened to him?

'What's wrong?' she asked, moving nearer and reaching out to touch his arm. He jerked back as if her hand held a syringe of poison. 'Has something happened?'

'No.'

'Where have you been?'

'I stayed on with Liz for a few days.'

He wouldn't meet her eyes, and fiddled with some papers on his desk.

'Why didn't you tell me? I sent you dozens of messages. Why wouldn't you take any of my calls?'

'I didn't feel like talking.'

'And what about how I felt?' Helen snapped. 'How could you? How could you ignore me when you kissed me like… like…'

'Like what?' His fingers stilled on the papers.

'Like you cared!'

'I did care!' For a second, the lights flashed back on in his eyes and she could see the emotion spilling out. 'I thought…'

'Thought what?'

'I thought I'd fallen in love with you.' A sort of shrug accompanied his words.

Love? He was in love with her? Helen hadn't expected that. She hadn't expected anyone to ever say that to her again, not the way she was now, and not after what she had done. And for *Joel* to say it… Her heart began to stretch, as if preparing to wake up. Then it occurred to her that he had used the past tense. Was that it, already?

'Kissing me changed your mind, did it? I know I haven't kissed anyone for five years, but I didn't think it was that bad.'

'It wasn't. The kiss was perfect.' His eyes were blank as he looked at her, but he couldn't disguise the ache in his voice. 'What changed my mind was discovering that *you* weren't perfect. That I didn't actually know you at all.'

395

'What do you mean? Of course you do.' But an icy drop of apprehension began to trickle down Helen's spine.

'I found out your secret.'

'I don't have a secret.' The lie pooled around the small of her back.

'But you did, didn't you? I thought Fliss' deception was as bad as it could get, but you take it to a whole new level. Because from what I've heard, it's a good job we stopped at a kiss. If I'd gone back to your room – if there'd been an accident and you'd ended up pregnant – it might have been four years before I'd known anything about it.'

Oh God, he knew. Helen sat down on the desk, her legs too numb to support her. She had chosen not to tell him, fearing exactly this reaction, but she saw now, too late, how much better it would have been to tell him herself, and to explain why she had done it.

'Who told you?'

'One of your friends. A good friend to me, as it turns out.'

'Kirsty?' Helen asked. She was the only one who knew the story, but Helen couldn't believe that Kirsty would have revealed it to Joel. 'When did Kirsty tell you?'

'Not Kirsty, Saskia. She saw us kissing outside the hotel. She sent me a series of texts with some information she thought I should know before it went further. Thank God she did.'

Now it all made sense. The figure Helen had seen darting into the hotel must have been Saskia: Saskia who had recently asked questions about Daniel, and who had never concealed her attraction to Joel and her resentment towards Helen. She had seen a way to scupper Joel's interest in Helen and taken it. But however she had found out about Daniel, she couldn't know the whole truth, and that meant Joel didn't either.

'What did Saskia tell you?'

'Everything. That you were a bored 'It girl' who wanted a baby as the latest accessory. That you deliberately got pregnant, and dumped Daniel as soon as you were. That you didn't tell him you were pregnant, and he only found out when he saw Megan for the first time last year. Are you going to tell me none of it is true?'

She couldn't, and he must have seen that in her face. Joel sank into his chair.

'It's all been distorted,' Helen protested.

'Did you want the baby?'

'Yes, there was no question of…'

'Did you end the relationship with Daniel when you found out you were pregnant?'

'Yes, but…'

'Did you tell him you were having a baby?'

'No, because…'

'Did you tell him that Megan existed before he saw her?'

'No,' Helen replied dully. She saw the disappointment settle on his face. 'Do you even want to hear the truth?'

'What more is there?' Joel's voice sounded duller

than Helen's. 'You've confirmed everything Saskia said.'

'Only the facts, not the feelings. I loved Daniel. I would have done anything for him.' Helen saw the pain ripple across Joel's face, but pressed on. 'We were about to start a new life in Hong Kong when I found I was pregnant. I knew Daniel didn't want children yet, and it would ruin everything he had worked for. I thought that if he heard I was pregnant, he would either come back to England for me, or persuade me to have an abortion, and I couldn't have lived with either of those alternatives. So I chose the third option. I didn't tell him. I let him go to Hong Kong and have the life he wanted, and I brought up Megan on my own. She's no accessory. She's everything. You must have seen that.'

'God, you're incredible,' Joel said, and for a second Helen thought that she had convinced him, until she saw from his face that it was no compliment. She wasn't incredible in the way she had been before. 'Do you really expect me to believe that you did this for him?'

'No,' she replied. It had been hope, not expectation, but as she looked at him, saw the ruins of his affection in his face, she realised that she had nothing left to lose. She might as well tell him the truth – the real truth, not the romanticised version she had told herself so often that she almost believed it. Perhaps it would even give her some peace to make her confession at last.

'You're right,' she said. 'I'm not perfect. And

Saskia was right. I was a bored 'It girl', if that's what you want to call me. I'd never had any real identity beyond being Patrick Walters' daughter, and Daniel Blake's girlfriend. And for a long time that was enough. But then it wasn't. I started sewing again, and designing crazy patchwork, but that wasn't enough either. I wanted something more, something of my own, some purpose to life. So I stopped using contraception, and no, I didn't tell Daniel.'

Helen looked at Joel. He was still listening, but it was impossible to know what he was thinking. She carried on.

'Then the job in Hong Kong came up, and it was going to be the most fantastic adventure. We only had a few weeks to sort it out, and in the excitement of it all, contraception never crossed my mind. I found out I was pregnant two days before I was meant to join him over there. You know what I did. I chose my baby over Daniel. I had found my something. My *everything*,' she repeated. 'So no, I didn't act entirely for Daniel; in fact I probably acted entirely for myself. I will never regret having Megan. And I will never stop regretting how I've treated Daniel. You can't possibly hate me for that as much as I hate myself. So now you know it all. I am selfish, inconsistent and completely imperfect, but I'm still the person you've come to know over the last few months.'

'You're not though, are you? You've lied about who you are from the start. All those times you told me you couldn't afford to improve your website, or expand the business – when I arranged reduced rent at the shop and the cottage to help you out, persuaded my friends to do your removal to save you money – and it wasn't bloody true! You've admitted it yourself, you're rich! As Saskia said, the shop and the sewing are nothing but a rich girl's hobby.'

'I'm not rich.'

'You can't deny it! Your dad has a bloody CBE!'

'That doesn't make me rich.' Helen banged her heels against the desk in frustration.

'I should have worked it out from what you said at Liz's house. The huge surprise party at Claridges, your dad flying around the world, and selling his business... It's not the background of someone genuinely struggling to earn a living. I admired you so much, for who you are, what you've achieved, and none of it's real. I can't believe I've been taken in again. Do I have "idiot" stamped on my forehead, or do you treat all men like this? Because you're good. You really know how to screw up a man. Perhaps you should add that to your list of classes in the Hay Barn.'

Helen jumped down from the desk. It would have hurt to hear anyone say these things about her. But from Joel... When only a few days ago his lips had persuaded her of such different feelings... She couldn't bear it. And there was only one thing left she could think of to offer him: another truth, that she hadn't even shared with Daniel.

'Yes, I've been spoilt and selfish all my life, but having Megan changed everything. If you were listening to me at Liz's dinner, you'll also know that

400

my parents are devout Catholics – devout to the extreme. I couldn't stand all their holiness and morality as I was growing up, and rebelled in every way I could: smoking, drinking, playing truant, going out with countless boys – you name it, I probably tried it. When they found out that I was pregnant, and that Daniel had left me, they were horrified. It was the final straw, as far as they were concerned. Instead of coming to the hospital themselves, as proud grandparents, they sent a stranger to persuade me to give up Megan for adoption. They said that I wasn't fit to be a mother, and that it would be best for both of us. Can you even begin to imagine how that felt?'

Helen could feel her heart breaking all over again as she remembered that time. Until then, she had truly believed that despite their initial disapproval, her parents would be thrilled as soon as her baby arrived.

'From that moment, I haven't accepted a penny from them. Adam lent me the deposit to rent a house and gave me a loan to open the shop – and I'm still trying to pay him back for both.' She took a deep breath. 'It's been harder work than I ever expected, and quite terrifying. I'm up until the early morning to get everything done. Sometimes I've lived for days only on toast, because I couldn't afford to feed us both. That's how real this is. So you can accuse me of playing at having a career, but it's not true. Not since I had Megan.'

She was at the door, the handle in her trembling grasp, when she heard him speak.

'Helen.' She turned round. He had moved in front

of the desk, and his knuckles shone white as he gripped the edge. 'Saskia said you're trying to make a go of it with Daniel again. Tell me it's not true. If our kiss meant as much to you as it did to me, tell me you don't love him, and that you wouldn't have him back if he asked you.'

'Joel, I...' The words stuck in her throat. The spark of hope illuminating his eyes died. She couldn't say the words he wanted, and he knew it. She couldn't deny her feelings for Daniel, even to please Joel. It was the one point on which Saskia was wrong, and the one point she couldn't even try to argue away. Would she go back to Daniel, if he asked? The truth was, she didn't know. It seemed unlikely to happen. But if it ever did, shouldn't she say yes? Wasn't that the only way to atone for what she had done to him, and to Megan, by restoring what she had taken away? So she took a final look at Joel, at what might have been, and walked out.

CHAPTER 29

February, a bleak month at the best of times, seemed even longer and bleaker this year. A combination of rain and snow kept casual visitors away from Church Farm, and it was hard to resist Malcolm's prophesies of doom. The atmosphere inside the Hay Barn was even icier than outside, as Helen tried her best to ignore Saskia, and especially to ignore the urge to go over with her sharpest needle, and sew up Saskia's lips so they could no longer form the smug smile that shaped them every time she looked Helen's way.

It hadn't taken long to discover how Saskia had found out about Daniel. A mortified Kirsty confessed to having told her the bare bones, after Saskia had tricked her into thinking she already knew. The rest she had made up, with an uncanny degree of accuracy. Kirsty was all for having it out with Saskia, but Helen stopped her. What was the point? She had done her worst, and it had worked. Joel avoided Helen now, at work and at home, and they hadn't spoken since the day he had returned from the London fair. Then one night, as she was going to bed, she saw him arrive home in a taxi with Saskia. He was wrapped up against the cold weather in a thick coat, but wasn't wearing her scarf. There was nothing more to be said.

'He would never be interested in Saskia, love,' Joan said, when she called at Helen's house one

403

Wednesday for coffee and a chat. 'He's too honest for her. That devious witch wouldn't know the truth if it bit her on the bum.'

'I think it's more than truth biting her bum now.'

'Oh love, you'll put me off my cake,' Joan laughed, nevertheless taking a large bite of the chocolate cake she had supposedly brought for Megan. 'I certainly won't be splashing out on a new hat if that wedding comes about.'

Helen put down the rest of her cake, her appetite gone. Though it was stupid: Joel could marry whom he liked. It was just galling to see Saskia's spiteful behaviour rewarded with the prize. Joan reached out and squeezed her hand.

'Where there's life, there's hope, eh?' she said, with a smile so sympathetic it almost made Helen cry.

'I never had hopes,' she replied. 'We were friends, that's all.' And now not even that. It was harder than she could have imagined to ignore the Joel-shaped gap in her life where that friendship had been.

Joan gave Helen's hand a pat.

'I had hopes,' she admitted. 'From the day he moved back from Bristol, months before you met. It seemed a perfect match.' Joan sighed. 'All this business about you being secretly rich and not who you seem... I could have told him it was nonsense. I've seen how hard you've worked. And if he'd been at Megan's first birthday party...'

'What was wrong with it?'

'Nothing, love, I know it was the best you could do at the time. But six of us sitting round a table in

404

the St Andrew's café, and her grandparents not there – it's not what you'd have done if you were rolling in cash, is it? I've half a mind to tell him...'

Crazy Little Things had turned from being Helen's sanctuary to a place of torture. She dreaded going to work and seeing Saskia, or seeing Joel with Saskia. There was no relief at home either, hearing Joel moving around next door, and trying to time their comings and goings so they didn't run into him. Megan asked every day when she could see Mr Cat, and where Joel had gone, and there was no possible answer Helen could give.

For the first time, Helen began to seriously consider Daniel's suggested compromise. She could give up the shop, concentrate on crazy patchwork, and perhaps even move again, somewhere nearer Broadholme. She would have to accept his maintenance payments, and it would mean giving up a large chunk of her independence, but it no longer seemed the wrench it once had. What good was independence, if it made her so miserable? She could put aside her own feelings, as she always had, and do what was best for Megan. Perhaps, at this moment, spending more time with her was the best thing.

'Would you like me to spend less time at work, and more days with you?' she asked Megan, as they snuggled together on the sofa in front of the fire one Saturday afternoon. Megan nodded.

'More days with Daddy as well?' she asked.

'More days with Daddy and Tasha eventually,'

Helen agreed, trying to sound cheerful about the prospect.

'Not Tasha, Mummy.' Megan giggled. 'Tasha isn't here.'

'Isn't where?' Helen asked.

'At Daddy's house. She's gone to her house.'

Helen had no idea what that meant, and it didn't feel right to interrogate Megan. When Daniel came round the next day, she waited until Megan was in the bathroom, and casually asked: 'Are you and Tasha taking her out anywhere today?'

Daniel hesitated.

'Tasha has gone back to Australia,' he said at last, glancing at Helen. 'She only had permission to be here for six months as a general visitor.'

'That's tough on you both. What happens now? Does she have to apply for a visa to come back?'

'She's not coming back.'

Helen took a moment to digest this, and then an awful thought occurred to her.

'Are you moving back to Australia?'

'No. We've broken up. She couldn't adjust to life here.' By which Helen guessed he meant she couldn't adjust to Megan. Tasha hadn't known she was crossing the world to become a stepmother. Now she was gone, and no threat to Helen's relationship with Megan, Helen was prepared to be sympathetic.

Daniel was watching her, one finger slowly tapping against his leg.

'Would you have minded if I'd moved back?'

'Yes, of course. Megan would be devastated.'

He gave a wry smile as Megan bounded into the room and jumped straight into his arms. The more time she spent with Daniel, the closer they became. It was Helen's recurring nightmare that as she grew older, Megan might choose to live with him. How would she ever endure that?

Daniel picked up Megan's belongings and took her hand.

'Do you want to come out with us today?' he asked, as Helen bent to kiss Megan goodbye. 'I thought the park, then lunch at Mum's.'

'I can't,' Helen replied, startled by the question and glad she didn't have to make a decision. 'I have to work. I have an appointment later.'

'You look tired. You need a break. Why don't we go on holiday? We could rent a cottage for a few days.'

'The three of us?'

'Of course.' Daniel smiled. 'You'd like that, wouldn't you Megan? A few days with Mummy and Daddy.' She nodded happily, and he looked at Helen. 'Why not?'

Her mind went blank, and if there were good reasons why not, she couldn't think of them. The prospect of a break – away from Church Farm, away from Pleasant View Cottages – was utter bliss, and exactly what she needed.

'That would be lovely,' she said, with a grateful smile. 'Shall I...'

'You don't need to do anything. I'll book somewhere. We'll go next Sunday. I'll let you know if that proves a problem.'

Smiling the Daniel smile she had dreamed about through the long years of his absence, he swooped to drop a lingering kiss on her cheek, and left.

Helen had never been on a self-catering holiday with Daniel before: it had been five-star hotels all the way in their previous life. So it didn't surprise her when they turned off a country lane in the Yorkshire Dales and pulled up outside what was clearly no ordinary holiday let. It was a picturesque stone cottage set amongst rolling fields, immaculately modernised, and with daily maid and chef services. It was like having a small boutique hotel to themselves.

'Like it?' Daniel asked, as he unloaded their cases from the car.

'Love it,' Helen replied, wondering if she ever needed to go home. She took Megan's hand, and led her round to the back of the house, where they found a large garden with a play area. But Megan was distracted by something else.

'Sheep!' she cried, and ran to the side of the garden, which overlooked a farmer's field. 'Lambs!' Megan squealed, her arm waving in excitement. Helen joined her, and watched as a mother lamb ambled away with two lambs at her side. Megan reached for Helen's hand. 'Joel would like this, wouldn't he, Mummy? Can we send him a picture?'

'Perhaps later,' Helen replied, checking behind her to make sure that Daniel hadn't heard. She must have underestimated Megan's perception of Joel, and of his role in their lives. Megan had been used to seeing him or hearing of him most days – as had Helen. Perhaps the break would help both of them come to terms with his absence.

The early spring weather was kind, and Daniel had prepared an itinerary of walks, farms, steam trains and garden trails that kept Megan amused in the day and ensured she was exhausted enough to tumble into sleep at night. Helen had worried that the evenings would be awkward, after Megan had gone to bed, and had brought a pile of sewing to keep her busy. But she hardly picked it up. Daniel had ordered three-course meals every night, which only needed warming up, and the nights drifted away as they lingered over the food and wine. For those few hours, it could almost have been old times; except for the separate bedrooms at the end of the night.

'Megan's having a great time, isn't she?' Daniel asked on the Wednesday evening, as they relaxed over the remains of a second bottle of wine.

'Yes, she is,' Helen agreed. It was only the second holiday Megan had ever experienced: everything was exciting. 'Thanks for arranging this, Dan.'

'It's good for her to spend time with us both together.' He leaned over and poured the rest of the wine into Helen's glass. 'We need to do it more often.'

'I suppose so, but it's difficult when I work on Sundays.'

'Have you thought any more about giving up the shop?' Daniel's index finger tapped rhythmically against his glass.

'Yes.' His head shot up, his eyes searching hers. 'I meant, I am thinking about it. I'm not sure it's working out at Church Farm.' She drank some wine, in the vain hope of drowning the anguish of acknowledging it out loud for the first time.

'Would you stay in that cottage if you weren't working there?'

'Probably not.' Her heart twinged again. She loved the cottage. It already felt more like home than her old house had ever done – than anywhere she'd lived had ever done. 'There'd be no point. I'd have to look for somewhere else.'

A long pause followed, during which jazz blared out of the iPod dock, Daniel stared into his glass, swirling the wine, and Helen sank deeper into misery.

'I think I'll go to bed,' she said, putting down her glass and standing up. Daniel stood up too.

'Move in with me, Nell,' he said. 'Let's be together. Let's do our best for Megan.'

She hesitated in the doorway, unsure about what he was suggesting. Did he mean together as a family, or together as a couple? And as she stood there, wondering what he meant, and what she wanted him to mean, he strode the distance between them and kissed her.

It was the familiar Daniel kiss, that she had never forgotten, but never expected to experience again. Already he was rubbing the back of her neck at her hairline, taking the shortcut that only he knew. And part of her swooned that he still remembered, her mind thrilled that what she had longed for was really happening, and she waited in anticipation for desire to stir...

But it didn't. He was doing the right things, but something was wrong. It was a good kiss. But it wasn't affecting her the way it used to do.

Perhaps her memories were stifling her reaction. How could it ever live up to what they had known before? But as Daniel's lips and hands tried to lead her in the routine direction, Helen understood what the problem was. It didn't live up to what she had felt with Joel.

Shocked, Helen pulled away.

'What's the matter?' Daniel asked, trying to draw her back. A faint frown clouded his brow.

'I don't know.' She tried a smile. 'Tired, I suppose. I need to think about this,' she admitted.

His eyes searched hers. A fact lay unspoken between them. She had never failed to respond before; never had to think about anything where he was concerned.

'We'll talk more tomorrow,' he said at last, and opened the door to let her out.

Daniel, Joel, Daniel, Joel... The thoughts tossed through Helen's head all night, keeping sleep at bay. What had she done? And what was she going to do? Joel had offered her everything, she couldn't doubt that, remembering his kiss; and she had rejected him, partly because of Daniel. And now Daniel had offered her *something*; and though she wasn't entirely clear what that something was, it was more than she had

411

ever truly thought would be hers again. Was she really going to reject him too? Could she, after loving him for so many years? Should she when, disregarding her own feelings, a reunion with him must surely be what Megan would want? Was she being selfish to even think about turning him down? Why was she still uncertain?

As the sun rose, and the sound of bleating lambs filtered through the window, Helen let herself out into the garden and sat on the swing, slowly rocking backwards and forwards in the early morning sunshine, the rhythm of the swing echoing the movement of her thoughts.

'Mummy!' Megan tore across the garden in her pyjamas, dressing gown and shoes. Helen stilled the swing, and Megan climbed onto her lap.

'Are you sad, Mummy?' she asked, looking up at Helen with curious wide eyes. 'You were swinging sadly.'

'Was I?' Helen kissed the top of her head. 'I was thinking, that's all.'

'You need Joel,' Megan said, kicking her legs to try to make the swing move. 'He makes you laugh, like Daddy makes me laugh. I like it best when you're laughing Mummy, not sad Mummy.'

She rested her head against Helen, and started singing. Helen rocked them both on the swing. Was it really that simple? Did Megan only need Helen to be happy, whoever she found happiness with? Had Megan noticed what Helen had been too blind – or too unwilling – to see herself?

Five years ago she had let Daniel go, but she had never let go of her feelings for him. Her heart was a patchwork of all kinds of love, and she had kept one patch for him; but it was no longer the largest one, or the most vibrant. The biggest patch would always be for Megan. But the next one was for Joel: Joel who made her laugh, who lavished her with support and friendship and who made her heart spin with desire, and sigh with tenderness. She couldn't go back to Daniel, even out of guilt, because she wasn't the girl who had loved him any more. The woman she was now belonged with Joel. But would he still want her, after all she had told him? And could she ever deserve to have him?

Helen looked up and saw Daniel leaning in the doorway of the house, watching them.

'I need to speak to Daddy, sweetheart, so swing yourself for a few minutes. I'll be watching to see how high you can go, okay?'

She crossed the lawn and joined Daniel. The sun was shining on him, picking out the grey at his temples. He was still one of the most handsome men she had ever seen. He always would be. They'd had an incredible past. She couldn't destroy the memory of that by following it with a mediocre future.

'You've decided, haven't you?' he asked, studying her face. She nodded.

'I can't do it. We can never recapture what we had, and I think we'd both be miserable trying.'

'Megan would be happy. Isn't that enough?' He took her hand. 'Think about it, Nell. We could give

413

her the proper family she's missed out on so far.'

'But there it is, even now. You can't help thinking about what I did. It will never go away. And that's not the only reason,' she rushed on, when he opened his mouth to protest. He deserved absolute honesty. 'I know you'd do anything for Megan. So would I. And I do love you, Dan.' She saw a lift in his eyes. 'But it's not the love I used to feel. Even if it was, I couldn't move in with you unless I was sure that you felt the same, and that you loved me as me, as who I am now, not just as Megan's mother.'

A flicker of consciousness whisked over his face, quickly gone, but she'd seen it and thought she'd hit the truth.

'Isn't it worth the chance, Nell?' Her hand was still in his, and his thumb was rubbing hers. 'Look at Megan. Look what we can do together. Let's try for Archie.'

The tears started when he said that, as she pictured the gorgeous little boy, the image of Daniel, who would never now exist – or not with her.

'Archie would be the end for us, Dan, don't you see? Witnessing his birth, seeing his first tooth, the first step, hearing his first word... They would be constant reminders that you missed all that with Megan. We would never survive that. Isn't it better for Megan to have us both around, as friends, than to have a few years together before going through a bitter separation? There's no way we can be together. For years I hoped you would come back and say all this, but if I'm honest, I knew when I kept Megan

414

secret that there could be no second chances.'

He let go of her hand, brushed the tears away from her cheeks, and pulled her into a hug. She could feel his ragged breaths, as he buried his head in her hair.

'Is it him?' he asked, drawing back to look at her face. 'Be honest, Nell. Are you in love with Joel?'

'Yes.' She couldn't deny it. She'd found her certainty now, too late. 'But it's no good. He thinks I'm a spoilt rich girl who ruined your life.'

'Not that rich…' Catching her eye, he laughed, and she laughed too. Though her heart still ached a little at the sight of him, it had become a good ache: an acknowledgment that they had shared something great, and had found a fresh way forward. They would be a team, but a team of parents, not lovers.

'Will you be honest with me, Dan?' she asked. She had tried to forget the conversation with Adam before Christmas, but she needed to know the truth. 'If there'd been no pregnancy, and I had come with you to Hong Kong, where would we be now? Would we be here, planning our future, trying for Megan and Archie?'

She knew the answer before he opened his mouth. The movement of his eyebrow, the tap of his finger, were tells that he couldn't disguise from someone who had idolised him on first sight.

'But you're so different now,' he protested.

'Only because of Megan. If I was the same person you left, she would never have existed, would she?'

He sighed, as if finally letting go of all the pretence of the last few months.

'Probably not.'

They both looked over at the beautiful little girl on the swing, who waved back at them, beaming with happiness.

'It doesn't bear thinking about,' Daniel murmured.

'And one more thing,' Helen continued. She took hold of his hand, for what she knew would be the last time. It was warm and solid in her grasp, and still carried a faint tan, a souvenir of their time apart. This hand had led her through some brilliant times, but she didn't need leading any more. 'No tricks, no blame, just tell me the truth. If I'd contacted you in Hong Kong, and told you I was pregnant – the Helen I was then – what would you have done?'

And again she saw the answer before he spoke it; but this time she needed to hear the words. He turned his hand so he was holding hers, and stroked his thumb along the back of her fingers.

'I loved you, Nell, you can't doubt that,' he said. 'But I had been working towards that job for over ten years. I couldn't have given it up.'

Helen nodded, and let her hand slide from his. Her nose prickled with unshed tears, and her heart stung as her memory of the past was scratched out, and a new version engraved in its place. Her guilt melted away, leaving her dizzy with relief and possibility. She really hadn't ruined Daniel's life. She hadn't ruined Megan's life. Perhaps she deserved her happiness after all.

'I need to go,' she said. Daniel nodded, understanding at once what she meant. 'Do you

416

mind? I'm sorry to cut short the holiday.'

'You should go on your own. Megan will be fine with me for one last night.' He took hold of her shoulders and twisted her round to face into the house. 'Go and pack. I'll ring for a taxi to take you home.'

A mile away from Pleasant View Cottages, the nerves crept in, towing wheelbarrows full of doubts behind in their wake. What if Joel wasn't there? What if he was there, but wouldn't listen to her? What if he was there with Saskia? Helen wished she was back in Yorkshire. What on earth had she been thinking of, rushing back here?

Her mobile beeped and she checked the message.

'Your Hong Kong is waiting for you. Be happy. Dan.'

Helen was still puzzling over the message when the taxi drew up outside the cottage and she got out. Daniel had already paid an extortionate fare, and as the driver lifted out her bag, she looked over at her house, and noticed even after a few days the changes that the spring weather had delivered in the garden. Crocuses and daffodils were bursting through the soil, bringing new life to the garden, and in a previously empty bed a couple of rose bushes waited for the summer. She stared at them, wondering where they had come from.

She opened the gate, and as she headed up the path she saw Joel waiting at the end, between the doors to their houses. Then she understood Daniel's message, and the tears sprang to her eyes again. He had done this. He had forgiven her. He had let her go.

Helen put down her bag and waited as Joel walked down the path towards her. The rogue curl sprang out over his ear, as if it had been recently tortured, and he was smiling, a faintly anxious smile, but it was still wonderful to see, and her heart swelled with relief.

'You knew I was coming back,' she said, as he halted in front of her. He nodded. 'Did Daniel ring you?'

'Yes. It was quite a surprise.'

'What did he say?'

'I'm going to have to be a hypocrite, and keep it secret. It was men's talk.'

'Was it about me?'

He laughed, and she soaked in the sound, marvelling at how much she had missed it.

'Stop fishing.'

She smiled, and bent down to read the label on the roses.

'Ingrid Bergman, a hybrid tea rose, deep red double petalled flowers. It sounds gorgeous. Did you do this?'

'Yes.' Joel moved beside her, his arm brushing hers. 'I bought them as an apology – and a declaration. But by the time they arrived, you'd gone on holiday and I thought it was all too late.'

'And yet you planted them anyway?'

'Yes. Because you are still the most amazing, incredible woman I've ever met, and you deserve to be

418

showered in roses, whether you're with me or not.'

And that was enough to bring hope to life, and Helen's heart began a glorious, dizzying spin.

'Why are you wearing two ties?' she asked, a smile bouncing round her lips.

'Another peace offering. I know how much you like them.' The cheeky grin flashed. 'I've a baguette in the kitchen ready for you to murder as well.'

Helen laughed and reached out to take Joel's hand. Long fingers wrapped round hers. It wasn't a hand that would lead her; it was one that would support her, as they walked side by side.

'Do you believe me?' she asked, searching his face. 'I'm just me, the good and the bad. I can't be perfect.'

'I believed you as soon as I'd calmed down, and long before a parade of people came to set me straight and tell me what an idiot I was.'

'Who?'

'Auntie Joan, Kirsty, Fiona, Malcolm...'

'Fiona and Malcolm? What did they know?'

'Haven't you heard? It's been a busy week. Kirsty told them everything, and Saskia's part in it. They'd guessed something was wrong. They threatened to leave Church Farm unless Saskia did. I gave her notice, but she's already gone. Apparently she made some contacts in London on the day of the fair, and has gone to make her fortune down there.'

The relief was immense. Helen could stay at the Hay Barn; she could continue to run Crazy Little Things. It struck her how unhappy she would have been to give it up as Daniel had wanted. It was part of her, and with Joel's support she could make it even better. But there was still one thing she had to clear up.

'I saw Saskia going back to your house one night. Have you been seeing her?'

'If you were watching, you'd have seen her leave not long after.' Embarrassment tinged Joel's face. 'It became obvious that she'd had ulterior motives in trying to put me off you.'

'It was obvious to everyone.'

He squeezed her hand. 'Everyone else, maybe, but I was only looking one way.'

Helen took a step nearer, and ran her fingers down the length of his ties.

'If you believed me, why didn't you come and tell me?'

'Because when I thought about what you'd done, the thing that hit me most was how deeply you must have loved Daniel.' Uncertainty lit his eyes. 'You share a history, and a child. We'd shared one kiss. How could I ever compete with that?'

'You're not competing. And it wasn't just one kiss. It was two, and they were the most magnificent kisses I've ever known.' She dropped his hand, let go of the tie, and put her arms round his neck. 'Daniel asked me to go back to him and I said no. I love you. I'm all yours if you still want me. And Megan.'

His arms slid round her waist.

'I never stopped wanting you. I love you both. Where is Megan?'

'On holiday for another night.'

420

'Is she?' A new smile was added to Joel's repertoire. It was decidedly wicked. Helen liked it. 'So we're on our own. What do you suggest we do now?'

'I suppose that depends on whether you need to go back to work.'

'Funny you should mention that. There is some business I need to sort out.' Joel tightened his arms, pulling her closer until it felt as if they shared each breath. 'It occurred to me earlier that I never did take your advice and negotiate perks with my favourite tenant. It's probably time I did.'

Helen's fingers tangled in his hair.

'It was excellent advice. And is that going to take you all day?'

'I think it's going to take me forever.'

'Forever?' Helen laughed. 'We'd better make a start then.'

And she kissed him, and took his hand and led him into the house.

Acknowledgements

I'm incredibly lucky to have some brilliant writing friends, particularly Julie and Catherine, who are unstinting in their encouragement, and always know what to say in the good times and the bad. Thanks also to the Beta Buddies for admitting me to the inner circle (at last!), and providing support, laughter and great books to read.

I'm grateful to everyone at the Romantic Novelists' Association for ongoing support, but special thanks go to Allie Spencer for kindness, excellent advice, and for giving me confidence when it was much needed.

It's been an amazing year since my debut, *The Magic of Ramblings*, was published, and I couldn't have anticipated how people would take Ramblings and the Ribblemillers to their hearts. Thanks to everyone who left a review or contacted me after reading the book. Reading has brought me so much pleasure over the years, and it means a lot to be able to pay a small part of that back.

KATE FIELD writes contemporary women's fiction, mainly set in her favourite county of Lancashire, where she lives with her husband, daughter and hyperactive cat. She is a member of the Romantic Novelists' Association.

Kate's debut novel, *The Magic of Ramblings*, won the RNA's Joan Hessayon Award for new writers in 2017.

You can find Kate on:
Twitter: @katehaswords
Facebook: /KateFieldAuthor

Praise for The Magic of Ramblings:

'A beautiful must read – magical!' **Emma Davies**

'This is one of the loveliest books I've read in a long time.'
Lynda Stacey

'*The Magic of Ramblings* is a book that I know I will be
reading again and again. A feel good book about the
goodness of human nature and the importance of
community, love and friendship.' **Jo Worgan,
Brew and Books Review**

'An absolute delight to read. I couldn't put it down. It's the
first book I've read by Kate Field, and certainly not the
last.' **Goodreads review**

'I really enjoyed this book and it's very obvious right from
the beginning that Kate Field is a very talented writer.'
JB Johnston, Brook Cottage Books

'Kate Field has captured brilliantly the essence of human
nature.' **Amazon review**

'I'm so glad I tried this debut author and can't wait for her
next novel to come out. More please!!' **Amazon review**

'Kate's writing is effortless and reading her work makes
you feel as you are wrapped in a cosy, warm blanket.'
Amazon review

'Character development is the key to any great story and
Kate handles hers with deftness and detail.'
Goodreads review

Winner of the RNA Joan Hessayon Award for new writers 2017

Running away can be the answer, if you run to the right place…

'A beautiful must read – magical!'
Emma Davies